THE ASSASSIN'S KEY

Also by Stephen B Smart

Whispers of the Greybull

Vanishing Raven

The Assassin's Key

Stephen B. Smart

Dedication

This book is dedicated to my good friend, Richard (Dick) Vandervert. Thirty-seven years ago I met Dick Vandervert and almost immediately he took me under his wing helping to guide, mentor and develop my abilities. I could always depend on Dick for just the right advice and a positive spin on the future. He set the bar very high and I have always tried my best to emulate his impressive personal skills.

Prelude

1822: Dublin, Ireland

"Hurry, get those boxes over to the wagon," said the smallest boy, as he wiped the sloppy mop of hair from his eyes. Scully stopped and looked warily around the alley. "Something doesn't feel right," he said in a thick Irish accent. "We need to—"

Numerous constables seemed to suddenly appear from the shadows wielding night sticks. "We got you now, you little beggars. Get 'em men!" yelled the closest man. The officers charged the four boys.

"It's a trap!" shouted Scully. The shock of the moment sent the three older boys instantly running down the alley. Scully quickly picked up one of the wooden boxes and ran toward the oncoming constables, throwing the box into the narrowest section of the alley. The unexpected action caused his pursuers to break stride as Scully made his getaway. In the distance he could hear men puffing and yelling. Just behind him he could hear a set of footsteps hitting the cobblestones. They were close. Scully knew he would have to be smart to elude this man.

This constable was fast. In the past he had easily outrun the out of shape officers but in the back of his mind he was worried. There was one place he might lose him. He broke from his normal escape route and veered down an alley. Leaping into the air over a pile of garbage, he landed in a brown puddle splattering its contents. He could still hear the man breathing as he continued to close the distance. If he didn't reach the corner soon the constable would catch him. Scully needed to make a hard left while hugging the building. A narrow patch of alley floor closest to the building was normally dry due to a small overhang. Past those cobbles lay the dried scum that hid the slimy floor beneath it. He could see the corner. Now if he could just make the turn without slipping. Suddenly he felt a finger touch his shoulder. He dodged and ducked as his foot hit the dry corner. The wall scraped his shoulder. Behind him echoed a startled scream as the man tumbled uncontrollably to the floor.

Scully smiled as he ran, smug that he had escaped one more time. He glanced back to see the officer lying on the ground grasping his leg and cursing in pain. There were still men behind him. He knew these alleys and was confident about his escape route. Down the next corridor, through a narrow alley, over a fence and he was free. Turning the corner at full speed, he collided with a burly constable coming from the opposite direction. Scully tried to stop as he glanced up and saw the downward arc of a truncheon.

* * *

It was late the following day when Scully slowly opened his eyes. He was lying on the damp, stone floor of a jail cell. He took a deep breath and almost gagged from the terrible stench. There were men of all descriptions sitting and standing in the tight quarters. No one seemed to be paying him any attention. Scully's elbow bumped something beside him as he staggered to his feet. He looked over his shoulder to see an overflowing chamber pot. Putting his dirty sleeve over his nose, he moved to an open space against the bars.

"So they finally caught you lad, did they?" said an old man with a scraggly beard, as he quietly chuckled to himself.

Scully gave him a disgusted glance and continued staring out between the rusted bars. His clothes reeked and greasy hair covered his face. After a few minutes his distant gaze suddenly focused on a gentleman descending the stone staircase. He was accompanied by a jailer whose small torch gave out just enough light to make the rest of the room visible.

The guard led the man to Scully's cell. "Where's the boy?" asked the gentleman.

"He's the small one standing by the bars," he said pointing. "Can't be more than twelve or thirteen but he's the leader of the worst band of thieving beggars in all of Dublin. Smart one he is. That little scoundrel eluded us for near on to two years. Always one step ahead, but we finally caught him."

The gentleman stared at Scully for a moment and then their eyes met. "Those are cold, blue eyes for such a young lad." He paused and turned to the jailer. "You say he almost outran the fastest man we have?"

"Yes sir, he sprained his knee badly chasing him. Says he's the fastest beggar he has ever chased. If it weren't for our trap we would have never caught him."

"Now you're sure he is an orphan with no kin?"

"None sir, at least none that anyone knows. It's been heard tell that his parents have been dead for a while, starved in the famine."

The gentleman walked over to the cell close enough to get a good look. "Boy, what's your name?"

Scully looked at the man defiantly. "Scully," he paused for a second, "Scully McCabe. Why be you askin'?"

The gentleman smiled. "You will find out soon enough." The man turned to the jailer and handed him a padded envelope. "As we agreed, now put him in chains and move him to my wagon. It's in the normal place. I take it there are no others?"

"No sir, he's the only one that fits."

"Good, let's be on with it." The man turned and headed back up the stairs. Minutes later two burly men shoved Scully into an enclosed wagon while a third man watched. Scully had seen a police paddy wagon before but this was unlike anything he knew. It looked more like a sheepherder wagon with bars. He immediately began thinking how to escape but he was still bruised and sore, and at that moment, he saw no opportunities.

Several other teenage boys sat chained in the wagon. Their clothing was worn and tattered and their eyes held an angry, empty stare. They were both older and bigger and didn't acknowledge him as the guards shoved him to the front of the wagon and chained him to a thick metal ring.

"There will be no talking," said the guard as he slammed the wagon door and fastened the padlock. The wagon jolted suddenly and Scully caught his balance by grabbing the metal ring. There was a small amount of dried blood on the planks of the floor and several small slits in the walls allowing for only the slightest breeze.

After hours on the bumpy road, the wagon came to a hard stop. The doors of the wagon slammed open and the three boys were dragged outside to relieve themselves as the guards watched. Scully was hungry and the cold bowl of stew they gave to each boy was quickly wolfed down. Their journey continued until nightfall when the boys were again unloaded, fed a small ration, and chained to the wagon's wheels. They had gained elevation and the night was colder than he was used to. Scully shivered as he curled into a tight ball trying to keep warm. Later that night one of the guards threw a tattered wool blanket to each boy and then went back to where he slept.

The next day the wagon worked its way through the rolling countryside to where the terrain became steep and rockier. As evening approached, the wagon veered off the road and slowed to a stop near a stagnant pond heavily engulfed by cattails. Scully could hear the key unlocking the padlock and the door opened with a thump as the wagon's heavy ramp hit the ground. One of the guards with a thick red beard escorted the first boy down the ramp and Scully could hear the sound of chains against the wagon wheel. He quickly returned for the second boy as Scully watched. The second guard was moving as if he were going to check the horses and the third man watched with his arms crossed. Scully heard the guard moving the second boy to another wheel and the sound of the padlock closing. Finally the man came back and ducked as he entered the low ceiling of the wagon. Scully sat perfectly still as he waited. The guard made his way to the front of the wagon, reached for the padlock, and unlocked it.

Just as he did, Scully kicked him and made his break. The guard yelled as Scully jumped. Immediately he felt a powerful arm knocking him to the ground. He hit hard and tried to stagger to his feet but before he could the two men were on him, pinning him firmly to the ground.

Scully was dazed but knew the men were mad as they grabbed him by the chains on each wrist.

"We will teach this lad some respect," the guard said angrily! The two men began dragging Scully towards the pond. Scully gagged and fought for breath as water entered his screaming mouth and the sharp edges of the cattails cut his skin.

"We will teach you respect and what happens if you little beggars try to escape."

Scully could feel the life going out of him when the guard on the bank yelled, "That's enough! We don't need him dead. O'Mahony didn't pay us to drown him."

The men dragged Scully from the water and threw him to the ground. The bearded man, wet from the waist down, gave a contemptuous look towards the third man standing by the wagon. "He may be better off drowning than the place he's going."

The Assassin's Key

March 20, 1861

There was a cold, damp feeling to the air, not unusual for early spring in Virginia's Piedmont. A dark depressing sky with a slight drizzle framed the leafless skeletons of maple trees that lined the road. Gillis McCabe smiled at his fiancée. Sandra Richards was considered one of the most beautiful women in all of Virginia. She laughed at his memories and description of his old dog, Blue Tick. She was all of 5'-2", slim, with long blonde hair that trailed down her back neatly tucked under her laced bonnet. The daughter of a prominent judge in Williamsburg, Sandra was known for her quick wit as well as her beauty. Gillis had met her only a year before in Williamsburg. He could clearly remember looking across the ornate dance floor and seeing this incredibly beautiful lady with a throng of eligible bachelors vying for her attention.

Gillis was a single, twenty-nine year old and it was not uncommon for him to attend the many balls thrown throughout Virginia. He was interested in making much-needed contacts for his growing shipbuilding business and considered it a bonus to meet and dance with the ladies. Now it seemed a lifetime ago that he ventured into Judge Richards's home and discussed being allowed to court his daughter. Richards was known as a tough judge with much power and influence. His name was dropped many times by the men in the know as a potential candidate for the upcoming Virginia governorship. Now a year later, Gillis had convinced the judge to allow his daughter to accompany him on this journey to his father's estate.

Their journey had taken six days across the rough and muddy back roads of the Virginia countryside. If memory served him correctly, there was a roadhouse a couple of miles further and hopefully they would be able to find shelter for the night. Gillis looked at Sandra. "I wish I had a better memory but I only traveled this road a few times and that was fifteen years ago. A good long ride tomorrow and I believe we should be at my father's estate."

"You haven't been back in fifteen years? How old were you when you left?" asked Sandra in her thick Southern accent.

"I had just turned fourteen." At that moment they rounded a sharp bend in the road and passed a lone rider. The man with his rain-deformed hat and dark slicker tightly pulled around his face rode past. Only the sharp whinny of his horse gave any acknowledgment that the rider existed.

"That was strange," said Sandra. "He didn't even look up or wave."

Gillis reached beneath the sheet of canvas covering the thick wool blankets that lay upon their legs and laps. His fingers touched the handle of his 1851 Navy Colt. Slowly he relaxed as he glanced back and saw the driver disappearing.

"There are still a few bad apples in this country and it pays to stay alert."

Twenty minutes later the clouds began to part to expose a rose-tipped sky on the horizon. Gillis pulled back the reins and the carriage began to slow as it approached the dark-timbered roadhouse. The building was constructed with a combination of logs and thick wooden planks that had needed painting for years.

"Whoa," Gillis commanded as he brought the horses to a stop near the wooden porch that signaled the entrance. In one quick motion he set the carriage's brake and stepped down. With both hands he pulled back the damp canvas and blankets and helped Sandra to the ground.

"I hope this will be all right." He quickly tied the horses to the hitching rail and the two of them walked up the wide plank stairs. A thick wooden door marked the inn's entrance with a faded, almost unreadable lettering. Inside was a large, dimly lit room with numerous tables. Men were scattered throughout and the room was thick with pipe smoke. Gillis glanced at Sandra concerned with what she was thinking.

"Don't worry, I'm fine. My dad is constantly smoking his cigars in his study and I am used to the smell."

Three men sat at a table in the corner, two in dark clothing and the other one in buckskins. The sound of an argument could easily be heard over the noise of the room. Several times the man in the buckskins raised his voice only to be calmed down by the other two men.

Kerosene lamps and cobwebs too high to easily be reached with a broom, hung from the rough-cut timbers that spanned the ceiling. A heavyset woman with a faded blue dress entered the room followed by a pungent odor that smelled like a mixture of dried sweat and wet dog.

"Greetings friends, come far?" the lady asked with a squeaky voice and a mouth full of yellowed teeth. She looked tired, but was making an effort to be pleasant.

"A fair journey to some, we need a couple of rooms. Adjoining, if possible, and there's an extra dollar in it if they're very clean."

"That's no problem, sir, cleaned them myself late morning. We only have six rooms and just a couple of guests, so it won't be a problem for you two to be room to room," she responded with a coy smile. "Nope, no issue at all."

"We would also like some supper, a mug of ale for me, and the best wine you have for the lady." He paused. "Is that all right with you?" Sandra gently nodded with a tired look of approval.

"Venison stew, fresh bread, and blackberry pie is what we have. Hope that matches your fancy," she said, as she wiped the counter off.

"Can you have someone take care of our horses, brush them down well and give them an extra portion of oats?"

"Sure can," she said as hollered to a man sitting alone at a table in the corner. "Willard, come take care of these folk's horses while I get them some dinner. Brush them down real good and give them extra oats."

The man was rough-looking. His long gray hair flowed down and melted into his beard. His hollow eyes and cracked face hid nothing of his hard life. The man nodded, stretched, and headed for the door.

"That will be a dollar for the rooms and dinner and two bits for the horses," she said. "I will collect for both after you have had dinner."

"Well, this is an adventure," Sandra said.

Gillis, with a partial smile, responded, "I hope you are okay with staying here. Tomorrow we will be at my father's home which is quite nice. His servants do an excellent job of keeping the place up."

"So your father has slaves?" Sandra asked.

"If I remember correctly, we had six adults and some children before I ran away. I'm not sure how many he has now. After my mother and brother died in childbirth, I was raised by one of our slaves, Letty." He paused. "Letty Brown is one fine woman. She raised me like her own. To tell you the truth, I have really missed her."

"You never told me why you left home. If I am to be your wife, there must be no secrets," stated Sandra in a firm voice.

Gillis was caught off guard by her direct line of questioning. "I guess you have a right to know enough to at least understand our relationship. My father and I were very close for years after mother died. I was nearing my fourteenth birthday, he started talking about sending me away to a boarding school in Ireland and what an honor that would be. Immediately, I became rebellious. There was no way I wanted to go away to some strange school across the ocean. It was difficult for dad as he was gone a lot with business. To his credit he did a great job of taking the time to teach me about the world. He taught me to read by the time I was four and we had a great library, something he was very proud of. Every day I had chores but when he was home he schooled me in math and science. He even tried to teach me how to defend myself.

The closer I got to fourteen the more forceful he got about me going away to school. One night we had a horrible fight with a lot of screaming and yelling. He suddenly changed from just talking about the opportunities of Irish schooling to demanding that I go. Things were said and the next day I ran off. After several months of traveling about and doing odd jobs for food, I ended up in Norfolk. I was lucky enough to find a job sweeping floors as a night janitor for a shipbuilding company. Every night on my break, I would study the latest blueprints of their ships and try to analyze how they functioned. I was fascinated that you could draw plans that would be turned into these amazing boats."

"Wait, you started at your company sweeping floors?"

"My father obviously had money but I certainly wasn't going to ask him for any. Anyway, one night I was studying a new boat design when in walks the boss, Mr. Ernest Peel. He was a funny-looking man. He reminded me of some sort of elf, small, bald, with a short white beard with a large round belly. Anyway he just suddenly appeared behind me and demanded in a loud voice to know just what in the hell I thought I was doing. He scared me so bad I thought I was going to soil myself."

Sandra laughed as Gillis looked up to see the barmaid bringing their food. "Here's your ale, wine, and hot stew. I will bring your pie in a couple of minutes and here are your keys." She placed two metal skeleton keys down on the table. "The rooms are one and two and both are on your left at the top of the stairs."

"Thanks. We would like to get an early start, so would you have your man harness the horses at first light?"

"Yes, sir. We will also have your breakfast ready and a packed lunch, too, if you like." Gillis nodded.

Just then the man in the buckskins yelled, "That ain't the deal, that's not what we agreed on." The two men across from him turned around nervously to see people staring at them, then quickly turned back to calm the man.

"Sorry for all of the commotion, I will ask them to hold it down," said the woman as she left to talk to the other table.

"I wonder what that is about?" asked Sandra.

"With so many states declaring their independence from the Union, I would guess that might be the topic."

"I don't want to talk politics, I hear way too much at home from father. Tell me what happened after this Mr. Peel yelled at you."

"At first I jumped out of my chair but when I regained my composure, I apologized for looking at the plans without permission."

"So then what?"

"He asked me if I even knew what I was looking at. I said, yes, sir. I told him I thought it was a beautiful design but I didn't agree with everything. You should have seen the look on his face. He wasn't sure if he should be mad, curious, or just fire me. Finally he just stared at me before saying, "Young man, if you understand this design, then tell me what you are looking at and what would you change?"

"I looked him right in the eye and said, 'I am looking at the bow, and if it were me I would reinforce the hull area here and here. Then I would sharpen its angle to cut better through the water, but those are just my initial thoughts.'"

"Then Mr. Peel asked if I had formal schooling in boat design. I said, "No, sir, just the teaching of my father, a schooled man."

Gillis smiled at the memory. "Mr. Peel mumbled something about amazing and told me to come to his office the next day. Then he ordered me to get back to sweeping and made the comment that he believed that was what I was paid to do. Then he turned and left."

"That's unbelievable, and it is all history from there?" Sandra asked.

"Pretty much, the meeting went well and I kept moving up in the business and when I turned twenty-four, Mr. Peel was ready to retire. He offered to sell me the business on credit, so I bought the company. I brought in some designers I respected and we began offering different styles of boats."

"So when did your father find out you were in the shipbuilding business?"

"I am not sure. But two months ago I got a letter from him asking for my forgiveness. He asked me to come back home and visit. I did miss my father—he is the only family I have and a lot of water has gone under the bridge. I knew he would appreciate meeting you so I thought it was time for a reunion. I think you will enjoy my father. He is a man of many talents."

They ate their pie and soon after headed upstairs and into their separate rooms. The night was quiet and they both slept well with the sound of rain beating on the cedar shakes.

* * *

The next morning they were up before sunrise for breakfast. Quickly they ate their biscuits and gravy before heading back up to their rooms to gather their luggage. It only took a few minutes for Gillis to carry his leather travel bag down the stairs and settle the bill. Willard, the older man who had tended their horses, struggled as he lugged Sandra's heavy suitcases down the stairs and out to the carriage. The horses stood quietly harnessed to the hitching rail as Gillis walked outside into a slight drizzle.

"I'll help you load your baggage," said Willard as he lugged Sandra's bags over to the back of the carriage. "Which way you be headed?" he asked.

"We are headed for Bedford Road and then on up to Three Forks. My father has an estate about five miles from there," said Gillis.

Willard looked at them for several seconds and then rubbed his gray beard as if he wanted to say something. "Been some mighty tough, salty men riding up that way in the last week. Nothing pleasant about that bunch, it would be good to keep an eye out, if you know what I mean."

Gillis looked at him for a moment and then dug into his coat pocket and tossed the man a coin.

"We'll do that," answered Gillis, as Sandra walked through the door and down to the carriage. Gillis helped her up into her seat, untied the hitching rope, and launched himself up onto the carriage. He gave the horses a gentle shake of the reins and loud, "Yaw!"

"Nice enough old guy, I wonder why he is worried about us," said Sandra.

"I don't know why he should be. We will be at my father's estate by evening."

"Your father sure lives out in the middle of nowhere. Is there a town anywhere nearby?"

"Not really. I talked to him once about why we lived in such an isolated place and he just said it was for the best. I'm not sure what he meant by that but at the time I didn't question it."

It was late afternoon when the rain finally stopped and the wind began to pick up as they turned off the main road onto a side road. "We are making good time, won't be long now. My father's place is about three miles from here. I am just a little worried how this is going to go. In the last couple of years I have only written him a few times and I never wrote a return address until the last letter, when I told him about you and wanting to visit."

"What did you tell him?"

"Not much other than I was engaged to the most beautiful woman in Norfolk."

Sandra smiled and nudged him. "Only Norfolk? It used to be all of Virginia."

"Getting pretty sure of yourself aren't you?" Gillis laughed, as Sandra smiled and then broke into a laugh.

"I was just testing you."

The road was smooth and gradual. The wind was blowing, quickly drying the road bed. Gillis was staring at the road ahead when Sandra looked at him with a puzzled look. "What are you looking at?"

"Probably nothing. It just seems like there has been a lot of horses on this road lately. My dad must have guests; I hope we don't disrupt anything."

"Don't be ridiculous! He's your father. He is going to be thrilled to see you. How many fathers have a son that has become so successful at such a young age?"

"Well I didn't tell him exactly when we would arrive and I hope that wasn't a mistake. My dad can be kind of different at times. He is brilliant, and to be honest, he's sometimes hard to talk to. I do appreciate all the things he taught me and how he encouraged me to experiment. I know my inventing spirit came from him."

"He isn't the only one that's brilliant if you ask me."

"I seriously doubt that I am anywhere near as smart as my dad. Anyway, from a young boy on I remember him saying that necessity is the mother of invention, and I live by that saying. He used to bring home drawings of all kinds of things and explain them to me. My dad is a patient man and would accurately explain how different machinery functioned. Once he even brought home engineering drawings of a ship. That was my first experience with learning about how a ship was constructed."

Gillis pointed. "See that large tree up ahead? We are really close to Kilmaar Glenn, my father's estate."

The huge estate loomed in the distance as the carriage passed through the two powerful brick columns at the entrance. As the carriage rounded the last curve in the road, they were both shocked to see the gruesome landscape.

"Whoa, whoa!" yelled Gillis as the horses dropped their powerful hindquarters and dug their hooves into the soft clay. Gillis locked the carriage's hand brake as he leaped to the ground. The bloody body of a man lay sprawled beneath an overturned wagon. Gillis quickly ran to the man, bending down beside him as a swarm of flies rose from the body.

"Is he dead? Are they all dead?" Sandra screamed hysterically.

Gillis reached down and touched the stiff body. "This one is and he has been for a while. The body is cold. My guess is he has been dead for at least a day, maybe two. He has a knife wound to his throat, and if that didn't kill him, I am sure the wagon landing on him did."

"Do you recognize him?"

Gillis took a moment to look at the gray-haired man. "Yes, I think I do. His name is Basil Legg; he was one of our servants. When my father left to go out of town, Basil ran the farm. He was a good man and a good manager, he wouldn't hurt a flea."

Sandra started getting out of the wagon as Gillis hurried to help her.

Once she was safely on the ground Gillis reached under the seat and retrieved his Navy Colt.

"What are we going to do?" asked Sandra.

"The first thing I want to do is to check out the other bodies and then the rest of the place. I need to know if my father is here. There is no way of telling if the men who did this are gone. Be careful! It's way too late to head back to the inn tonight and the roads aren't safe after dark. We will need to barricade ourselves in the barn for the night."

Gillis looked at the house as the soft, silk curtains blew in and out of the shattered windows. The front door hung unnaturally from one hinge. Gillis pointed his pistol towards the doorway. Another man's body lay twisted on the porch, his arm dangling unnaturally over the edge. Gillis took a moment to look around and then cautiously checked the dead man before working his way up the steps with Sandra following.

"Are you sure you want to go in?"

"My father could be in there. I understand if you need to stay with the carriage, but I have to find out what is going on."

"No, I want to go with you."

Gillis pushed what remained of the finely crafted door fully open and pointed his pistol into the darkness. He cautiously set one foot inside and waited a second as he watched for movement and let his eyes adjust to the dimly lit space. The inside of the house had been violently ripped apart and debris littered the foyer and hall.

He slowly shook his head. "Whoever did this was very thorough. There isn't one piece of furniture that isn't broken. I have never seen anything like it. The way this looks I think it would be smart for you to stay here until I search the entire house."

Sandra nodded and moved up against one of the walls in the hallway.

Pointing his gun into the next room, Gillis moved quietly inside. He was met with the same destruction as the first room but with the addition of hundreds of books strewn across the floor. Whoever had done this was thorough. They had taken the time to open every book before discarding it onto the floor.

A scream came from the other room as Gillis whirred around and charged back to Sandra.

"What, what's wrong?" he asked.

"I heard someone move in that room," said Sandra, pointing to an open doorway.

Gillis focused his pistol in that direction and began cautiously walking forward. He was not a man who had used a gun much and he was sweating. "Stay here, I will see what it was," Gillis said. The silence was broken by a quiet pitiful moan.

Quietly he stepped over the debris as he moved down the stucco littered hallway but it was difficult. Chunks of plaster had been torn from the wall and whoever had done this wanted to make sure that the walls weren't concealing anything. Finally he entered his father's bedroom. Stacks of bed parts, goose feathers from the mattress, and broken furniture lay heaped on the floor. He stopped and listened for a moment. Then he heard the sound again, a soft moan coming from the far corner of the room. Quickly throwing items aside he worked his way towards the corner. He removed a long board that had once been part of the bed and lifted it from the pile. Then he saw her, the aged and beaten face of Letty, the servant lady who had raised him. He carefully removed the debris from around her chest and head. Her face had several deep gashes and dried blood covered one side of her face.

"Letty, what happened?"

Her battered brown face was badly swollen as she tried to open her eyes. It had been years since Gillis had left and even in the poor light she seemed to recognize him. A slight smile came over her cracked lips.

"My baby. Master Gillis, you came home. Oh, how I have missed you."

Gillis felt the tears welling up in his eyes as he stared at the woman that for every meaning of the word had been his mother. A deep gash in her throat was now filled with dried blood and Gillis could tell that even the slightest movement caused extreme pain.

"I'm here now, you'll be all right."

Gillis knew in his heart that was a stupid thing to say but words were coming hard and he didn't know what else to do.

"You being here is enough. Oh, my land child, how I have missed you."

"I know I should have come back sooner. I'm sorry, I am so sorry."

"It's all right, Master Gillis." She coughed. "Seeing you after all these years is truly wonderful."

"What happened here? Do you know where my father is?"

"He's gone," said Letty in a quiet, hoarse voice as she reached her hand out to Gillis. Their hands almost touched when suddenly the life left her body and her head fell to one side. Gillis reached over and carefully closed her eyes. He held the tight little fist she had raised into his hands for a moment before setting it back down close to her side. The movement seemed to loosen her grip just enough that something metal fell to the floor. Gillis looked down in the dark room and noticed a small, worn medallion about twice the size of a silver dollar. It was oval with a key-like neck and a strange-looking pattern. It was unlike anything Gillis had ever seen. He looked at it for a moment in the dim light and then slipped it into his side pocket.

"Is she dead?"

Gillis whirled around to see Sandra standing in the doorway. "Yes, she's dead. Her name was Letty Brown. She was the one I told you about that raised me when my mother died. She was a wonderful, kind-hearted woman and why anyone would do this to her is beyond imagination. These men aren't amateurs, this was a professional job and they meant business. They obviously didn't want to leave any witnesses to their deeds. I don't know what is going on but there is something terribly wrong and I plan to find out what. Let's move the carriage and the horses into the barn and lock everything from the inside. I doubt anyone is coming back tonight but I don't want to take any chances. I'll try and find some blankets in the bedrooms. Don't worry, honey, we will be fine."

"I'm scared, Gillis. I don't think I have ever been this scared in my whole life."

"We don't have much choice. I think it would be far more dangerous for us to travel tonight. I am a decent shot with a Colt and I guarantee you no one is going to harm you."

Gillis led the team of horses pulling the carriage inside the barn and stripped the harnesses and collars. After leading each one into separate stalls, he gave them water and several pitchforks of hay as Sandra watched. "We will put a board across the main doors and we can lock the side doors. If anyone tries to get in here I will hear them long before they make it in."

"I trust you, Gillis, but I just haven't ever seen this side of life. To tell you the truth, I haven't ever even seen a dead person up close before."

"You'll be fine. We will make a place in the hay for you to sleep then I am going over to the house to see if I can find something to eat. Tomorrow we will head out for the sheriff's office. There's a small town about six miles or so east of the roadhouse. Hopefully the sheriff can bring some men back and help us figure out what happened."

Sandra just nodded.

"That should do for a bed," said Gillis, as he flattened out some clean hay inside a corral stall. "It won't be like your feather bed but it should work at least for one night. Now when I go out the door put the board back in place and I will knock three times as a signal to open it."

"I understand—be careful, Gillis!"

Gillis opened the heavy barn door and went outside carrying a lantern. He could hear the plank being shoved into place by Sandra on the other side of the door. The sky was quickly losing the last of its light as he entered the dark house, lit the lantern and moved toward the kitchen. The room was torn up but not nearly as bad as the rest of the house. With the help of the lantern he began searching for food. Most of the contents of the cabinets lay scattered on the floor. Broken jars and chunks of glass were strewn throughout but with a little searching he found a half a loaf of bread wrapped in a white cotton cloth, an unopened jar of jam, and a kitchen knife. Holding the lantern as high as he could, Gillis took a second to scan the room. The cupboards had been ripped from the walls and like the other rooms, no furniture was left intact. Gillis shook his head and climbed over the destruction as he headed toward the back door.

He was at the doorway when he thought he heard the distant sound of a horse whinny above the howl of the wind. He stopped. Hearing nothing more, he shook the sound off as his imagination. At the back door he took a moment to look around before proceeding toward the barn. He hoped Sandra could handle this. Her life had been protected and he knew she hadn't ever seen anything even close to this horrible scene. Were the rest of the servants dead or even worse, severely injured and lying out in the woods suffering? He couldn't take the chance of searching in the dark and leaving Sandra alone. Hopefully he would get some answers in the morning. He was reaching to knock on the barn door when he heard the quiet crunch of a leaf behind him and quickly turned toward the sound. He saw the silhouette of a large man and then everything went black.

Chapter 2

Straining to open his eyes, Gillis felt the pain of his throbbing head. He could feel the soft texture of grass hay around his head and knew he was no longer outside. He tried to focus and as he did he saw an enormous man with his back turned standing next to him. Suddenly Sandra appeared from behind the stall wall, bent down and began gently rubbing his forehead with a wet cloth.

"Is he coming around?" Gillis didn't recognize the deep voice as he tried to focus.

"I think so, but I'm not sure."

Gillis felt fuzzy but he could now see a large black man, thick and wide standing over him.

He struggled to speak. "Who are you?"

"I'm Roper, Roper Taylor, Master Gillis, we used to play together. I'm sorry I hit you so hard but I thought you were one of them. The only reason I didn't kill you was I thought you might have some information on where they took your father and why they did this."

"*You* hit me?"

"Yes sir, I did and I am sorry. It's just that I haven't seen you for so long I didn't think you would ever come back here."

"What happened?"

"I don't rightly know for sure but from all the evidence I have found there were four or five of them and they waited at least a full day before they attacked. I found where they kept their horses and their lookout."

"You didn't find my father?"

"No sir, I didn't. He must have been away on business or something."

"Letty said just before she died that my father was gone, but it is a little hazy right now. I do remember you, Roper. It's been so long but I remember you as skinny and tall. Now you are, well, you are really big!"

"Yes sir, Master Gillis, I grew up just like you. Neither one of us recognized the other. I wish I would have known it was you."

"I understand—we are past that. I forgive you in light of the situation."

Sandra interrupted, "Those men killed his wife and four-year-old son."

Gillis looked at Roper with a cold stare. "Is that true?"

"Yes, sir. I found both of them slaughtered like pigs. They not only killed them, they cut them."

"I'm sorry, Roper, I am so very sorry."

"They can't get away with this. They even killed children and they didn't steal a thing."

"Nothing?"

"Nothing, Master Gillis."

"Why did they do this? It doesn't make sense," said Gillis.

Roper struggled to answer. "I don't know."

"I'm so very sorry."

"I understand how you feel, Master Gillis. I know that Letty was like a mother to you."

"Yes, she was, and no matter how long I live, someone is going to make these people pay dearly for their sins. You have my oath on that."

* * *

The next morning with the help of Roper and Sandra, Gillis struggled to walk outside where he took a seat on a bench by the door. Gillis looked over and noticed the wagon was now up-righted and the body that had lain beneath it was gone.

Gillis looked at Roper. "Boy, am I glad you only tried to knock me out. I don't think my head would have withstood a harder hit." Gillis looked over where the overturned wagon had been. "Did you lift that wagon by yourself and move the bodies?"

"Yes sir, Master Gillis, I did. I turned the wagon back up and then loaded the bodies and took them up to the family cemetery. I have all but two graves dug."

"You are one strong man. I want you to help me up there. And would you mind just calling me Gillis or Mr. McCabe from now on. I am not your master nor do I ever intend to have slaves."

"Yes, sir." He paused. "Mr. McCabe, but you is my master if your father isn't alive."

"As far as I am concerned you will be treated as a free man. You can work for me from now on but you will receive your wages every two weeks like every other person who works here. Hopefully, my father is still alive and it might be best for you to work for me until we find out for sure."

"Sure thing, Mr. Gillis, sir."

Gillis looked at Roper for a moment and then motioned him over to help stabilize him as they walked up to the cemetery. The bodies lay in a row in front of the small plot of land filled with aged white crosses and a few granite head stones. Roper had dug six new graves behind the crosses and had laid the eight bodies in a neat row.

"Shouldn't we say a prayer or something, Gillis?" asked Sandra.

"Yes, we can certainly do that. It's the least we can do for them until we can have a real funeral." Gillis took a step forward and bowed his head. "Dear Lord, we stand here in front of you today with these innocent victims of a horrible crime. We ask that you bless their spirits and take them to a better place, amen."

The three of them stood there for a minute with their heads bowed before returning to the house. Gillis seemed to finally be walking better despite his throbbing head and his balance was coming back.

"I don't want them buried until the sheriff gets a chance to see them. The way some of them were mutilated it is almost like a killer's signature. If any other crime was committed like this it may give the sheriff a clue. Roper, I will need you to ride to town this afternoon and get him."

"Yes sir, I can. The sheriff surely needs to know what happened here. I will gather up some lunch for us and then I will take off."

"Sandra, I'm still in no shape to ride. You can go with Roper if you would feel safer or stay one more night with me here. I know those are tough choices but it's all I've got. I still feel fuzzy at times and I wouldn't want to be driving on that road and have an issue."

"Of course I will stay with you. Who else is going to take care of you?" Sandra asked.

"I guess that settles it, Roper. The sooner you can take off for town and the sheriff, the better. We will be fine, I'm sure."

"I don't know if that is best, but I will do as you ask, Mr. McCabe."

"I guess you don't plan on calling me Gillis, do you?"

"No sir, you and your family come with a lot of respect for me and I need to show it back. I will be back with the sheriff tomorrow one way or the other."

Roper went to the house's root cellar and after a few minutes returned with enough food to make lunch, as well as extra for that night.

"This ain't what you are probably used to but it is all we got that didn't get broke or ruined. Hope it is okay."

"We will be fine, Roper. You go ahead and take off. We will see you late tomorrow."

"I will fetch one of the mules and I will be out of here."

"You ride a mule?"

"Yes sir, Mr. McCabe. Best damn creature God ever created. The thoroughbred mule I plan to ride is big, strong, and fast. He's real smart and will eat and drink less than a horse. There isn't a finer animal I could be riding alone on these roads. That mule always seems to know if trouble is out there—those big ears of his have saved my bacon a few times."

"I guess the choice of an animal you ride is up to the man and you obviously have chosen. We will see you back here tomorrow. Be careful."

Ten minutes later all six foot-two, two hundred and twenty pounds of Roper launched into the saddle and headed down the road at a trot.

"I need to look around some. This whole thing doesn't make sense. There has to be some reason behind this killing. Too many men were involved for there not to have been an objective."

"You sound more like a detective than someone that has just lost your home and the people that raised you."

"There is no use in letting my emotions take hold of all my thoughts. This murder was done by someone that meant my family tremendous harm and wanted to set an example. I am pretty sure they planned on killing my father. Roper said it looked like they had watched the place for a couple of days before they struck. My father often rode out after dark, and if I was to guess, I would say they got frustrated he wasn't here. They sent him a message, but why? Why on earth would they feel they needed to kill everyone, even the two dogs?"

"Do you think your father is dead?" Sandra asked.

"No, he is a survivor. He has always been a cautious man. Even at dinner he would sit where he could see the doorway. He always had a couple of watch dogs roaming the place and it was one of the servants' responsibilities to patrol the place at night. I never asked him but I knew he wasn't a normal business man. He always refused to answer any questions about his business."

"Was he trying to hide something from you?" asked Sandra.

"Who knows for sure, but I think so. I have no idea what. He has always been guarded and secretive. I will say he was open to my questions about life and how things worked. In many ways he was a great father and teacher and I knew he loved me."

"My dad wasn't secretive about anything except the court cases he was working on. He said those conversations were off limits. The problem with being a judge was how political it was and how much of the time he was gone. We didn't have dogs or anyone standing guard but I do think a couple of our slaves may have served in that capacity as well."

"So your dad, the judge, taught slaves to use guns?" Gillis asked.

"I was told never to admit that, but he did. He always felt they were loyal to him and we treated them much better than any slaves we knew."

"I need to go back to the house and look around better. Tomorrow Roper will be back here with the sheriff and probably a few others and I want to think as much of this through as possible."

Gillis walked from the barn over to the house and cautiously entered the front door with Sandra a few steps behind him. He headed down the hall toward his dad's study, a room he had given little time to during the previous night's inspection. In the doorway to the study Gillis reached down and picked up a picture frame that was face down on the floor and turned it over. He stared at it for a moment and then handed it to Sandra.

"This is a picture of my family when I was just a baby with my dad and mother. My mother passed away about two years after this picture was taken during the birth of my brother."

"I'm sorry, Gillis."

"It was a long time ago. Notice the floor, there isn't even an old letter, no correspondence at all. They must have picked up every scrap of paper that could have been a letter or who knows what. Let's go outside in the back and look around. I have a hunch."

The two climbed through the debris and down the stairs of the back porch. Gillis immediately began looking around and it didn't seem like he was finding what he was searching for.

"What are you looking for?" asked Sandra.

"I'm not sure but I will know when I find it," Gillis said as he walked around back of the carriage shed.

"Right here, see it! They tried to burn up every scrap of paper they could find right here." Gillis took his foot and gently moved the ashes. He reached down and picked up a small piece of paper but there wasn't anything on it. After ten minutes of sifting through the ashes, Gillis had several dozen partially burnt fragments of paper.

"Here, this one has a partial word on it, Alexandri. That must stand for Alexandria, Virginia. I can't be sure but that is the only location anywhere near here with a spelling like that. Alexandria is just out of Washington and I know my father mentioned being there in the past."

"How do you know that isn't just a business letter? How does it tie into these murders?"

"I don't, but I don't have many clues and I need to follow up on anything I can."

Gillis stuck the scrap of paper in his pocket and went back to the house and began searching for any information he could find but after two hours he had found nothing. Gillis walked out of the house and found Sandra sitting on the porch. "Are you all right?"

"Yes, I have just been sitting here thinking just how unreal this whole thing is—all this killing and for no reason, at least none that we can figure out. Roper losing his family, and then having to come back to nothing, it's not right."

Gillis sat down beside her and put his arm around her shoulder. "I know I've found life to be unfair a lot."

"Until now I have always been protected from life. I was never made to go to a funeral, not even if it was a relative. I never had to deal with the dark side and now I need to face the worst of life. I don't know if I can handle it," said Sandra. She put her head down into her hands.

"You are doing fine. This isn't something most people could handle and you have been very strong. Let's walk back down to the barn and fix something to eat. I am feeling better and I seem to have my balance back. That Roper is one powerful man, I'm glad he is on our side."

The two walked back to the barn and made do with what they had for a meal. Afterward they sat down on a bench in the barn. "Sandra, I want you to know how proud I am of you. Not many people could see what you have seen in the last couple of days and retained their composure like you have."

"Thanks, Gillis, but I really don't know how well I am doing. I feel like I need to run and hide but I don't know where."

"You will be fine. I'm not leaving your side."

Gillis reached in his pocket to look for the scrap of paper he had found and touched the small metal item that Letty had clutched in her dying hand. "I forgot about this."

"What is it?"

"I'm not sure. Letty had it in her fist when she died. I don't know if it means anything or even what it is."

"Can I see it?"

"Okay," said Gillis as he handed it to Sandra.

"It's an unusual shape and there appears to be a worn MU etched into it. In some ways it looks like some sort of unfinished key."

"Let me see. I must have not looked hard enough." Sandra handed the metal object back to Gillis who tried to examine it closer.

"Yeah, I see it. It's certainly worn, but now that you point it out I can see the lettering. I am surprised I missed that the first time I examined it."

"What do you think it is?"

"It might be some type of tool but I have no idea what for. Why someone would have their initials on it is curious, and it appears well made, probably by a craftsman. I guess I really don't know what it is."

Gillis put the medallion back into his pocket. "Alexandria is a big town, hell it's a city and there's probably over five thousand people living there."

"So you thought about having a factory in Alexandria?"

"It's close to Washington and I thought we might be better able to market our ships to the War Department but I sold the business before I got that far. Let's call it a day and get some sleep. I am still kind of worn out from the hit to the head. Hopefully everything will go back to normal with a little rest."

Gillis fell into a deep sleep and when he awoke he could hear the birds chirping outside and rays of sunlight streaming through slits in the boards. He leaned over and put his hand on Sandra. "Wake up, it's morning."

Sandra struggled to open her eyes. "I sure had my share of nightmares last night. I will be glad when Roper gets back here with the sheriff and we can head back home."

"I'm sorry I put you through this. I can't believe this whole thing is happening myself."

"Let's get some breakfast and go outside and soak up some sunshine. The drizzle from the past two days has been depressing."

"Roper should be back here about 1:00 and we can spend the night back at that inn we stayed at. It isn't home but at least you can have a hot meal and possibly a bath."

They ate the remaining food Roper had found in the house and then headed outside into the sunshine. "Now that the bodies are gone this place is actually quite beautiful. I can see why your father decided to build here."

"It will never be the same. These men weren't after valuables or things would be missing. No, they wanted my father and maybe more importantly something he had. But what could be so valuable that they would kill innocent people? The only way to find out what happened here is to find my father. He has to be the key to this."

"You can't be sure. Your father could just be gone on a business trip and might not know a thing about this."

"Sandra, I love you dearly but sometimes you are a bit too much on the trusting side and maybe a little naive."

"You are too quick to judge. Your father could have nothing to do with this, whatsoever." Sandra just shrugged her shoulders and walked further out into the yard with Gillis slowly following her.

"You know I pretty much checked the house but I think I will do it again, since I have the time," Gillis said.

"You go ahead. I'm going to stay here."

Gillis entered the house and it was a good two hours of searching before he stuck his head out the front door again. "I didn't find a clue, not a single one. These guys did a pretty fair job of destroying anything that would help me."

"Look, Roper's coming with some men," said Sandra, as she pointed toward the road. "Hopefully one of them is the sheriff."

A man on a stout, blue roan rode up ahead of Roper and pulled back his reins. Both Sandra and Gillis took a step back trying to put a little distance between them and the snorty horse. In one smooth motion the sheriff slid from the saddle and stepped to the ground.

"You Gillis McCabe?"

Gillis glanced in Roper's direction before looking at the squared-jawed man wearing a badge who stood in front of him.

"Are you the son of Scully McCabe?"

The two quick questions caught Gillis by surprise. "Yes I am and I appreciate you coming so quickly."

"Did you find your father's body?"

"No, I don't think he was here when this happened or they took him."

The sheriff turned to one of the men he had ridden in with. "Tie Big Blue up over with your horses. I think this is going to be a long day. Roper here says he came back from town and found you two here and all the bodies. He also told us how they were mostly all butchered. Tore the living hell out of the place is what he said."

"Someone wanted something, and we don't believe it was a robbery."

"How do you figure?" asked the sheriff, taking a couple of steps toward the house as he looked around.

"Nothing I remember is missing," Gillis said.

"It was gruesome—everyone was dead," chimed in Sandra.

"Who do you think did this?" asked the sheriff.

"I haven't been back here in fifteen years and I have no idea what is going on."

"Seems to me, years ago I heard something about you running off, but I don't quite remember the details. It was a long time ago, back when I was a deputy. I met your dad on one dang cold, rainy night when I was tracking a fugitive. Stopped in here and he made sure I got a hot meal and let me sleep in the barn. Nice man. We visited for about an hour before he turned in, never forgot his hospitality."

"My father was a nice man, at least the part of him I knew."

"So what do you mean by that?" demanded the sheriff in a rough tone.

"Only that he was gone so much that I saw very little of him. When he was here he was the best father a boy could ever want, but he wasn't around that much. He was out of town on business a lot and would never tell me what he did or what the job was. Whoever killed all of these people and didn't steal anything was sending a message as far as I'm concerned. They were serious about their business. These men were professionals. They didn't leave a single clue that I can find as to where my father is or who these killers are."

"I need your address and where I can get a hold of you. We plan to do a full investigation here. Roper says he gave you quite the hit to the head—are you all right?"

"No, not really, but I need to get Sandra back home and away from all this. It wasn't the homecoming we were expecting."

"With your dad missing, you are in charge of this place. Who will do the talking for you while you're gone?"

"I have known Roper since we were children. I plan to have him clean everything up and get the place back on its feet while I take Sandra home. As soon as I get her home and settled, I will return."

"Give me the information we need and you two can be on your way."

Gillis met with Roper for a few minutes to discuss plans and then gave him a hundred dollars in currency before hitching up the carriage and leading the horses out of the barn.

"Thanks, sheriff. I appreciate you getting here fast. Roper, I will see you in another week or so. Leastwise I will be back here as soon as I can. We will let the dust settle and hopefully know more about what happened and why."

Sandra climbed into the carriage with Gillis's help. He climbed in the other side, picked up the reins, and released the brake. He took a moment to look back before snapping the whip lightly and sending the carriage down the road.

It was several hours before sunset when the carriage rounded the bend and Gillis could see the roadhouse they had stayed at earlier. Gillis turned to Sandra. "Would you like to stay here for the night? At least we know we can have a bath, and the food wasn't bad."

"That's fine. I am exhausted by this whole thing, and it's really drained me."

"I'm sorry—it was meant to be an enjoyable meeting with my father. I have no clue about what is going on but I will."

As the carriage approached the front door, Gillis saw Willard was sitting on the porch. "Howdy folks, you came back."

"Unfortunately not by our choice," replied Gillis.

"Same oats and good rub down for the horses?"

"That would be fine. Go ahead and take the carriage. I will get the baggage myself."

"Sure thing, sir."

Gillis helped Sandra down and went back for the two large and one small bag. He climbed the stairs and went through the door held open by Sandra.

The two walked to the front desk and the heavy lady with the yellowed teeth walked out to greet them from the kitchen. "Well, well, looks who's back, hope you had a good trip."

"Let's just say it wasn't what we had expected. Anyway we need two rooms, dinner, and a couple of baths."

"We can get the first bath started right away. I will have my girls start heating the water. It will be at least an hour before the second bath is ready."

"Sandra, I'll take your bags up to your room. You relax before your bath and I will sit down here and have a whiskey. Once you are ready, we can have dinner and then I will have my bath."

Sandra nodded and headed up the stairs with Gillis following behind with her bags in tow.

For the first time in his life Gillis looked for a table that gave him a good view of the inn. He sat down and ordered a scotch and tried to think through what had happened. He felt miserable. What was meant to be a great outing had become a total nightmare. As he sat staring aimlessly forward he saw a middle-aged woman come in and look around for a moment before proceeding to a table of men she seemed to know. They talked for a moment and then she moved on to another table and finally the front counter. She talked for less than a minute to the heavy woman who had gotten Gillis the rooms before heading back out the main door.

Willard walked up. "Got the horses all taken care of and they got their extra oats just like you requested."

Gillis was shaken from his thoughts for a moment. "Thank you," he said as he flipped the man a coin.

"I saw you looking at the woman. Lost her husband the night you and the lady stopped in a few days ago, just disappeared. He never came home to the missus and the kids. A man like that just doesn't come up missing without a trace if you ask me."

"What do you mean?" Gillis asked.

"Well him being an ex-scout and all. He knew this country like the back of his hand."

"So he went missing. What did he look like?"

"Pretty much like all the others with beards, medium in build, wore buckskins most of the time."

"I remember him. Wasn't he the one having the argument with those other men?"

"Yeah, he is a little cantankerous when he drinks but he's a good man," said Willard. "I hope the wife finds him soon. That family was already in poor shape before he disappeared. They are being foreclosed on by the bank. It's been a hard row for them since his knee injury. He could ride okay but he couldn't farm. Some of his friends have been helping when they could but then he comes up missing and well, I don't know what's going to happen."

Gillis listened and took the whole thing in. "I hope they find him." He then reached into his pocket and pulled out some coins, singling out a five-dollar gold piece. "Give this to the wife, I hope it helps."

"That's awful generous for a man that doesn't even know them folk."

"I have had some rough times myself lately. I hope they find him. I do have a question though."

"What's that, mister?"

"Has anyone said anything about a whole lot of murders at the Scully McCabe farm?"

Willard stood there and shook his head, "Nope, haven't heard a thing."

* * *

For the next four days they rode back towards Williamsburg. At night they would stop at different roadhouses but during the trip Sandra talked little. Gillis continually tried to find new and interesting topics to discuss but Sandra seemed distant and in no real mood to converse. Finally on the fourth day of their journey they could see the outskirts of Williamsburg and Sandra began her normal chatter. Gillis felt relieved that Sandra seemed to finally becoming more herself and out of her terrible nightmare. Several times she mentioned seeing her father and how nice it would be to get home.

The carriage made a sharper than normal turn in the street as it rounded the corner to Sandra's home. Suddenly Gillis pulled the reins back hard as he yelled, "Whoa" in a loud voice. In front of Sandra's house was a small crowd including five or six policemen.

"Oh my God, what happened?" asked Sandra in a desperate voice.

Gillis walked the team closer to the crowd when a man came up to the carriage. "What's going on?" asked Gillis, as Sandra stared at the man.

"You haven't heard? Judge Richards was murdered."

Chapter 3

Sandra jumped from the carriage and ran toward the house. A thick-shouldered guard stood at the door blocking people from entering and for a moment looked as if he might stop the crying Sandra. At the last minute he seemed to recognize her and pulled back as Sandra ran through the door and into the house. Gillis turned the carriage around and drove back to an unoccupied hitching post several hundred yards away from the noisy crowd and tied the team. He had a knot in his gut as he got down from the carriage and started walking toward the house not knowing what he would say or do. He was convinced that this was not just a coincidence.

He walked to the edge of the small crowd alive with chatter over what had transpired and began asking questions. Gillis saw a man standing in the back and said, "Excuse me, sir, but can you tell me what happened?" The man seemed to carry himself with more presence than most which is why Gillis chose him.

"I really don't think anyone knows the whole truth, but from what I have heard they found the judge dead in his chambers, the victim of a stranger. One of the men that helped carry the judge's body out of the courthouse said he had a small bloody hole in the back of his head the size of an ice pick. Whoever killed him must have been part ghost to walk past that many people and into his private chambers."

Gillis stared at the man for a moment, then thanked him and started toward the Richards's front door. As he climbed the steps the police officer stationed beside the door abruptly stopped him. "Sorry, sir, but my boss says no one is allowed past this point without authorization."

"I understand, but I am Miss Richards's fiancé. Can you get someone to allow me to join her?"

"Just a minute, sir, and I will check. Would you mind waiting here?"

"That will be fine."

The guard opened the door and closed it behind himself as he disappeared into the house. Moments later a black servant that Gillis recognized followed the guard back out the door.

"Hamilton, would you mind telling this guard who I am so I can come in?"

"Master Gillis, Miss Sandra asked me to tell you that she would be in contact with you as soon as she feels up to it, but she needs some time alone right now."

A feeling of confusion and anger filtered through his body as Gillis turned and slowly walked down the stairs and through the crowd toward his carriage. What had just happened? Why was his world crumbling around him? Nothing made sense.

The ride back to Norfolk was gut-wrenching as he tried to sort out the week's events. Everything had been going so perfectly in his life and now everything was turned upside down. Why would anyone kill the judge and in such a public place? He knew the judge was looking at running for governor but to his knowledge he hadn't even given formal notice of his intent, so why would he be a target? Why had his father's estate been attacked and with such savagery? And where was his father? Was he dead, a captive or maybe hiding somewhere? Gillis tumbled the questions through his head but it was no use. Without more information he wasn't going to find answers.

The gates to his estate, Glen Hollow, were wide open as he steered the carriage through the entrance and toward the carriage house. The heavy clicking of the horse hooves on the stone pavers could easily be heard in the house. Several of the servants quickly appeared as he pulled the reins back and came to a full stop. Gillis had no slaves but many employees and servants and he paid them well to maintain his estate. After the shipyard took off financially, he would sometimes go to the slave market and buy certain slaves, and let them work off part of their sale price. He would then offer them a job as free men. He trusted these men and women and they were extremely loyal. His head servant, Lawrence, had been with him for almost six years and he did a great job of managing the staff and grounds. Even though it was against the law, Gillis had secretly tutored him in reading and math.

"Mr. Gillis, nice to have you back. Did you have a nice trip?" asked Lawrence.

"Regrettably I didn't, Lawrence. I think someone may have killed my father and when I took Miss Sandra home someone had murdered her father. I don't know what is going on but we need to station guards around the property and if we don't have enough people, we need to hire more. But make sure they can handle a gun and you trust them."

"Yes sir, Mr. Gillis, I will see to it right away."

Gillis walked up the wide stairs of the grand porch and entered his house. Walking past the kitchen he plopped himself down on a dining room chair. There had to be a reason, an answer to what was happening. Murders weren't an everyday occurrence and to have Letty and Sandra's father both killed so close together couldn't be just a coincidence. He poured himself a tall whiskey and drank a small amount before Lawrence walked through the hallway entrance. "Sir, Dr. Bennett is here to see you. He saw you ride up."

Doc Bennett had been a close friend for the last five years. They met at a dinner party in Norfolk and hit it off right away. Standing almost six foot three and close to one hundred and seventy pounds, he was skinny and narrow but was stately in his presence. It didn't take Gillis long to recognize the doctor was blessed with a kind heart and a quick wit.

"Hi Doc, come on in."

"Gillis, did you hear that Judge Richards was murdered in his chambers?"

At first Gillis just nodded and then spoke. "I have been with Sandra for a little more than a week and brought her home this afternoon. She found out her father was dead by a loud mouth gent on the street in front of her house. She jumped from the carriage and ran into the house. After I tied up the team, I hurried to her front door and was told by her servant that she didn't want to see me and that we would talk later."

The doctor pulled out a chair and sat down. "Sorry to hear that, Gillis, I am sure this was extremely hard on her. She will need some time to assimilate the whole thing. Surely, she isn't blaming you for a murder that happened while you two were up visiting your father?"

Gillis proceeded with telling Doc Bennett the whole story. His friend nodded before he slowly spoke.

"Did you ever figure out where your father was?"

"No, from what I can tell he either escaped or was lucky enough to not be there."

"Really, why would anyone do such a horrible deed? What possible motive could they have?"

"The only thing I can think is that they were looking for someone or something and they intended to send a strong message. I have no clue how this puzzle fits together with the judge or the disappearance of my father, but whoever did this certainly knew what they were doing."

"Is that what Sandra thought too?"

"She didn't say but Roper and I talked and he agreed with me. He is one of my father's slaves. I grew up with him. He's a very capable man and ran the estate in my father's absence. In the next couple of days I will need to head back up to his estate and get this figured out. I may be gone for some time."

"Did you find anything that might give you a clue?"

"Not a thing. These men did a thorough job."

"What can I do?"

"You're a good friend, Doc, I appreciate you asking. I may need some assistance in the future but not now. I will be using my father's estate as my base until I understand what I am up against. Lawrence will be checking the telegraph station every day around four for my messages and he will contact you if I need your help. Right now I just need to get back up there."

In a tone slightly louder than a whisper, Doc spoke. "Regrettably, we all might have some large problems shortly. The rumor in town is the South has declared war on the Union. People are really getting fired up. For a long time I held out hope that somehow a peaceful solution might be found."

"You think it has gone that far?"

"I do. Unfortunately the level-headed people have been shouted down. When President Buchanan left office and President Lincoln began saying that no new territories will have slaves, the talk of war became a heated topic."

Moving forward in his chair, Gillis replied, "I love the South but I side with Lincoln on this one. I don't agree with slavery. The South is foolish to think they can win a war against the North. They have all the factories, the raw materials, and the vast majority of the shipping, not to mention the money."

"I don't think they are looking at this with a clear head, they're emotional and mad. They think they can win the war in six months and be done with it."

"That's crazy. Can't they see what they are up against?"

"Most aren't well traveled or as thoughtful as you. Anyway I need to get home. I saw you in your carriage and thought I would extend you a dinner invitation. I know how you love my wife's cooking. We would enjoy having you over if you're available. It's been a while."

"I appreciate the offer but I don't see myself having much time for a while. Tell her thank you and I look forward to having dinner with you two when I get back."

* * *

The next day Gillis rode one of his Morgan horses to Norfolk's largest bank, Citizens United of Virginia. He maneuvered his horse through the maze of carriages occupying the muddy streets until he saw an empty hitching post and tied up. Dismounting, he walked up the wide stairs of the bank's entrance and toward the door. An armed guard dressed in a uniform similar to a police officer stood to one side of the door with a musket. "Greetings, Mr. McCabe, nice to have you back."

Gillis tipped his hat and went in. The main part of the bank was a large room supported by tall granite columns that were ornately carved and decorated. Gillis walked up to an oak desk where an older lady in a black dress sat busily working until she looked up.

"Well, Mr. McCabe, I haven't seen you in far too long. What can I help you with?"

"I need to make several withdrawals. Is Mr. O'Malley in?"

"He sure is, just give me a moment and I will announce your presence. I am sure he will see you right away."

Within seconds a tall, well-dressed man with graying sideburns and a mustache walked out of the room with his hand extended.

"Gillis, how is the bank's best customer?" asked the man with a thick Irish accent.

"I'm good, Jake, nice to see you. Do you have a couple of minutes that we can visit in your office? I need to conduct a little business."

"Sure, sure, come in, how might I be of service?" he said as the two men took seats opposite of each other.

"You probably won't be too happy with what I have to say but I need to transfer half of my assets to the Bank of New York. My attorney will be getting ahold of you first thing tomorrow to handle the details that might arise. I'm sorry I have to do that but there is a business deal I am working out."

Mr. O'Malley looked at Gillis for a moment with a stare of disbelief. Finally he nodded his head. "Certainly, I will have my staff get the money ready as soon as possible. We will miss not having all your business."

"One more thing, I want five thousand in U.S. currency and the other forty five thousand in gold bars."

The banker looked perplexed, and then nodded again. "That may take me a day or so to put together—is that all right?"

"Do the best you can, the sooner the better. One last thing, today is Monday, would you mind having the money delivered to my home just before sunrise on Wednesday? I want to draw as little attention to this as possible."

"Yes sir, we will have several armed guards deliver it Wednesday morning."

Gillis shook the man's hand and walked back down the wide stairs of the bank to his horse. He lifted the stirrup and tightened the cinch as he carefully scanned the street before launching himself up onto the stout sorrel. The past week had rattled him and he was determined to being aware of his surroundings. He hadn't felt this sense of vulnerability since his early days when he lived on the streets before finding a job. His fingers felt the pocket of his coat and he was comforted by the bulge of his handmade miniature revolver. He would be alone on his ride back to his father's estate and he planned to pack some firepower just in case.

* * *

It was almost noon on Tuesday and Gillis had just finished packing. He had a change of clothes and blankets for his stay in the woods. He planned to by-pass the normal inns on his route and sleep in the woods. This would draw the least amount of attention. It had been a while since he spent time in the woods and in some strange way he was looking forward to the challenge. He heard a gentle knock on the door as he finished packing and saw Lawrence standing in the doorway.

"A letter just got delivered from Miss Sandra, Mr. McCabe. I thought you would want to know as soon as possible."

"Thanks, Lawrence." Gillis cut the seal and quickly removed the letter.

Dearest Gill,

The past week has been the hardest of my life. I really don't know what is happening and what I have to say is very difficult. In my heart I will always have a place for you but I can't be engaged right now. I need time to heal and figure out where I am going. I hope you understand.

Love, Sandra

Gillis put the letter back into the envelope and slipped it into his inside coat pocket. A feeling of frustration and confusion came over him. He just sat and stared for a moment before regaining his composure and finished packing the last couple of items. The letter took him by surprise. Finally, he decided he would stick to his plans and hope Sandra would change her mind. Feeling like he had been kicked in the stomach, he walked down the stairs from his bedroom carrying his two bags. After arriving at the carriage house, he set the bags down beside the two reinforced bags that would carry the gold. He threw two canvas manties out on the floor, then carefully placed his supplies and clothes on them. He tightly secured the manties around the gear with rope and weighed both sides to make sure they were very close to matching weights. He struggled the rest of the day wondering if he was doing the right thing.

*   *   *

It was the crack of dawn on Wednesday morning when three armed men in heavy wool uniforms brought a wagon through the gates of Glen Hollow.

Gillis walked out into the cobblestone courtyard to meet them. One of the men held a double barrel shotgun. "Good morning," said Gillis.

The three men almost in unison responded, "Good morning, sir." The slightly overweight man driving the wagon spoke, "Sir, where would you like this unloaded?"

"Just inside the carriage house door will be just fine."

The heavy man who drove the wagon handed Gillis a paper, pen, and a small ink well. Gillis looked at the document for a minute, then signed it and handed it back. The other two men unloaded the wagon quickly and stacked the two bags by the door of the carriage house.

"Thank you, sir. Be careful and have a nice day," said the guard. With a gentle snap of the reins the horses turned and headed back out into the street.

"I will be taking one hundred and fifty pounds of gold bars with me and all the cash. Put the rest of the gold in front of the safe. I will be there shortly to unlock it. I will need you to go to the livery later today and buy two good pack mules in the fourteen or fifteen hand range. I want them stocky and old enough that they have their heads on straight. Pay a little more if you have to, but bring back good, experienced animals. It's going to be important that I get to my father's estate without issue. Lock the gold and cash I am taking in the carriage house for the night and have two men you can trust guard it. I will also need a good sawed-off shotgun. If I am not mistaken, we have one downstairs in the gun closet."

"Will there be anything else, sir?"

"No, not right now. Get the money and gold taken care of. Then head into town and buy those mules and a couple of pack-saddles that fit."

Later Gillis went out to the carriage house and got two heavy pack bags that were in storage and laid them beside the gold. He then cut two, half-inch-thick boards to length to place on the insides of each pack bag to protect the mule's side. Next he carefully put an even number of bars in each bag to make sure they balanced. Grabbing some old burlap sacks he stuffed several in each end of the pack bag and laid one loosely on top to disguise the contents. He took him an hour adjusting the loads until they looked more like ordinary pack bags that hopefully no one would notice.

It was almost dark when Lawrence rode in leading two well-muscled, black mules. Gillis could see from the look on Lawrence's face that he was proud of his purchase. "How did you do?"

Lawrence smiled from ear to ear as he looked back at the two mules he was leading. "Two of the best pack mules in all Virginia. A little on the expensive side but as you know, mules go for a lot more than plain horses."

* * *

The next morning Gillis was up hours before sunrise putting together the last of his gear which included another rifle and scabbard, as well as additional ammunition which he placed in his saddlebags. It was still dark when Gillis walked outside where Lawrence was putting the pack saddle on the mules.

"Lawrence, I see you have this under control. Is my horse saddled and do I have those extra rations as we discussed?"

"Yes sir, extra rations and ammunition for you and extra oats for the stock. I think you are really going to like these mules, sir. The man that owned them was real proud of them. Hopefully you will find them more than acceptable. Are you sure you don't want me or some of the men to accompany you? It's a long trip."

"I will be fine, Lawrence. I plan to slip out of here before anyone even knows I am gone. With these mules I won't have to stick to roads. I think that will be an advantage considering the circumstances. Let's check the cinches one last time and then load."

With a quick good-bye Gillis mounted and quietly led the mules single file out the gates. Their shoes were a lot noisier on the cobble stones than he would have liked. He quickly headed for a dirt strip covered by dark shadows and away from the generously spaced street lights. With everything else going on somehow it felt good to be alone. He was scared and excited to be leaving as he knew this trip could be dangerous. After riding for a little over a mile, he left the dimly lit streets and headed into the darkness, never noticing the hidden figure that quietly watched.

It was an hour after sunrise before he finally passed his first person, an elderly man driving an old wagon pulled by two tired and thin horses. He gave a casual wave and kept going. Over the next eight hours he passed numerous wagons and people walking and on horses. This was exciting for Gillis and he found himself a bit smug that he had vanished unnoticed into the darkness. With the exception of some people very close to him, no one knew he was gone. He would need to find an isolated spot for the night where he could hide the stock and still provide some graze. The mules were everything Lawrence thought they would be and Gillis could see they were already bonding with his horse.

It was quickly becoming evening and he had ridden all day without a problem. On a narrow curve in the dirt road Gillis noticed a lightly used game trail that dropped off the road. He carefully led the string down into a small gulley and then began working his way up the other side. He was careful not to make his path visible from the road. Leading his animals up the hill on the other side, he made sure that the vegetation hid his route. As he rode over a small hill he noticed a small protected meadow hidden in the trees. The spot was almost perfect to hide a small fire and give the stock enough grass for the night.

Gillis picketed the horse and tied one mule to a rope highline so the lead rope could slide as the mules fed. The second mule he hobbled and then let loose. He still wasn't sure the mules wouldn't decide to leave but having one tied was reasonable insurance. He had vague memories of the summer of his thirteenth birthday and how he and his father had gone on a number of camping trips. Like many of his childhood memories they were vague and almost forgotten. Gillis hoped he wouldn't have problems with the stock and later that night he planned to exchange mules and tie the second one up.

The camp spot had an old, dry stump where he could get enough wood to keep a tiny fire burning. Gillis felt comfortable and was sure the wood would put out little to no smoke. The mules and the horse settled down almost immediately as Gillis fixed himself some supper. Two hours later he exchanged mules and put the slightly taller of the two mules out on hobbles.

This feeling of being alone in a strange place was a long-lost memory to him, but it was strangely appealing. He pulled out his pipe, stuffed it with shredded tobacco, and lit it with the end of a stick from the fire. He took several puffs and then listened to the hoot of an owl several hundred yards up the ridge. He glanced over to see the mules staring at him. Suddenly he felt the cold barrel of a pistol against the back of his head and heard the pistol being cocked.

Chapter 4

"You move one muscle before I tell you and you're a dead man. Do we understand each other? You need to know I'm not your enemy but I believe the three men out there that have been trailing you all day are. Now slowly stand up and turn around. I am good with a knife and gun and if you do one thing before I tell you, it will be your last. Now slowly stand up, turn around, and keep your hands up."

Gillis deliberately took his time standing up not wanting to give this man, whoever he was, a reason to shoot.

"Tell me, sir, who might you be and what are your intentions?"

"I go by Wooly. I was the man you saw in the inn near your father's estate. I was arguing with those two men that were dressed in black clothes. I saw you glance at us. Those men baited me there and then tried to kill me."

"I still don't know what that has to do with me."

"First of all I want to thank you for giving my family that gold piece, it was much appreciated."

"You are welcome but I know you didn't hunt me down just to say thank you for a coin."

"I really need to start at the beginning. About three weeks ago three men rode into my farm. My family has really been struggling since I hurt my knee, and to tell you the truth, we are real short on money. Well, this stocky fellow gets down from his fine horse and tells me that he heard that I knew this country like the back of my hand. He asks if I might be willing to be hired out as a guide for a few days and he was willing to pay top dollar."

"Did he say who he was or why they were there?"

"He just reached in his pocket and gave me a ten dollar gold piece and said that should be enough to answer all my questions. The way I saw it I didn't have much choice. We were late with the taxes, and if it weren't for the neighbors, we wouldn't have gotten by."

"To do what?"

"He asked me if I knew the country up around your pa's place. I knew that area pretty darn well because I used to run hounds there. Your pa has a real nice place, well-kept and beautiful. When we got on this hill overlooking your place we dismounted and they used an eyeglass to look things over. They asked me a lot of questions about the roads going in and out and if I knew anyone that lived in those parts. I had heard of your family but I sure hadn't rubbed elbows with them. They just kept asking questions until I plum ran out of answers. The leader said something quiet-like to one of his men and then they rode out. I was getting a real uneasy feeling about the whole thing—something just wasn't right."

"Did you recognize any of these men or had you seen them before?"

"Nope, never seen them before, but the more I was around them the worse my gut feeling was. The man that stayed behind with me was real quiet and tough-looking. He went over to his saddlebags and started to open them. That's when I knew something was up. I kicked out his knee, and as he fell, I punched him in the face and jumped on my horse and got the shuck out of there."

"So do you think he intended to kill you?"

"I sure as shoot did. I think he was overconfident. In a fair fight he would be hell to handle."

"Did they say anything about killing my family?"

"Nope, not a thing. By the way, you can put your hands down. Just don't reach for anything real fast until we work through this. Anyways as I was saying, I have done a few things in my time that I am not proud of but I never killed no one except maybe an Injun or two out West. When I left there, I knew they weren't going to leave no witnesses and it was then or never. I high-tailed it down the road and took some trails I knew would lead me close to my farm. I waited back in the trees, watching as my wife fed the chickens and hogs. I wasn't sure what if anything would happen but I didn't want to take chances. I just stayed hidden until the next day when I saw them riding in. The two men that led the way were at your pa's place. They rode in towards the front porch while my wife was getting water from the well. I had taught my boys since they were young'uns how to shoot and when a stranger approaches to hide and get a good rest until they know if they are friend or foe."

"I kept my musket on them the whole time as they talked to the missus. Just seeing those men again made the hair on the back of my neck curl. I knew I had made a mistake helping them but the money kind of blinded me. Anyway, they left a message with my wife for me to meet them in the inn the next night and then left."

"What was the message?"

"It was a bunch of crap, fresh from the outhouse and I knew it. They said they just wanted to meet and give me the other half of the money they owed me. Hell, if they really wanted to do that they would have given it to the missus and been gone. I'm not so sure they didn't see one of the boys sticking their gun barrel out from the barn, but they didn't give the missus any trouble and rode off."

"So when my fiancée and I arrived at the inn it was you and those two men that were arguing?"

"Yeah, I knew it was a trap but I had to figure out how to play the hand I was dealt. As soon as they rode out from the farm I had the wife and kids go stay with the neighbors. I had to get to the bottom of what was happening. I knew they didn't intend to pay me but I had no intentions of running the rest of my life. I thought the inn was as good a public place as any to try and find out what was going on."

"Did you learn anything?"

"Not really. I went back to the inn a couple of hours before I thought they would arrive and snuck in and talked to Molly, she's the heavyset woman that runs the place. Anyway I knew she had a trap door on the back porch that someone originally built years ago in case of Indian attack. One day when I unloaded a wagon for her and accidentally sat a heavy box on the door, I discovered it. Otherwise I would have never known about it. I figured that once I got in there they would lay a trap outside in the dark where no one would see who done the killing. These men are hard bred. I wasn't around them for a long but in a scrap, my bet would be these men would have been as good as any fighting men I have ever gone against. The way I saw it I only had one advantage and that was a big one."

"What are you talking about, what advantage?"

"These men are born and raised city folk, you can just tell. They might be good with a knife or a gun but they were lost in the back country. I noticed it right away when I saw their tracks following you out of town.

Their track showed they rode straight ahead, three abreast. Never checked their back trail or dismounted to check out other tracks on the road. I watched them from a little distance and only occasionally did they check the hillside. When they did, they didn't see anything. It was pretty obvious that they never spent much time in the woods. Heck, they never even tried to hide their direction or how many of them there was."

"What did those men say to you in the inn?"

"They were all pleasant and said there had been a misunderstanding of their intentions and they certainly didn't mean for me to feel threatened. I knew they were up to no good. I lost my temper a couple of times. I wanted them to know that I wasn't afraid of them. They said they had the other half of my money out in their saddle bags. Told me we should have a couple ales and then let them pay me for a job well done. I certainly didn't let on that I wasn't buying anything they were selling. When it came time to leave, the three of us got up and I said I would meet them outside. I told them that I had to tell Molly something. As soon as they went through the door, I snuck out the back door, dropped to the floor and began crawling out onto the back porch. I made my way to the trap door, opened it and slid down inside to the ground. In the moonlight you could actually see pretty well. I stayed in the darkest corner under the porch for close to ten minutes before I heard footsteps on the porch that walked down the steps and out into the yard. I could tell from the shiny tall, black boots that they belonged to one of them fellows from the inn. He went from one side of the yard to the other before another man in dark gray clothing joined him. They were really mad and cussing up a storm as they continued to search. I bet they were out there for close to an hour before they gave up and rode away."

"The afternoon of the next day I checked out the inn real good before I snuck back through the back door and that's when Molly told me about the massacre at your father's place. I felt real guilty that in some way I may have helped these men and wanted to tell you to your face what happened. That's why I came to Norfolk to talk to you. I hear you're a good man and I appreciated your generosity to my family. Maybe I could tell you how sorry I was and help you in whatever way I could."

"I finally made it to Norfolk late afternoon and found someone that gave me directions to where you lived. It was getting pretty dark as I led my horse towards your place and from a distance I saw a guard standing at your gate. I knew with what had happened you would probably be real nervous. So I thought I would bed down at the livery stable until morning. Then come see you at first light. As I stood back in the shadows I saw some movement across the street from your home. There was a man dressed in black and he seemed to be watching your house. I watched for at least twenty minutes but he stayed right there in those bushes watching, so I headed over to the stable and bedded down for the night."

"In the morning I got up early and waited until light to head over to your place. I left the horse in the stable so I could walk and kind of just slip out if I needed to. When I finally reached your home, the man I had seen the previous night was gone and I had a gut feeling you were in trouble. I walked to the gate and asked the man that was guarding it if I might speak to you and he said you weren't taking visitors. So I got my horse and rode to the edge of town where I saw fresh horse and mule tracks. One of those mules was carrying an extra heavy load. I knew the tracks were from early that morning or late last night, so I bet that you were headed back to your folks' house. But I also noticed something else. There were three more sets of tracks following you. I could tell by the make of the shoe that the tracks were made by some of the same horses those men rode that tried to kill me. Their tracks were right over yours."

"So you think they are after us?"

"No, right now they are after you. I'm pretty sure they don't know I am here, but if they did I am sure they would enjoy doing away with me too."

"But you don't know who they were?"

"No clue, they were always careful not to talk much in front of me. I surely didn't see a thing that would lead me to believe they planned to kill someone."

"Did you hear that my fiancée's father, Judge Richards had been murdered?"

"No, I didn't. I just got into town last night and I really didn't talk to anyone while I was on the road and slept nights in the hills."

Gillis slowly sat down. "Well, where do we go from here?"

"I'm pretty sure they don't know we are here. I got ahead of them and took a branch and wiped your tracks where you got off road. Tomorrow early we can make a detour up through these hills and try and get moving without being seen. If it is all right with you I will bring my horse over and tie him close to the others. We will have a long day tomorrow. It's a lot slower route but one heck of a lot safer."

* * *

The following morning they ate a little breakfast and began saddling the stock. Wooly was done quickly with his horse and grabbed a blanket and sawbuck for one of the mules. Thoroughly smoothing the wrinkles from the blanket, he laid it on the mule's back and carefully settled the pack saddle. He was so quick he had started on the second mule before Gillis could finish with his horse.

"I see you must have done this a time or two."

"Yeah, I ran a pack string out West one summer for some miners. Made good money until some robbers decided to bushwhack them. Robbed and killed them both and I was out of a job."

"You say you never met my father?"

"Nope, heard of him though. Heard he raises good mules. He bred to good mares. Not like most places where they breed their ass to the ranch's raunchiest stock. He was known for quality and it's told that he asks a pretty penny for them too."

"I didn't know my father had started raising mules, that's news to me."

"Mules fetch good money, more than your average horse, at least for people that are headed west. There is a real demand for them critters on wagon trains and men planning to mine."

Wooly took a quick glance in Gillis's direction after he picked up the first heavy pack but never said a thing. A few minutes later the small troop headed out around the hill on a seldom-used game trail and headed north away from the road. Even with the dead falls, the pace was good and the loads rode well. They only needed to adjust the pack once when one of the mules snagged a pack bag on a red oak sapling. Wooly quickly dismounted, straightened the pack that had been leaning to one side and added a small rock for balance.

The spring day was cool but rays of sunlight broke through the canopy of mature maples and oaks. The wet leaves on the trail made the going quiet but left an easy trail to follow. Gillis could tell Wooly felt good that they were headed away from the main road. According to him there was a lightly used road to the north that paralleled the one they left. Unfortunately the reason it wasn't used much anymore was because of the difficult river crossing caused by the bridge being washed away years before.

Three hours later they broke from the forest of deciduous trees onto the grassy, overgrown road. The road bed was firm and fairly dry and small shrubs encroached on both sides. Wooly pulled back on the reins of his horse and stepped down from his saddle. For a few minutes he studied the road and woods on both sides before mounting back up.

"There hasn't been anyone through here for quite a spell. What do you think about catching a bite to eat? We can make good time this afternoon. There is a place not more than ten miles from here that would make a good safe camp for the night."

"That sounds great," said Gillis as he dismounted and led his mules over to copse of small trees and started tying the lead ropes.

"You might want to tie that quick knot a mite higher in case we have a roller amongst them mules. I would hate to have to repack them again. Tying high keeps their head up enough that most animals don't think they have enough length to roll—just my thoughts."

Gillis gave Wooly a bit of an indignant look before loosening the knot he had just tied and retying it higher on the tree.

"I really haven't packed for years. I won't forget again."

"Don't mean to insult, just trying to save time."

"I appreciate that. Sorry for the look. I guess I just haven't had much criticism in my life and don't handle it well."

It was close to dark when the two men stopped and Wooly pointed. "Over in those trees is water and plenty of grass. That's the meadow I was talking about."

Less than thirty minutes later the stock was quietly grazing on either a picket line or hobbled. Gillis was collecting wood while Wooly filled both their canteens and the coffee pot. The sound of the wood crackling on the small fire was comforting and Wooly set the coffee pot on a flat rock strategically placed to take advantage of the coals.

Gillis slowly sat down beside the fire. He was tired and sore and he knew his face showed it. The air was clear and the night was slightly cold. Using his saddle as a pillow he relaxed and let his mind wander. In the course of two weeks he had gone from being engaged and carefree to losing his fiancée, having his father come up missing, the woman that had raised him was dead and now his fiancée's father had been murdered. And to add insult to injury, he was being pursued by three men he didn't know.

"The coffee is ready, would you like some?"

Gillis extended his cup and Wooly filled it halfway. Wooly turned and began to stir the brown beans that simmered in the shallow pot against the fire. Minutes later he handed Gillis a plate of steaming beans, a chunk of pilot bread, and some slices of dried apples.

"Thanks, Wooly. I didn't really mean for you to wait on me. I guess I have had it pretty easy for the last few years. Having someone fix dinner was just normal." Gillis quickly ate his dinner and gulped a second cup of coffee before taking Wooly's empty plate and heading down to the stream. Putting the plates into the small creek, he used a little sand to wash them. He had to find his father or if needed, his father's killers. Gillis had the resources to hire good fighting men to help and he would if need be. He had told Roper that he would be back as soon as he could and directed him to hire more men that could be trusted and knew how to fight. If this group of mystery men decided to come back they would find their greeting totally different.

Gillis walked back to the small fire and sat down. Wooly sat quietly sipping his coffee. Gillis was impressed with this man he barely knew. He could handle or avoid trouble, but more important was the fact he knew how to survive. Gillis had learned from his father to take your time when judging a man and now he wondered if he could trust the stranger across the fire. Certainly there were more than a few opportunities to do him in, and he probably knew about the gold. Riding all the way to Norfolk to say he was sorry and thank a person for a gift was far out of the range of most men. Yet he had warned him that he was being followed. Wooly didn't strike him as a mean man, more of a man of character, one who could take care of himself and put up with little nonsense.

* * *

The next morning they got up and Gillis found himself sore and tired but he rose quickly to make a fire. Wooly was tying the two mules to trees close to the packs. The skill and speed of which he saddled the two mules was impressive and Gillis almost stopped to watch before turning and walking down to the stream for water. By the time Gillis was back, the two mules had their sawbucks snuggly fitted and the horses were ready except for their bridles. They quickly ate some salted beef and pilot bread before loading the mules. Again Wooly chose not to comment on the heavy packs that carried the gold and Gillis was glad he didn't. There was a small fortune in gold. Gillis remembered his father saying gold spoke volumes; it loosened tight tongues and opened doors.

For several hours they rode making good time. At first it was almost unnoticeable in the distance but the closer they rode the more the sound of crashing water met Gillis's ear. It was a good ten minutes before they actually could see the foaming, thrashing water. The swollen creek raced through a thick bed of boulders on its way down the mountain. Gillis, who was leading the two mules, gave his Morgan a slight nudge to catch up beside Wooly's horse.

"How in the hell are we going to get across that river?" asked Gillis.

The moss-covered remnants of a heavy wooden bridge that once spanned the gorge were all but gone and now only a few beams and logs remained.

"We aren't, at least not here," Wooly said. "Trying it here would be suicide and I don't think either one of us are headed on that course. We need to head downstream about a half a mile to where the river spreads out a mite. I have crossed there many times but I don't remember ever crossing when it was this high. Anyways, it gets better downstream a ways."

Gillis tried to take the whole thing in. The water looked like it would have no problem swallowing a man and his horse, never to be seen again. The going for the next hour was a little rough following the overgrown trail that paralleled the river. Finally Wooly took one of the mules from Gillis and nudged him into the water onto a sandy bar.

"I think we have our best chance here. The footing looks good and the water is moving right along but it doesn't appear more than a couple of feet deep. I hope those loads aren't too heavy for them mules. They may have to swim if it gets any deeper."

When Lawrence had come back from buying the two mules he said they were athletic and strong, and hopefully he was right. Gillis followed Wooly into the current and as the water began to reach the horse's stirrups. Suddenly the powerful gelding threw his head back as his eyes bulged at the sockets. All of the animals struggled for footing as the force of the white water pounded and swirled around their legs. One of the mules pulled back and the lead slipped from Gillis's grip as he turned in a desperate attempt to grab it. Gillis leaning backwards was just enough to put the large Morgan off balance as he fell into the foaming water. The impact threw Gillis to the side and into the water and the next thing he saw was water going over his head. He felt a rock hit his leg and then another one hit his back as he attempted to swim toward the surface. The icy water pelted his body. He was desperate to break to the surface. He could see the sunlit water of the surface. Now he knew which way was up. His heavy clothing was pulling him down. He knew the crashing water would kill him if he didn't get a breath soon.

His head broke through to the surface and he gasped for air before being immediately pulled back into the powerful current. Again he was under the water and he launched himself toward the surface, extending his arm, searching for something to grab. He was quickly becoming exhausted. He had to work himself toward shore. Another rock tumbled him back under the water and his foot touched bottom again. He was losing his strength. There was energy for one final attempt.

Suddenly he felt something on his wrist and it was digging deep into his exposed skin. He never saw the boulder that the rushing water smashed him against. His whole body went limp.

Chapter 5

Gillis fought to open his swollen eyes. He could hear the crackling of a fire and the scent of burning wood. He was wrapped tightly in several wool blankets and when he tried to move they restrained him.

"It's okay, Mr. McCabe, just trying to warm a little life back into you. Thought you were a goner until I saw your arm pop up and I threw a rope on it. The stream plum beat the snot clean out of you. You are bruised from stem to stern."

"You're lucky I am a boat person or I probably wouldn't understand what you just said." Gillis coughed a couple of times. "Help me out of these blankets. I feel like a can-packed with sardines. And where are my clothes?"

"They're dry and ready. You been out since we crossed the creek, almost a full day. You banged your head real hard and it don't look like the first time."

"The way my head is throbbing I am sure I banged it pretty good. Thank you for saving me. It seems like it is becoming a bit of a habit for you lately."

"I'm sure if you were in my place you would have done the same. Anyway I bandaged all of your wounds that were still bleeding. You're lucky, you didn't break anything. You will be sorer tomorrow."

"You're really not telling me anything I didn't know. Now if you wouldn't mind bringing over my clothes I would like to get back to the world of the living."

Wooly walked over to the base of a nearby tree and picked up the folded pile of dry clothes and set them down beside Gillis.

"That's a lot of gold to be carrying in these parts without armed guards. You're lucky you didn't lose it to those men in black or that river."

"So you saw the gold?"

"When I unpacked the mules one of the sacks was damaged and a bar spilled out. None of my business why you have that gold but that might be the reason you were being tailed."

"I am pretty certain no one knew that I have that much gold with me."

"So you trust the person you got it from and people that helped you load it?"

"Absolutely I do. I have worked with the same banker for close to fifteen years. He has helped me with my estate for over ten years without issue."

"Well that being said, how else would they know you were packing gold? "

"That's certainly a good question. When you add my father's estate being attacked and everyone killed, my fiancée's father being assassinated, and now these men in black doing their best to rob and probably kill me. I guess I really don't have any good answers."

Gillis struggled as he pulled his pants on and moaned as he moved his shoulder. "Kind of hurts when I move."

"Are you going to be able to ride?"

"Oh, I think so. Where's my horse?"

Wooly kind of looked down and then tossed the stick he had been whittling into the fire. "Yep, lost him. He rolled under a log and never resurfaced."

"Damn good horse to lose like that. At least he was fine to look at."

"What do you mean by that?" asked Gillis in an agitated voice.

Wooly looked up. "Only meant that he probably never was going to make a good mountain horse, he was too high strung for the woods. In sheer panic when he got in that water."

"I don't feel like taking on this argument. I can smell coffee and I'm hungry. Let's eat and then head out. Do you know where I can buy another horse and saddle?"

"Sure do, the Miller place. He's an old friend and may have some stock he could part with."

Gillis walked over to the fire and picked up a tin mug and poured himself a steaming cup of coffee.

"Wooly, you said you spent time out west?"

"Sure did, seen a lot of places. Take the Kansas Territory for instance, the wind constantly blows there. Hell, I heard tell that one day it stopped for a moment and half the town's people fell over." Wooly smiled as he looked down at the ground.

"I seriously doubt that, but it's a good story. So what is your favorite place?"

Wooly gently scratched his beard for a moment before looking straight at Gillis. "Probably the place I like best is that Wyoming country. She's big and wild, full of game, and wide open to a man tough enough to take her. I kind of planned on moving there once we got on top of our bills."

"Sounds real nice, but I'm more of a city person."

"To each their own. Now let me ask *you* a question. You say they attacked your father's ranch. Was your father amongst the dead?"

"No, fortunately to my knowledge he wasn't."

"So he escaped?"

"I'm not really sure."

"Do you know where to start looking for him?"

"I think I have a clue, but I'm not sure."

"So where's that?"

"I don't know what's going on or how he is tied into all this but until I figure things out better, I am keeping things to myself."

"I guess we are done with that talk," said Wooly as he stood up.

Gillis rode while Wooly walked leading the mules as they left camp. They broke from the oak and maple forest and traveled across yawning canyons of thick grass. There was a well-used game trail they followed and soon they could see a narrow road down below in the valley.

"We'll be back on our road soon," said Wooly.

"Do you think we gave those men the slip?"

"I think so but it depends on how good they are. We wouldn't have given me the slip. The way I figure it is those men aren't familiar with how to travel in this part of the country, but I wouldn't want to bet my life on it."

The game trail worked its way down the hill and soon the men broke onto a narrow, mud-covered road.

"Jacob Miller lives about two miles down this road. Hopefully he's home. Been a mite since I saw him last."

Soon the two men came to a weathered log cabin with smoke curling from a crude stone chimney. "This is his place," Wooly said.

They were a couple of hundred yards from the house when the hounds tied in the yard cut loose. "I suspect everyone in three counties knows we are coming," said Wooly, as he turned and spit a wad of tobacco to the side of the road.

A heavy-set man with a dirty shirt and a belly that draped down over his belt was standing on the porch. He carried a double-barrel shotgun nestled in one arm and he looked curious as to who was coming up the road that led to his house.

"Jacob, its Wooly."

"Wooly, is that really you? Hell, I haven't seen you in a coon's age. Where have you been hiding yourself?"

Wooly walked up to the hitching rail and tied off the mules before walking up to Jacob and shook hands vigorously. Gillis gingerly got down and tied the horse to the make-shift hitching rail. "Jacob it is nice to see you, how's the wife and kids?" Just as he said that two young kids' heads popped out from behind the door.

"Oh we are all fine but did you hear we are at war? We attacked Fort Sumter. They say the war will be over in a couple of months. Yesterday we saw a whole troop of Confederates ride by here headed north. They sure looked fancy in those new uniforms and those good-looking horses. Hope them fellows are right that this war ain't going to last long."

"Yeah, we heard."

"From what they said down at the store, we attacked the fort and it surrendered the next day."

"Jacob, its real nice seeing you but Mr. McCabe here is in a real hurry. We desperately need a good horse. Do you have any for sale?"

"Hell yes, they are all for sale for the right price," he said as motioned for Gillis and Wooly to follow him around the back.

Thirty minutes later Gillis was riding a not so pretty sway-back gelding with high withers. "This isn't much of a horse. I think your friend took advantage of me."

"He may have but that's a mountain horse, bred and broke here. He surely will get you to your father's estate. He ain't much to look at with the Roman nose and all but he has good feet and he's still got decent muscle on his hindquarters. Anyways, we didn't have much choice in the matter. We are a ways from anywhere and we needed a horse and he knew it."

"The saddle isn't much either."

"It fits the horse and that's all that matters. Hopefully in three or four days we will make it to your father's place and as I remember there is plenty of good horse flesh there."

For the next couple of hours they rode along quietly with little conversation. Gillis was deep in thought but no matter how he twisted it he couldn't figure out what was going on. Finally, he broke the silence. "I can't put any logic to what happened so I have decided to quit trying, at least until I find some sort of clue."

"Might be the best thing you can do for now."

Wooly pulled back on his reins and raised his arm in a motion to stop but it was too late. Two men dressed mostly in dark clothing were trotting their horses around the bend about fifty yards in front of them. They seemed to come out of nowhere. Wooly quickly motioned for Gillis to follow him. He firmly yanked on his horse's left rein and led the mules into the forest with Gillis hot on his heels. Their reaction was swift and seconds later they were hidden in the vegetation of the forest. Wooly had almost immediately found another game trail and was following it. Gillis looked back hoping the men hadn't seen them and the trail would lead to their escape. They had gotten less than fifteen yards when the sound of a pistol cocking stopped both men. There in the shadows of a large maple, stood a third man with a revolver pointed right at them.

"Don't move. I'm damn good with this Colt, especially at this range. I can take the eye out of a chicken at twenty yards and you are quite a bit bigger than any chicken I know."

Chapter 6

Wooly and Gillis pulled back their reins and sat back in their saddles with their hands up. Gillis was desperately trying to figure out a way to escape but there just wasn't one. The vegetation and dead fall on both sides of the trail would make it almost impossible to make a break for it and the sound of the other horses galloping up from the road told him they were surrounded.

"Just turn those horses and mules back towards the road and slowly ride out. I have nothing against shooting a man in the back if you try anything."

Wooly pulled on one rein and spun his horse and the mules around. Gillis followed as they made their way back out to the road. There on the hard pan gravel of the road sat two men on their horses with their pistols drawn and cocked. They rode fine-looking Thoroughbred horses, the type a man could easily outpace most horses with. Both men had strong sculptured faces, with prominent scars that flowed into their beards. All three wore black hats and slickers but the rest of their clothing was various shades of gray.

Gillis glanced at Wooly. He looked nervous. These men had come a long way to do whatever they intended to do and Gillis was sure he would find out soon. Sitting on their horses they looked smug in their victory. The man who had caught them walked out of the woods leading his horse behind the mules. He had a square jaw and piercing blue eyes, and a solid look of confidence. At one time he had been a handsome man but the injury to the right side of his face robbed him of that.

"You two, get down off those horses. Dolan, grab them two pack mules. The boss will be happy with the bonus of gold. Tie both of them up real tight. It may take us a while to get the information we need and I don't want to do it on this road." Dolan handed the lead rope to the other man and grabbed a piece of rope from his saddle bags. Walking over to Wooly, he began tying his hands behind his back. Next he took out his knife and cut the rope he intended to tie Gillis with. The man yanked Gillis's arms behind his back and he could feel the rough rope taking skin as it was dragged deep into his wrist.

The sound of trotting horses suddenly disrupted the men as a troop of soldiers dressed in gray uniforms rode into full view. The third man back carried a Confederate flag that waved in the breeze as they rode. Everyone froze for a moment as the troop of riders quickly descended on the group. Gillis immediately saw his chance as his captors hastily tucked their pistols inside their slickers. The young lieutenant raised his hand for the troop to stop while his eyes fixated on Wooly and the fact that his hands were tied. Gillis seized the moment to yank his hands free from the man and launch himself towards Wooly. The shove pushed Wooly between a horse and the mules. Reacting to the movement the scared mules yanked back as Wooly rolled into the ditch. Gillis yelled at the top of his lungs, "They're Yankees!"

Almost by reflex, the two men who had been holding their guns on Gillis and Wooly pulled the pistols from their slickers and started firing. A thick cloud of black smoke blurred everyone's sight as Gillis dove for the side of the road. The man they called Dolan had released his grip on the mules and was quickly leading his horse back into the woods. As he entered, he spun around and made a quick shot at Wooly. Wooly screamed in pain and doubled over. Dolan launched himself onto his horse and made a hasty escape into the forest. Gillis yanked himself around to see one of the men in black fall from his horse as the other man grabbed his side and kicked his stout horse into a full run.

Almost instantly the other horses of the soldiers were rearing and prancing through the thick black haze. Several troopers gave chase but the man's horse quickly outpaced their common grade stock. There weren't many horses in this part of the county that would be a match for that big Thoroughbred, thought Gillis as he saw the man quickly disappear.

Gillis tried to stand. His whole body hurt and he felt dizzy. Suddenly, a hand grabbed his arm and turned to see a soldier helping him catch his balance.

"You okay, sir?" asked the soldier.

Two other soldiers were helping to move Wooly to a flat spot beside the road. Gillis saw a crimson stain on his left side as the two soldiers gently lowered him to the ground.

The lieutenant was walking toward Gillis totally focused. "Damn Yankees are sending spies all over this part of Virginia. Thank God we got here when we did. Why were they taking you two prisoners?"

Gillis straightened up and looked at the man. "Lieutenant, to tell you the truth I'm not positive. I'm a shipbuilder and designer from Norfolk but I believe they wanted to know if I knew where my father was."

"Why would they be looking for your father?"

Gillis noticed one of the soldiers looking at the pack bags containing the gold and he was about to peer into the bag when the mule took a crow hop. It was just enough that the soldier abandoned his thoughts of inspecting the load and returned to his horse.

"Again sir, I am not certain. A little over a week ago my father's estate was attacked by some men that I believe were part of this same group. They killed everyone there, eight in total. I arrived at the estate a half-a-day later and it was gruesome to say the least. At first I didn't have a clue why but now I believe they wanted my father for something but I just don't know what. They must have wanted him pretty bad. They did some torturing before they killed some of the slaves and hired labor. Damn Yankees might just have been on a raiding party but I don't know why they went after us."

"What's your father's name?"

"Scully McCabe."

"If I am not mistaken his estate is northwest of here. Nice, big place, well kept."

Just then the two soldiers that had given chase rode up to the lieutenant. "Sir, the man got away. We had his trail for a while but we lost him."

"That will be all, men. I didn't think we would catch him. He had too good a head start."

One of the soldiers lay in a pool of blood with several other soldiers kneeling around him. Gillis could see the man was dead. Over at the side of the road Wooly quietly lay in the grass. The man who had given the orders to tie them up lay sprawled in the middle of the road beneath his dark slicker.

"I want that man searched. Look for anything out of the normal. Feel his clothing for any hidden pockets that might contain a map," said the lieutenant in a commanding voice. The lieutenant then turned and joined Gillis as they moved over to where Wooly lay on the ground.

"How bad is it?" asked Gillis.

"Nothing I can't live with," Wooly said. "That bastard decided to shoot me before he escaped. It took a nice chunk of flesh out of my hide. It stings like crazy but I don't think it did any permanent damage."

"You're lucky. If that flesh wound had been a little deeper it could have been a hell of a lot worse."

Several troopers began working on Wooly as he raised his arm to give them access to his wound.

The lieutenant looked hard at the wound and then at Gillis. "Sir, I think he will be fine. Take it real easy and just change the bandage every couple of hours if possible. If it were me, I would soak the wound when you get to some place you can boil a little water."

"Easy for you to say," said Wooly in a grumpy voice to the soldier, as he slowly stood up and started walking around with a painfully sour face.

"Sergeant, did you find any papers on that man?"

"None, sir."

The lieutenant turned to Gillis. "Do you need any further assistance before we depart?"

"We aren't hurt that bad. I am sure we will make it but we appreciate you showing up when you did. It could have been a lot worse if you hadn't," said Gillis.

"I hope you two men make it without further problems. Sorry that we can't be of more assistance," said the lieutenant in a quieter voice. "Sergeant, have Trooper Sanson scout up ahead and make sure there isn't any sign of those men."

The lieutenant watched the trooper ride off and then turned to Gillis. "Good luck."

"Thanks, lieutenant, we are sorry you lost a good man."

The lieutenant just nodded and then tipped his hat as a small salute before he turned to his men. The bodies of both dead men had been tied on their horses as the lieutenant shouted, "Mount up!"

In unison the men got on their horses and with military precision they trotted off down the road.

"That was way too close," said Wooly with a look of relief on his face. Gillis nodded in agreement. "Thank God we were able to pawn those guys off as Yankees."

Painfully both Gillis and Wooly mounted their horses and started once again down the dirt road. "With your side and my body, we make a great pair," Gillis said.

"Yeah, I know but I got to give them men some credit. Never thought they would look for us on this road or I wouldn't have let my guard down. One of those men either knows this country or knows someone that does. It won't happen again I promise you."

Both men slumped slightly in the saddle as Gillis led the mules behind Wooly for the next three hours until they had had enough for the day.

Gillis and Wooly struggled to unload the mules before setting up a highline and starting a small fire. The tiny campsite they chose was at least a quarter of a mile off the road and they both felt it would be safe for the night. The dancing fire and the quiet popping of the branches were comforting as the men found themselves exhausted. They were too tired to cook so they ate jerky and drank from their canteens for a makeshift dinner.

Gillis looked over at Wooly whose eyes were already shut. "I will do the first watch and wake you in about four hours."

"I appreciate that. Giving a little blood to that road has me kind of beat but I will be fine with a little sleep."

*   *   *

The next morning Gillis awoke to a gentle drizzle. He wiped his face with his coat sleeve and sat up. "Morning Wooly, you sleep okay?"

"Hell no I didn't sleep okay."

"How's that side of yours?"

"It's fine, just fine, it only hurts when I move. A day or two of rest and I will be as good as new."

With great effort they hurriedly packed the gear, saddling the mules first and then the horses. The mules always held their breath on the first tug of the cinch and tightening them a second time always saved time later. For the next four hours the rain came down as they continued on their course.

"Leastwise we don't have any more of them swollen creeks to cross between here and there. I don't know if we can afford to lose another good horse," Wooly said with a smile.

"I appreciate your concern, I really do."

Four days later the road broke from the trees into an open field and Gillis knew where he was. "Dad's place is about another hour's ride up this road to our left. I used to have a friend that lived in that burnt-out cabin years ago. I would ride down there and visit. His house burned down about six months before I left. Never saw that buddy of mine again. He was a good friend." Then it began to rain.

An hour later the twosome crested the muddy ridge top, their bodies soaked to the bone. Wooly shivered almost uncontrollably. They rode in through the main gate and Gillis could see Roper looking from the porch and came running to meet them.

"Mr. McCabe, you alright? It looks like your friend here is in real rough shape."

"His name is Wooly Nielsen. Get him to my father's room and have a good fire built. He will need some hot towels and some clean bandages. He may have a fever."

"Yes sir, Master Gillis."

Gillis just looked at him. "I mean Mr. McCabe, sir."

"Mr. McCabe will do just fine, now let's get him in the house and then I will unload the mules in the barn."

"I will get a couple of men to help you."

"No, I don't want any help. After you are done taking care of Wooly, have someone draw me a warm tub. I need to soak this nick and then get a good night's sleep. But first I have some work to do in the barn and I don't want to be disturbed, do you understand?"

"Yes sir, Mr. McCabe."

Gillis pulled the rein to the side and began leading the two mules toward the barn. He was cold too but not to the point that he could leave the gold out for someone else to handle. Gillis rode his nag of a horse through the barn doors followed by the mules. The stone foundation of the barn rose a good ten feet above the ground. The craftsmanship of the barn's masonry was amazing, far nicer than the house. The barn was a lot older and Gillis had never known its history. He dismounted near one of the six massive wooden posts that spanned the center of the barn and tied his horse. He loosened the ropes on the packs and let them slide to the ground. He unsaddled all three and led them into individual stalls. Using a pitchfork he tossed some hay into each stall and poured a can of oats into a bucket for each animal. He would have someone water them later.

The large barn doors shut with a louder than expected bang as Gillis used a thick plank to bar the door from the inside. There were no real windows in the barn but a number of shooting ports had been carefully laid into the stone. Obviously the people who owned the place before his father expected trouble. Gillis leaned against the closed door and tried to catch his breath. He was tired, wet and cold, and his energy was fading quickly. He needed to figure out a place to hide the gold for a while. He carefully scanned the large dirt floor analyzing each area for a spot that would meet his needs. He picked a logical place near where there were numerous piles of old crates, barrels, and other items common to a barn. After studying it more, he changed his mind.

Finally he walked to the hay pile and looked at the stout stone wall rising above the pile of dried grass and started moving the hay with a pitch fork. Soon he exposed the hard dirt floor of the barn. He set the pitchfork down and retrieved a pick and shovel from against the wall and began digging. His plan was to dig down about four feet and place the boxes of gold in the hole and bury it. When he was finished he would use hay to hide any traces of his work. He still had several thousand dollars in United States currency in his saddle bags and wouldn't need the gold for a while but what he planned to do could cost a lot of money.

For the next hour he dug as the sweat ran down his face mixing with the dust from the dirt. He was almost to four feet deep when he hit something. Not hard like a rock, but almost like wood with a slightly hollow sound. His mind was racing as to what it could possibly be as he continued to dig. Shortly after that his shovel hit something that sounded like metal and he kneeled down in the hole and brushed the dirt away. What he saw shocked him.

Chapter 7

There in the dirt was what looked like a door with a rusty four inch metal ring connected to a heavy plank by corroded bolts. Gillis straightened up and looked at what he had uncovered and wondered what he was looking at. He knew it was a door but to where and why it was there he had no idea. His body ached. Exhaustion rolled through him. He was shaking with fatigue. If he didn't get some food and rest soon he knew he was in for trouble.

Climbing out of the hole, he walked over to the two boxes in the pack and with great effort removed them. One by one he dragged them to the hole and lowered them down onto the wooden surface. He was too tired to dig anymore and where the door went would have to wait until he recovered. He set the two boxes containing the gold side by side, climbed back out of the hole and began filling it in. When there was a foot of dirt over the two stout boxes, he stomped on the mound to compact it. Then he filled the final two feet and stomped on it as well. Sweat poured down onto his brow as he took his dirty handkerchief and wiped his forehead. He struggled to stand as he spread the hay back over the spot where he had dug. It seemed to take forever but he made sure that no fresh or loose dirt was visible on the barn floor. It had to be done well.

When he finished removing even the smallest piece of dirt he took some old hay full of mouse chewed clippings and gently sprinkled it over the entire area. If he hadn't carefully mapped out the location in his mind, even now he would have a difficult time locating the exact spot.

He removed the plank that stretched across the two doors of the barn and leaned the thick beam against the wall. He gently pushed against the heavy door trying not to make any noise. Gillis looked around and then began walking to the house. He was slow to climb the three stairs of the porch before quietly opening the front door. The last time he had seen the inside of the house it had been in shambles and he was surprised to see everything clean and new pieces of furniture in the foyer. Two kerosene lanterns lighted the hall and Gillis saw Roper coming from the kitchen as he entered.

"Welcome back, Master . . ." Roper hesitated. "I mean Mr. McCabe. It is nice to have you back."

"Thanks Roper, how is Wooly doing?"

"Good sir, I think. We changed the bandages and he is asleep. He lost some blood from the ride but I believe he will be fine in a couple of weeks."

"Good. I need something to eat and drink. I am hoping that tub was drawn for me. That and a good night's rest and I should be fine. Quite honesty I am really tired of sleeping on the ground and I will greatly appreciate the luxury of a bed."

"Hot soup and bread fresh baked is in your room waiting for you. The new maid put hot rocks in your bed. By the time you have taken your bath your bed should be nice and warm."

"Thanks again, Roper. Now I think I will eat," said Gillis as he started to walk out of the kitchen. "Tomorrow I have a lot of things to go over with you."

Gillis ate slowly in the quiet of his room and then soaked for a good thirty minutes before finally getting dry and bandaging his head wound. He lay down and was immediately asleep.

The next day Gillis woke mid-morning to the sound of birds chirping. His body still ached as he sat up too fast and felt a little dizzy. He moaned quietly as he rose to his feet and pulled on his pants. There was a sudden knock on the door and then a woman's voice: "Sir, are you all right?"

"Yes I'm fine, who are you?"

"My name is Lucy. Mr. Roper brought me in to do maid work, cooking, and to help with the cleanup. Is there anything I can get you?"

"Yes, I'm ready for a good breakfast and some really hot, black coffee."

"Yes sir, we have all that. Is there anything else?"

"Yes, have Roper meet me at the table for breakfast."

"Oh yes sir, I will tell him. He said earlier that he has a man coming to buy one of your father's mules this morning."

"Hmm," muttered Gillis.

Gillis quickly washed his face in the porcelain bowl on the dresser and shaved the long stubble from his face. He found a freshly washed and ironed shirt on a chair and guessed it was his father's. He pulled on his boots and headed out the door to the kitchen. Roper was walking through the back door as he entered.

"Good morning, Roper. I hope the coffee is as good as it smells."

"I'm sure it is, Mr. McCabe."

"You have done a fine job cleaning up the place. How is Wooly doing?"

"He's still sleeping real hard."

"Were you able to find some good men?"

"Yes, sir. I got three men that are mainly farm help and another four men that are decent with a gun. The three farm boys I have known for a while. The men with the guns are fresh faces that I met by visiting a few towns and asking a lot of questions."

"So, did you find it difficult to get men to come here to work, especially when it was a Negro man trying to recruit them?"

"Money speaks real loud, sir. Fifty dollars a week is a hefty sum and men were willing to quit other jobs for that."

"Good, that is more than I like to pay but these are certainly strange times. Have you seen anything more of those men that dress in dark clothing?"

"I have a couple of men watching up in the hills. Two days ago he saw a man by the edge of the timber but he quickly disappeared. We went looking for him but found nothing."

"Did you come up with anything that might shine some light on why this happened? There has to be a clue somewhere."

"No sir, I didn't. Your father kept to himself about his business. I don't even remember him mentioning what he did for a living other than raise and sell his mules and horses. Only once did I hear him ever say where he was going but right after that he shut up real quick, like he had said something he shouldn't have. He said he was going to Washington."

"That's a big place. A man could search a long time and cover a lot of ground and still not run into who he was looking for."

"Sorry, Mr. McCabe, but we all kept an eye out for any clues when we cleaned the house. Unfortunately, we didn't find anything that seemed important or mentioned any location in particular other than what you found."

"Anyway, would you like to have breakfast with me?"

"I would, sir, but I ate breakfast three hours ago."

"Well thank you for doing such a good job of putting this place back together. You're a man that can be depended upon. You seem more than capable. How did you learn so much?"

"Your father, sir, he taught me pretty much all I know. He is a great man and he treated me more like a son than a boy bought off the blocks."

"I am impressed."

"Thank you, sir. Until the buyers get here I will be outside rebuilding the cabins. I know it's only spring but winter be will here again before you know it. Those men destroyed three of the cabins completely and I am surprised they didn't burn the whole place to the ground. A couple of the other buildings look like they tried to burn them too but that rain we had must have saved them."

Gillis murmured to himself.

"What's that, sir?" responded Roper.

"Nothing. I was just talking to myself. Go ahead and get back to work. We will discuss things later. Oh, I do have one more thing."

"What's that, sir?"

"I want you to send a rider over to Wooly's ranch. Tell his wife he's safe and give her this envelope. There should be enough money there to pay any back taxes they owe," said Gillis, as he handed Roper a small, brown envelope.

Gillis finished eating, got up, and went outside. Roper had proven himself to be a very good manager and a leader. Gillis stood looking at the different men working throughout the small estate. Everything looked so different from the night he and Sandra had driven their carriage into the grounds. In the past couple of weeks, everything had changed. He almost enjoyed the normalcy that was the moment. He wondered how Sandra was doing and if he would ever see her again. How strange it was to have her father killed just days after the men attacked here. Was there really a connection or was it just a coincidence? He had the scrap of paper that had the partial name Alexandria but that was a big area outside Washington. If nothing else was found he would have to start his search there. At least he felt comfortable in that he had the money needed to open doors and find the information once he found a decent clue.

He thought about the previous night, the rain, and burying the gold in the barn. What had that heavy planking and metal been doing down there three and a half feet below the barn floor? He was sure the rusted handle had to be for a door but why would someone bury a door in the floor of the barn? He had no answers and that bothered him. The splinter of wood he had broken from the plank looked to be oak with a generous layer of pine tar. Even if he did dig it up would it really be a door or just the remains of an earlier barn burned to the ground by Indians or the like? Sooner or later he knew he would need to find out.

Just then he saw Lucy coming out of the main house and looking around. Their eyes met and she hurried over to him. "Mr. McCabe, Wooly woke up and he was asking for you."

"Thank you, Lucy," said Gillis, as he followed her over to the house. She was a very attractive Negro lady, slender, and in her twenties. She appeared to have had some schooling. Gillis entered the bedroom where Wooly lay and saw him sitting up on the edge of the bed. His bandages were visible but not blood- stained.

Wooly's eyes met Gillis's and he smiled. "Guess we both made it. That was far too close. If it weren't for those soldier boys, I don't think we would be alive. I am lucky that I happened to move just as he shot but he still took a larger chunk of flesh than I would have liked."

"Leastwise you're here, and for the time being we are both safe."

"So have you found any clues?"

"I haven't but I am hopeful that will change soon."

"I should be ready to go back home soon. I will say I have enjoyed your company and I wish I could continue to work for you."

"Well, I am hiring. My father lost a lot of good men when the estate was attacked. I don't know much about your farm, but I have Roper building cabins for the men and women that will service the ranch. There's a job here if you want it."

"I haven't worked for anyone for a fair spell because of this knee. But God knows I could use the money. I don't intend to get into this here war.

I don't have a dog in that fight. First chance I get I want to take the family out west. Yeah, I will take that job and I guess we can see where it goes."

"Glad to hear it, now you spend another week or so getting your wound healed. As of now, you work for me officially and that's an order," said Gillis as he turned and walked out the door, closing it as he went.

Gillis mulled over the situation. He had no clues, at least nothing that he had any confidence in.

He walked to the front of the barn and hesitated for a moment as he looked around before entering. He slowly walked around, examining the floor for even the slightest change. Everything was as he remembered, even the small piece of wood that lay several inches above the ground covered with hay. Gillis had carefully placed the hay to make sure he would know if someone had disturbed his hiding place. He walked back to the door and peered out. Everyone was still working and he saw no evidence that anyone knew he had returned to the barn. Slowly he closed the door trying not to make a sound as the two doors swung together. He picked up the heavy plank and carefully placed it in the metal brackets bolted securely to the doors. The supports were old but whoever had made them years ago intended them to last.

Next he went into the back of the barn and emerged with the tools he had used the night before. He had even been careful to clean the fresh red clay from the shovel so no one would guess that it had been used recently.

Walking to where he had stored his two pack bags, he retrieved a canvas manty that was ten by eight feet and laid it on the ground beside the hay pile. Slowly and carefully he removed the hay from the area until it was just clean dirt. He took two edges of the manty and shook it gently in the air. As he pulled back, it descended to the ground almost perfectly flat. Gillis smiled at the trick Wooly had shown him. After cleaning the site, he began digging and shoveling the soft soil onto the manty. Soon he had reached the boxes containing the gold. He pulled them from the hole and dragged them over to another stack of hay where he hid them from sight. Shortly thereafter, he heard the sound of solid wood beneath his shovel. It took a hard hour with his knife to carefully remove enough dirt before he knew for certain it was indeed a door. Carefully he began expanding the hole so he could try and open it. Finally, he exposed the complete blackened door with its rusty hardware. The door measured approximately six foot by four foot. He stood to one side and tried to pull up as hard as he could on the metal ring but nothing seemed to move.

He could feel frustration setting in and the heat from the humid day getting the better of him. Finally, he climbed out of the hole and sat on a chest that was part of a bunch of dusty discarded items that had accumulated in one corner of the barn. His guess was it would take at least a couple of men to break the jammed seal and dislodge the door. Down deep he knew that there was no one else he wanted to share his secret with except Wooly and he was in no shape to help. He scanned the room until his eyes settled on a pulley, a part of a block and tackle set used to lift heavy grain bags to the second floor of the barn. With a little shifting he was sure he could reconfigure the blocks to the beam over the mysterious door.

Gillis quickly inserted the hook from the block and tackle set into the large ring of the door. He was exhausted from the effort but his adrenaline had taken over and he began to tighten the ropes with great effort. He pulled hard on the rope and when it didn't budge he jumped up and grabbed higher on the rope, letting the weight of his whole body and gravity power the pulley. But still the door didn't open.

He stopped for a moment, sweat running down his face. He needed to think this through better, so he sat down on the edge of the hole and stared at the door. Getting up, he continued over to where an assortment of tools hung and grabbed a short broken pitchfork before hurrying back and climbing down into the hole. For the next ten minutes he dug around the door's frame going deeper and deeper with the narrow iron spine until he was finally satisfied and climbed back out. Again he tried pulling the door open but again it didn't move. He was tired and frustrated and wasn't sure he would ever open this door by himself. He stood up again and walked over to the thick rope and extended his arms as far as possible and took a solid grip. Gillis launched himself in the air while bending his elbow and grabbing the rope higher up. The result sent his full body weight as well as his momentum pulling down on the rope. With a loud, graveled bang the door sprung open, showering the floor with small pieces of damp dirt and black wood splinters. Some of the soil made its way down into the black opening created when the door opened and Gillis could hear the sound of water splashing.

In places the wooden frame had exploded into small pieces of wood from the impact. The momentum caused Gillis to almost fall into the newly exposed opening. He lay there moaning slightly as he struggled to catch his breath. His bruises hurt and even though he had opened the door, he struggled to get up. His legs felt wobbly as he pulled himself up using both the rope and his legs. He stood beside the open door and looked down into the hole but he could see little. A well-built set of rotting stairs disappeared into the darkness. There was definitely a room below filled with water but where it led Gillis had no idea. He had been born on this estate and the idea of coming back after all these years and finding a secret room was almost unbelievable.

Walking back over to where a kerosene lantern hung on the wall, he lit it. Turning it up, he walked back to the doorway and looked down. There was a flight of stairs, gray and covered by moss. There were no hand rails and the light didn't penetrate far enough for Gillis to see much. He was uncomfortable with the thought of descending. He had to have a way to get out if for some reason the old stairs collapsed. After getting a smaller rope he tied the lantern's handle to it and began carefully lowering it further into the darkness. He thought he could see faint ripples in what looked like water. Carefully he swung the lantern around the opening allowing the light to cast its glow across more area. The rope bumped into a small rusted metal bracket that Gillis thought might be for hanging a lantern. Its color blended in perfectly with the black bottom. He couldn't be sure but he thought he saw more ripples in the water with what looked like a small light colored objects moving away. Then they were gone. Gillis had no idea what could have caused the ripples but something definitely made them.

He took the excess rope from the block and tackle and flung the end down into the water. Then he tried the first step. The old oak tread creaked but appeared firm and easily held his weight. He took several more steps and tested each one before transferring his total weight. He began a routine of setting the lantern on the step below, while keeping the other hand on the rope. Then he would stomp on the next step before shifting his weight. The old wood seemed remarkably strong as he carefully continued down to where he could hang the lantern from the rusted hook. He counted seventeen steps in all before the stairway seemed to melt into the brackish water. A stale, moldy smell gripped his nose the further he went. He was two steps from the foul-smelling water before he noticed the thin layer of moss that coated the last step. He stomped on the step and with a loud crack, the stair gave way flinging Gillis into the darkness.

Chapter 8

He flailed his arms trying to regain his balance as he fell forward into the black water. Almost immediately his whole body hit bottom and he quickly struggled to his feet as he spit stagnated water from his mouth. He was relieved to find the water was slightly below his knees as he slowly regained his composure. A steady stream of water dribbling from his soaked clothes was the only thing that broke the silence. He stood there staring up the stairs for a moment before catching his breath and wading toward what remained of the staircase. He sat on the third stair from the bottom and took a deep breath.

Then he heard it, a threatening hiss from the corner, one that made the hair on the back of his neck standup. Gillis scrambled up the stairs reaching for the lantern. Swinging the light in the direction of the sound he saw what looked like an arched, rock doorway made of stone with a stack of broken furniture piled in front of it. His eyes focused on something moving.

Tangled around a chair leg was a huge snake, at least five feet in length and extremely thick through the body. The snake was slowly moving down and through the rotting furniture toward the water. Gillis had seen large snakes before but never one of this size. The huge water moccasin seemed to stop for a moment and stare in his direction. Its pale snout streaked with two dark lines that almost seemed to point in his direction.

Gillis suddenly pulled back as he realized that there were numerous other smaller snakes swimming around him and they were close. The tips of the small snake tails were light in color and as they swam the rest of their olive black bodies almost completely disappeared into the dark wavy water. This had to be her brood Gillis thought as he began to panic. He knew this was a dangerous place: water moccasins were known for their deadly, aggressive behavior especially near their dens. Just then the large snake slithered into the water, slowly moving its body back and forth as it swam toward Gillis.

Spinning around, he launched himself up the stairs before grabbing the lantern and looking back. The large cottonmouth water moccasin silently swam to the bottom stair with its head several inches above the water. Then it slithered a foot of its body up upon the first stair and stopped. The snake seemed to glare as it kept most of her body in the water gently rocking back and forth, in a slow undulating motion. Slowly the snake raised its head a good six inches above the stair riser. The snake made a loud threatening hiss. The sound petrified Gillis. The inside of the snake's mouth was cotton white and almost glowed in the dark. He had often heard the snake referred to as a cottonmouth but only now did he get the full meaning of the expression. Gillis climbed up two more stairs, never letting his eyes leave the snake. The cottonmouth just sat perched on the stair gently moving its tail back and forth. Its eyes seeming to never break their silent stare.

Gillis hurled himself up the last remaining stairs before turning and shining his lantern back down the shaft. The large snake was still perched on the stair. Gillis stood and found that he was shaking and tried to calm himself. This snake was of unusual size and Gillis was glad he wasn't standing down in the brackish water. Finally, after regaining his composure, the thought came to him that this large, poisonous snake might serve a purpose. Tying rope slings on both boxes, he then guided the first box down the staircase shaft and into the water. The splash seemed to disturb the snake as it glided back into the darkness. With a splash Gillis swung the rope to the right into open water as the snake slithered back into the darkness. Then he lowered the second box and began swinging the box attached to the rope until he let go at the right spot. Again the box landed with a splash and sank beneath the dark water.

Gillis took a deep breath and shut the heavy wooden door and began shoveling. He shoveled for almost a half an hour until the hole was filled. Tired, he collapsed on an old bench that sat against one of the heavy wood pillars of the barn. His heart was still pounding from the experience and he wondered what the room was that he had just found. Why was this room under a barn that was at least eighty to a hundred years old? His father had never mentioned it and Gillis hadn't known it existed. His clothes were still dripping. The stale smell of stagnant water saturated his clothes. Again he carefully tried to compact the soil as he covered the shaft entrance by hitting it with a flat shovel. When he was through filling the hole he sprinkled small shards of dry hay over the disturbed soil.

Gillis scanned the area one last time looking for even the slightest clue he had been there and concluded he was confident with his work. He was a man of detail, a man who would rather work with his mind than his brawn, and so far it had worked for him. His soft hands were blistered. It had been years since he had done so much manual labor but he was proud that he could still handle the task.

It was almost dark when he opened the locked door of the barn and slipped out walking briskly to the house. He could hear an owl's hoot deep in the forest but other than that he heard nothing. He quietly opened the back door and headed toward his father's room. He slipped down the hall and quickly took off the wet clothes beside the closed door. He dried himself with the towel laid out next to the bowl and pitcher for his night wash. Clean and hungry, he changed into dry clothes and made his way down to the kitchen. After gorging himself on a chicken he headed to bed. For a while he just stared at the ceiling thinking about what had just happened until his mind finally moved to other things.

He was impressed with how Roper had hired and organized people to get the house back together. He had found skilled men and women who had rebuilt when possible or bought new when needed. Some of the walls still showed damage but overall the entire house was quickly becoming the home he remembered. A kerosene lantern had been turned down to a mere glow that gave off just enough light to find the bed. The sheet and covers had been laid back and carefully straightened and Gillis knew that Lucy was doing everything she could to make him comfortable. It took almost an hour before the exhausted Gillis fell asleep.

* * *

Early the next morning the sound of a distant rooster and the sun shining through the silk curtains stirred him awake. He poured water from the pitcher and scrubbed his face. He looked over the place he had piled his wet clothes and they were gone. Walking out into the hall he could smell fresh bread. He stopped at the room where Wooly was sleeping and knocked softly before cracking the door open. Wooly was gently snoring and Gillis closed the door quietly. He turned the corner on his way to the kitchen and noticed a man with his back to him. He immediately froze before realizing that the man was working on repairing the wall.

"A bit jumpy, Mr. McCabe?"

Gillis spun around to see Lucy standing behind him with a pile of freshly washed and folded bedding.

"Sorry if that man surprised you. Roper has them working throughout the house ever since you left. They were told to be very quiet until you got up. Wooly seems to just sleep through the noise. If you ask me, they are doing a great job."

"Yes, I had thought that earlier when I had a chance to look around. Roper is a pretty amazing man."

Lucy just smiled. "Are you ready for some breakfast?"

"Yes, that sounds good. I don't remember pushing myself this hard for quite a while. I have much more of an appetite than normal and the smell of that fresh bread cooking this morning really woke up my taste buds."

"Well, have a seat, I have a pot of tea and honey bread for you. I will have some bacon and eggs ready soon."

"Thanks, Lucy. I suppose it was you that picked up my wet clothes from my room and got my bed ready."

"Yes sir, it was. You had a small puddle that made its way under your door. I hope it was all right that I picked them up and put them to washing?"

"Certainly, again I appreciate your actions. How is Wooly doing?"

"He had a bit of a fever last night but he is getting better. He thinks he is ready to travel but that gash still looks a bit angry to me."

Gillis was almost finished when he heard the back door open and in walked Roper. "Master," he paused, "Sorry, it's a hard habit to break, Mr. McCabe."

"Good morning, Roper. I must say I am more than impressed how you have put this disaster of a ranch back together. When I do find my father, I am sure he will appreciate your efforts as much as I do."

"Thank you sir, it's been a challenge but there are good men to be found for the right price. I came in hoping you were up so we could talk about selling some of the stock. We have a couple gentlemen waiting outside that want to buy a few horses and three mules, and maybe a saddle or two."

"I guess I am not quite up in my knowledge on selling mules."

"Your father has some mighty fine mules and horses. He got into that business a couple of years after you left. We usually sell around forty mules and about half that many horses a year. Most of them are Thoroughbreds but also a few Morgans. Those big stout Thoroughbred mules out there are hard to beat if you want to cover a lot of ground."

"I only wish my father was here to tell me what I should be selling them for. It is more than frustrating not knowing what I am doing. Roper, I am sure you know the business so treat it like any other sale. My father had a lot of confidence in you to carry on in his absence. I have some questions but they will wait until you are done with those gentlemen."

"Actually, Mr. McCabe sir, I usually do make all the deals. Your father is away far more than he is here."

"From what I have seen he picked the right man. We will visit more this afternoon. Before you go, are you sure you and the men haven't found anything that might give us a clue?"

"Nothing, Mr. McCabe, we searched everywhere."

"There is no other place you could possibly look?"

"There is only one place we didn't look, but your father forbids us from ever setting foot in Brown Haven without his permission."

"I had forgotten. The cabin down in the meadow?"

"The one named after your mother's family. Once or twice every couple of years your father would use it as a guest house for his business associates. With it being at least a mile from here and in that isolated meadow, a person just forgets about it. Do you remember your father's strict rules about no one going down there? Well, that never changed. Your father and his guests were the only ones allowed to use the cabin. None of the staff was to mention it without permission."

"I totally forgot about that place. Is it still standing?"

"Yes, it was built well. It seemed like every few years a couple of men that aren't from around these parts show up for a couple of weeks or so for repairs, painting, reroofing and the like. Then as sudden as they appear, they're gone. Your father would tell me when people were down there but there wasn't much else said about the place. Sometimes the men would stay there for a month or more but they never bothered anyone. They were far enough away that no one seemed to ever hear them. I do remember a couple of times your father bringing one of their horses up to the blacksmith to be shoed or doctored."

"So you haven't checked it out for clues?"

"No sir, but we will if you want us to. We all want to find your father and to know who these killers are." Roper paused. "Especially me."

"I have a couple of things to do but later I will walk down there and take a look. Do I need a key?"

"Yes, there should be a key in the library. I guess we aren't supposed to know its location but Lucy accidentally found it hanging under the desk top when she was cleaning. According to her if you get down on your hands and knees you can see the key tight up against the back corner."

"Thank you, Roper. After breakfast I think I will head down to Brown Haven and give my father's guest-house a thorough look."

Roper was obviously a powerful man but he was smart, too. He seemed to know a lot about what happened around the place, as well as its business. Gillis stopped at the doorway to the library and peered in. The last time he had seen the room piles of torn books were scattered among various sized jars and dumped in the middle of the floor. This time everything was carefully organized, cleaned, and neatly placed on the shelves. He remembered the thousands of books from the many hours he had studied in the room as a youngster. Roper had done a great job of organizing things back to almost what they had been. The original three bookshelves were back in place and looked like they had never been disturbed.

The back wall where the window stood was surrounded by shelves containing jars with various labels. Now the whole room seemed to take on new meaning. Someone had even taken the time to redo the subject categories encased in tiny metal frames identifying the topics in each section. There were books on almost every subject from horse care to doctoring, from building to economics, and numerous strange topics. A painting of a huge mastodon hung above the shortest shelf that contained hundreds of labeled jars while a chunk of tusk stood propped against the corner of the book shelf. Taking a few minutes he scanned the room from floor to ceiling, absorbing the massive collection of literature.

A small section titled "toxins" caught his eye. There were three books under the label and Gillis picked up the largest and thickest of the three. From his quick scan of the first chapter he could tell that this wasn't a normal book for a family library. Gillis didn't remember these books as a boy and to his surprise the next three chapters covered the art of poisoning. Why would his father possess these books he thought, as he carefully replaced the book on the shelf. Having one book like this was strange but to have three, all on this bizarre subject, brought more questions than answers.

He walked behind the large oak desk and looked underneath the desk top for the key. Just as Roper had said, a skeleton key hung on a single square nail hidden from view in the sanctuary of the darkness. Someone had carved a neat little depression that did a great job of hiding it. With effort he reached under and took the key off its nail and slipped it in his pocket. He sat on the large padded chair and leaned back, allowing his eyes to slowly scan the room. Finally, Gillis opened a drawer of the desk and pulled out a quill and paper. The ink well had been replaced and was sitting in its normal secured spot in an inlaid piece of wood. For the next hour he worked on a drawing and when he was finally done he blew on it until the ink was thoroughly dry. Taking his time he carefully folded it. He stood and headed back to his room where he put on his coat and gently placed the paper in his inside pocket. He stopped in the kitchen and looked for Lucy but she had already gone, so he headed out the back door. As he opened the door he saw her hanging clothes and quickly went over to her.

"Do we still have a blacksmith or was he one of the victims?"

"No, Mr. Pruitt was away visiting kin when those men attacked. He should be down at the shop working. I thought I heard him pounding on horseshoes only a few minutes ago."

"Thanks. I'm glad we didn't lose him."

"Me too, sure seems like a really nice man."

Gillis headed down through the barnyard and past several of the smaller buildings. In the distance he could hear the dull clank of a hammer hitting metal. Turning the corner he could see a short, burly man pounding on an anvil. As he got closer Gillis was struck by the thick black hair that covered most of the man's bare shoulders and arms. His tan, leathery face showed of age and was darkened from years of working over a fire.

"Mr. Pruitt?"

"That would be me and I am guessing you are Mr. Gillis McCabe," he said, smiling and holding out his hand.

Gillis shook the powerful hand that almost totally swallowed his own. Gillis reached into his coat pocket and handed the man the paper he had drawn in his father's study and handed it to him. "I have a project that I need completed in the upmost haste. Can you have it to me in the next couple of days?"

The blacksmith took the folded paper. "Let's take a look at what you got there." He carefully unfolded the paper and took his time examining it. "I really don't think I will have any trouble making this. Have you heard anything from your father?"

"No, not yet, but I am sure I will find him or a clue sooner or later. It's tough not knowing even where to start looking," said Gillis. "Hopefully, you can read all my notes."

"Yes sir, I am a learned man. So what is this?"

"It's a kind of a tool for grabbing, somewhat like tongs but that is all I want to explain for now."

"I will have it done in a couple of days for sure. Nice meeting you, sir, and welcome back to the farm. I understand it has been a while."

"Thanks, I will be back."

Gillis began walking down through an open pasture gate. The field was a foot high in grass and as he walked, an occasional bird flushed in front of him. The ground had been harrowed and manure had been spread creating exceptional pasture growth. The carpet of green followed the gentle topography of the ridge as it snaked its way smoothly down the hill. The top of the ridge had been cleared years before with most all the rocks and stumps removed. Here and there the remains of the more massive, stubborn stumps still stood. An effort had been made to burn most of the stumps but it hadn't been totally successful. In other areas a boulder that was too large to be moved protruded up into the soft landscape. Finally the pasture edges faded into a thick tangle of vines, brush, and deciduous trees as the ground became too steep to farm.

Gillis thought about his younger years when his father demanded without reason, that he never visit this secluded place. Like most kids he was curious and finally one day he decided to make the journey to the far reaches of the farm. He waited until his father was gone on a trip, and when he was done with his chores he disappeared down over the hill, keeping close to the cover of the tree line.

The memory of peering through the window into a dimly lit room and seeing a table and chairs and a door to another room stayed with him. The cabin had a massive stone fireplace with thick wooden beams holding up the mantel and it was beautifully carved. Unfortunately, there was but one window without faded curtains and viewing any detail at a distance was difficult. Several months later on another visit he saw two stout horses tied to the hitching post in front of the small, adjacent shed. He hid for several hours in the brush watching the place before seeing two men in dark clothes come out, go over to the hay shed, saddle their horses and ride out. He could still remember one of the men pulling back on his reins and looking in Gillis's direction as he dropped flat into the brush, hoping the man didn't see him. When he looked again the men were gone. The experience scared him and that was the last time he visited the cabin.

He had been walking for a good forty-five minutes through the fields before he saw the small opening in the forest he was looking for. Changing direction, he began to follow the seldom-used path that led to the cabin. As he got closer he could see the chimney of the cabin sticking up amongst the tangle of overgrown vegetation that threatened to swallow it. The cabin seemed to have gotten lost in a mass of English laurel, dogwoods, and mountain maples. It no longer looked as he remembered. Its strong shell remained but it needed maintenance badly. Long drooping branches screened the entrance as Gillis pushed back several branches to gain access to the front door.

Pulling the skeleton key from his pocket, and with a little effort, the key turned in the lock as he shoved the door inward. Several cobwebs dangled from a rusty chandelier that hung over a dust-caked table. The cabin certainly hadn't been used by anyone in a long time. He stared at the fireplace. It was wide and powerful and filled most of one wall. The mantel appeared to be an amazing work of art with fine details carved across it face. The stone of the fireplace was beautiful, carefully cut, and tight jointed. But what was really amazing were the scores of fossils embedded in the rocks and carefully placed into the masonry design. He remembered that at one time his father's hobby had been paleontology. The fossils brought back memories of being very young and one day noticing his father's collection had disappeared. Now he knew where they had gone. Many of the fossils were large and impressive in their detail. Gillis took several minutes looking at an ancient fish and then at a trilobite. There were fossils of leaves, small creatures, butterflies, ammonites, and strange unknown plants.

Gillis went back to examining the place but found no papers or anything else that might gain him a clue in his father's disappearance. A little discouraged, he opened the mysterious door that from the window had always intrigued him. His hopes of what he would find were quickly dashed by the Spartan furnishings of two beds, a lone chair, and a dresser. On top of the dresser sat a dusty wash basin and pitcher but nothing that would help him in his search. He opened all the drawers finding nothing but dried mouse droppings. Disappointed, he closed the bottom drawer and headed into the main room. All hope of whatever he thought he might find was gone. Finally, he walked out into the sunshine as he closed the door, locking it behind him. His venture had been a waste of time and energy.

It took a while to walk back up through the fields to the farmhouse and he had raised a sweat by the time he arrived. He stopped momentarily to see if he could spot Roper then turned and headed back toward the house. He felt the need to relieve himself and quickly. There were outhouses spaced throughout the farm but he had paid little attention to their locations. The outhouses were built on skids and their locations changed every couple of years. Glancing around he was lucky enough to locate one with a star cut into the wooden door. The odor was a little overpowering as the door swung shut. To one side he noticed a pile of corn cobs in the corner and beside them a mound of corn silk husks. When he was done with his duties he used the cob to clean himself and then a small amount of corn silk. He remembered when his father first began requiring a daily pail of water be placed beside each door and somehow that becoming part of his everyday chores.

A tall man carrying some wire and a hammer was walking past when Gillis shut the door and fastened the latch. Gillis didn't recognize the man but there were many here that were new.

"Excuse me, sir. Do you know where Roper is?"

"The last time I saw him he was headed over there behind the log barn at the corrals with several gentlemen," he replied.

"Thanks," said Gillis as he headed in that direction. There were four barns on the property but only the massive stone barn was built using masonry. The thick walls rose up high above the ground until finally merging with the wooden beams of the roof. Whoever originally built it had planned for the worst and maybe that was why they had gone to the effort of building the secret room underground. He thought about falling into the brackish water. Did he really see part of a stone arch behind the rotting furniture? If it was a stone doorway, where did it lead? In the excitement he wondered if his mind hadn't just played a trick on him.

Gillis suddenly could see Roper and his mind snapped back to business. Roper and the two men were walking in his direction. The group stopped and huddled around talking as Roper noticed Gillis.

"I hope you are finding what you need," interjected Gillis somewhat awkwardly. He really didn't know the business of buying and selling stock and he didn't want to mess up any deal that Roper was putting together.

Both men smiled and the taller of the two men spoke. "Your stock is very impressive, Mr. McCabe, and your man Roper here seems to know his stuff."

"Thank you, but he's not my man. At least to me he is a free man, and a knowledgeable one at that."

"Sorry sir, no insult meant."

"None taken," said Gillis as he turned toward Roper. "So have you negotiated a deal?"

"We were just about to close it," Roper said. "They want three good mules and two of the Thoroughbred geldings. They also wanted to buy your father's old saddle, the bridle set, and the matching saddle bags. Your father switched his personal riding horse about two years ago and the back on the new horse was a bit longer and wider so he had a new saddle and matching tack made. I believe we have come to agreement on the stock, now all we need to do is figure out the gear."

"Sounds like everything has been handled. When you are done can you see me at the house? I have a few more questions."

"Yes sir, Mr. McCabe, it shouldn't take me much more than a half an hour to finish up here."

"That will be great, I will see you then."

The sun shone brightly as he walked back toward the house and his wandering mind enjoyed remembering the many experiences he had as a child. The thought of his dad being gone and maybe dead felt like someone had ripped a large hole in his life. Even though he had not needed his father's help for over fifteen years the reassuring thought that he was there had never left. Now in the course of last month he had lost his fiancée and possibly his father.

With both hands in his coat pockets, he continued toward the house in a slow controlled walk. He felt something in his pocket. Reaching inside, to his surprise, there in his hand was the metal medallion that Letty had dropped as she died. He stopped and in the good light took another look at it. It reminded him of an old skeleton key but this had no teeth and was larger and fatter at the base than a normal key. There was basically just a short shaft and at the end with a small notch cut into the lower side. For the first time, he stood and studied it. Suddenly he noticed faint stamped letters worn by time on the side of the oval base. They were not easy to see but a faint capital "F" was stamped into the flatter oval part of the medallion. Maybe this identified the owner but only they knew what the key and the letters meant. The object looked worn and handled and Gillis thought it was probably pretty important. At least it had been to Letty. Gillis couldn't help but believe this small medal object was somehow tied to the whole disappearance of his father. How, he didn't have a clue.

All of a sudden Roper came running up from the barn. "Mr. McCabe, Mr. McCabe, we found something."

Chapter 9

Roper was waving a letter in his hand as he ran, quickly covering the ground between them. "It's a letter from a lady named Miss Annabelle Smith in Alexandria. It has her address on it! One of the men found it when he was looking through Mr. McCabe's old saddle bags. Apparently your father had forgotten to remove this letter or he didn't see it. It was kind of stuck in the bottom. It's a little water-damaged but it says right here to Mr. Scully McCabe."

Roper was excited and pointed at the address as he handed the letter to Gillis.

Gillis stared at the letter for several seconds before looking back up at Roper. "Good work, Roper. I'll leave for Alexandria in the morning. I need you to do two things. I will write out a telegram to a friend, Doc Bennett in Norfolk telling him of my journey and where I believe I will be staying. Also, I need to have someone accompany me but with Wooly still hurt and having a fever I am not sure who. Roper, I trust your judgment so I need you to stay here and manage the place while I'm gone. Do any of the men stand out as being able to handle themselves in a bad situation?"

"Yes sir, Luke Wright is smart, honest, and good with a gun. My gut says he has had a hard past but he's a good man."

"Send him to the house as soon as possible. Thank you. This is the first real lead I have had. I have to believe that the burned paper and the letter both having Alexandria on them is no coincidence. Roper, while I am gone, I want four log towers erected around the farm so we aren't surprised again. Make sure they build them stout with plenty of protection for the sentries."

"Yes sir, Mr. McCabe. Are you going to travel by carriage or with horses and a couple of pack animals?"

"As much as my sorry rear end would like to ride by carriage I think horses would be a lot safer."

"I agree but you might consider using some of our Thoroughbred mules."

"Mules to ride to Alexandria? I have never considered such a thing. Gentlemen usually don't ride mules."

"I guarantee you that those big ears of theirs will hear things well before those horses do. I have a six year old named Brandywine that is as well trained as any horse and will tell you if anything is within a hundred feet of her. You would be amazed."

"All the way to Alexandria?"

"Yes sir, mules live off the land better and drink less. They are amazing beasts."

"At this point I am open to anything. I will try, and pray you're right. Now hurry and go get that Luke, what did you say his last name was?"

"Luke Wright. You will be impressed; there is no backup in the man."

Gillis headed over to the house and met Lucy at the door of the kitchen. He hesitated for a moment, his eyes fixed on the slender woman before softly telling her what he needed. "Lucy, I am leaving in the morning and need enough supplies for two weeks of travel. Can you start putting that together?"

"Yes sir, Mr. McCabe. I'll start on it right after dinner."

Gillis had been impressed with this young, black woman since she arrived and God only knew how difficult these circumstances were that she had walked into.

"I am expecting a Luke Wright. Please show him into the library when he arrives."

"Yes sir, Mr. McCabe."

He didn't like the sterile tone of their conversations but she had been raised a slave and he knew it would take years to break her of the habits that at some point were probably whipped into her. Walking down the hall and into the library, he began examining the long lines of shelves. He knew the book was there, at least he remembered it from his childhood. The book contained hundreds of maps showing all the roads and trails all the way up to New York and as far south as South Carolina. He went to his knees and searched the travel section but after several minutes gave up in frustration. Gillis knew at one time the book was there because he remembered studying it when his father and he had anticipated a trip to Asheville when he was young. The noise in the hall startled him as he rose from the floor to see Lucy standing there.

"Mr. McCabe, this is Luke Wright."

Luke was tall and slender with a certain air of confidence that showed in his dark eyes. He had the look of a man who could handle himself and had probably earned every inch of the respect he expected.

"Please to meet you, Luke. Roper speaks very highly of you. Says you're smart and a good hand with a gun if needed. Can you give me a little history on yourself?"

"Yes sir, I was taught early by my pa. He died young and I needed to know how to defend my family and myself. I try and use my brain first and my gun second but sometimes that isn't possible. I was born northeast of here. After my ma died a couple of years back I started drifting, mostly working on farms and ranches. I even spent a little time working as a deputy, but I always felt the need to move on."

Gillis noticed that Luke had several scars that aged his face and a Navy Colt strapped to his hip.

"Did Roper tell you what I needed you for?"

"A little, he said your father's place here had been attacked by somebody but no one knows who or why. Roper said you found a clue that your father may have had a girlfriend in Alexandria and would probably need some help getting there. He said you were city folk and might not know your way around the woods and when you get to Alexandria you might need some help."

"I can't say I like what he said but he is probably right. It's been over three weeks since my fiancée and I rode my carriage in here and found just about everyone dead. Whoever did that took the time to tear up everything looking for something. The real mystery is why they didn't steal anything. Roper was gone and survived but few others did. There were eight men, several women, and even a couple of children that were brutally murdered in the attack and my father is missing."

"So someone took your father?"

"I don't know that. Until today I hadn't a clue were my father could be or where to start looking. Fortunately, Roper was out selling some mules and tack when one of the buyers found a letter tucked into the bottom of an old set of saddle bags."

"So why me? You have Roper and other men that probably know this country just as well."

"You're right," said Gillis glancing down at Luke's scuffed and worn boots. "But I need Roper here to keep things running. Wooly is hurt and you know the country. According to Roper you have a sixth sense about you that keeps men alive."

"So what is in this for me to be your scout and bodyguard?"

"An extra hundred if you get me to Alexandria and back safe. Another fifty if we find my father."

"Sounds fair enough, when—"

Roper walked into the room. "Looks like you two have already met."

"I like your choice and I think Luke and I will do just fine. I want to leave tomorrow morning early and I spoke to Lucy about getting our grub together. Keep a good eye on Wooly and if he doesn't get better, fetch Doc."

"Mr. McCabe, this place is still being watched. One of our men got another glance of someone and he also heard a horse in the distance. We need a way to quietly get you two out of here and away safely. I have been thinking on just how I could do that and I think I know how. There are a number of roads that work their way towards Alexandria and Washington but I am pretty sure whoever those men are out there, they are watching them. There is a trail I once walked with your father that was the roughest, nastiest, rocky goat trail you have ever been on. I asked your father why we were going that way and he said it saved over a day and a half of riding and he needed to know if it was still passable. It took us over four days on foot but the trail does just what he said it did."

"So you think we should climb up over this goat trail on foot to make our way to Alexandria?"

"Not on foot, ride the mules. You need to leave here and not be followed and I have figured out how I think that can be done. If you and Luke will head to the bottom of the meadow and follow a game trail north for a couple of miles it opens up at the base of the mountains. From there you curl around and follow what I swear is a trail a goat made. If you are followed, those mules will leave them in the dust. There is only one exposed road you will need to ride on for a couple of miles before you reach that trail up the mountain and you will need to be careful there."

"I guess we have decided. I don't know what to say but it makes sense to lose these men no matter how we do it. I trust you Roper that these animals are what you say they are." Roper started walking toward the kitchen. Gillis looked at Luke. "Is he saying a horse can't make it on this goat trail he was talking about?"

"No, some can, but a mule is just put together better and can do it without getting into trouble. A lot of horses would give you hell on a trail like what he is talking about. It isn't like riding down a road—it's going to be dangerous and with a couple of pack mules you'll be able to carry everything you need."

"It appears you two think this is the route we should take. I guess I am up to trying anything once, even if it is riding a mule. Can you have everything ready first thing in the morning? I'm going to look around some more and hopefully find a map."

"No problem, Mr. McCabe, come sunrise we'll be ready."

* * *

The next morning Gillis walked to the barn and quietly opened the door to the large barn lit only by a single lantern. Inside two saddled mules and two mules with fully loaded pack mules stood.

"Morning, Mr. McCabe," said Luke. "I want you to meet Brandywine—she will be your mount for the trip. According to Roper, she is one of your father's best mares. She seems to be tough, cut, and smart. Listen to her through her body movements and she will get you through. Those long ears of hers are the best watch-dog you have ever had. I will be riding one of your father's johns, Scotch Dandy. He's a good mule too but not near as smooth as Brandywine."

An hour later Luke led the way as he held the lead rope connected to the first pack mule. Gillis followed in silence. Down through the meadow they walked hugging the tree line before disappearing on a hidden trail behind a large gray rock at the forest's edge. For the next hour Luke kept to the rough game trail as if he rode it every day. Even in the dark shadows of early morning the mules stayed glued to the trail's indentation that to the common eye didn't look like much. Finally the sun began to rise and Gillis could see the faint imprint of the path meandering along the forest's floor.

Luke turned to Gillis and whispered, "We have another three hour ride before we get to the goat trail. The first part of it is through traveled country. As soon as we go around this next bend we meet up with another trail that is almost wide enough to be a road. It can be well-traveled at times. Keep real alert. I will feel a whole lot safer when we get on the goat trail and start up the mountain."

They rode around a small rock slide and then worked their way through two overgrown bushes that almost completely hid the trail. In front of them was a wider trail, wide enough for horse and pack but too narrow for a carriage. The dirt was torn from use and Gillis wondered who was ahead of them. For the next half an hour they rode silently until they reached a small creek they needed to cross. The two lead mules plunged their muzzles into the cold, clear water but Brandywine kept her head up and her ears pointed up the trail. Finally she drank after the other mules were done.

"Something is bothering Brandywine," Luke said quietly. "She either heard, seen or sensed something up the trail. Could be just a deer or a fox or the like, or it could be a man. We will take out of here real slow and careful like, and hope whatever the burr under her saddle is isn't anything we can't handle."

They continued for another twenty yards when Luke pulled back on his reins and raised his arm in a silent signal to stop. Brandywine instinctively stopped and Gillis nudged her ahead with gentle pressure to her side. "What is it?" whispered Gillis. In front of them another trail merged with the one they were on.

"Tracks and a lot of them, at least five horses have been through here in the past day or so. It looks as if they may have stopped up here for a while. I want to take a look around—no use taking chances if we don't have to. Maybe they left a clue and we can figure out who they are. Why don't you tie up over there and I will use these other trees."

Gillis rode his mule off the trail several yards and could see where someone had cleared a few branches from the tree in front of him and headed toward it. The rubbing from a lead rope had scarred a young maple tree and it was recent. He threw his leg over the mule's back and dismounted onto the dark soft ground pulverized by horse tracks and tied Brandywine.

Whoever had used this spot had taken their time and maybe rested there for a while. Luke was already scouting the little site so Gillis walked away from the mule and behind a large bush to relieve himself. He was partway through when he noticed some fresh dirt mingled with the leaves. He suddenly jumped back. There amongst the leaves was a battered grayish-white hand sticking out of the ground.

Chapter 10

The hand was bent and dirty and the fingernails and tips of the fingers were coated in dry blood. Gillis jerked back throwing a stream of urine across a wide area before controlling himself enough to tuck his privates back into his pants.

"Luke, come here quick, there's a hand."

Luke quickly turned and jogged over to Gillis. "Where?"

Gillis only pointed as Luke turned his head and stared at the gruesome sight. Both men just gawked momentarily before Luke pulled his gun from his holster and motioned Gillis to follow him back into the trees. Tucked behind a large oak Luke whispered, "These tracks are probably at least a day old but who knows, they might still be out there. You stay here until I can search around and make sure they are gone. We don't need any more surprises."

Gillis nodded and moved closer to the large tree. His mind raced. He knew he was out of his element. For the past fifteen years he had worked and enjoyed city life and since the moment he had entered the grounds of his father's estate his life had changed. He was no skilled woodsman and if it weren't for Luke he would probably be hopelessly lost. How would he ever find his father? For the next few minutes he hugged the tree thinking about everything that had happened in the last weeks and wondering when the nightmare would end. He was lost in thought when he heard something behind him as he jerked backward to face the noise. It was Luke working his way silently through the brush and when he saw Gillis he put his thumb up into the air. Within a minute he stood beside Gillis breathing hard. "I circled the opening and their tracks lead out. There is no one here but us and that dead guy. I wonder who he is."

"I certainly plan to find out," said Gillis in a firm voice as he walked over to the blood-stained hand and reached down with both hands and pulled on the wrist. It barely moved. Luke quickly joined him and with his help and some digging they began to expose more of the arm.

"They sure didn't bury him very deep."

"I doubt they thought they needed to—they disguised the grave by putting leaves and debris on it. Its way out here in the middle of nowhere and what are the chances of someone coming along and happening to relieve themselves at this exact spot? I think we were lucky to have stumbled upon him. If it weren't for the hand sticking up, I am sure we would have never seen it."

For the next ten minutes they worked at digging and pulling the corpse out of the makeshift grave before dragging the stiff body into the small meadow. Mud caked the man's face and dried blood mixed with the dirt covered the ends of his fingers. All but one of his fingernails was missing and appeared to have been ripped off in a frantic attempt to free himself. Gillis walked back to his mule, untied his canteen and removed it from his saddle. Opening his saddle bag he retrieved a small cloth.

"What are you doing?" Luke asked.

"There is only one way for us to see his face and that's if we wash it off. That is what I intend to do." The victim's face was so caked in mud that only a small patch of skin was visible.

"They must have tried to kill him during or just after a rain storm to get this guy that dirty. Probably some local guy would be my guess," said Luke staring at the body.

Gillis began pouring water over the man's face while washing the mud off. Finally, the effort revealed the clammy white features of the dead man, his gaze frozen with a look of terror. Gillis kneeled beside the body and for several minutes examined it. Then he stood back up and went over to the stream and refilled his canteen to finish the job.

"That man went through hell and that's quite the scarring on his face. Do you know this fellow?" asked Luke.

"In a way I do. This is one of the men that attacked Wooly and me when we were coming back from Norfolk. I don't think I could forget his face or his scar if I wanted to, but what I would like to know is why they beat and killed him."

"I sure don't see any blood on his skin or clothes and I don't think they meant to bury him alive. Let's roll him over and take a look." Carefully they rolled the man over onto his stomach. With the back of his head exposed they could clearly see an area about three inches in diameter of matted bloody hair. Gillis took a moment to examine the rest of the man's back but couldn't find any additional wounds.

Again Gillis examined the body for moment before leaning over and closely smelling the wound. Then he reached for his canteen.

"What on earth are you doing?" asked Luke.

"I'm not sure but this man wasn't shot—there isn't any smell of gun powder. Let me see your knife."

Gillis bent over and skillfully cut back some of the bloody hair from the scalp. Luke stood close by carefully watching the grisly procedure.

"So they stabbed him in the back of the head?"

"I don't think they stabbed him. Look at this clean hole, perfectly round. It almost looks like someone used some type of tool to finish him off. I know of no tool that will cut through bone like that and leave such a clean mark."

"What about an ice pick?"

"God only knows, but whatever it was I don't think it killed him as quickly as they anticipated. My guess is that whatever was used knocked him out for a while and then he came to shortly after they buried him. There was just enough dirt to make it impossible to dig his way out. He finally died from either his wound or suffocation or both."

"That would explain why only his hand made it above the surface."

"I am afraid it would. Whatever this man did or saw must have been considered a death sentence by the rest of his group." Gillis stood and gently shook his head. "I know we don't have shovels but let's try and bury him."

"Mr. McCabe, I don't think that is a good idea. Time is our enemy. These tracks tell me they are in the area and we need to make it over those two steep ridges and down onto that road to Alexandria before those men find us. I say we just drag him into the woods and pile leaves on him."

Gillis stood there thinking for a moment before nodding his head in agreement. "You are probably right Luke, let's get it done."

An hour later they were still on the overgrown trail when Luke pulled back the reins and stopped. "Over there is the main trail. It's hard to find the trail we are on, but that pile of rocks stacked there is how I remember." Luke pointed to a small pile of rocks about eighteen inches high on the far side of the trail. He smiled. "Whoever built this trail knew what he was doing. Marking it but not at the entrance, he knew that it would throw off all but the most experienced."

"I don't see any trail."

"Exactly, and that is just exactly what we want."

Luke stepped down and tied the mule Gillis was leading to his. He mounted and led the two pack mules across ground littered with leaves before rounding a large mountain maple. The men took a sharp turn between two huge boulders and were immediately on a very old and seldom used trail.

"Good, there aren't any new tracks on the trail so we should be getting a decent head start."

"I can see why this trail doesn't get much use, it's pretty nasty," said Gillis as the trail began gaining elevation through a field of sharp boulders and maple trees.

"How does your saddle feel? You might want to tighten your cinch for the next couple of miles. It's going to get pretty rough and steep."

"I tightened her up good just before I mounted."

The trail was no more than eight to ten inches wide and Gillis could see the mule's smaller hooves were an advantage in finding a place wide enough to step. The route stayed to the trees as it worked its way over slick moss-covered rock and piles of wet leaves. Gillis found himself staring ahead not wanting to look at the steep drop off to one side. Several times his mule stumbled slightly but caught itself right away with a quick jerk. The trail continued to be rocky but finally gave way to a less dense part of the forest with burnt oaks. Soon it began to meander through a thick maze of ancient, rotting snags and more boulders before leveling out on top of the ridge. The flat ground didn't last long before diving back down into another valley. It was almost dark before they made it to the last ridge where Luke stopped and dismounted.

"There is a storm gathering behind us and we need to find a shelter soon. I camped in this area a long time ago. If I remember right there is a nice clear spring about sixty yards over this hill. We should be able to hobble the stock and hopefully there is enough grass for the mules to put a little something in their bellies for the night."

Gillis nodded as he slowly dismounted. He had never healed up totally and now his butt hurt worse and he felt sore all over. The ride was long and hard and was all he wanted. If it weren't for those men he knew were hunting them he would have much preferred the springs of his carriage. By the time he had tied Brandywine to a tree Luke was already untying the pack ropes of the diamond hitch.

Looking over at Luke, Gillis feebly said, "Is there anything I can help you with?"

Luke stopped for a moment and looked back. "I got it, boss. Why don't you take that log over there and put it so we have a place to keep the saddles off the ground. I will use this canvas to cover the gear. I also brought along some spare canvas for us. I agree it does look like it might rain a bit."

Gillis was slow at moving as he put part of a tree up between two rocks to keep the saddles off the ground. Then he worked at gathering firewood. He had gotten soft and now he was paying for it. Every move was an effort as Luke seemed to fly through things getting one chore done after another. The mule's hobbles were burlap sacks twisted to fit their ankles and Luke made short work of getting two of the mules done and removing their lead ropes. The other two mules remained tied to stout trees.

Gillis sat down and moaned quietly as he did. Luke sat a pile of small, dry branches down in front of Gillis."

"I ride stock all the time and I'm used to it. Those are new muscles you're finding Mr. McCabe, and nobody enjoys finding them. You're doing fine. Hopefully we will be riding flatter ground again. We will keep the fire low and at the base of that turned-up stump. It will be hard to see there. No use inviting strangers if we don't have to."

After supper Luke took all the mules to water and firmly tied the two mules that had eaten to trees near camp. Quickly, he untied the other mules and let them graze in hobbles.

Gillis held a steaming cup of coffee in his hand and offered it to Luke. "Thanks," he said as he sat down beside the fire.

"Did they all drink?"

"All of them drank except your mule, Brandywine."

"Really, why not?"

"Mules only drink if they are thirsty and apparently she wasn't thirsty."

"We did go over some pretty rough country and your mules did a great job. Hopefully if we need to outrun someone, they can do the job."

"I'll let them answer that question if it arises."

Later that night Gillis woke to the pounding of rain on the canvas sheet strung above the high ground they had chosen between two trees. The rope had stretched and the canvas hung down far lower than Gillis remembered before falling asleep. They weren't getting wet but the sheer sound of the pelting rain hitting the stretched canvas made it too noisy to sleep. Gillis could barely see the mules tied beneath the other trees. Their ears were rolled back and they look miserable. Gillis turned to look at Luke who was rolling a cigarette. The fire had long ago been drowned by the rain and Luke seemed satisfied to just hold the unlit cigarette in his mouth. Gillis sat and wondered if this whole thing was just a terrible folly. He thought of Sandra back home in her bed and wished he was beside her. How could everything change so fast and why were these men so intent on killing everything close to him? Many thoughts went through his mind including the loss of Letty before he tightly pulled his damp wool blanket around his neck. Finally he dozed off as the rain began to slow.

* * *

Gillis woke to the sound of a crackling fire. He tried to stand but the soreness of his body slowed the process.

"You're looking a little stove-up this morning."

"I'm fine, just haven't ridden that much over the years. So what did you make for breakfast?" asked Gillis in an aching voice.

Luke opened a small mason jar that sat beside the fire and poured what looked like scrambled eggs onto a frying pan. "How does a couple hard biscuits, bacon, and a couple of eggs sound to you? Don't have the luxury of having a pack mule with me often and it's remarkable what a man can carry when you do."

An hour later the two men and their stock were packed and headed northeast down a trail that meandered through a mixture of thick maple and oak trees. It was close to four hours later when they finally broke from a thick deciduous forest into another meadow. If a person didn't know this trail existed there was little chance of finding it. The remains of a large logging wagon with several rotting logs sat close to the tree line at the back of the meadow and Gillis glanced at it, wondering how it got there. Across the meadow on the muddy road was a man driving a team of horses pulling a loaded wagon with tied-down canvas. He looked surprised as he glanced their way and then waved. The driver pulled back on the reins easing the team to a stop and waited until Gillis and Luke had ridden up beside him.

"Howdy, you two lost?"

"Nope but if that storm last night had gotten any worse I think we would have washed away," Luke said in his Southern accent.

"Hell of a storm wasn't it? Washed out a lot of the road back a piece, going to make it harder for the wagons that are coming up after me."

"Where you headed?" asked Luke.

"There's a big camp of soldiers about ten miles from here and they go through a lot of supplies. If we're going to beat them blue bellies we will need to feed our troops. There sure is a lot of truth to the saying that an army marches on its stomach."

Gillis looked at the man for a moment and then spoke. "Mind if we tag along? We are headed towards Harrisonburg and this road will take us near our cut-off road. That is if I am reading the map right."

"Sure thing, join up. We should be at the camp in about three hours or so. It will be nice to have some company. I feel pretty lucky I got this job. It pays well but I doubt it will last long."

"How's that?"

"Everyone thinks we will beat them Yankees in less than six months. They say they don't have the stomach to fight like we do. My bet is they are right but I guess we will see."

"War between brothers is never good. Have you heard any news on the fighting?"

"A little, President Lincoln called for a blockade right after the South declared war but from what I heard they only got five ships to cover the whole East Coast and the Mississippi. That can't be much of a blockade with only five ships if you ask me."

"That Abe Lincoln is a smart man and I wouldn't think he would bluff about a thing like that."

"I guess we will find out soon enough but things are surely getting tense close to Washington. I wouldn't be surprised if they have a big battle somewhere up there." For the next six miles the men talked over the steady clumping sound of their horses and mules working their way through the muddy road surface. In the distance they could see a large flag blowing in the wind, red with a blue cross and white stars.

"That must be our new flag," said Luke with a smile. Down deep the flag made a powerful impression on both men but they were different impressions.

"Look at all those tents. I'll bet there are over five hundred and twice that many men."

Gillis looked from side to side at the perfectly aligned tents and men moving everywhere. Some were around campfires, others cleaned their muskets, and still others marched in unison as their commanders barked orders.

For most of the trip the two rode beside the wagon driver but now Gillis motioned Luke to fall back behind the wagon. Gillis subtly turned to Luke as they rode side by side followed by their pack mules and whispered. "If you make eye contact, be sure and smile and wave. We don't need a lot of questions right now."

"But Mr. McCabe, I really don't have a dog in this here fight and these boys are on our side."

"Luke, we will always be Virginians but we need to remember we are headed toward Washington and I don't want anything holding us up."

Luke looked over with a confused look but nodded regardless. Several times the two of them waved to soldiers that showed an interest in their presence. Abruptly the wagon veered to the right and the driver looked back to make contact.

"This is where I turn off to deliver them supplies. Hope you two have a good trip the rest of the way."

"We will and God speed to you. Long live Dixie," said Gillis as he gave a gentle tug of salute on the front brim of his hat and kept riding forward down the road. Gillis was surprised that the two guards stationed on the perimeter of the camp just gave them relaxed salutes as they passed.

* * *

For the next three days they rode towards Alexandria. They passed numerous patrols of soldiers and only received occasional waves as they passed. At night they slept under the stars, trying to leave as little a trace as possible of their path.

On the fourth night they camped on a bluff overlooking Alexandria with Washington just a few miles further beyond the Potomac River. At the edge of the woods they found a small meadow with a creek and a beautiful view of the lights of the city. They picketed out two mules and put the other two in hobbles before lighting a fire and starting dinner. Luke was soaking up what little juice there was from his meat with a small piece of biscuit when he spoke.

"Mr. McCabe, I rightly don't think I know where you stand in this here War Between the States. You don't want the North to win do you?"

"The United States is thirty-four states as we speak. We are a big country with plenty of opportunity for anyone who wants to work hard. This war will pit brother against brother and will hurt this country more than anything imaginable. I was raised by a wonderful lady after my mother and brother died in childbirth. For fourteen years this lady raised me as one of her own while my father was gone on business. I owe so much to Letty but unfortunately for her she was born a Negro slave. I consider her my mother and miss her as any son would." He paused.

"I love Virginia and its people but because of Letty and others I have known I could never take the side of slavery. No man should own another man regardless of color or politics. I won't fight against my beloved Virginia but I won't help the North defeat her either. I guess in a way I am a man caught in the middle with no place to go. I am going to find my father and then try and figure out what to do. Don't get me wrong, I'm not feeling sorry for myself. I believe there will be a lot of this country far worse off than me after this war ends."

Luke poured himself another cup of coffee from the metal pot precariously balanced on two rocks that circled the fire and took a sip as he looked at Gillis. In almost a whisper he said, "If you value your life I suggest you don't make any sudden moves. I have been hearing them for the last couple of minutes and my guess is there are at least a dozen men out there and they sure as hell aren't here for the coffee."

Chapter 11

In the darkness the two men could hear the cocking of muskets. They couldn't see anything but they knew the meaning of the sound.

"Hold it right there, stay close to the fire and slowly raise your hands high where we can see them," said a firm voice from out in the blackness.

By the light of the campfire Gillis could make out the shape of a dozen soldiers, all wearing dark blue uniforms.

"Corporal, light the torches so we can see these spies better and have two men tie their hands behind their backs. I don't want any dead prisoners, leastwise until we interrogate them."

Several soldiers firmly grabbed each man and spun them around before tying their hands tightly behind them. "Nice spot you picked to view our troop movements. I will be curious to hear your story," said a soldier with lieutenant's bar on his shoulders. It was hard to see the man's face in the dancing light of the campfire and the shadows of the torches. He had a wide-brimmed hat with golden tassels and dangling against his side was a well-polished sword. A look of achievement showed across the outline of his hook-nosed face as he silhouetted himself in front of the fire.

Gillis turned and looked at Luke. "I'll handle this Luke. Lieutenant, my name is Gillis McCabe."

The lieutenant interrupted in a voice heavy with sarcasm. "Am I supposed to recognize that name?"

"No, I didn't really believe you would but I believe the Secretary of War, John Floyd will vouch for me."

Even in the low light of the torches Gillis could see the officer had a puzzled look.

"If you would be so kind as to raise the right side of my saddle bags and take a close look you will see a patch of leather sewn on the backside. It is meant to appear as a repair. Take a knife and carefully cut open the stitching and I think I can explain everything."

The lieutenant stood there for a minute looking at Gillis and then at Brandywine the mule before shouting to one of his men. "Private James, remove those saddle bags from that mule and see if there is a patch on the back side." Brandywine turned her head and carefully studied the man as he cautiously approached. Gillis could tell the soldier was not comfortable with mules. He slowly untied the leather strips from both sides of the saddle and pulled the saddle bags off and set them on the ground. He turned the saddlebags over and began examining them with the help of the campfire.

"Sir, there is a fair-sized patch on the right side just as he said. Do you want me to cut it open?"

"Yes, and hurry it up. This could be some kind of trick so keep a sharp eye out."

The soldier pulled a six-inch knife from a black leather sheath that hung from his belt and began systematically removing the stitching. Finally, he pulled back the flap of leather and removed what looked like a letter.

"Sir, it appears to be a letter," he said as he stood and handed the battered envelope to the lieutenant.

The lieutenant studied the letter for a moment and then pulled a pair of wire-rimmed spectacles from his coat pocket. His face had a stern, serious look as he scrutinized the seal on the envelope before carefully opening it and removing the letter. The letter appeared to be two pages long and the officer took his time absorbing its contents before turning to Gillis and giving him a smart salute.

"I am very sorry to have disturbed you, sir. Corporal, untie these gentlemen." The lieutenant paused. "How can I be of assistance?"

Luke looked at Gillis and then to the lieutenant with a look of disbelief.

"Lieutenant, I am actually here looking for my father. He's gone missing and I have reason to believe I might be able to at least get a clue as to his whereabouts from a lady who was a friend of his and lives in Alexandria. If you could possibly help me find West Oak Street or point me in that direction I would be very appreciative."

"My pleasure, sir, my men and I will meet you here first thing tomorrow morning and escort you to the outskirts of town. It will be our honor and again sir, I am sorry about the spy thing. We have orders to stop and interrogate anyone we find near this ridge."

"That's not a problem, lieutenant, I understand and we will see you in the morning."

The man tipped his hat in a form of salute and then took one of the torches and began leading his men down the hill. The light from their torches danced in the darkness as it slowly disappeared amongst the trees.

Luke turned to Gillis with a look of amazement. "Mr. McCabe if you don't mind me asking, what in the hell did that letter say that got those Union boys acting that way?"

Gillis looked at Luke momentarily before answering. "First, I want to know how you knew those men were down there and were surrounding us. I certainly didn't hear anything and I have excellent hearing."

"It was a lot of things. First the mules ears, they all were pointing in one direction and then another. They are great watch dogs and can tell you a lot if you watch and listen."

"Let me get this straight: you could tell we were being surrounded by the mule's ears?"

"That and listening to the crickets and leaves. On a calm night you always hear crickets and the gentle rustle of leaves when the wind blows but the crickets stopped and there wasn't but the mildest of breezes. You shouldn't have heard any leaves rustling but sometimes I could."

"So why in the hell didn't you say something?" Gillis asked.

"There were a lot of them and just two of us. They knew exactly where we were and I only knew they were out there in the dark. Any quick moves and they could have opened fire. They had the drop on us from the beginning and there wasn't a whole lot we could do."

"In the future I would like to be part of the plan but I understand why you did it. I guess I am greener than I thought when it comes to the woods. You are probably right. I may have gotten myself killed if things hadn't gone right."

The thought of Luke growing up in the woods in poverty seemed to sink in. The woods were his world and he understood them. Deep down it made Gillis jealous and he knew he wanted to get a whole lot smarter quick.

"Mr. McCabe, I know it isn't any of my business but I sure would like to know what was written on that hidden letter. It really made that lieutenant and soldier boys stand up and take notice."

"It's a little bit of a long story but I used to own a shipbuilding business and the government bought a lot of my technology as well as a number of completed ships that my company designed and built. Less than a year ago, I sold the business. Since then the government has been trying to get me to come to Washington and do consultation work for the Navy. I have thought a lot about it since the war broke out and I can't take up arms or supply the Union with ideas that would destroy my beloved Virginia or the South. The Union is going to try and blockade the whole East Coast and the Mississippi River at some point in this God-forsaken war. Unfortunately, most of the ships they plan to do it with are ships my company either built or were designed by us."

"So you're neutral and you believe a Negro slave is as good as a white boy?"

"I do. I believe there will come a time in our future when color will no longer matter as it does today. Unfortunately, I am afraid that time is still far into the future. I won't help the Union anymore but I won't help the South either. I am the worst of people, a man who won't take a stand for either side. The letter is from the Secretary of War, John Floyd. It is a request for me to come to Washington."

"You know the Secretary of War?"

"Yes, quite well. He is a straightforward man and he has become a good friend over the past seven years."

The rest of the evening Luke talked about how he grew up and learned about the woods, prompting Gillis to discuss how he got into designing and building boats. Finally the two rolled up in their blankets and fell asleep.

* * *

Gillis's eyes slowly opened to the dim light of early morning. A small fire crackled and the first sign of steam began to rise from their blackened coffee pot. The smell of bacon filled the air and Luke kneeled beside the fire cutting up some hard bread with his knife.

"Well, good morning Mr. McCabe, breakfast is almost ready. Hope you're hungry?"

Gillis sat up and squinted. He rubbed his eyes a second time before answering. "Good morning Luke. I must have been more tired than I thought. For some reason I didn't sleep that well."

He took a second to listen to the sounds around him before standing up and walking over to the coffee pot that had started to boil. With his glove on, he moved the pot back to a rock out of the flames.

A bird flew up about a hundred yards away and Gillis jerked his head around. With confidence Gillis said, "Must be the lieutenant and his men coming back." Luke nodded and smiled. Gillis looked at the mules, all their heads were turned and their ears were pointed in the same direction. Minutes later the sound of horse hooves could be heard as the lieutenant and his men rode up the narrow, steep trail that led to their campsite.

The lieutenant saluted and then spoke. "Good morning, Mr. McCabe, is there anything my men and I can help with?"

"We are doing fine but thank you. It will be a few minutes before we are ready. We were just finishing up with breakfast, care for a cup of coffee?"

"Don't mind if I do," said the officer as he dismounted, leaving nine mounted soldiers alert in their saddles. "Alexandria is a small place compared to Washington. Most of the houses are built near the Long Bridge that crosses the Potomac. Anyway, we can take you to the postmaster and I am sure he can give you directions on how to find the address and lady you are looking for."

Gillis ate as he and the lieutenant talked. Luke stayed busy saddling the mules and packed up the gear. With skill long learned, he was done in less than ten minutes. Finally he led Gillis's riding mule over to him as Gillis finished his inquiries of Alexandria. The lieutenant rode up beside Gillis and waved his arm and Luke, the two pack mules and the soldiers followed. It was on the long side of an hour before the small troop finally left the last stand of forest and started seeing houses. The further they went the closer together the houses had become and Gillis knew it indicated a town. Most of the homes were not log cabins but were made from planked overlapped lumber and if painted were done with white-wash. Within twenty minutes the quality of the homes and the streets began to improve. Abruptly the lieutenant raised his hand in the air and the column halted.

"There she is, the post office. I am sure the postmaster can help you locate the lady's house you are seeking. Good luck and Godspeed, sir." The lieutenant saluted smartly then led his troop in a semicircle and headed back in the direction they had come.

Gillis looked at Luke. "Well at least we got here. Now I hope we can find this Annabelle Smith's residence." The two rode up to the small, post office, dismounted, and walked through the door. A narrow-faced woman with grayish hair and small eyeglasses perched on the end of her nose appeared to be just finishing. The postmaster was middle-aged, balding and overweight.

"What can I help you gentlemen with?" he asked as his eyes scanned the men, not missing a detail.

"I am looking for a Miss Annabelle Smith on West Oak Street. I believe she lives in a boarding house in Room Three if I am reading the envelope correctly. It got a little wet and the number is difficult to read. We were hoping you could give us directions on finding her place."

"What would be your business with her?" asked the man as his body stiffened and his face went from a smile to a stern, serious look.

Gillis thought the response was odd but he had come too far to not accomplish his goal. "Sir, she is a friend of my father and he has gone missing. We are trying to find clues as to his location. Did I say something wrong?"

"No, no you didn't, it's just . . ." He paused and looked down at the counter.

"It's just what?" asked Gillis, his voice showing some annoyance. "What is the problem with getting directions to her house?"

"Obviously you haven't heard. They found Miss Annabelle Smith dead a week ago. As brutal and grisly a murder as these parts has ever seen, the type of brutality that got the whole town locking their doors."

"This happened last week?"

"Yes, someone tortured and murdered her. Police said that the cause of death was some type of wound to the back of the head. Whoever murdered her even sewed her lips shut after she was dead."

Chapter 12

"How do you know she was dead first?"

"The neighbor told me. Said there wasn't any blood on her face so the killer must have waited until she stopped bleeding. One of the first police officers on the scene told me the killer even poured himself a drink of Scotch and probably just sat there watching."

"Did you hear anything else?"

The postmaster looked uncomfortable. "No, other than within a few hours soldiers got there and took over the place. No one has heard a thing since they posted guards outside her door."

"Why would the military take over the murder scene and post guards outside her door?"

"Dang if I know. She worked across the river in Washington but I don't know what she did or who she worked for."

Gillis took a deep breath. "Well, I still need directions. My father is missing and there may be a clue there."

"The best thing I can do is probably draw you a map. The boarding house is only a couple of miles from here on one of the side streets. It's a large two-story house with a white picket fence around it. Whatever Miss Smith did she was well paid for it. She lived in one of those really nice neighborhoods, cobblestone roads, flower lined walkways. The kind of place most people can't afford."

The man reached under the counter and pulled out a sheet of paper and moved the ink well and pen closer to himself. "This may not be the best map but I think it will get you there." Gillis stood quietly not interrupting as the man drew a crude map. Finally, he blew on the paper for a moment signaling the map's completion and then slid it across the counter. "There you go. Hopefully you won't have a problem finding it."

"I appreciate your time, thank you."

"It can be a strange world out there. I hope you find your father."

Gillis nodded, turned, and walked out the door. Outside, the mules were quiet with their heads down while Brandywine tried to finish off a tall weed that grew between the hitching rail and the first stair. Gillis mounted his mule and by the time he gathered up the reins Luke was already in the saddle. "Mr. McCabe, this whole thing with your father is getting stranger by the minute. Do you have any idea what is going on?"

"Wish I did, but whatever it is, I worry my father is in over his head."

Gillis had studied the map and stayed on the road that was quickly becoming more of a street with houses packed closer together. He could still see horses and cattle out in the fields and most homes had a few chickens wandering about. A man was pulling his buggy out from a carriage house and was harnessing a horse that stood motionless yards away.

"It's been a while since I was in the city," Luke said. "It always strange to me how close the houses are. Hell, you can't even take a piss off the back porch without the neighbor watching."

"I suggest you get used to it for a while, Luke. Remember there are outhouses. I don't think what we came for will be easily found if it plays out like all the rest of what has happened." Gillis looked up as they approached an intersection and stopped after noticing a wooden post with several hand-painted street signs. The sign was partially hidden by a large drooping willow. "We turn here and go six blocks and then take a right on Oak Street."

"Whatever you say boss, lead on."

Twenty minutes later they turned onto Oak Street and immediately noticed the red cobblestones of the street. Trees and flowers lined the lane and the houses looked freshly painted and well kept. Two young boys not yet in their teens came running up to them and motioned Gillis to stop.

"Hey mister, why you riding those long-eared mules, can't you afford a horse?"

Gillis was uncomfortable at first but then smiled. "At one time I thought the same as you boys but these mules here are real smart and they can go places few horses can." He paused. "And they make very good lookouts."

Luke's face went into a smug smile as Gillis nodded his hat to the boys and gave his mule a slight nudge to the ribs.

"I never thought I would see you spouting the virtues of a mule. I would have bet good money that would have never happened," said Luke with a smirk on his face. Gillis didn't respond as he looked from side-to-side hoping to find a name or address on a mailbox.

Gillis pulled back on the reins. "That's got to be the place—see that soldier standing guard?"

The two men rode their mules over to the hitching post in front of the white picket fence that surrounded the yard. Dismounting, Gillis took a second to read the mailboxes. Of the four boxes one read Sam Schultz and the other one read Annabelle Smith. The other two boxes had small signs stating "For Rent." He headed to the small arbor entrance that announced the yard and began to unlatch the gate.

"Hold it right there, gentlemen. This building is off limits by order of the U.S. government. The only people allowed in or out of here are the residents and you two aren't residents, so be on your way."

Gillis saw an old man sitting on a swing just to the side of the building. "Private, I'm here to visit with Sam, the gentleman in the swing over there." The private looked confused and seemed to pause for a moment, his thick handlebar mustache hiding a puzzled look. With his musket tipped with a bayonet he motioned them to come ahead and go directly to where the old man was sitting.

"You can talk to him for a minute or two but you may not enter the house. Make your business short and sweet and then be off with you."

Luke followed Gillis as he walked over to the man who was gently swinging back and forth on a white wooden swing buried amongst the rightly cut hedge of laurels. The swing hung from a branch of a giant oak tree that dominated the tight corner of the house and gave views to the street. As they got closer they could see the man was elderly, probably in his mid-seventies. He was impeccably dressed in a faded and worn white suit that almost matched the color of his beard and mustache. The old man just stared into the street as if in his own world while gently swinging back and forth. Walking up to the old gentleman, Gillis gestured Luke to move up beside him so the guard couldn't see what they were saying. Gillis stumbled, "Sir, excuse me, sir. May we talk for a minute?"

The elderly man turned and looked at him with a slight smile. "You can call me Sam like you told the private there. Pretty smart of you, young man to read the mailbox and put two and two together."

"I guessed. I figured it was a pretty good gamble that you were Sam."

"Very smart, most people wouldn't have made it past that guard. Quick thinking, I like that in a man."

The man's quick wit and power of observation caught Gillis off guard and the look showed on his face.

"Just because you are old doesn't mean you can't pay attention to the world around you. You boys went through a fair amount of effort to talk to me, now what can I do for you?"

"I apologize, I should have never assumed—"

The old man cut him off. "Quit apologizing, I know what I look like sitting here, it's no wonder that you—" He stopped. "Anyways what can I do for you?"

"My name is Gillis McCabe and this is Luke Wright. First of all we were sorry to hear about what happen to Miss Annabelle Smith. We had hoped she might give us a clue as to my father, Scully McCabe's location. We found a very personal letter from a Miss Annabelle to him. We thought maybe her home or someone around here might have some information as to my father's whereabouts."

The man cleared his throat. "Since we are getting all acquainted like, my full name is Sam Schultz. We are all very sorry about what happened to Annabelle. I remember several months ago that she had a male guest come by and if I remember right she called him Scully. Nice looking fellow, older, strong build, seemed confident and cordial enough. I don't remember much more. So you two know she was murdered? "

"Yes sir, when we were asking for directions from the postmaster, he told us. We are sorry for your loss."

"She was no kin to me but she was a nice lady. She never shared her personal life but some days she would bake little treats and come by and visit. She was an extraordinary lady, kind and warm. There isn't anything I would rather do than get my hands on the dirty bastard that killed her." Gillis saw the man's eyes watering up and then one small tear work its way out of his swollen eyes and down over the cracked skin of his cheek.

Gillis just stood there for a moment. "Sir, I regret to confess that I haven't seen my father in over fifteen years. From what I can remember he has no real distinguishing characteristics except a small scar on his left cheek, a slight, Irish accent and an impressive use of the English language. Would you by any chance know where I might find the man she called Scully? He might be my father."

"He also could be the killer. Those soldier boys were asking me the same thing, like I might know where he was hiding or something. I saw the man she called Scully only a couple times over the last three years. When he did come by it was usually late at night and I go to bed early. As I told you and I told them, it was only by chance that I ever saw him." Gillis could see there wasn't anything else the man was going to offer as to Scully's whereabouts.

"Can you tell me anything about the murder?"

"I will tell you Miss Annabelle didn't deserve what that killer did to her. She was a good, solid person and when she was out of town I fed her cat and used her room to read. She has a big south-facing window and the light was always better there."

"So you had access to her room?"

"Of course I did. How do you think they found out she had been murdered? I hadn't seen her for a couple of days and I could hear her cat meowing like it was hungry. I got my key and went in like I normally do and there she was, tied to that chair with her lips sewed shut like one of those South American shrunken heads. It was grotesque."

Gillis looked puzzled. "Was there any kind of note or something that would give a clue why?"

"No, nothing, whoever did it took his time."

Gillis looked at Luke with a questioning expression before returning his gaze to the old man. "Did you hear anything the day or night before that would have seemed out of the ordinary?"

"No, I can't say I did but there were a few things that I thought were interesting. There were two shot glasses, one empty and one still full. You could see a little bit in the bottom of the second glass, the amount that always seems to stick when you kill a shot fast."

"The postmaster told us that the killer drank whiskey while he watched her die."

"It wasn't just whiskey. It was Glengyle Scotch, some of the best you can buy. The bottle is still there half empty unless one of those half-wit federal guys drank the last of it. The other thing that was real strange was the way the killer murdered her. There was a small hole in the back of her head with only a minimal amount of blood that bled onto her hair, very clean. It must have been the same killer that has been working over Washington for the last few years."

"There have been other murders like this?"

"Oh yes, a number of them. I believe the man that murdered Anna has been killing people for at least the past three years, but this is the first one on this side of the river. The government always seems to be one step behind this butcher and most of the murders seem to be kept hush-hush."

"Why would the government not want people to know about the murders?"

"Something about a secret society. Apparently there have been more than a few well connected people in high places that have either been murdered or vanished. It doesn't give the common folk much of a sense of security."

"I am a little shocked that you know all this. Where did you get this information?"

"From my son-in-law, Detective Logan Fritz. He comes by here every couple of weeks to visit and he told me. He flat out hated the sheriff so he retired from the law a couple of years ago and took a job as a private detective but he still has plenty of ties. He said that over time he had heard things, really bad, strange things."

"Was there anything else you can remember?"

"Yes, it looked like the murderer tortured her before he killed her. He had pulled several of Anna's fingernails out, left a lot of blood. It was a nasty sight, one I wish I had never seen."

Just then the guard walked over. "Time's up. If the captain knew I let you even talk to the old man this long he would have my hide. Now I need you two to get on your way."

"Thank you private, we will." Gillis turned to Sam. "It was nice seeing you again Sam, thanks and take care."

"You boys be safe," said Sam as he raised his hand from the swing rail and waved goodbye. "Come by anytime."

Gillis and Luke walked back through the gated arbor and over to the hitching rail. "The Scully he mentioned has to be my father. Glengyle

Scotch is very rare and expensive, not the type of drink most men drink. I don't believe it's a coincidence that the Scotch they found was father's favorite."

Luke looked at him. "It sounds like it may have been your father he talked about. The thing that struck me strange is the lady's mouth being sewn shut. Why would the murderer take the time to do that?"

"He was sending a message."

"What kind of a message?"

"I believe he was sending a message to my father. Keep your mouth shut."

Chapter 13

The two men rode deeper into the main town of Alexandria. "I would like to stable these mules for a while and rent a carriage. We need to blend in. The last thing I want right now is attention. Let's find a store so we can stock up on some supplies just in case we need to leave in a hurry. Hopefully there is a stable near our hotel. I could use a bath and I know you could too."

Luke glanced over with a scowl, but finally let the comment pass. "So what are we doing tomorrow?"

"We are going to visit an old friend of mine and hopefully get a few more answers."

"Sure seems we are getting more questions than answers."

"It does seem that way."

Twenty minutes after getting supplies they came to a stable that looked well-kept with a small fenced pasture behind it. Down the road they could see the sign of a hotel Gillis knew was there and would be convenient for what he had in mind. "This place should suit the mules. Let's take them inside."

A heavyset man in a sweat-stained shirt grinned as they entered. "Morning gents, what can I do for you?"

Gillis straightened up in the saddle. "We want to board these mules for a few days, maybe more, and rent a carriage if you have one."

"Fine looking mules but we don't usually see gentleman riding them. You're not from around here are you?"

"No, we are not. The rough country we came through made riding a mule sensible. That's the Brinkmoore Hotel down the road, isn't it?"

"She's a pretty good hotel and I haven't heard many complaints. I will take good care of your mules during your stay. I assume you want the carriage delivered to the hotel in the morning?"

"Yes, please bring the carriage by first thing after breakfast. I need to leave most of our supplies and packs here. Do you have someone available that could take us and our bags to the hotel now?"

"Can do, the mules will be ten cents a day, each. The carriage of course is extra."

Gillis just nodded and flipped the man a five dollar coin and then dismounted as Luke led the two pack mules over to a post in the barn and began stripping the packs. Gillis turned to Luke. "I didn't mention to bring any finer clothes by chance, did I?"

"No sir, Mr. McCabe, you didn't. But even if you did, I only own two shirts and a couple of pairs of pants and one pair of socks. I haven't owned any Sunday best clothes for probably ten years."

"First thing tomorrow we will get you some more appropriate duds before we meet the colonel and the people of Washington."

"We are meeting a colonel?"

"Yes, Colonel Morris Dougell, a friend of mine for some years. Hopefully he can shed some light on what has been going on here."

Within minutes the man had a carriage and horse ready. The buckboard springs groaned as the men took a seat behind the driver. The young man driving obviously worked at the stable and the smell of freshly mucked stalls seemed to linger upon him. At the hotel they grabbed their bags and Gillis tipped the man two-bits.

"Thank you sir, you just tell me if you need anything. I will have your carriage waiting here first thing in the morning."

"We will see you then. By the way, in a few days we won't be of need of a driver. I will give you plenty of notice so we don't waste your time. In the future I will need you to find a place that's okay with the hotel and leave the horse and carriage tied there."

Luke carried both bags and followed Gillis up the porch stairs to the front desk. The hotel was clean but the furniture and rugs showed wear. Gillis stood at the front desk for several minutes and was about to ring the bell when a blue-eyed lady who looked to be in her mid-thirties appeared. "I would like two rooms preferably in the back of the hotel away from the street." The lady passed the registry to him and watched as Gillis signed.

"So you are Mr. McCabe. We have been expecting you." Gillis was caught off guard by her comment.

"You have? And why is that?"

The lady knelt down and then stood up holding a telegram in her hand. "This came for you a couple of days ago so we figured you would be by." The telegram was from Sandra Richards. Gillis picked the letter up from the desk and quickly stuffed it inside his jacket.

"How did anyone know we were going to be staying here?" asked a stunned Luke.

"I told Roper where I thought I might stay. I drove past this place years ago on a tour of Alexandria. It was in the spring and the cherry blossoms were amazing. I had lunch here on that tour and remembered the name. I like how it is just outside Washington and something about it works for me. But I also told my doctor friend in Norfolk."

Gillis sat a small bag down on the counter. "Please put this in your safe for the length of my stay."

"Yes sir, Mr. McCabe. Happy to do that."

Several minutes later they were up on the third floor trying their key in the lock. "Mine works," hollered Luke from down the hall. "When do you want to meet for dinner?"

"Let's meet in the lobby in another hour and then we can eat here or find a place that works." Gillis hesitated at the doorway before entering and looked back down the hall. Luke had already disappeared into his room but Gillis took in the stairway they had come up and a door at the end of the hall that had a small sign stating "exit." For a minute he studied the layout of everything before entering his room. Gillis set the bags down by the door and then turned and locked it. Sitting down on the bed he opened the telegram as if it were fragile. He lit the kerosene lantern beside the bed and began to read.

Dearest Gill,

Life is not what it once was. With my father gone thieves broke into the house and stole many of our valuables. I no longer feel safe there and now I am staying with my aunt. Gill, I have been a spoiled fool and losing you has been the worst thing that has ever happened to me. Forgive me Gill. I still love you very much.

Love, Sandra

Gillis refolded the paper and stuck it back into his coat pocket. One side of him wanted him to leave immediately and ride to her rescue but what about his father? For now Sandra sounded safe and he knew his father was in trouble. What kind of trouble and whether he could help was still a question?

An hour later Gillis was standing in the lobby when Luke came down the stairs. "Been waiting long?"

"No, not really. I checked the little restaurant and their menu and if you have no objections I think it will work for at least tonight."

"Fine by me," said Luke as he headed toward the small separated restaurant. As Luke walked Gillis noticed that his pistol showed under his coat. "First we will go to a clothing store and get a low-hanging coat for you, one that will hide your gun."

The rest of the night was quiet and both men retired to their rooms.

The next morning after a quick breakfast the two men went outside into the bright sunshine. Gillis glanced over and saw the man from the stable sitting in his carriage waiting.

"Good morning, you're right on time. I hope you can give us some directions to a decent men's clothing store and a gun store."

"Yes sir, if you follow this road another half a mile north you will find both on the left hand side of the road. The place is called Barman's but they sell both clothing and guns."

"We appreciate your help," said Gillis as he tossed the man a coin and stepped into the empty carriage. "We will see you back here about six tonight so you can pick up the carriage."

"Thank you sir, I will be here."

The shoes of the horse clicked along on the cobblestone street and soon they were in front of a large store bustling with activity. Luke looked at the sign in amazement. "That must be the biggest sign I ever did see."

"You haven't visited the city very often?"

"Not really, never had much need to."

Shopping for new clothes for Luke went reasonably quick but the search for a small, concealable derringer dragged on. Gillis examined, held, and pointing at least forty guns before choosing a four inch, double barrel pistol.

"Well are you satisfied?" asked a bored Luke as he pulled and twisted, trying to find comfort in his new suit.

"It's as close to perfect for me as I can get. Next, we need to visit the bank and then we will go and visit the colonel. He will be surprised to see me. The last time I saw him I told him I didn't see myself ever coming to Washington again." Gillis hesitated. "But life does change. He is a good man and even a better friend. If he knows anything I am sure he will clue me in. I finally have a pretty good idea of where I am and I think I can lead us right to his office. They have added more than a couple of buildings since I was here last but the building he works at is very stately. It's much like the flavor of ancient Greece with their tall stone columns and wide stairs."

They finished their tasks and rode across the Long Bridge which separated Alexandria from Washington and finally arrived at a tall stone building. Finding a hitching rail under a maple tree, they tied the horse. Luke looked down at the sidewalk. "Quite the stuff they make these paths out of," said Luke.

"Concrete is an amazing product. It will grow in use in the future."

Luke looked at him. "How do you know so much about everything?"

"I don't know about everything but I am well-traveled and enjoy reading."

They walked up the twenty stairs and entered through a tall door where two guards stood. Strangely, they didn't say anything as they entered but an officer just inside the door sitting at a large table motioned them over.

"State your business please," said the man without looking up.

Gillis took a step forward and cleared his throat. "I'm Gillis McCabe and this man's name is Luke Wright. We are here to see Colonel Morris Dougell." The over-weight man behind the desk momentarily looked up and made eye contact. Long sideburns covered most of his angular face.

"Do you have any papers?"

Gillis's eyes never left his as he reached into his coat pocket and retrieved an envelope and handed it to the man. The officer studied the contents then refolded the letter and handed it back to Gillis.

"Do you know where the colonel's office is sir?"

"Yes, I have been there a number of times."

"I need you two to sign in and then please check in with his secretary," said the officer as he slid a registration book towards Gillis. "Please sign out when you leave."

Gillis nodded and the two of them headed down the hall. "That was easy," said Luke with a slight smile.

"This is Washington and everything is on the formal side. That man has seen me numerous times in the past and I am sure he recognized me but they pretty much stay to their routine." They had passed at least a dozen offices when Gillis stopped in front of a dark oak door with a plaque that read "Colonel Morris Dougell."

Gillis looked at him for a moment and then opened the door to the sweet smell of tobacco. An attractive middle-aged woman with long red hair sat at her desk near the back wall. A large picture in a gaudy frame of a Revolutionary War Officer leading a charge hung above her. Gillis walked up to her desk with Luke slightly behind. A small name badge set on the desk in front of her.

"How may I help you gentlemen?"

"Miss Caden, if I remember correctly. I'm Gillis McCabe and as you may remember I'm an old friend of Colonel Dougell. We have worked on numerous projects together. I was hoping I could visit with him for a minute or two."

The lady looked at him again and then slowly stood. "Yes, I remember you, Mr. McCabe. Would you be so kind as to have a seat for a moment? I will see if the colonel is available." She went through the door and quietly closed it.

"Hell yes, I will see him," came a booming voice from behind the door. The secretary opened the door as a big man in full uniform followed her out. "Gillis, my friend, it has been such a long time." The colonel reached out and shook Gillis's hand which immediately disappeared into his enormous grip. "Come in, come in, it has been way too long." The colonel towered over Gillis and Luke as his uniform buttons strained at his middle. His thick copper hair had patches of white, as did his beard and sideburns. His jovial smile immediately reduced the impact of his loud and commanding voice.

Plush leather furniture filled the room and the colonel walked over to a side table with numerous glasses and several bottles of whiskey. "What will be your poison?"

"You know I don't drink this early in the day, at least not hard liquor but I am sure Luke here would enjoy a glass."

"You know, I remember now, it has to be evening," the colonel said as he poured two glasses and handed one to Luke. "So what brings you to Washington? The war I imagine?"

"No, I am sitting this one out. I love Virginia and could never fight against her but I don't believe in slavery and want no part in its continuance. Unfortunately, many good and brave Americans are going to die because of it."

"From everything I have heard it will be a very short war, maybe six months at the most. We have all the factories and man-power to produce the weapons needed. The South has literally nothing that can stop us."

"They have heart and a lot of it. This is not a war that I would have wished to happen."

"Gillis, you were always a man of your convictions. So if it isn't the war then to what do I owe the honor of this visit?"

"About two months ago I decided to settle my personal issues with my father. I hadn't seen or heard from him in over fifteen years and I guess my maturity finally kicked in. My fiancée and I ventured out to surprise him and allow me the opportunity to introduce my future wife. When we arrived, we found the place ransacked and most of the staff dead. Fortunately my father wasn't one of them. That night one of the hired men returned but my father didn't—he seemed to have just disappeared. I finally got a clue from a personal letter that a woman friend of his had penned. It had her Alexandria address and I decided to go track her down and see if she could help but when I arrived I received news that she had been murdered and in a very brutal manner. I am concerned that my father is somehow tied into something very bad but I have no idea what. At the deceased lady's room, I met a man that said a number of murders had occurred in Washington over the past four or five years but this was the first one committed this side of the Long Bridge. I was hoping you might shed some light as to what is happening."

"I am sorry to hear that. If your father is anything like you I am sure he is a good man caught in unfortunate circumstances."

"That may be but I need to find him. Can you tell us anything about the murders?"

"Not much. Unfortunately your friend here will need to come up with some top clearance papers or he will need to wait in the other room while we talk."

"No problem, Mr. McCabe," said Luke as he turned and walked out the door, closing it behind him.

Colonel Dougell stood staring out the only window in his office. "Gillis, I am sorry to say it but there have been more than a few murders and some high-profile abductions. This group or gang, whoever they are, even kidnapped a prominent senator. It's been close to five years now and we don't seem to be any closer than when it started. The whole thing has Washington on pins and needles. Even President Lincoln requires a briefing daily on the status of the investigation. Washington has put a Major Cates in command of the investigation. And to be frank Gillis, he is one of the biggest assholes I have ever have ever met. And to make matters even worse, the higher ups believe there is a mole inside the investigation and they have given Major Cates complete control. Even with my rank, I am told little of what is going on and few others know either."

"So what is going on?"

"No one is sure. They appear to be working in pretty systematic way."

"You said gang, so you know there is more than one individual involved?"

"Yes, in some cases we are sure the assassins had help in their getaways. We don't know if they are a gang or what but they are good at what they do. I can tell you this, the murders are well planned and whoever is involved in this is running it like a fine-tuned machine."

"So do you believe they might be Southern spies?"

"At first I did but several of the men in the earlier killing had strong ties to the South. No, I think this is much more complex than that. It has me baffled and nothing I have come up with makes sense. They assassinate someone in a busy place with dozens of witnesses and then they just disappear as if they can fly away. I'm not sure how we got this information but three months ago we got news that they might strike in a certain part of town. We didn't know the target but we were confident that we did know the approximate day and maybe the location."

"So you have a mole in their operation."

"Again I'm not sure and I don't have access to how they received the knowledge of the attack. So it may very well have been someone on the inside of their operation. I have told you about everything I know and it isn't much more than you could find if you read the local paper."

"I would like to go back to your comment about them vanishing. What did you mean by that?"

Colonel Dougell walked over to his desk and retrieved a box of cigars. "The really good ones can only be bought in Cuba, so I have them shipped in." He extended the box to Gillis who shook his head. "It is my understanding that in the information they received they knew the day and what part of town the assassination attempt would occur. Unfortunately they didn't know who the victim was or the exact time. So they hid undercover men on both ends of the street and waited. The plan was at the first sign that something was afoot the closest man to the attack would shoot his pistol into the air. That would be the signal for everyone to converge."

"Later that afternoon, a very ordinary looking man wearing a derby hat entered a small tea shop with outside seating. He walked back outside and casually strolled up behind a man engaged in conversation. Without anyone noticing he used an unknown weapon to punch a small hole in the back of the man's head, killing him almost instantly. The man's head simply fell to his chest and it took a moment for his small surprised party to even realize he had been murdered. Only when a lady seated directly behind them noticed the blood coming from the wound and screamed did anyone realize he had been murdered."

"Later the victim would be identified as an assistant cabinet chief, out for his morning coffee with his wife and another couple. In the shock of the moment the man casually walked out of the establishment and back onto the street. That's where he ran into trouble. He collided with an undercover man running towards the screams. One shot was fired and the undercover officer lay dead while the assassin seemed to just vanish into the confusion." The Colonel took a long draw on his cigar and Gillis noticed the unique smell of the tobacco.

"So you did figure out what type of weapon he used?"

"No, it is unlike anything we are familiar with. Whatever killed that man was completely silent and had enough power to send some sort of projectile deep into the man's skull. These assassins have not discriminated as to their victims—some have been young, others old. Some had high positions in the government, some were only slightly associated, others had no association at all."

A gentle knock on the door stopped the conversation as the secretary cracked the door. "Colonel Dougell, you are late for your meeting with General Drake. The general's messenger is here to find out if there is a problem."

"No, no there isn't a problem, please tell the general I will be right there. I am sorry, Gillis, but I am scheduled for another meeting that I must attend. We will have to get together sometime and have a drink or dinner. Sorry I have to cut you short."

Gillis walked over to him and shook his hand as he opened the door wider. "I appreciate the time, and yes, I would enjoy having a meal together."

At the last minute the colonel turned back to Gillis. "I hope you find your father." He walked out the door and turned to go down the hall.

Gillis found Luke sitting in one of the plush chairs of the outer office. He immediately got up as Gillis followed the colonel out of the office. Gillis said little as the two men walked back to the carriage, untied the horse and started back to the hotel. Luke looked out toward the street and spit a little chew. "Luke, you don't spit in the streets of a city like this."

"That is the first time you said anything about spitting, Mr. McCabe. What's wrong with spitting?"

"You just don't do it here. It's fine in the woods or back at the ranch but society here frowns on it and it brings unwanted attention to us. I would appreciate it if you would refrain from doing it again and if you have to do it, do it where no one can see."

"Yes sir, Mr. McCabe, you are the boss but I don't see the harm." It was almost dinner time when the two men rode up in front of the Brinkmoore and Luke stepped down from the carriage and tied the horse. "The man from the livery should be here soon to get the carriage so just leave it tied." Gillis paused for a moment. "Would you like a drink before dinner?"

"Yes sir, I would appreciate that."

Smiling at the answer Gillis entered the building and walked over to a table by the bar. Almost immediately a young lady came and took their order of a glass of whiskey and a glass of sweet tea. "Luke, I can't make heads or tails of this but whatever it is, I think my father is in up to his eyeballs. I'm frustrated. Here I am trying to find a father that I haven't seen for nearly fifteen years and making no progress. My father is obviously tied up with this group in some way or they wouldn't have attacked his estate. What I can't figure out is how this all fits together?" Gillis paused and took a long drink of his tea.

"I have no idea, boss. What are you thinking we should do?"

"We are going to go back and talk to that old gentleman Sam, at the boarding house. Hopefully, we can find out where we can get ahold of this Detective Logan Fritz. I think he could be helpful."

* * *

The next morning the two men ate breakfast and then headed outside. The day was sunny and the harnessed horse and carriage sat tied to one side of the steps as agreed. "Well our stable boy hasn't forgotten us."

About forty five minutes later Luke pulled back the reins in front of Sam's boarding house. They noticed the guard was no longer there as they stepped down from the carriage and tied the horse. Even before they opened the gate they could see Sam's head above the laurels in the garden and a trail of smoke rising above his head. As they approached Luke glanced at Gillis. "Looks like Sam enjoys a good smoke." Luke paused. "Hope he knows not to spit."

Gillis didn't acknowledge the remark as he headed straight toward the man. "Morning boys, glad you were able to make your way back here. Much friendlier without those pesky guards, don't you think?"

Gillis nodded. "It's nice to see you again Sam."

"Such a fine day. Sun shining, a good pipe and now some friends show up for a talk. I take it you two haven't gotten anywhere in your search and if it makes you feel better the federal guys didn't find anything either. One of the guards talked to me before he left. Those boys were really frustrated."

"Well Sam, you were right, we haven't figured out much. You have helped us more than anyone else to this point. We were hoping you could tell us how to get ahold of your son-in-law, that Detective Logan Fritz you spoke of. We would like to hire him."

The old gentleman swung his arm around and stopped with his hand motioning the two men to sit on two unused garden chairs.

Gillis and Luke sat down. "Do you think my father Scully had anything to do with this murder or for that matter the other murders?"

The old man struck a match and puffed while restarting his pipe more out of habit than the pipe really being out. "No, Mr. McCabe, I don't. I think your father loved Annabelle. I didn't see much of your father but the one time I saw him glance at Annabelle there was nothing but pure love in his eyes. She was a fine woman and a great judge of character. Annabelle never spoke to me about your father and I never inserted myself in her business. If I was a betting man, I would wager your father was deeply hurt by this whole thing."

"I appreciate you saying that. It's difficult to truly know your father when you haven't spoken for years but I too still believe he is a good man and probably has been dragged into something way over his head."

"You may be right, you may be wrong but my gut feeling is your father is a decent man."

Gillis stopped and tried to regain his composure. The strain of this whole ordeal was settling heavily on his shoulders and he fought to remain stoic. Finally he looked up at Sam again. "Is there any chance we could see her room?"

"Now that the guards are gone, I can't see why not." Sam struggled with his cane as he got up and began leading the two men toward the house. As they got close to the stairs Sam turned. "These stairs are a bit hard on this old body. It will take me a minute or two to make it to the top."

Luke reached down and put his hand under Sam's arm and helped balance the old man as they climbed the stairs. "Thank you, young man, I can do it myself but I really don't know how much longer. It's just around the corner. Her room was above mine. She lived in 2A and mine is 1A."

Gillis tried the door but it was locked and he turned and looked at Sam, who handed him a key. "Try this."

The key immediately slid into the lock and the click told Gillis it was open as he turned the door knob. "Well I guess we are in."

"That is interesting," said Sam.

"What is interesting?" asked Gillis.

"Everything is like the last time I saw it. Those federal boys didn't tear the place up. From the stories I have been told by my son-in-law that isn't like them."

Gillis took a minute to scan the room, trying to take in as much as possible. Two shot glasses sat in front of an almost full bottle of Glengyle Scotch. One shot glass was empty and the other was still full, the way the federals had found it. Gillis picked up the shot glass still filled to the top and turned to Sam. "Can you tell me a little more about Miss Annabelle?"

"Well, she always looked, dressed, and acted like a lady."

"Sam, when you walked in on her you said her lips were sewed shut similar to what a head hunter would do. Do you remember if there was blood around her mouth?"

"It was hideous but to my recollection there wasn't any blood there."

"Did you hear anything that night?"

"Nothing, my hearing is not as good as it used to be but I don't remember hearing a thing."

Gillis continued to look around until he noticed a pile of books sitting on the desk. He began going through the pile and then suddenly stopped. He read the cover and then opened the book. "It was written Charles Darwin on paleontology. Interesting, this was my father's favorite hobby. Would you mind if I borrowed it?"

"To my knowledge Annabelle had no relatives so I don't think she will need it for a while. Your question brings another problem I have been thinking about, what to do with all her stuff. My guess is letting you borrow one book wouldn't upset anyone too much. You will bring it back won't you?"

"Yes and thank you, I have seen enough. I appreciate you letting us look around Sam. You were a lot of help."

Sam stared at Gillis. "What help did I do?"

"You told me the killer was probably a gentleman in society and he enjoyed Glengyle Scotch. He respected the quality of the Scotch and only had one drink. With no blood around her lips, that told me the lady was already dead when the executioner sewed her lips shut. He knew that by brutalizing her body with stitching her lips together that people would talk and he would get his message out to his intended target. Granted, it is a very weird way to do it but it was certainly morbidly clever and deliberate."

Luke looked at Gillis. "Who was the message intended for and what was the message?"

"I have my theory but at this point I'm not sure for whom it was intended, but the message is very clear. If you talk, you die."

Chapter 14

The two men thanked Sam for his help and the address of the detective. Gillis walked to the back of the carriage and carefully placed the book inside the small leather chest securely attached to the back. Moments later they were headed back to the hotel for lunch and directions. Gillis was quiet during the ride and Luke took his lead. Their lunch consisted of a couple of sandwiches and a drink. Quickly they were off again to S. 412 Lancaster Street, the home and business address of one Logan Fritz. Gillis turned to Luke. "I am tired of hearing this crap about the assassin vanishing after each murder. People don't vanish and they don't sprout wings and they don't fly away. This is certainly a well-trained group, but whatever their motives are still escapes me. Why would anyone kill young and old, important and irrelevant, and all in such a public place?"

"Mr. McCabe, if I remember right the man at the hotel said we were to turn right on Vick Street and we are here." The statement seemed to break Gillis from his thoughts as he pulled hard on the right rein almost unbalancing the carriage.

"Sorry Luke, I have a lot on my mind. Sometimes my brain focuses so hard that I ignore everything else."

"No problem to whatever you just thanked me for, glad I could help."

Gillis knew that Luke had little to no formal education but his common sense was something to be admired. He was smart and skilled in the ways of the woods and if it weren't for him Gillis knew that he wouldn't have made it safely this far. He wore his new tailored clothes well and for the most part the longer jacket hid his Colt. Gillis was glad he had Luke along and was beginning to really like the cut of the man.

They took another right on Lancaster Street and quickly found the unkempt home of Detective Fritz. His house was small needed both paint and a good carpenter. Gillis stepped from the carriage and tied the horse to the hitching rail in front. Even the hitching rail needed replacing as the past horses had gnawed it down to half its original diameter. A wooden plank sidewalk led to the front door and by the time the two were close to the porch the door suddenly opened. A heavy-set man with a neatly trimmed beard stood in the doorway.

Gillis looked up and met the man's eyes. "Are you Logan Fritz, the detective?"

"That I am, come in."

The two men entered the dimly lit home. It had a stale, smoky smell, the kind of smell you get from something that hadn't been cleaned well or hadn't been allowed to air for a while. The main room was small and packed with old police memorabilia. Several cigar butts filled a dirty ashtray. The man walked with just the slightest of limps and though not really fat his pants strained to hold his belly in. He closed the door quietly as he pulled his last suspender strap over his shoulder.

Logan caught their glances. "I worked my way up from sweeping jail cells to working as the number one deputy. The final ten years I went out on my own and worked as a detective."

"I assume Sam told you I was looking for my father. We had a letter from a lady in Alexandria that sounded like they had a very close relationship but when we got here she had been murdered."

"I happened to drop by my uncle place shortly after you two left. He told me of some of your questions. From what he said happened when you visited her room, you must have a little detective in you. Anyway, have a seat at the table and I will put on a little coffee."

"I certainly have not been professionally trained like you but since Sam has clued you in on my visit, what can you tell me about this whole thing?"

"You mean the murders?"

"Yes, what can you tell us about them?"

"Even when I was a beat cop we had murders, mostly on the fringes of the city, seedy bars and the like. If I was to guess we had a murder every six months or so but with no real drama and most of the time the culprits were quickly apprehended. It wasn't until after I was promoted to detective that this new type of murder seemed to come around. It was more of an assassination than a murder. Clean, quick and well thought through. In fact, to my knowledge they haven't caught a single perpetrator. Instead of bar room fights that become murders, high society people are being killed and for no apparent reason. Many an investigation was launched but we never could really find a thing that led us anywhere. It almost became routine—every few months there would be another murder or abduction and sometimes it would be in their homes and other times it was in a totally public place. There was no consistency other than the rough time factor."

The coffee pot on the stove began to boil and Logan slid back his chair to get up.

"So the police have never even found a suspect, never tied any of the victims together, and never found any reason why these people were being targeted?"

"That is pretty much it."

"I need information if I am going to find my father. I want to hire you."

"I'm pretty expensive: five dollars a day plus expenses."

"I think I can handle that. The first thing I want is a chronological order of each murder you believe was committed by this group." Gillis stopped for a moment. "Have you ever heard any name for this band of thugs?"

"I have heard them called several things but the one you hear most is a nickname the public gave them, the Ghostly Butchers. Not very clever, but it seems to fit. In three years Major Cates hasn't come up with one damn clue to report to the brass. He is the type of fellow that thinks government has all the answers and it makes him so mad that he hasn't found a good clue that he could spit. If you spend any time investigating this case sooner or later you will run into this guy and it won't be pleasant. He has sole control over the investigation and doesn't have to report to anyone except Secretary of the Army. It's one extremely tight investigation."

"And how do you get your information?"

Logan just smiled. "I have my ways."

Leaning back in his chair Gillis looked hard at Logan. "I need their name, age, nationality, race, and anything else that comes to mind. If they were in a public place I want to know who they were with and if possible what business they had together. I want descriptions of the dead and whatever description we can get of the killer. And before I hire you, I want to know how you plan to find out this information."

"To tell you the truth I have a source close to everything and with a little financial incentive, he usually comes through."

"As incentive, you mean money?"

"That always seems to open doors for me. Anyway, information is valuable and people with good information know that."

"I especially want to know as quickly as possible if any other murders occur. I have a gut feeling if I can figure this out, I will find my father. I also want you to put the word out on the street that there is a large reward for information about Scully McCabe. I will write out a physical description for your knowledge."

"Is there anything else?"

"Yes, I want to meet you every three days or sooner if you find anything valuable. Time is of the essence."

"I understand. I need a hundred dollars to start, is that a problem?"

Gillis reached into the inside pocket of his coat and pulled out numerous bills, counted and folded them, and handed the money to Logan. He quickly counted the money before shoving it inside his coat.

"That's a lot of money for a man to carry around. People have been known to kill for less," Fritz said.

Gillis smiled. "That is one of the reasons I have Luke with me. He is excellent with a gun and not afraid to use it."

The two men walked back out to the carriage and untied the horse. "Logan is an interesting man," Gillis said. "I sure hope he is all he says he is. We need to remember to stop by the blacksmith's place and check on the mules. I don't want him to think we abandoned them. They should be well rested by now."

The two men got in the carriage and Luke quickly asked, "Mr. McCabe, how would he have a secret source the government wouldn't know about?"

"That's the problem with government, they always think they are the smartest people in town and often they get their butts handed to them by common folk. My guess would be this Major Cates is one of those."

They pulled up in front of the livery stable. The blacksmith met them at the door as Gillis pulled out his wallet. "I guess it is about time I settled up and give you some money for the next week. By the way, is there a way you can have your man put a little time on the mules so they don't get fat on us? I want to keep them in good shape."

"Sure thing, my man can do that. There is a small field out back with a round pen for training. I will have him work each one of them for twenty minutes each morning. Why don't you give me another ten dollars and then we will settle up when you leave town or your next visit here. My man, Liam is up at the hotel waiting for the carriage, so just take the carriage up there and I will see you when I see you."

The fast clatter of the horse's hooves echoed off the four large buildings that loomed close to the road as the carriage headed toward the hotel. When they arrived Liam sat on the far end of the steps in a shady spot and stood at they approached. "Nice to see you, Liam. Give me a second to get something out of the back and then the carriage is all yours." Gillis walked to the back of the carriage and undid the three thick leather straps that kept the weathered chest closed. He quickly reached in and pulled out the book he had found at the scene of Annabelle Smith's murder and covered it with his coat in one motion.

Luke walked up to Gillis and in a quiet voice asked, "Mr. McCabe, is there something special about that book?"

"To be honest, I don't know but there might be. When I was a child I remember reading a book similar to this one with my father before bed. I found it to be an interesting coincidence that there was the same book on paleontology in her room. I will at least take my time and get a good look at it. Let's get cleaned up and I will meet you in about thirty minutes for dinner."

"Sounds good boss, see you then."

Gillis walked upstairs and put the key in the lock and entered. The maid had been in and the bed was tightly made. Gillis walked over to a hardwood chair in the corner that was well served by the passing sun. He opened the cover of the book and looked at the writing on the inside as he had quickly done in Annabelle's room. The single word "Peanut" was written in ink inside. It had been a long time but there was something in the back of Gillis's mind that recognized this book and Peanut, the nickname his father called him as a child. Could this be just an uncanny coincidence or could this have been the book he read as a child? Gillis turned another page of the book and examined it. Carefully he began turning each page until he had worked his way to the back cover. He could see no marks, no writing, and no clues, nothing that would communicate a message of any sort. By the time he set the book down on the table it was time to go meet Luke. He knew how impatient Luke was when it came to food. He slid the book under his pillow and locked the door as he left.

The second stair from the top creaked as he walked down the staircase to the first landing. In magnificent fashion it flared as it merged with the worn lobby. Within moments Gillis saw Luke standing at the bar, obviously watching for him. He quickly threw down the remainder of his beer and began walking his way. "Boy, am I starved," said Luke. A quick-moving waitress seated them and Luke seemed anxious to talk. "Well Mr. McCabe, did you find anything in that dinosaur book?"

"I thought I would but maybe the whole thing was just a coincidence. My imagination sometimes gets the best of me and maybe this is one of those times."

"So what are we going to do tomorrow?"

"Tomorrow we are going to make a visit to Major Cates and see if the gentleman is as difficult as everyone says he is. He must have information that he isn't telling the press or colleagues and maybe with my clearance he might share some information."

"From what I have heard you are barking up the wrong tree, Mr. McCabe. He isn't described kindly by folks."

"I heard the same thing you did. I am not overly optimistic that he will welcome us with open arms but I need to try."

After dinner the men retired to their rooms and Gillis couldn't sleep due to a loud ruckus from people partying in the street. A number of new patrons had occupied the hotel and they seemed to enjoy sitting on the front porch, sharing their stories and laughing uncontrollably. It was almost midnight before the men decided to retire and finally the quiet was restored. He lay in bed thinking of Sandra and how everything had gone wrong but maybe with her letter she wanted to get back together.

Normally he could think his way out of most problems. Usually the answers came quickly. But now he found no answers and even the small number of clues he had seemed to have nothing in common. Maybe he should just head back to Norfolk and then to Williamsburg and try to find where Sandra was staying. He dreamed of her beautiful face surrounded by soft, blonde hair blowing wildly in the wind as the fast carriage carried them to their secluded rendezvous. Those dreams quickly turned to a nightmare about his father.

* * *

The next morning he awoke to rays of sun lighting his room through the thin curtains. At least it will be sunny, he thought as he put on his pants. Gillis gave a disgusted look at the chamber pot sitting inside the wooden cabinet on the far side of the room. He had seen one of the maids lugging a pot down the back stairs and thought what a terrible job. With pants on and a light undergarment coving his upper body he made his way down the stairs to the outhouse that hung over the fast moving creek. At least it didn't stink up there but he felt sorry for those living down at creek level.

Later he found Luke fully dressed and already sipping a cup of coffee at one of the tables. "Good morning Luke, you sleep well?"

"Like a baby. Closed my eyes and didn't open them until I heard the birds chirping."

"So all that noise on the street and that loud argument in the restaurant didn't wake you?"

"Nope, I had nine brothers and sisters growing up and learned to sleep when I needed to. It's different in the woods. I never go into a deep sleep there but here with those feather beds, it's like heaven."

"You're a fortunate man. I wish I had your constitution."

"My room is in the back and quiet. You want to switch rooms?"

"No, but I appreciate the offer. I may take you up on that tonight. God only knows I could use a good night's sleep."

"Are we headed to see the major?" Luke paused.

"Yes, if you mean Major Cates. Hopefully he is willing to discuss things."

"I don't know why but this Major Cates fellow sure seems to have a chip on his shoulder."

"I wonder if Detective Fritz has found any of the information I requested. I want to visit the sites of some of the murders today. Maybe I'll see a pattern.

It sure doesn't seem to bother the murderer to do his deed in the middle of the day and that bothers me. It is almost as if they want to be noticed and I don't buy off on the vanishing act. There has to be a more logical answer."

It was then that Detective Fritz walked over to their table with a small leather brief case under his arm. Setting a folder down in front of Gillis, he pulled back a chair and sat down. "Morning Mr. McCabe, Luke, I have some interesting information for you. I compiled a number of accounts but also included both papers that ran the stories on the more visible murders. I will meet with my source in the next couple of days. Hopefully he will have some interesting information to share. They are pretty tight with their investigations and the recorded accounts. Normally a bit more leaks out. The files have maps and I included as much as I could find."

"I appreciate your work. I will look over these papers. I look forward to our next meeting."

Detective Fritz scooted back his chair and stood up. Gillis reached into the inside pocket of his coat and retrieved an envelope which he handed to the detective. "Until next time, Mr. Fritz," said Gillis as Fritz nodded and walked away.

After breakfast the men walked to the front of the hotel where their horse and carriage waited. Liam was on the edge of the porch and stood when they approached. "Good morning, Mr. McCabe, Mr. Luke."

Gillis smiled. "Good morning, Liam, right on time."

"I'm kind of here for a couple of reasons, sir. Heard you were looking for your father and had an interest in all these murders that are going on. Sometimes I hear things with all that waiting I do for different gentlemen and such. If you made it worth my while, I might be able to help."

"Let me think on your proposition. Maybe when you bring the carriage back tonight we could visit for a minute or two?"

"Yes sir, I will be waiting, just like normal."

The map Detective Fritz had supplied was excellent and Gillis followed it to a small diner called Dockery's which provided outside seating. After tying their horse to the metal hitching rail, the two men walked to one of the tables facing the street. Gillis motioned Luke to take a seat. Shortly, a young lady with slightly buck teeth and a pretty blue dress came out to get their order.

"What will it be, gentlemen?" she asked in a cheerful voice.

"Two things: two cups of coffee and some information," said Gillis.

"We have fine coffee, sir, but it depends on what information you are looking for."

"You had a murder occur here about three months ago. What can you tell me about what happened, and did you see anything?"

"Not a lot, sir. I was waiting on this lady that had just spilled tea on herself when all of a sudden a woman screamed and I looked up to see the back of this man hurrying out from among the tables and onto the street. I really didn't see much, it happened so quickly. I told the police and those Army officers the same thing."

"The police and the Army were here?"

"The police were here first but when the Army officers got here they took charge and did the questioning. They wouldn't let anyone leave until they interviewed everyone."

"Did you hear anyone give any information that you would have considered useful?"

"Nobody seemed to see anything. As I say it happened so quickly. I saw the bloody hole in the back of that gentleman's head that was killed but I didn't hear a gun or anything. Whatever killed that man was pretty much silent or I would have heard it. The whole thing happened less than three yards from where I stood. By the time the lady screamed the man was walked past me."

"So the assassin was almost beside you before anyone realized that a murder had been committed but you didn't see his face?"

"No sir, I didn't. It happened so quickly. He was a nice man, the one that was killed. Came in regularly like, wore nice clothes and was a good tipper."

Gillis leaned back in his chair and scratched his chin like he was churning over what happened. "Thank you. Please bring us two coffees, one with cream and the other black. That is the way you like it, isn't it Luke?"

"Yes sir, Mr. McCabe, only learned to drink it one way. When you get a chance to drink fresh coffee like this, you need to enjoy the flavor." Luke paused for a minute like he knew he had said something wrong. "But I understand people wanting that cream flavor too."

Gillis just smiled as he watched the waitress coming back with their order. As she set the two coffees on the table Gillis paid for the order and handed the lady a one-dollar coin. "A couple more questions if I may?"

The waitress looked at the tip as she picked it up and put it into a pocket in her dress. "I don't know that I have anything more to offer."

"The newspaper says the man vanished into the street heading east."

"Yes sir, he did and several gentlemen got up from their tables and tried to give chase but by the time they slid their chairs back and worked their way through everyone, he seemed to have just disappeared."

"So the pursuers lost him. Can you tell me what he was wearing and how tall he was?"

"It looked to me to be of normal height and he was wearing some sort of light trench coat, but it could have been a rain coat, I'm not sure. And he wore a hat, a derby with a small brim, sort of a dark color, maybe even black."

"Just a couple more questions, I know you have to get back to work. Did you smell or hear anything?"

The lady stood there moment thinking. "Yes, now that you mention it, I did. As I told you when he hurried out he almost ran into me. I remember smelling an almost musky odor like you would smell in a basement or a crawl space. Funny I forgot that until you mentioned it. I also heard something I can't place, kind of a clicking sound, not too loud and only for a moment but I did hear something."

"Thank you. If you remember anything more, we are staying at the Brinkmoore. I would gladly give a reward for any useful information."

The two men finished their coffee and proceeded to visit the next two diners where murders had taken place in broad daylight but didn't find anything. In each location, witnesses said the assailant quietly assassinated the victim and within seconds disappeared into the street before anyone realized what had happened. "I finally figured out the answer," said Luke.

"Yes and what's that?"

"Do you think they just want attention?"

"I see no humor in your comment. People are dying, good people with families, and no one has any clue who these people might be."

"That's my point. No one knows who they are and with them committing their crime in such open places they are trying to get noticed."

"Well put, Luke, I agree. These people are making a statement but whatever that statement is, I'm not sure."

The carriage pulled up in front of the building where they had earlier visited Colonel Dougell. "Well, let's give this a shot and see if Major Cates will see us." The two men tied the horse and started down the concrete walk in front of the building and up the multitude of stairs and past the guards. The office for Major Cates was in a different hallway than Colonel Dougell's office and the oak door was nowhere near as fancy.

Gillis knocked on the door and then reached for the knob and entered with Luke one step behind him. He squared himself with the desk and addressed the surprised sergeant. Gillis handed him the letter he had sewed in his saddlebag as an introduction before addressing the man.

"Sergeant, as you can read I have top clearance. If Major Cates is in, I would like to speak to him as to your investigation into the murders that have occurred around Washington for the past five years. I believe my father may be tied to them in some way and I would like to offer my help."

The sergeant never rose from his chair as he looked both Gillis and Luke up and down. "You don't say. Well give me a minute to read your letter." Finally, the sergeant seemed to finish as he scooted his chair back and with letter in hand he stood up. "Please take a seat and I will see if the major is available."

Gillis noticed how immaculate the room was. Even in areas where the sun shone through the room's only window, the furniture appeared to be free of dust. "Do you think he will see you?" Luke asked.

"I think he will, if not for any other reason than to satisfy his curiosity." Several minutes later the door opened and the sergeant reemerged followed by an officer in his mid-thirties. The sergeant went back to his desk and the major stood there for a moment seeming to evaluate the two men. His face was angry, rough-hewn and imperfect, just the way Gillis had imagined.

"Would you mind stepping into my office?" he said with a wave of his arm. "It is my understanding that you two gentlemen would like to meet with me."

Gillis and Luke followed the major into the room as the officer walked behind his desk and sat down without shaking their hands. Again, the room was immaculate and the papers on the desk were all in tight order. "I have read your letter—very impressive—but I have no intention of sharing what information I have no matter who has spoken on your behalf."

"Not exactly the welcome I had hoped for but the one I understood I would get. Let me get right to the point, Major. People are dying in your streets and no one seems to have a clue who is doing it or why. Obviously these are highly trained individuals with a strong agenda. There seems to be neither rhyme nor reason to these killings and somehow my father appears to be tied up in this whole thing."

"So how may I be of service to you, Mr. McCabe?"

"You have seen my clearance and history and for the last month, like yourself, I have been trying to solve what is going on. As I get nearer to figuring this whole thing out I may need your help. I prefer to have at least some type of history between us. I have solved little to this point but it is just a matter of time before more information and clues become available to me. I would very much like us to be on the same team and when I find that information I could share it with you."

"Mr. McCabe, I certainly don't intend to share a federal investigation with a rank amateur such as you. Why would you even think I would consider your proposition? This is an Army matter and it will stay an Army matter, am I clear?" The major rose from his chair and clasped his hands behind his back and moved from behind his desk.

Just then two quick knocks could be heard on the door and before the major could answer it the door swung open and an Army Corporal ran through the door and made a bee line to the major. "Sir, there has been another murder minutes ago at Dockery's Diner."

The corporal could see the angry look on the major's face. The corporal slowly turned to see Luke and Gillis sitting in the chairs in the far corner. "Sorry sir, I thought you were alone and would like to know immediately."

"Isn't Sergeant O'Reilly out at his desk?"

"No sir, I saw him going down the hall and it appeared he was headed to relieve himself. Sorry again sir, I didn't know you had guests."

In a disgusted voice the major turned to Gillis and Luke. "Would you mind excusing me? Our meeting is over." Then he turned to the corporal. "Get my horse saddled immediately and have a troop of soldiers ready to escort me to the scene in the next five minutes."

Gillis and Luke got up and walked out the door and as they did Gillis turned and addressed the major. "Remember, major, we are both on the same side."

Chapter 15

The sergeant was walking up the hall as Gillis and Luke hurriedly exited the office. The major stood in the hall for a moment while looking sternly their direction and then rushed toward the back of the building.

Luke smiled at Gillis. "I guess I know where we are headed!" he said, as the two men rushed for the door. With their carriage ready to go they quickly headed down the street. The sound of the horseshoes and a whip followed in their wake. It took less than seven minutes at a full trot to make it to the little diner known as Dockery's where a small crowd had already gathered. Gillis turned to Luke. "Let me off here. Go tie the horse down the road so we don't get caught in the crowd. Then come find me."

Gillis hopped from the carriage and charged toward the small group surrounding the diner's outside seating. He assumed the murder was probably carried out the same as the last one with a well-planned route of escape. Pushing his way through the noisy group of gawkers, he found himself staring at a dead man lying face up. He appeared to be in his forties. His top hat rested on its rim in a pool of blood that oozed from the back of the man's head. Gillis kneeled down and took a good look before gently rolling him over. Immediately he noticed the small hole in the back of the victim's head similar in size to the one he had found on the dead man on the trail. He moved the victim back to his original position and then stood and scanned the crowd but he could see little in the crowd of gawkers. Pushing and shoving, Gillis worked his way back through the crowd. The waitress he had spoken to earlier was sitting in a chair by the building. She was noticeably shaken.

"Miss," Gillis said in a gentle voice, "are you all right?"

"Yes, I guess. Twice I have been right there when people were murdered. Who could do such a horrible thing?"

"It's a good question. The people we are dealing with aren't normal, they are assassins. For whatever reason they are picking their victims based on some crazy criteria that no one has figured out. I have no answers; it's a mystery to me too."

"Well at least they wounded the man this time. He was definitely bleeding. He had a red spot on his side when his coat flipped open. Some man was walking on the street and when everyone began screaming, he came running and shots were fired. The man that tried to help is over there." She pointed in the direction of the boardwalk.

"Is that the direction the murderer ran?" asked Gillis.

She nodded and pointed again, "He ran down the boardwalk that way!"

Gillis walked toward the wounded man who tried to stop the attacker. He was being attended to by several people and he looked pale from loss of blood. Gillis hoped to ask the man a couple of questions when Major Cates and his men seemed to appear out of nowhere and began moving people out to the side of the restaurant, creating a kind of detainment area. Gillis quickly saw what was happening and moved in the opposite direction, the course the murderer had used to escape, and began walking down the sidewalk. There were soldiers in every direction. He would be fortunate to find any evidence that would help but he needed to at least make the attempt.

Most of the exits were blocked with well-armed soldiers. More troops were arriving while others with their muskets and mounted bayonets kept the original crowd of about thirty people isolated. The soldiers had moved tables from the diner to the edge of the street and several men seemed to be getting papers organized. Gillis looked at the whole thing from the shadows thinking that at least this Major Cates was a thoroughly organized man—not the smartest, but organized nonetheless. Gillis continued walking slowly down the sidewalk looking carefully at the worn planks beneath his feet. He tried to put himself in the shoes of a wounded murderer trying desperately to escape to a known sanctuary. He had only walked a couple of yards when he heard a shout.

"You there, stop and raise your hands," said a soldier pointing his musket toward Gillis. "What are you doing?" he demanded.

"Just heading back to my hotel, why do you ask?" said Gillis in an innocent voice.

"I will do the questioning here. You need to turn around and join that group of people up by that diner and you need to do it now!" he ordered.

Gillis turned and walked back toward the group. The small crowd was nervously standing behind the ranks of the soldiers who kept them pinned against the building. The soldier who led him was somewhat taller but far stronger as he shoved Gillis forward breaking the blue line of uniforms.

"Now stay here until it is your turn to be questioned," he said in a commanding voice.

Gillis stood there looking at the confined group and then turned and noticed Luke standing out past the ring of soldiers. He was in the shade leaning up against a large oak tree with a slight smile on his face. He looked around for a moment and then gave Gillis a movement of his hand that was more of "I am here" than a wave.

For the next hour Gillis watched as the soldiers took different individuals out through the ring of soldiers and down to where Major Cates was conducting his interrogations. From what Gillis could see a soldier was taking down a statement from each person and a lot of people were putting their palms up making visible hand signs of "I don't know." Even from a distance Gillis could tell that Major Cates's frustration level was beginning to rise. After over an hour of waiting, two soldiers walked up to Gillis and grabbed each arm and firmly escorted him to the table where the major sat.

"Well, Mr. McCabe, I know it is not by accident that you are here, take a seat please." The major slowly rolled a cigarette and then lit it. "I also know that you were in my office or at least the building when this murder occurred. Therefore you are fortunate that I can't arrest you as a suspect, but in the future if I find you in the middle of any part of my investigation I will take great delight in throwing you in jail no matter who wrote you a letter, do you understand?"

Gillis didn't like the tone of the conversation and held himself back from what he really wanted to say. "Yes major, I understand what you said. Is it okay for me to leave now?"

The major just stared at him for a moment and then turned to a corporal who stood behind him. "Escort this man to our perimeter and if you see him again at our investigations, I want him arrested immediately for interfering in a federal matter. Now get this man out of my sight."

Gillis rose to his feet as the corporal grabbed him by this arm and the two men escorted him to the street and through the barricade of soldiers.

The soldier turned to Gillis. "Mister, I don't know who you are but the major has a real nasty side to him and I would suggest you take his advice and stay out of this."

Gillis looked at the man. The soldier's face was stern and firm and Gillis could tell from his stone cold blue eyes that the man was telling him the truth. This Major Cates was not a man to be messed with and Gillis could expect no help of any kind from him.

"I will remember that, corporal," said Gillis, as he started walking to where Luke stood patiently waiting.

"That didn't seem to go well. Did you find out anything, Mr. McCabe?"

"I appreciate your astute observation. Now where is the carriage?" Gillis was mad. This Major Cates had treated him like trash and he certainly wasn't used to being talked to in that manner. Sooner or later the tide would turn and then the major wouldn't sit so high in his ivory tower.

The ride back to the hotel was quiet as Gillis digested all that had happened. Finally, as they neared the hotel he turned to Luke. "Tomorrow, after I meet with Detective Fritz we go back and take a better look at everything at the diner. I am nowhere near done with this investigation."

Luke stared ahead. "Whatever you say, Mr. McCabe."

"When we get back to the hotel I want you to check our mail and see if we have any messages. I want to eat in another hour or so. If I have any messages bring them up to the room, otherwise I will see you in the restaurant."

"Yes sir, Mr. McCabe. If there isn't anything I will be in the bar having a beer, if that is okay with you."

"That's fine," said Gillis, as the carriage came to a stop in front of the hotel. He handed the reins to Luke before stepping down. As he started to the steps he saw Liam walking up the street toward them.

"Sorry I am a little late, Mr. McCabe, I had one of your mules get out. Somehow that long-eared beast figured out how to undo the stall latch. That's one smart animal."

"I assume you did catch them?"

"Yes sir, I did, and if we still got the deal on information, then I have that too."

Gillis looked back at Luke who was still in the carriage. "Just tie him off over there and join us at a table," he said as he pointed to a hitching rail down in the shade. The two men walked up the stairs and over to the open-air porch used for outside seating. "Have a seat, Liam," said Gillis as he pulled out a chair and sat at one of the more isolated tables.

As soon as they were seated a waitress approached the table and Gillis turned to Liam. "Would you like a beer or something?"

Liam smiled. "Yes ma'am."

"Bring us three beers, thank you." Gillis turned back to Liam.

"So what do you have for me?"

Liam looked around like he was searching to see if anyone was watching or listening. "Well sir, the word on the street is that the group that is doing the killing is some type of secret brotherhood. No one I talked to knows how they pick their victims but they are definitely picking certain individuals. I hate to admit it, sir, but some of the people I run with are from the wrong side of the tracks, if you know what I mean. According to them they ain't doing these killings, it's these people."

Gillis sat back in his chair and sipped his beer and motioned for Liam to have a drink. He hoped the beer might relax the young man and help the information flow. Just then, Luke walked up to the table and Gillis motioned him to take a seat. "Liam here has a little information that he would like to share with us."

Even with the beer Liam seemed nervous. For a moment he looked like he wanted to say something but was struggling. "Mr. McCabe, from what I hear you are dealing with a really dangerous bunch, people that kill for little or nothing. Whoever stands in their way either ends up dead or goes missing. Even in the toughest part of town people are afraid and careful. Talk is that these people like to kill quietly, and with great skill. Lots of times the victims have their throats cut clear to the bone, other times the victims are found with nothing more than a small hole in the back of their heads. It's like they were sending a message to not mess with them."

Gillis raised his hat and stroked his hair backwards before continuing. "Unfortunately we know what kind of men we are dealing with but I have little choice."

"Sir, I did find out one more thing. A friend of mine was working late in a bar in the middle of town. Two men had been drinking most of the night and were talking in a whisper. My friend listened in on the conversation.

He didn't hear everything but they were talking about the murders and a group called something like the Fenian Mu or something close to that. One of the men talked about how Murphy wouldn't be happy. That's about all I know right now but with a little incentive, I believe I could find out more."

Gillis stood up from the table. "Liam, will you excuse me for a minute? I need to get your money from behind the desk."

Liam just smiled and nodded. Gillis walked over to the hotel desk. Concealing a twenty dollar gold piece under his hand he slid the coin across the counter to the desk clerk. He used his body to hide the motion in such a way as neither Luke or Liam could see and in a quiet whisper he said to the desk clerk, "Now reach under the desk for a moment and act as if you are getting something, then hand this gold piece back. I want those two men at that far table to see. When I check out, there will be a good tip in it for you if you keep your mouth shut about what I just did."

"I certainly will," responded the young man as he reached down behind the desk and in full sight of the two men handed Gillis the gold piece back.

"Thank you, good sir," said Gillis in a louder than usual voice as he walked back to the table. He glanced across the street and noticed a well-dressed man with a tight manicured beard seated on a bench across the street reading a paper. He gave it little thought as he sat down and slid the gold piece across the table to Liam in a subtle movement.

"I hope we are good until tomorrow," said Gillis as he smiled at Liam.

"Yes sir, we are and then some. Your carriage will be waiting as usual."

As Liam walked down the steps of the hotel, Luke took a short swig of beer and then turned to Gillis, "What was that all about, acting like you got the gold from the front desk?"

"Well Luke, if he thinks I keep the gold behind the front desk then there is more of a chance that whoever knows I am carrying money will stop there first." Luke nodded and then took another swig of beer.

Luke reached into his coat pocket. "There were a couple of letters for you, Mr. McCabe. Would you like them now or would you prefer I put them in your room?"

"No, I would like to see them, thank you," said Gillis as Luke handed him the letters. Gillis looked at the first letter and he was sure it was from Wooly. He looked at the second letter, it was from Sandra. Gillis stared at the letter for a moment. "Would you mind giving me about ten minutes to read this letter in private?"

Luke looked startled by the comment but shoved his chair back and stood up. "No problem, Mr. McCabe. While I am killing time would it be all right for me to look at the book you have on them dinosaurs? I have never seen anything like that before, hard to believe those things roamed the Earth before people."

Gillis reached in his pocket and handed Luke the key to his room. "After you get it, come back. I want to discuss plans for tomorrow." Luke nodded and went toward the main staircase of the hotel. Gillis took his time as he stared at the large thick brown envelope that contained Sandra's letter. He thought of her constantly and missed her beyond words but he was a man of logic and he needed to solve what had happened to his father. Hearing from her was in some ways almost magical. The reality was that he would have to wait to see her again. Gillis pulled his pocket knife out and slit the envelope open with a quick motion. As he removed the letter two dried rose petals fluttered onto the table. The letter had the gentle fragrance of rose and for a moment he held it up against his chest.

Dearest Gillis,

Life here with my aunt and uncle has become very difficult. Already there is a food shortage and even though I try every day to do what I can, I believe I have become more of a burden than a help. I hope you will understand what I am about to say. I miss you so very much and I know you are searching for your father but I must see you again. Tomorrow I am leaving for your father's homestead. I was so confused when father died. I really miss and love you.

Sandra

The letter was dated almost three weeks ago and Gillis read it several times before carefully shoving it back into the envelope and putting it inside his coat. As he tucked the letter down into his pocket he felt something and pulled out the key-like object that Letty had held before she died. It was almost like she meant to tell him he had to find his father. The light was good as he looked at the object and turned it over. It was such a strange, almost round at first then turning into an oval shape before a small stem-like projected out. In some ways it looked like a key but it had no teeth and Gillis was sure it had never been a key, at least not the type of key most people were familiar with.

Something about it caught his eye and he looked hard at the two letters on the front, a large F and smaller M, both stamped in a bold style. The smaller letter M at the base of the F appeared to be newer, like it had been carved into the key at a later time. Gillis looked at the key for a moment and stuck it back into his pocket.

It was close to ten minutes later when Luke approached the table with the book he had borrowed. "This book has a lot of great drawings of dinosaurs. Who would have ever thought such creatures existed." He paused. "Oh by the way, did you know a couple of pages seem to be stuck together? I tried to get them apart but I couldn't."

Gillis about jumped out of his chair. "Let me see that. What pages?" he asked reaching for the book.

"It's pages 46 and 47 I think."

"If this is what I think it is, it will be amazing. My father used to take great pride in hiding messages in plain sight where others wouldn't notice. Great job Luke, now run and find me the sharpest straight edge you can." Luke headed back towards his room and within minutes was back at the table with a straight razor.

Chapter 16

"How's this, Mr. McCabe?"

"That will work great," said Gillis as he began to surgically split the pages. "These pages are stuck together with a very fine layer of glue and almost invisible to the average eye reading this book."

"So what does it say?"

"Nothing at this point but let's take a look." Luke looked at the pages with a puzzled expression.

"What's that?"

"I am not positive. Right now it is nothing more than a series of numbers, letters, and symbols." The writing was done in pencil and it was extremely light and small. The letters were so strategically placed up against the picture of a dinosaur's head that even in the light it would be impossible to see from the previous page. In front of him were two sets of symbols. The first one was the word "red" then a slash. The second word "green" is followed by a dot. Just after the word green is the crude line drawing of a house. The second line of symbols starts with the number "3" then a dot and then two arrows on top of each other pointing in the opposite directions. It is followed by the word "high" and then another dot. Finishing the last line of symbols was a drawing that looked like a set of human teeth.

Looking up at Luke, Gillis said, "It is definitely a code."

"That makes no sense to me. Are you sure you can break this code?"

"Maybe with time, my father was very clever and every now and then as a child he would test my ability to solve different types of puzzles. We didn't do them often but when he did, I took great delight in trying to solve them. This may take a while but I will solve it."

That night alone in his room, Gillis read Sandra's letter over and over. There was something missing in his life and he knew it was her. Finally, he set the letter down and looked at the book with the code. He would spend the next two hours studying it before closing his eyes for the night.

* * *

The next morning Gillis was up early. He headed down for breakfast and was surprised to see Luke already eating. "Well good morning, did you sleep well?" Gillis asked.

Luke smiled. "Like a baby. I closed my eyes and don't remember hearing a thing until morning."

"I wish I could say that. The street noise kept waking me up. It's amazing how many people are up and around at one in the morning. You have to wonder when they sleep."

"Any luck on the code?"

"A little."

The two hadn't quite finished breakfast before Detective Fritz appeared in the lobby looking a little lost as his eyes searched the dining area. Gillis raised his hand and immediately Detective Fritz acknowledged him and began walking their way. The distance between chairs was tight and the cigar-smoking detective took his time finding the least obstructed route.

In a quiet, almost concealed voice he began. "Mr. McCabe, here are your reports. First there is a list of everyone that has been murdered. Their ages and the dates of the murders are all in chronological order. Each murder has a folder of what the individual did for a living, why they were there, if known, and any other facts I could find. Unfortunately, I wasn't able to find any common denominators."

"I appreciate the effort," said Gillis as he reached into his front coat pocket and retrieved an envelope. "Hopefully this will cover all your expenses."

"Happy to be of service," said Logan as he took another puff on his cigar. "My contact said that everything is tightening up over at Major Cates's office. They are really getting frustrated."

"Keep me abreast of what is happening," said Gillis.

"Thank you, Mr. McCabe. Just send a messenger if you need me or if I find out anything additional I will come by the hotel."

"Thanks again, Mr. Fritz," said Gillis as the detective made his way into the busy street. Gillis noted the second patrol of five soldiers going past the hotel in the last twenty minutes. The heat had been turned up.

An older lady, her face marked and puffy, refilled his coffee cup and seemed to linger by the table until Gillis turned to her. "Thank you. I really won't be needing anything else." She turned and slowly walked back toward the door leading to the restaurant. Gillis watched her leave and then turned and looked at Luke. "I wonder where Liam and the carriage are. He has always been right on time. I wonder if one of our mules got out again and he is late because of them."

Just then Luke turned and saw their horse and carriage coming up the street. "There's the carriage but that isn't Liam driving it—isn't that the blacksmith?"

The blacksmith got out of the carriage and tied the horse to the hitch rail in front of the hotel and looked around. "Luke, why don't you go and find out what's going on while I look at this list and the folders Detective Fritz gave me." Luke scooted his chair back and hurried down the stairs and over to the blacksmith. Gillis could see them talking and blacksmith's hand movements.

Shortly after, Luke made his way back to the table and seated himself. "I guess Liam didn't show up for work today, first day he has missed in two years. As soon as the blacksmith is done with us I guess he is going to check out where he lives and see if he is sick or something. Anyways the carriage is ready anytime you are."

Later the carriage passed through several neighborhoods on its way to the Dockery's Diner. "Do you want to question the waitress again?"

"No, I think everyone including me has covered that fairly well. What I want to do is figure out how that assassin was able to disappear. I am quite sure by now that Major Cates believes they can fly." Luke laughed as he pulled up in front of the diner.

"What do you want me to do, Mr. McCabe?"

"Just stay with me and listen. If I miss something in my observations I would like it pointed out. The killer ran down through the crowd and disappeared into the people walking on this wooden boardwalk. The sound of gunshots should have gotten most people's attention. Someone had to have seen something and I plan to find that someone." The two began walking up the boardwalk as Gillis closely examined the planking while looking under the decking.

"What are you doing?" asked Luke.

"If the killer was actually wounded and I believe he was, then there should be some evidence of that." Gillis pointed at a small dark oval spot on a board next to a building. "That's what I was looking for, a spot of blood. He definitely passed through here."

For the next two hours Gillis and Luke walked the boardwalk visiting with each business owner or the store manager. Everyone seemed to remember the event, the crowd and its excitement, even hearing shots but no one seemed to recall a man running down the street. The block was several hundred yards long with no open access to the service alley that ran parallel behind the buildings. The only area without a store front was a narrow ten-foot alley that ran back about sixty feet and stopped, creating a dead end. The solid brick-lined alley floor was littered with scraps of all sorts and rotting pieces of old boxes.

Gillis continued on to the far end of the block where an Army recruitment center was located. Numerous soldiers were milling around the entrance. Gillis walked up to a group of soldiers and tried to begin a conversation. "Any of you men see anything of the man that murdered the gentleman at the Dockery's Diner yesterday?"

Almost immediately a large bearded sergeant appeared to take charge of the conversation while Luke went and sat down with a couple of soldiers. "No murderer made it this far yesterday. Several of us heard the shots and went running toward the commotion but we never saw the killer. Before I left this station, I ordered the corporal here to seal off the street and not let anyone in or out. No one came through here. It's like the guy simply vanished. By the way your name isn't McCabe is it?"

"Why no it isn't, my name is James Brink, why?"

"Major Cates would have my hide if I talked to a man named Gillis McCabe. I guess he is some big shot that is well connected and sticking his nose in Army business."

"I will sure keep my eye out for this McCabe fellow." Luke didn't say anything as he just looked at Gillis and then at the ground. "Terrible crime, I hope you find the murderer," said Gillis, as he started walking back towards the diner.

"Mr. McCabe, you sure must have placed one hell of a burr under that

Major Cates's saddle for him to have ordered his men not to even talk to you."

"You are probably right, Luke. Now there is one more thing I want to look at over here and then we can move on to the dead end alley. If all the shopkeepers are telling the truth, that's the only place he could have gone unless he really did vanish."

"I heard one of the soldiers tell another that they thoroughly searched every store from top to bottom," said Luke.

Gillis walked back down the street toward the alley and diner and past the alley entrance to the store that sat on the corner next to the entrance. About ten crates of apples sat neatly stacked on several pallets from the floor standing about four feet above the boardwalk. The same thick-looking man they had talked to earlier was now standing with a white apron on and polishing each apple.

"Good morning, sir. Perhaps you remember me from this morning and my questions on the murder that took place at Dockery's."

"Yeah, I remember you. You might have another question but I really don't have any more answers for you or those Army boys."

"When we were talking earlier I noticed you adjusting one of these crates of apples. Is there any chance that you put these out here this morning?"

"Yes, just got them in late yesterday, probably an hour after the shooting."

"If I gave you a dollar would you mind moving those apples boxes to the other side of the store front so I could examine the surface below them? I probably won't find anything but I will pay for the exercise and give you a hand."

"Why sure, I can do that. Easiest dollar I'll make today."

It took about five minutes to move the crates with all three men helping. Gillis stood and examined the space where the crates had been removed. Almost immediately he dropped to his knees and pointed. "Here's what I am looking for. It has been walked on a bit but here's another drop of blood. Now we know the assassin came at least this far."

Luke looked down on the eroded spot of blood and shook his head. "That's pretty amazing, Mr. McCabe, that you figured out that there may be blood under those crates."

"Sure is," said the shopkeeper. "Everyone including myself missed it—who would have thought?"

"It tells me he went this way and as close as the blood spot is to this corner my guess is he turned into this alley." Gillis hesitated for a moment before turning to the shopkeeper. "I would assume you can restack these crates yourself and if you keep quiet about what we found, there is another couple of dollars in it for you."

"No problem Mr.—"The shopkeeper looked straight at Gillis.

"Brink, the name is Brink. Remember to keep our discovery to yourself," said Gillis, as he pulled two dollars out of his coat for the man.

"Luke, let's go check out this alley."The two entered the narrow brick-lined alley. A few smashed crates lay strewn across the ground and in a couple of places people had relieved themselves. Gillis stood and scanned the site for a few minutes before moving up and down the wall examining it. Minutes later he went to the back wall and repeated the process but still found nothing.

The final wall was almost exactly the same as the other two with four-foot wide brick panels inlaid several inches with a two-inch brick header. The only difference he could find were the staggered rusty gas lights that hung on every fourth panel. He looked at all the walls again, studying every detail. It was almost twenty minutes later when he turned to Luke. "If you look carefully, Luke, you will see where someone has moved this light slightly to one side. The question is why? I can only ascertain that it may have something to do with how the assassins vanished."

Again Gillis stared at the first rusted light fixture. He slowly moved down the line examining each one as he went. After ten minutes of staring at the wall, the fixtures and the floor, Gillis got down on his hands and knees and began crawling along the foundation. Suddenly he stopped. Luke bent over to see what had caught Gillis's eye. "Do you see the small drop of blood here?" said Gillis pointing.

"Yeah, I see it. Good eyes, Mr. McCabe!"

"Do you see something different about it?"

"No, not really," said Luke looking more closely.

"This blood spot is unlike all the rest. The others were oval like a man bleeding while he was on the move. This one is perfectly round. The assassin stopped here and stood for a moment, but why?" Luke just looked puzzled as he knelt down looking at the spot.

"If I am correct, somehow this single drop of blood has led us to how the murderer escaped unnoticed."

Chapter 17

Gillis stood slowly and stared at the rusted lantern frame that years ago had been abandoned. It was now late afternoon and the wall was beginning to fall into the shadows and the thought occurred to Gillis that it would actually be nice if the lantern worked. He stared at the rust-caked light, so well-constructed that even the majority of rivets were still holding each individual metal component tightly together. Gillis reached up and with a firm grip pulled outward on the ornamental mounting of the glassless lantern. It was steadfast and didn't budge.

Again he tried pulling the lantern, this time down against the wall but it still didn't move. The base of the lantern was close to six feet above the ground and Gillis reached up and tried moving all parts of the lantern in every conceivable way but again nothing moved. Gillis took several steps backward and lowered his hands to his hips and said loudly, "I know it's here, I just know it's got to be here somewhere. This wounded assassin didn't run down a dead end alley to stand here bleeding. Somewhere here lies the key to his escape."

Down deep Gillis was convinced he was right. The man stood there long enough that a perfectly round drop of blood fell to the ground. With new vigor he pushed on each brick starting at the bottom and working his way to the top of both the recessed panels. Still nothing moved. Each brick was firmly in place and Gillis's frustration was beginning to mount. There were at least twenty slightly recessed panels of brick in the alley but the fact that the wounded man stood here under this exact panel had to hold the answer.

"Mr. McCabe, it is starting to get dark and we may want to think about getting the horse and carriage back. Do you want to just come back tomorrow when there is more light and we can see better?"

The comment broke Gillis from his trance-like stare at the wall. Taking a deep breath he turned to Luke. "You're probably right and we do need to get the carriage back. I still have a lot of work to do on those folders Detective Fritz brought and hopefully figure out my father's code." The two walked out the alley and down the boardwalk until they reached the tied sleeping horse that woke with a snort.

"This is actually a pretty nice piece of horse flesh they gave us today. I wonder if Liam finally showed up. Nice young man but a tough background. Hopefully he is back to work and has gotten us some more useful information."

The ride back to the hotel was quiet and uneventful as Gillis directed the horse over to the hitching post they had been using. A skinny young man walked up to them as they dismounted the carriage. "You Mr. McCabe? I was sent over here to get the horse and carriage."

"So where's Liam?"

"You must not have heard?"

"No, we have been out all day."

"They found Liam floating in the mill pond about four miles from here. The boss said it looked like someone gave him a terrible beating. I guess they found him late this morning. The boss went and met with the police and identified him early this afternoon. Been so many murders in this town in the last couple of years, the folks around here don't even seem to get real riled up anymore."

Gillis looked into the man's eyes. "I am truly sorry. Did he have a family?"

"Yes sir, a wife. It was her birthday today. She just turned sixteen."

Gillis reached into his coat pocket and took out a couple of tightly folded bills and handed it to the man. "Please make sure his wife gets this."

The man nodded. "Yes sir, I will."

Gillis walked up the stairs of the porch, entered the building and went straight to the desk clerk. "Is there any mail for me?"

"Sorry Mr. McCabe, none today."

Gillis turned to Luke who was standing about ten feet behind him. "I want to clean up a bit and scan those folders. I will meet you down here for dinner in an hour."

"That's fine, Mr. McCabe. I will be here."

Gillis walked to his room and used the key to enter. He lit the kerosene lantern by the bed and the two additional lanterns he had requested from the desk clerk. Filling the water bowl on the dresser, he washed his face, and dried it off with a clean white towel. He was frustrated and the strong feeling that he had missed something today persisted, but what? He had tried every conceivable way to move the rusty lantern with no luck. He had checked every brick to see if it somehow triggered a secret door but there was none. What was he missing? Why would a single round drop of blood be in front of that panel of brick unless the assassin stopped there? Gillis kept pondering the situation.

The killer had to have known his escape route, and if Gillis was right, there were far more than one of these killers. The witnesses to the different murders had described the assassin as tall, short, heavy and thin and one even believed it had been a woman. Gillis was sure that the assassin ducked into the dead-end alley knowing there was a way out.

If there were more than one person in on these murders, then there had to be some noticeable object or something that could be easily seen in plain sight. Each member of the group would know exactly where the escape route was located, but what? Gillis knew he had missed something and hopefully by studying the alley again he might find a clue.

He decided to let it drop for the night and sat on one of the two comfortable chairs adjacent to the table and spread out the contents of the folders. It was the finest room in the hotel and probably the most expensive. He was sure that was why it was still available. According to the desk clerk it was twice as large as any of the other rooms and from Luke's comment, the difference was huge. The room's window commanded a beautiful panoramic view of the street below as well as the distant hills beyond. Gillis made no secret of his arrival and he knew if his father was still alive, he would be easily found.

It was thirty minutes past the agreed upon time when Gillis finally walked into the dining area and pulled back a chair. "Sorry I am late. I got caught up in those folders and the descriptions."

"Did you find anything?"

"I'm not sure but one thing for certain is extremely odd. When I hired Detective Fritz I asked him to give me the names of each person that was murdered, their age, the location of the murder, what they did for a living, and who they were with at the time. From what I gleaned from our conversation, Detective Fritz has someone working with him on the inside. I am not sure how much the Army and the police share information but there is nothing lost in asking the question. Therefore, I sent him a note asking him to try and acquire information that may have been obtained by the police at each murder site."

"So what struck you as odd?"

"At first nothing, but the more I read and looked for similarities something jumped out at me. The people who were murdered were in their early thirties clear up to one individual that was seventy."

Gillis set the pile of folders down on the table. "I couldn't figure out why there was such an age discrepancy and I still don't have the answer but then something else stood out to me, their names. Robert Parson, merchant age 35, William Smith, shipping, age 51, Edith Cole, merchant, age 42, followed by Jonathan Porter, and men named Steward, Nelson, and Woods, and so on. So do you see the similarity?"

"Not really, Mr. McCabe."

"Every one of these people has an English name. Maybe it is just coincidental but I would guess that fifty percent of the people living in Alexandria and Washington aren't of English ancestry. Of all the many assassinations that have occurred to date, the victims were all between thirty-five and seventy and all of them had an English name. What are the chances of that?"

"I don't know," responded Luke.

"Exactly, different ages, different professions, different friends but all of them have English names. We know at least several were killed by some type of tool or weapon that fatally punched a hole into the back of their heads. Tomorrow, I want to go back to that alley and take another look. I truly believe I am on the right track here."

"Whatever you want to do, Mr. McCabe, but we looked that alley over pretty hard. What do you think we missed?"

"I don't know yet but there was a reason the killer was there. You can bet he studied his get-away carefully and knew exactly where he was going and what to do. I need to figure out his escape, what he did, and how he did it."

Just then the young lady who had waited on them before began moving toward their table. "By the looks of that pile of folders, you have a lot of work ahead of you, Mr. McCabe."

Gillis smiled and straightened the pile into a neat stack. "I'll have an order of coffee, roast beef, corn, and a potato." Luke ordered the same.

Luke pulled a small pamphlet from his pocket and started looking at it. "What do you have there?" Gillis asked.

"Oh, it's a map of all you can see in Washington. They have a stack of them on the front desk."

"I guess I have been working you pretty hard. Would you care to take the day off tomorrow and visit some of the sights?"

Luke jumped at the opportunity. "That would be great, Mr. McCabe. I would really like that, but don't you need me to watch your backside?"

"You have been working pretty hard for a while now and we haven't seen any of those men that followed us on the trail. I plan to do most of my work in my room tomorrow and the following day we can check out that alley again. I feel pretty safe here in the hotel and you do remember I carry a pistol." Luke smiled. "Let's have breakfast here tomorrow at seven, then you can take off and see the sights."

* * *

The next morning both men met on the stairs and exchanged greetings as they walked down to eat. The stairs, although old, had been hand carved and showed a lot of interesting detail. These fancy front stairs and the narrow back stairs were the only sources of access to the floors above. The back stairs were used by staff and the hotel customers who didn't want to use the chamber pots. After several cups of coffee and a big breakfast Luke stood up. "I can't ever remember eating this good. Are you sure you're still good with me leaving for the day?"

"Absolutely—you can't come to Washington and not see the place. I have toured almost every building of importance and enjoyed all of them. When I was building ships I was constantly coming up to Washington for meetings and trying to promote my business. This is a fascinating city. I will plan on seeing you back here sometime late this afternoon."

"Thanks, Mr. McCabe."

Gillis thought what a good man Luke had turned out to be and how he had learned to trust and accept his judgment. He reached over and picked up a paper, more to scan for information than read it. He found nothing of interest and finally headed back up to his room where he unlocked his door and walked in. Once inside, he locked the door before flopping into a padded armchair.

For the next couple of hours he poured his energy into the different folders that Detective Fritz had brought but found nothing new of interest. Then he thought about the alley and all the different descriptions of the assassins. One thing he was fairly positive of was these people were connected. There had to be a way they could maneuver throughout the city by seeing some type of symbol or sign that identified escape routes. Regardless of the many hours he spent thinking and staring at the walls of the alley, he knew there had to be a clue he was overlooking.

Taking a short break, he stood and looked out the window. He wondered what Sandra might be doing. He missed her. Finally, he sat back down and opened the book he had found and decided to work on the code. This was a cryptic message and Gillis believed that his father had meant it for him to find. The top message had the word red, with a slash, then green, and then what looked like a building or house. He thought about a red and green building or house, but nothing came to mind. Even if he could think of a red and green house, he didn't know in what city or town the code was referring.

No, he wasn't thinking right. What if they were simply the colors, red and green? If you blended those colors together, they would make brown. Certainly there were a lot of unpainted brown houses; that couldn't be the answer. Slowly, he began working on the house. Maybe it was meant to depict a house, maybe a home or a building but that certainly didn't limit the possibilities. Next he considered the definition of a house or home and he came up with numerous words such as residence, dwelling, domicile, and many others. None of these made any sense if the first word was actually brown.

The thought of the actual definition of a home brought to mind a place where one lives, where you belong, a safe place, a refuge or sanctuary. Gillis played with each word and seemed to get hung up on refuge or sanctuary.

A brown refuge or brown sanctuary made no sense and finally he stood and decided to go downstairs for a cup of coffee. After spending over an hour and a half trying to piece things together, he needed to clear his mind. He walked down the stairs and into the dining area where he sat at a table near the rail. The sky was blue and the day warm without much wind. The waitress who had waited on him most of his visits walked up to his table and Gillis looked at her and excitedly said, "Brown Haven—of course, the house is a haven."

"Pardon me, Mr. McCabe, but were you talking to me?"

"Sorry, no, I figured something out that I have been working on. Thank you. Would you mind getting me a cup of coffee?"

"Of course not, sir. Will there be anything else?"

"No, not now, just the coffee."

As the waitress walked away, Gillis smiled. At least now he knew where his father wanted him to go, the small isolated cabin at his estate, Brown Haven. He felt confident that now he had a rough outline of how to solve the rest of the puzzling code. He sat sipping and thinking. What did the number three, opposite arrows, the word "high" and a drawing of teeth mean? Could it be a group of three objects? Possibly, but he didn't think so. What about another way to say three? "Tri" immediately came to his mind. It's a starting point he thought. He looked at the two opposite arrows and tried to remember why they were familiar to him. He had to really think but then it came to him. Those were one of the many symbols for opposite. The opposite of the next word high would be low. I got it, he thought, the last symbol has to be teeth or something associated with it. Triloteeth, it has to be trilobite. From these clues it appears my father wanted me to visit Brown Haven and look for a trilobite. Where in Brown Haven? He had no clue. Maybe his father wasn't in Washington after all but waiting for him at Brown Haven.

Gillis looked up from his cup of coffee and nearly spilled it all over himself. There in front of him stood Sandra, smiling with a bright butter-colored dress. He launched himself from his chair and quickly the two embraced with a passion only known by people deeply in love. Finally, Gillis pulled back never removing his hands from hers. "How did you get here?"

"It was hard getting to your father's ranch but after I got there, Roper helped me catch a stage headed north. After many miles and a lot of stops the stage took me to the Alexandria Depot which is only a few miles from the hotel. After cleaning up a little, I hired a carriage to bring me here."

"Thank God you did. I have missed you terribly," said Gillis as he hugged her firmly.

"Can you ever forgive me for blaming you for everything, especially for my father's death? How a person can screw up their own mind that badly is beyond me."

"Please come and sit down. What can I get for you, some sweet tea?"

"Yes please, that sounds so good. It's wonderful being here but it's been hard. Williamsburg is really struggling. What is this world coming to?" she asked in her thick Southern accent.

"I don't know but I am so glad you're here. Let me go over and make sure I can get you a room."

Sandra smiled as Gillis stood. "Thank you, but I already checked in. They said you weren't in and probably wouldn't be back soon. But then I saw you sitting out here at this table."

"I want you to switch rooms with me. Mine is much bigger and nicer."

"That's sweet of you but maybe tomorrow or the next day. For tonight it will be fine. I already have my luggage in the room."

Gillis couldn't believe she was there and his memories of her beauty were not exaggerated. He had dreamed of this moment. "Did you find your father?" she asked. "Roper told me all about what has happened, at least as much as your letters explained."

"No, I haven't found him. My father is smart and capable and I believe he is still alive. After a few days, if you are rested, we will start back to the ranch. I believe he left me a clue to where he may be found."

"I sure hope he is okay. I am looking forward to meeting him."

"Hopefully you will. I almost hate to leave here. I have so many unanswered questions. This group of assassins is working the city, and the police and the Army have no idea who they are. There is a part of me that feels uncomfortable leaving. I believe this is the same gang of individuals that murdered Letty and the others. This group of killers appears very skilled, well trained, and dedicated. Not a single one of them has been captured and no one seems to know how they are able to vanish after a murder but I believe I may be close to solving the mystery. From what I know of the city's attacks, all of them have occurred in a five-mile radius and that may be a big clue in itself."

"Let's talk of happy things. This is one of the most special days of my life and I want to enjoy it."

Gillis smiled at Sandra, as he held her hand.

"Have you had dinner?"

"No, and I am starving. The food along the way wasn't very good and it's a long way between stage stops. And besides, I was far more interested in seeing you than eating." Gillis reached over and kissed her.

"Oh have I missed you too. Let's go have dinner. I know you are hungry and you are probably exhausted too." The two of them drank the best wine the hotel had to offer and later they enjoyed a prime rib dinner at one of the restaurants in town. Sandra shared the story of her journey from Williamsburg up through two military lines and a lot of rough country.

They finished dinner and made it back to the hotel when Luke showed up in the lobby. "Sorry I'm late, boss. I guess I got carried away by all those sights." Luke's eyes went to Sandra.

"No problem, Luke. I know you have never met her but this is my fiancée, Sandra, the most beautiful woman in all Virginia."

"Oh, Gillis," Sandra blushed.

Luke smiled, "Nice to finally meet you, ma'am. Mr. McCabe has spoken of you often."

"It's a pleasure to meet you, Luke. I appreciate the good job you did keeping Gillis out of trouble."

"I'm not sure I kept him out of trouble, ma'am, but I have enjoyed our time together. You are getting a good man." Luke turned to Gillis. "Mr. McCabe, what time do you want to meet tomorrow?"

"I plan to have breakfast with this beautiful lady and after that I will decide what to do next."

"I understand. I will see you in the morning. Have a great night." Luke headed upstairs to his room.

Sandra and Gillis talked for several more hours but Gillis could see the exhaustion begin to flow across her face as she struggled to stay alert. Reluctantly, Gillis walked her to her room on the far end of the hall. The room was one floor down from his and Gillis wished he could be closer.

He passionately kissed her for most of a minute before releasing his tight grip. He would have to wait on the bonding of body and spirit, for she was a proper woman and he was a respectful man.

* * *

The next morning at breakfast was like the night before with nothing but smiles. As breakfast ended, Sandra, in her thick accent, said, "Gillis, I am still so pitifully tired that I am almost sick. The trip thoroughly wore me out. Would you mind if I sleep until noon and then we can go out, see the town, and celebrate?"

"Certainly, I can only guess at how difficult this trip was on you. I am flattered and blessed you made the journey. I am one extremely lucky man and I know it. You can sleep until the afternoon if you want and I will wake you in time for dinner. If you are going to nap, I need to keep my mind busy so I think Luke and I might go and visit a place where I believe I may find a clue as to the strategy of these assassins. It would be a huge help to the police and Army if they had some answers or at least some clues as to how these murders are committed." Gillis walked Sandra to her room and kissed her softly.

Gillis couldn't help but continue to smile as he made his way back down the stairs. He had become accustomed to sitting at the same table and for the first time he found it occupied. Oh well, he thought what a beautiful day this would be. Gillis took a seat at another table with a completely different view. He found himself gazing over the street and the angle revealed a small bench sheltered by a large maple tree but what got his attention was the man reading the paper on the bench. Gillis felt like he had seen him before but where he had no idea. He shook off the thought as he sat down and Luke joined him soon after.

It was shortly after breakfast that Detective Fritz showed up with another file of paperwork. "So detective, what do you have for me today?" Gillis asked.

"Well, more information on each of the victims and the individual murders, some of their personal backgrounds and something that may really interest you."

"What's that?"

"I was talking to a friend of mine who works on the New York police force. We were able to visit for a few hours before he had to head back to New York. It appears we aren't the only big city experiencing rampant execution-style murders associated with assassins. They had a dozen people in their city murdered over the last couple of years and numerous others that disappeared. But the big difference is that they caught one of the bloody bastards and found out the group's name."

Chapter 18

"The hell you say," said Luke. "Who are they?"

"They didn't get as much information from the man as they would have liked. Seems a big German sergeant was doing the interrogating and got a bit rough. Originally the man refused to talk. Stout Irish lad I was told, had the misfortune of slipping and breaking his ankle while making his escape. Murdered an English gentleman in his forties in broad daylight with a clean, deep cut across his neck and then tried to disappear into the crowd. Unfortunately for the lad, one of the first people murdered in New York was a close friend of the sergeant's family. He at least got the name of the group before the young man died. They called themselves the Fenian Mu. From what he said they are a secret Irish brotherhood. The bigger problem is actually coming from a much smaller, far more violent group. They broke away from the original Fenian brotherhood and they are bent on speeding up their revenge." "Revenge—revenge for what?" "The Potato Famine of 1845. Seems a lot of Irish families died over a six-year period when the potato crops failed and the English landowners did nothing to help. There wasn't much money in the hands of the peasants. The estates were owned mainly by Englishmen and their companies. With no profit to be made in Ireland they chose to sell their food supplies elsewhere leaving these people to slowly starve. This secret Irish society known as the Fenians began from a hatred of anything English. They started in Ireland but for the last fifteen years they have been quietly building their numbers in America and subtly doing everything they can to get revenge against anyone English whose ancestry played a part in this. Some of the victims are sons, and even daughters, of the original people who owned the farms or made the decisions. They are a well-organized and funded group that has been working on something major, according to their prisoner. Unfortunately he died before revealing anything specific."

"The prisoner said a man named Aidan McMurphy is the leader of this breakaway group. This fellow McMurphy is one powerful man, intelligent, and mysterious. He leads a younger more vicious group that are ready to follow him into hell if need be. When the prisoner was asked to describe him, it got a little strange. The leader always wears a mask at their meetings and only a few really know his true identity."

"So the sergeant beat him to death getting the information?"

"Unfortunately yes. I took good notes when I talked to my colleague and now you know as much as I do. The man was a stubborn fellow but the sergeant was damned and determined to get the information—probably a little too determined." "I appreciate the information since it puts more pieces of the puzzle together," Gillis said. "I may be close to solving how these assassins, at least here in Washington, are able to keep vanishing. Until I am sure, I'm not going to discuss it. I also believe we are being observed by someone, but I have no proof of that either." Detective Fritz took that moment to subtly look around as if to verify Gillis's statement. "Detective, you have done a great job for us. I plan on looking into a couple more clues and then we will probably be heading out. I need to pay you for the rest of your time. Do you have a moment to make out a bill?"

"Certainly," said the detective as he fumbled with his small notebook, unlocking the buckles that secured it. After a couple of moments of shuffling through papers, he handed Gillis a bill.

Gillis looked at the rough handwriting and then opened his coat pocket and retrieved his long flat wallet. Pulling several bills from the wallet he handed the money to the detective. "Thank you."

"That would be fine, Mr. McCabe. It's been a pleasure working for you." The detective headed out of the dining area and into the lobby.

Gillis turned to Luke. "Well, are you ready to go? I saw the carriage."

Luke drove the carriage as they headed toward the alley. "Mr. McCabe, if you don't mind me saying I have never seen you look so happy. I am glad things seem to be working out." "I appreciate that Luke. It has been a couple of rough months but I believe everything is starting to get better. I would still like to figure out how the assassins were able to vanish so easily and I think I will today. I have been thinking about the whole premise of their vanishing and I believe I may have at least one part figured out."

"What's that, Mr. McCabe?" "It will be easier to show you. We are almost there and it shouldn't take me long." Luke tied the horse and carriage to one of the many hitching posts along the street before the two men headed for the alley. "That perfectly round drop of blood keeps leading me back to the same spot in that alley. The wounded man stood still there long enough to disappear and I think I know how he did it."

Gillis walked straight to the masonry panel of recessed brick that he had stood in front of before and pondered without results. "I was looking for the wrong sign in the wrong location. Whoever came up with this method of communication was very cunning." Stopping in front of the panel where they had found the drop of blood, he looked at the numerous, seemingly duplicate panels on both sides of the post. He continued to stare for a moment until he finally turned to Luke. "Do you see that dark brick on the second row from the top, the one that looks like it may have charcoal on it, like it has been in a fire?" "Yeah, I see it." "There isn't another brick that color on any other panels or bricks in the entire alley. When you know what you are looking for, it actually stands out. If I am not mistaken that is a sign that tells them where the entrance is. There is no other rational reason why one lone charcoal-covered brick would be standing up on that wall. I made the mistake earlier of not looking high enough. I was looking where a normal man might view. All along I should have at least looked at the sky line. Hiding the symbol there is pure brilliance. Anyone looking for some type of sign or symbol would only by the best of luck, ever look that high. I believe that is the answer and now I have to figure out the key."

"What key?"

"When Sandra and I arrived at my father's farm right after the massacre we found everyone dead and the house torn apart. Some of the victims were just outright murdered while others were tortured. Whoever did this was obviously looking for something and now I think I know what. If I am not mistaken it was this key-like medallion, a kind of special access tool that allows its holders to come and go without anyone knowing how. This medallion that Letty gripped in her hand as she died has to be the access tool that allows the Fenians to come and go undetected. The burnt brick shows them where and the key allows them access." Gillis reached into a pocket of his light coat and pulled out the medallion. "The other day I stood here and analyzed this rusted light fixture for at least a half an hour and was impressed with how well it was built and how every stout rivet was still firmly in place except one. I looked at each lantern in this whole alley but this fixture seemed to be in slightly better shape and I believe the reason is that it is newer. The rust is not as thick nor does it seem to have aged with the exact same patina. If you look at the other lanterns they have some yellow algae growing in amongst the rust but this one doesn't. And after you thoroughly examine them, why is this lantern in better shape than the others? I believe this lantern is newer and the missing rivet is not from age but by design."

Gillis took the key-like medallion and stuck it in the missing rivet hole. Without turning it he heard a delayed click inside the four-foot-wide brick panel. "Mr. McCabe, did you hear that? The wall just clicked."

Gillis smiled and with his shoulder pushed on the panel of brick and it began to move inward with a quiet creaking sound.

"Wow, Mr. McCabe, you figured it out," said Luke in an excited voice. "You figured it out!"

"I have figured out at least one piece of the puzzle. Whoever was smart enough to come up with this amazing feat of engineering and masonry was good, very good. Look at this swing joint: it's exceptionally handcrafted and someone has kept up with the greasing. See this joint? It's been lubricated recently. The mechanism can only be opened by a shaft that is a certain diameter and length. If the shaft is too long it sets off a second mechanism and the door locks shut. Letty must have known something about this key before she was murdered. There had to be an important reason she lived long enough to place it in my hand before she died."

Gillis looked at the locking mechanism of the door before shifting his eyes to the brick walls of the inside. Several wooden torches hung on the wall in iron holders and he could see no further into the darkened tunnel than twenty feet. In the darkness it looked like a narrow flight of stairs began to descend. Reaching up, he took a torch from the rusty holder and searched his pockets for his small box of matches. "There is a lot of moss on these walls and some of the floor. If I am not mistaken that has something to do with the fact that I can hear running water."

"Me too, I can hear it—almost sounds like a slow-moving creek, but a ways off."

"If that is the case it would explain the moss and the dampness and gives us clues as to why this tunnel was originally built. Luke, do you remember the waitress saying the man smelled slightly musky?"

"Yes, I remember."

"Well, this would explain that too. I want you to stand guard at the door. I need to take this torch and explore this tunnel but I don't want any surprises when I come out."

"Are you sure you don't want me to go with you?"

"I will be fine, just be sure and watch my backside. I don't plan on going in very far. I need enough information that when we get the Army involved they know there is actually something down there."

"Be careful, Mr. McCabe."

"I will. I should be fine as long as this torch lasts. I have my pistol in my belt and I honestly don't think anyone will be in there. If I am correct, they use this more as a way of traveling throughout the city rather than a place to hide. Explaining it to Major Cates may be a challenge. How that man ever rose up through the ranks baffles me. I should have enough information now that he will follow this up." Luke nodded more in a manner of submission than agreement.

Gillis struck a match and ignited the two-foot-long torch. It took a minute for his eyes to adjust before he began to examine the brick passage. The masonry on the ceiling was done in a fine arch shape. Moving forward, he looked from floor to ceiling as he slowly progressed down the hall that seemed to narrow with each step.

The floor had a thin coating of mud and Gillis could see the tracks of various sized shoes. As he continued, he could see the start of a narrow set of stairs that dove down in front of him. The access was steep and the light from the torch wasn't bright enough to see far. Connected to the side of the stairs was a rusty cable that was anchored to the wall every few feet. Gillis grabbed it with his free hand as he descended. The stairs kept dropping until he was a good thirty feet below the elevation of the alley. Ahead of him, he could now clearly hear moving water as it echoed throughout the tunnel.

Finally, he reached a landing and took a moment to scan the area around him. He was on a six-foot-wide gangway that disappeared in both directions as the tunnel curved. Stacked against the wall were gray, aging crates, old barrels, and several coils of rusted cable. Gillis looked at the materials before deciding to continue following the shallow muddy footprints. The air smelled stale and musky as he placed the torch over the smooth flowing water.

"What is this place?" he thought. It certainly had been built years before but why? It had to be part of some type of water or sewer project. Keeping tight to the wall, he continued on as the passage made a gentle curve. In front of him was a wooden bridge, its timbers old and gray from age. It appeared to cross the water and disappear into another tunnel that could only be clearly identified by the pitch-black hole of the entrance. Then he saw a faint light coming from farther down the passage and for the first time he noticed he was sweating.

The light suddenly alerted him to his dangerous course. He had dismissed the fact that he might run into a trained killer, an assassin with enough experience to elude police and the Army successfully for over three years. He took his torch and without thinking doused it in the slow-moving stream beside him with a hiss. The near total darkness brought his fears to a terror level. He had never placed himself in such a dangerous situation. Gillis kept asking himself, what are you doing? You're no hero.

Somehow he found the inner strength to continue down the gangway toward the light like a moth drawn to a flame. He was scared and excited all at the same time; never in his life had he felt so alive. He told himself he would find the source of the light and then turn around and silently make his way back up the tunnel to where Luke was waiting. For a moment he thought he could smell the sweet odor of tobacco and then it was gone. He pressed his back against the damp brick wall and scanned the tunnel in front of him as he carefully continued.

The tunnel was getting brighter the closer he got to the light source and he could see more detail around him. He stopped and studied the brick boardwalk that he intended to sneak along when he heard the sound—a sound so close it took his breath away. Someone was only yards behind him and he started to awkwardly reach for his pistol even though he knew it was too late. Grabbing the pistol he swung around quickly knowing whoever was there would have little problem beating him to the draw.

The loud squeal of a huge rat shook him to his core as it bounced off his boot and scurried across the floor before diving into the water beside him. Gillis could hardly breathe as he stood motionless for several minutes before getting himself back together. Finally he began inching forward. Deep down the tunnel he thought he could hear the sound of a chain being dragged but then it was gone. He inched forward, his back pasted against the damp wall that was his only protection. Then he heard it, a low quiet moan that stopped him in his tracks. The sound was one of pain and it sent shivers up his spine. He began to feel panicked as he placed his hand on his forehead and felt the clammy perspiration. By reflex he reached into his pocket and pulled out his handkerchief and wiped his brow.

As he tried to shove the damp handkerchief back into his pocket he heard a distant voice and immediately turned and started silently retreating back down the tunnel. He had gone too far in his adventure and the authorities needed to handle this. Why risk losing everything when he was finally getting some answers and Sandra was back in his life. He was careful with his steps. The further he moved from the light, the darker the tunnel became and soon he was in total darkness.

For close to thirty minutes he crept along the damp wall, testing each step and feeling the wall, hoping he would find the opening that led back to the stairs he had entered from. Several times he found small hollows in the brick of the tunnel that he hadn't noticed initially. Each time it gave him false hope that he was close to the stairs and safety. Finally, his hand felt a sharp corner of brick and as he turned the corner he could barely see the faint outline of stairs. Minutes later he reached the top of the stairs relieved by the sight of a small beam of light from the crack in the brick door. Pushing the heavy door of brick outward he saw Luke standing outside in the sunshine and he struggled to adjust his eyes.

"You were gone a long time, boss. Did you find anything?"

Gillis took the medallion from Luke and put it back into his pocket before he spoke. "You could say that. There is a maze of tunnels down there and everything is designed around some type of water channel from what I could see. Those tunnels are well-built, large, and old. People would have noticed their construction. There is even cable on the stairs for hand holds like it was a government job, but I'm not sure why no one seems to know it's here. Anyway, I want to go see Major Cates tomorrow and tell him what I found. I didn't find any hard evidence but I am convinced the assassins were able to vanish through this series of tunnels."

Gillis reached for his handkerchief and searched one pocket and then the next. "What's wrong, boss?" Luke asked.

"My handkerchief, I had it in the tunnel and I shoved it in my pocket but I can't find it."

"Handkerchiefs are cheap, Mr. McCabe. We can stop on the way back to the hotel and get you another."

"You don't understand, Luke. It's a special handkerchief. It has embroidery with initials in the corner, initials of my father. If whoever is down in those tunnels finds it, they may be able to trace it back to me or my father. There is a lot of old, decaying junk down there but otherwise it is pretty clean. I only hope that when I dropped it that it fell into the stream and was carried away."

Luke looked at Gillis for a moment. "I hope you're right. I would hate to have those men know we somehow stumbled into how they vanished."

Gillis used his shoulder to push the door closed and heard a click. "I need to get back to the hotel. Tonight is to be very special. I am going to take my future wife out on the town and have a nice dinner. Early tomorrow morning you and I will visit the Army and tell them what we found. I can't wait to see Major Cates's face when we show him this secret door. If everything goes as planned, we will be all packed up and headed back to my father's estate by early tomorrow afternoon. I want to get some ground between us and those Fenians before they figure out we were the ones that told the Army. When we get back to the hotel, I want you to ride to the livery station and make sure the mules are shod and ready. Buy a good sure-footed horse for Sandra. I don't know how well she rides."

"Sure thing, Mr. McCabe. I can't say that I'm not anxious myself to head home. Washington is interesting with all the history and such, but the people here are not near as friendly. They are a different sort."

The two talked more about what they thought would happen the next day and soon were in front of the hotel. To Gillis's surprise, Sandra was on the porch dressed in a soft blue dress that accented her sparkling blue eyes. As they pulled up to the hitching post she waved and Gillis waved back with a huge smile. Luke slowed the carriage to a stop and Gillis stepped to the ground and in a lively jog headed up the stairs. He had waited so long for a moment like this and he almost couldn't believe it was happening. Gillis threw his arms around Sandra and they embraced with a long passionate kiss that most of the people on the porch stopped and stared at. "Come, let's go sit for a minute."

Sandra stopped and looked at Gillis's coat. "Where have you been? You are wet and muddy and you smell musky like you were in a cellar or something."

"Sorry if I got any mud on your dress, it was—"Gillis paused. "You look so beautiful that I forgot that I am wearing these dirty clothes."

"Did you fall in a mud puddle?" asked Sandra.

"No, none of that. I figured out how the group of assassins has been escaping. I found a secret door and I had to see if it led to anything and that's how I got dirty. I didn't get hurt or anything. Now I can show the Army and finally arrest these murderers. Honey, would you mind having a glass of wine while I get cleaned up and put on some other clothes? I want tonight to be so very special and I plan to take you to the fanciest place in town for dinner and I will tell you everything then."

"You go. I will be right here when you return, but don't linger."

"I won't," said Gillis. "You did pack up your clothes so we could change rooms, didn't you?"

"Yes, everything is in my two suitcases but I am still fine with the smaller room, Gillis."

"My larger room will allow you to spread things out."

"Are you sure?"

"Yes, I want you to have my room. I want to make this trip as special and comfortable as I can. I will be right back." At that he turned and headed toward the desk clerk. It was a different older lady with silver hair who now manned the desk and Gillis leaned across the countertop and explained the situation to her about changing rooms and the two sets of baggage that needed to be switched. As he walked up the stairs he thought about how gratifying it would be to show the arrogant major the secret door. If it wasn't for his wonderful bride-to-be, he would be tempted to knock on the man's door tonight.

He unlocked the door and entered his room. Quickly, he filled his washbasin and then cleaned up. He hastily put on his other suit and placed his dirty clothes in a laundry bag. It only took Gillis fifteen minutes to make it back down to the table where Sandra was sitting.

"Well, you ready to see the town?" Gillis looked at his pocket watch. "The carriage and driver I hired should be here in another ten minutes. He is supposed to be an excellent tour guide as well as driver. I set it up yesterday to celebrate you making me the happiest man in Virginia."

The tour of the town and the evening lights were beautiful and finally the carriage stopped in front of a fancy building with two men standing in front to help with the carriages. One immediately went to hold the reins of the horse while the other helped Sandra down. Lanterns decorated both sides of the wide stairs that ran up to the restaurant and a smiling Negro man opened the door for them as they entered.

"Oh, Gillis," said Sandra when she entered the lobby. "This is so wonderful."

Gillis could tell her mind had gone somewhere else. "Are you thinking of Williamsburg?"

"Yes, and I shouldn't. This night is so perfect that bad memories shouldn't be allowed to spoil it and they won't." Sandra gracefully walked inside as the maître d' greeted them.

"Reservation for McCabe, hopefully you have a table overlooking the river with a little privacy. I have a lot of catching up to do with this lovely lady."

The waiter smiled. "Right this way, please." Gillis couldn't keep his eyes off Sandra and before they knew it the waiter informed them that the restaurant would be closing and he hoped they enjoyed their meal. How fast the night had gone. The carriage ride back to the hotel was romantic as Sandra cuddled against Gillis in the cool evening air.

As they neared the hotel, Gillis could hear fireworks as they rode around the corner. Much to their surprise they saw about a dozen boys firing off a variety of fireworks in front of the hotel. "They must have known that it was a special night for us," said Sandra, as Gillis smiled and nodded.

The carriage stopped in front of the hotel and the driver climbed down and helped Sandra. They walked close together as Gillis kept his arm around her waist. They made it up the stairs, through the lobby and up towards Gillis's old room. They hesitated for a moment at the door as he pulled her close and passionately kissed her. Regrettably, he let their embrace loosen and Sandra smiled as she looked into his eyes.

"Gillis, I had a wonderful time tonight. I never thought I would feel this type of happiness again. Thank you for dinner."

"Having you back into my life is beyond words. Sleep well. We have a big day tomorrow. I think you will find that bed very firm and comfortable. I know I have enjoyed it. Anyway, I hate to leave but I know you are tired and we will be up early tomorrow. I will have the desk clerk wake you around seven to get ready. I have some business to do first thing in the morning with the Army and then we will head back to my father's estate."

Sandra stood on her tippy toes and kissed Gillis one more time before spinning around and saying, "I love you, Gillis McCabe," as she gently closed the door.

Gillis practically floated back to his new room one floor below, his heart and mind full of a love that he thought he had lost. How great the next day would be traveling back to his father's ranch and hopefully finding answers to where he had gone. As the fireworks continued outside, Gillis slipped out of his clothes and into bed and was almost immediately asleep.

A loud pounding on the door woke Gillis from a deep sleep as he jumped from his bed and scrambled to put on his pants. A voice came from the other side of the door. "Mr. McCabe, please come quickly! Mr. Wright has had a terrible accident."

Chapter 19

Gillis grabbed his shirt and with one arm in the sleeve he tore through the doorway opening and headed toward the stairs. With speed he didn't know he possessed, he took two stairs at a time as he flew up to the landing and then to the floor above. Four people stood gathered in front of Luke's open door and they were all talking excitingly. Gillis pushed his way through the small group and into the room. There on the floor with his eyes staring at the ceiling was Luke lying in a pool of blood.

An overweight man in a top hat was talking loudly and Gillis could hear his voice but his words seemed blurred as he stared at Luke. "I woke up early this morning for a meeting and that's when I heard something dripping in the middle of the room. I walked over and saw an area the size of a frying pan with blood on it. It was dripping through the floor boards from the room above. Of course that is when I hollered for the manager."

Gillis looked at Luke, his face pale from blood loss. Slowly he rolled him over. Unfortunately, he anticipated what he would see next, a small perfectly round hole. The wound looked similar to the wound of the dead man they had found on the trail and others they had since encountered. Gillis rose to his feet, forcing his way back through the growing crowd and headed at a full run for Sandra's room. He frantically knocked on the door for several seconds before reaching for the crystal knob. To his surprise the door wasn't locked and turned easily in his hand as he shoved it open.

"Sandra, are you okay?" screamed Gillis.

The room was torn apart as if a struggle had occurred and Gillis dropped to his knees in desperation. Both chairs that had been against the table lay scattered on the floor. Sandra had put up quite the fight but why didn't anyone hear the noise? Instantly he then thought of the boys playing with the fireworks and threw on his shirt as he headed downstairs.

Continuously he hit the bell on the counter as if he could make it louder with each hit. The manager came running down the stairs. "What, what, what is it?" cried the man in an angry voice.

"Those children last night that were outside shooting off fireworks, do you know any of them?"

"Yes, a couple. One of them lives a few houses down in the second alley. Nice young man, Jerome is his name but why do you want to know where he lives? The young man is harmless."

"If I am correct, that fireworks display was used to disguise any sounds from the murder and kidnapping. Now what does the house look like?"

"It's more like a boarding house. He and his mother live there with a couple other children. The father died in an accident last year and they have had it tough ever since. I think their room number is four, if I remember correctly."

Gillis kept telling himself not to panic and stay focused. He grabbed a sheet of paper from the counter and started writing as the manager watched. "Look, this is very important. I need you to get this over to the police right now. Then, I need you to have one of your boys take this note to Major Cates—he will understand the meaning of it. Tell your boy he can find Major Cates at 320 West Chanticleer Street, Office 305. Have the major meet me at the corner of Gilmore and Birch. Tell him to bring men." Gillis handed the man the note and began to turn and whipped back around.

"I also need a horse and I need it now!" He spun around and headed back upstairs to the group of people that continued to gawk and discuss the body.

"Did anyone see anything last night that could be a clue as to who might have done this?" asked Gillis in pleading voice. Most people just shook their heads as several looked down to avoid making eye contact. "Please, someone must have seen something."

There was a pause of silence before a boy of about twelve stepped forward. "Last night late I was headed to the privy and I saw a couple of men. One was helping a real sick woman down the hall and the other man came out of one of these rooms. I think it was this one." He pointed to the open door where Luke lay dead. "I don't know if he was the murderer or not and I never saw his face."

Gillis squatted down to eye level with the boy. "Son, do you remember what he was wearing?"

"Yeah, they were real nice fancy clothes and he wore a long black jacket. It could have even been a rain coat but it was real black."

"Was he wearing a hat?"

"Yeah, it looked like the hat that man's wearing." The boy pointed to a heavy bearded man wearing a derby hat. "Like that one except darker. The man never saw me and he never turned around."

"Do you remember anything else?"

"I'm not sure." He hesitated for a moment. "Oh yeah, he wore gloves but one of his hands looked funny like it was fatter than it should be."

"Which hand looked funny, the right or the left?"

The boy hesitated for a moment and then turned and faced the opposite direction. "His left."

"Are you sure?"

"Yeah I'm sure, it was his left."

"Did you see where they took the sick woman?"

"Only that they took her down the back stairs. I had to go real bad so I went down the front stairs."

"Okay thanks," said Gillis, as he turned and hurried to his room to get his coat. He figured the police would be there in twenty to twenty-five minutes. He would need to leave and find a mount or carriage to meet Major Cates and his men to show them the alley and the secret door. Grabbing his coat, he raced down the stairs and took a right at the bottom. It only took minutes to find the run-down boarding house before knocking on the dilapidated door with a hand-painted number four. After several rounds of knocking, a small girl cracked the door.

"Do you have a brother named Jerome?" asked Gillis in the calmest voice he could muster.

The girl turned and hollered back into the room, "Jerome, there is a gentleman here to see you—you in trouble again?"

It seemed like an unreasonable amount of time before a young man, probably in his teens, stepped into sight. He was skinny and dirty and didn't look comfortable. "Mister, I didn't do anything, nothing, honest."

"I'm not accusing you of anything. I do have a question though. It's my understanding that you and some of your friends shot off fireworks in front of the hotel last night. Jerome, you're not in trouble for that, all I need to know is if someone paid you to do it."

"Yeah, but how did you know he paid us?"

Gillis paused for a moment. "There was a crime committed in the hotel last night and I believe the noise from the fireworks was meant to disguise the sounds created by the crime."

"I didn't know, mister. Some man gave us two big boxes of fireworks and a dollar to light them all off over a couple of hours. He said to have fun, that he wanted a little light show in the street to celebrate. We didn't know any crime was being committed, honest mister, we didn't."

"I believe you, Jerome. I don't think you or your friends had any clue you were helping a crime be committed. You could help me though. Can you remember what the man looked like and what he wore?"

"He had a thick mustache that curled a bit at the ends and he wore a derby hat, well-dressed man he was."

"What was he wearing?"

"Some kind of jacket, long and black."

"Like a rain slicker?"

"Could have been, but it was a fancy one. He looked like he had money, real well-dressed. I remember a couple more things too—he had a square jaw and his hand looked funny."

"When you say funny what do you mean?"

"It just looked funny, unnatural like. It almost looked like he had something besides his hand stuck in his glove, maybe his hand was deformed or something, I don't know."

"Can you think of anything else?"

"Well, he had a nice smile."

"He smiled at you?"

"Yes sir, he did."

"I really appreciate your straight answers, young man," Gillis said as he reached into his pocket and pulled out a silver dollar. "Keep this and if you remember anything else come see me at the hotel. There will be another just like this one and remember my name, Gillis McCabe." Gillis took one step and stopped. "The hand, the hand that didn't look right, was it his left or right?"

The young man thought for a moment. "It was the left, sir, I am sure it was the left. Thanks for the dollar, mister. I will keep my eyes open and tell my friends to do the same."

Gillis headed back to the hotel. It tore him up inside to think of Sandra in the hands of killers and what they might do to her. He was angry, angrier than he had ever been. In the matter of one night he had lost two people he really cared for. He had grown to like and respect Luke and most of all he considered him a friend. He thought he had lost Sandra, his first and only love. She had come back to him only to be kidnapped and held who knows where. As he walked toward the lobby he could hardly believe that somehow they were both gone.

Walking up to the desk, Gillis saw several policemen with their bell-shaped hats and large badges standing there, talking to the clerk. "Are you Mr. McCabe?" asked the guard with a straight mustache and beard, who seemed to appear out of nowhere. The man's dark blue uniform smelled of sweat and its tightness fought with every move he made.

"Yes, I am. Luke Wright worked for me and Sandra Richards was soon to be my wife. Thank you for getting here so quickly."

"We were only a block away when this young man came charging over and said there had been a murder in the hotel."

Just then the manager walked up, "Excuse me, Mr. McCabe. We have that horse you wanted. It is saddled and ready in front. The man we rented her from lives behind the hotel and was about to take her on a ride himself when we arrived. She is the big, stout gray mare tied to the hitching rail to your right under that big oak tree. The man that was saddling her is a good three inches taller than you so you might want to adjust the stirrups."

Gillis was frustrated by the man's wordiness. "Thanks. I will be back as soon as I can. I need to meet with the Army investigators."

One of the policemen was walking briskly towards Gillis as he stood at the counter.

"Hold on, sir, you aren't going anywhere until my partner and I thoroughly question you. Then we are going to sit here and wait until the lieutenant shows up. He will get to the bottom of this."

"You don't understand. They kidnapped my fiancée and I think I know where they are holding her. I have to meet the Army to show them the access point for the entrance to a secret tunnel. I believe this is the same group that has been assassinating people here in Washington for the past three years, and if so, the group holding her might kill her."

"Calm down, a secret tunnel system you say? I am sure the lieutenant will want to hear all about it but for now you are going to sit right here and talk to us." He reached inside his jacket and retrieved a pencil and a small pad. "Your name, please?"

"Damn it, my friend is lying dead upstairs and my fiancée's room has been torn to pieces and she has been kidnapped and you want me to calm down? You don't get it, this gang of assassins might kill her any moment if I don't show the Army where this tunnel entrance is," screamed Gillis.

"Calm down, calm down, sir. Don't worry this shouldn't take more than an hour. They have already sent for the lieutenant. I am sure he will help you and the Army will find this kidnapped fiancée of yours. What did you say her name was?"

"I said her name is Sandra Richards. Please, I have to go show the Army where the entrance to this tunnel is and I need to do it now!" Gillis pulled the copper medallion from his pocket. "See this, it's some type of key or something but it opens the tunnel door and I believe I can lead the Army right to where she is being held."

"I'm sure you can but if we let you go before the lieutenant gets here, he will have our hide. I'm sorry, but I am sure no one will hurt her until you get there."

"For God's sake, man, let me go meet the Army. Can't you understand that they kill people?"

"If you don't settle down I may have to put my handcuffs on you, so sit down and quietly wait until the lieutenant gets here. I don't want you to say another word about the Army or some secret entrance to any tunnel." The older police officer began pulling his handcuffs from his belt when Gillis's anger got the best of him. He stood and in one quick action threw the table into the sergeant's body, knocking him backwards to the floor. The hotel chair he was sitting on broke on impact adding to the force as Gillis jumped to his feet. The other officer reached for his nightstick.

Gillis moved toward him and with all his might swung his fist into the man's nose, dropping him to the floor beside the stunned sergeant. He turned and ran to the front door as the two men lay moaning and trying to stand. Flinging open the door of the hotel, he saw the stout gelding standing under the oak tree and began running toward it. He flew down the hotel's stairs, untied the horse, and with one hop launched himself into the saddle. Pulling hard on the right rein he soon had the horse charging down the street at a full gallop with the sound of metal on the cobblestones echoing between buildings. Gillis had no idea of how much time had actually elapsed. He hoped he could make it to the corner before Major Cates and his men got tired of waiting and left.

Gillis's mind was racing with what to do next. He knew that so far the street had been a straight shot but soon he would need to turn and he pulled back on the reins to slow the horse. The metal shoes would have little traction on the turns and the last thing he needed was the horse to lose its footing. Five minutes later he took the final turn that would lead to the corner and the alley. He could see at least eight soldiers mulling around as he yanked back the reins and slid to a stop.

Gillis jumped from the saddle and ran up to Major Cates. The major stood by his horse with his hands on his waist and a scowl on his face.

"Thank God you are here. They kidnapped my fiancée from the hotel," said Gillis in a loud voice.

"Why wouldn't we be here? You said you knew where this den of assassins was operating from," said the major in a condescending voice.

"Major, if you give me a chance I can clear everything up. We need to go over to the alley and I will show you," said Gillis as he pointed to the opening. "I figured out how they could murder someone and then disappear minutes later. Follow me and I will show you, I swear!"

"Mr. McCabe, for some reason I have never liked you. For your sake, I hope this is what you say it is."

The major and his men followed Gillis to the opening and started walking down the dead-end alley. Gillis stopped at the base of the brick and looked up. "There, see that, the charcoal colored brick, it's the only brick of that color in the whole alley." Gillis reached into his pocket and pulled out the medallion. "See how this old rusted light fixture is missing a rivet. It's how they open the door to the tunnel that leads under the city." Gillis took the medallion and pushed it into the discreet opening like he had done earlier but this time it wouldn't go in all the way and there was no click.

"I don't understand," said Gillis as he looked again to make sure the charcoal brick was still there. Once more he stuck the key into the rivet hole of the fixture but again there was nothing. "Major, you have to believe me. This is a well-designed door made of brick and metal and hung on huge swivels. I even went down into the tunnels and could hear people talking."

"If what you say is true then why didn't you immediately contact me?"

"It is a bit of a long story. I didn't contact you because I thought I had enough time to finally take my fiancée out on the town. They must have seen me find this door and blocked it from opening. I swear to you it opened yesterday and there is a stairway that leads to a network of tunnels."

The major looked at Gillis and then back at his troops. "Corporal, is this the man that introduced himself to you and used the name James Brink?"

"Yes sir, it is."

"Thank you, corporal, that will be all," said Major Cates as he turned and faced Gillis.

"Mr. McCabe, your story is more than far-fetched that these murderers vanished underground through solid walls, not to mention the number of names you go by. Assuming Gillis McCabe is your real name, why should I believe you?"

"Because if you don't those men may kill my fiancée."

"Mr. McCabe, I think we have wasted enough of our time here today. I know what I should do to—" The major's words were interrupted by Gillis.

"Get me a sledge hammer—the door can't be very thick, we can just break it down. Obviously they knew we were coming and sabotaged the opening mechanism," said Gillis as he slipped the medallion back into his pocket.

"I say not," said the major. "Do you really expect me to tear down the wall of a business on the word of a crackpot like you? If you weren't so well connected I would have thrown you in jail long ago for meddling in Army affairs. Maybe now you will finally—"

The hit from the tackle sent Gillis to the ground with a thud. Two policemen in their navy blue uniforms started punching Gillis as he lay dazed on the ground.

The major threw up his hand and hollered at the two policemen. "That will be quite enough. What is the meaning of this?"

"This man punched two police officers and then escaped from a murder and a possible kidnapping scene."

"Pick him up and put your handcuffs on him but that will be enough of the beatings. Mr. McCabe here says his fiancée was kidnapped. Can you back up any of his story, any at all?"

The heavier of the two men was still breathing hard as he spoke. "Yes sir, it appears that a man was killed at the Brinkmoore Hotel last night and there may have been a kidnapping too."

Just then an enclosed wagon pulled up with a large star on the side. The driver yelled out, "Is this the place that needs a paddy wagon?"

Gillis charged at the major, screaming, "You can't let them take me away. They will kill my fiancée and it will be your stupid fault for not listening. Please, I am begging you. Let me go and help me." Gillis now had three policemen fighting to keep him under control as they dragged him toward the paddy wagon that stood at the entrance to the alley.

"This guy has to be crazy the way he is fighting," said one of the policemen as he pulled out his night stick. Gillis never saw the blow as everything went black. He fell to the ground and the policemen began to drag his limp body toward the paddy wagon.

Chapter 20

The three men lifted the limp body of Gillis onto the wooden floor of the paddy wagon while a stream of blood ran from his head and another from his mouth. Another prisoner of middle-age with a rough look sat in the front of the wagon chained to the wall. He quietly watched the whole affair and as they slammed the cell door of the paddy wagon. He yelled to the policemen. "You might want to do something for this man! He is bleeding badly. If you don't do something he may die."

One of the other policemen that had helped drag Gillis to the cage paused for a minute as he looked at Gillis's bloody head. "He may be right, this guy is seriously bleeding and he may die before we get there. Didn't someone at the hotel say this guy was kind of important?"

"Yeah, I heard that too," said another one of the men, reaching for a handkerchief from his pocket. "You there." He pointed to the man sitting in the front of the wagon. "Reach over there and if you can, put this handkerchief on that wound and keep it there until it stops bleeding. If you know what's good for you he better not die, do you understand me?" The man nodded and pulled Gillis close enough that he could reach his head. It was difficult but he held the handkerchief tightly against the wound as the wagon lunged forward.

"Should we take him to the hospital before we take him to jail? We wouldn't want the lieutenant all mad."

"I don't think so, head wounds always bleed a lot," said the other guard. "Serves him right for fighting us but we have to go by the hospital anyway. Once we're close let's take a look and determine if we should stop or not."

Just then the lieutenant rode up on a short chestnut horse and glanced through the bars of the door. "What in the hell happened to this prisoner? Are you trying to kill him before I can question him? Take him to the hospital immediately," said the lieutenant in a cold, firm tone. "You better hope for your sake that this man doesn't die. I need some serious answers and I won't get any if he is dead. There is a real possibility that he was nothing more than an innocent bystander in this whole affair. You knocked him senseless. If you have killed another blameless bystander, I will see you men thrown out of the police force, do you understand me?"

A chorus of "Yes, sir" rang out from the men as they grumbled to themselves. The driver gave a quick flip of the reins and hollered "Yah" sending the horse into a trot.

Less than ten minutes later the paddy wagon pulled to a stop in front of the small hospital and the lieutenant directed his horse over to a hitching rail and dismounted. "You men get him out of there, carefully. Private Yates, go inside and see if you can find a stretcher. God knows you have abused him enough today."

With great care the police officers moved the prisoner into the hospital and onto an examining table. After a short wait a man dressed in a white coat entered the room.

"This man took a hell of a blow to the head. What happened?"

"He was resisting arrest, sir."

The doctor looked at the three policemen and the lieutenant for a moment and shook his head. "Three men couldn't subdue this slightly built man without nearly killing him? You should be real proud of yourselves."

"He put up a whale of a fight, sir."

The lieutenant looked at the three men with an angry face before speaking. "What do you think, doc, does he need admitting or just stitches?"

"Oh, he's in bad shape all right. He could still die from these wounds. He needs hospital care immediately. I won't know more for a while. In the meantime I need to clean and stitch his wounds." A tall nurse with brown hair tied in the back entered the room and immediately started helping.

"Yates, I want you to stand guard outside the door while the prisoner is in here. Have Stewart stand guard in the courtyard in case he has friends. Corporal Benson, I want you to come back to the station. I can't wait to read your report why three police officers needed to beat this little man near death to stop him. Do all of you understand me?"

"Yes sir," said the three men as they moved through the door and into the hallway of the hospital.

The lieutenant looked at the bloody head of Gillis and then at the doctor. "I understand this man is in really bad shape. I apologize for my men's overzealous restraint of him, but if you break the law bad things happen."

"I could certainly see why you came to that conclusion. You are lucky we aren't dealing with a corpse instead of a half-dead man."

"My apologies again but he was fleeing from police."

"What is he charged with?"

"Nothing at this point but he did flee a murder scene and in my experience that usually is a sign of guilt."

"Well, he won't be fleeing anywhere soon. I hope he wakes up at some point and remembers who he is," said the physician with a lingering disgust in his voice. The man turned his back to the lieutenant and began going through instruments on a tray. The lieutenant stood there for a moment, then turned and walked out.

In a woozy haze Gillis partially opened his eyes and could make out a room. He vaguely remembered hearing two men arguing about taking something from his clothing when they were interrupted by a firm woman's voice threatening them and ordering them to get out. Then he lapsed back into his silent, black world.

Gillis slowly opened his eyes trying to focus. His head felt like it would explode. The pounding was terrible as he tried to make sense of the environment around him. The room's walls were covered in faded white wallpaper and the windows were covered by grayish drapes that blocked what little light tried to enter the room.

Gillis slowly scanned the place. No one seemed to be around as he tried to focus his eyes and absorb every detail of the small room. He could see a pile of clothes neatly folded on a darkened oak dresser in the corner. The room had a sterile appearance and he couldn't remember how he got there. His head throbbed with every movement as he carefully put his hand up and touched his head. He could feel a soft linen bandage and slightly pushed on it. He pulled his hand away and saw a spot of blood on his finger. "No wonder that hurt," he said quietly to himself.

As much as he tried he couldn't remember anything about how he had gotten to this place but his thoughts were interrupted by a quiet knock on the door. The door slowly opened in the direction of his bed, blocking his view until the person had cleared the threshold. A woman appeared. She was an attractive, tall woman dressed in a white nurse's uniform. Her face showed an expression of surprise as she spoke. "So, you finally woke up did you?"

"How long have I been asleep?"

"You are going on a little more than two days now. To tell you the truth, I was wondering if you would ever wake up."

"What happened?"

"I am sorry to say the police got a little carried away with their night sticks. According to them you fought like a mad man. They said you beat up two officers over at the Brinkmoore. But for some reason you don't look the violent type to me."

"I'm not, it's just that I needed to—" Gillis stopped in mid-sentence.

"What did you need to do?" The nurse looked at him intently.

Gillis looked lost for a moment, his head throbbed, and he felt confused. "I needed to save Sandra."

"Who's Sandra?"

"My fiancée, they took her."

"Who took your fiancée?" she asked with a look of concern.

"I am not positive but I think it was the group that is behind all the murders and assassinations that have been happening throughout the city. I came to Washington looking for my father and somehow got myself mixed up in these murders. Now I believe they are also after me." Gillis groaned. "Might you have anything for this headache?"

A half smile came to the nurse's face. "Yes, the doctor left me some willow bark tea if you woke up. Here, take a drink from this cup. There is water in this pitcher beside your bed." The lady walked around to the far edge of bed where a blue and white porcelain pitcher sat. She reached down and with two hands picked up the pitcher and poured Gillis a glass of water. "They always fill these pitchers too full, gives them an excuse to not have to fill them very often. Anyway, drink this. I am sure you are a bit dehydrated. Have you tried to use the chamber pot? Or, if you would like, I could see if one of the policemen could walk you to the privy."

"There are policemen guarding my door?"

"And the window, apparently the sergeant you struck is in pretty bad shape and police are none too happy."

"I didn't mean to hurt him. For some reason I don't remember the whole thing, only bits and pieces. But to answer your question I would prefer that one of the policemen walk me to the privy." In the back of Gillis's mind he wanted to see the outside of this place and what was happening around him. Guards outside the window and door weren't a good sign that he would see freedom in the near future.

The nurse interrupted his thoughts. "If you're not dizzy and feel like putting on your clothes they are on the dresser. As soon as you are comfortable, open the door to the hallway. I will be outside talking to the guard and taking care of some cleanup."

Gillis carefully stood, steadying himself against the bed. He felt wobbly and sick to his stomach as he carefully walked across the room to where his clothes were stacked. They were neatly folded and with the exception of his derringer everything seemed to be there. He even felt the padded pockets skillfully sewn into the back of the jacket and the slight bulge they produced, a bulge created by a stack of fifty dollar bills.

It took almost ten minutes for Gillis to get dressed but finally he knocked on the door. With one hand he steadied himself as he turned the crystal knob of the door and ventured into the hallway. In front of him stood the nurse and an armed guard holding a shotgun draped over one arm. Gillis staggered for a moment and almost fell before the guard reached out with his free hand and grabbed him.

"Easy there, fellow," said the guard. "Let's head back into your room and get the chamber pot if you feel that dizzy."

"No, I want to go to the privy," he said firmly. To his surprise the guard actually seemed to care if walking down the hall was comfortable or not. The two shuffled out the back door as the nurse stood behind and watched. The back of the hospital was mainly dirt with a couple of red oaks shading three wooden outhouses that stood in a row. When Gillis was done the guard helped him out of the small cramped building by firmly holding his arm. Carefully, he led Gillis back to his room and the waiting nurse.

"You feel better now?"

Gillis only smiled in response before sitting down on the bed. "Looks like I got myself into a lot of trouble. My rash decisions may cost my future wife her life."

"What do you mean?"

"My hired man was a friend and they killed him in the hotel and kidnapped my fiancée. I panicked when the police wouldn't let me go and meet the Army. I needed to show them the secret door where they took her. The door leads to a series of underground tunnels. If I am correct, I believe they are part of some type of abandoned water system."

"You do realize how your story sounds?"

"Nothing about this whole thing makes good sense. If only I could find my father and—" Gillis stopped and looked at the nurse. "This doesn't sound very plausible does it?"

"It does sound a bit far-fetched but you were struck pretty hard on the head and you seem to believe what you are saying. I don't know what to believe but it doesn't really matter."

"It matters to me!" shouted Gillis.

The nurse looked at Gillis. "Anyways, now that you are awake they will probably be moving you to the jail tomorrow. They hit you pretty hard. The truth is most people didn't believe you would live through the first night. You have nine stitches but hopefully the jail will have someone there to change your bandages."

Gillis was groggy but he needed to know. "Do you believe my story?"

"I only work here. Almost every man they drag into the criminal ward says they aren't guilty of whatever they are being charged with. It isn't my job to believe or not believe you. It's my job to get you better and take care of you while you are here. But for whatever it may matter, I do believe you."

Gillis limped over to the window and pulled the curtain back. There, ten yards away, under a large maple, sat a guard with his rifle lying on his lap. He looked asleep until he swatted at a fly. Gillis let the curtain fall back in place as he turned to the nurse. "So you think they may be transferring me tomorrow?"

"That's what the guard said. As soon as you are up and about they are going to move you to the main jail downtown."

"Is the main jail over on Jefferson Street?"

"So you have stayed there before?"

"No, but I remember passing it when I took a tour of the city a few years back. It's a big white two-story building with a statue of a lion in front."

"Your memory serves you well, that's it."

"Would it be possible for you to get a message to a friend of mine? He's in the war department. His name is Colonel Dougell and I believe he might be able to help me explain this." Gillis reached into his pocket and to his surprise felt several silver dollars that still remained in his pants. At least the policemen were honest enough not to take his money or they didn't find it he thought, as he tried to hand the nurse one of the dollars. A vague memory came shooting back to Gillis. "You stopped them—you stopped the police from taking my stuff."

"They have no right stealing a man's possessions even if you are a prisoner. Keep your dollar until I find out if there is someone willing to deliver your message."

"Do you have someone in mind?" asked Gillis.

"I know one of the boys that work in the kitchen. He would be happy to make that type of money delivering a letter. He should be getting off work in a few minutes and I will give it to him. Quickly write down your message I will try and catch him before he leaves. There's paper and a pen in that drawer," she said as she pointed to the small table that held the water pitcher. "Be quick. I need to visit one of the other patients but I'll be right back."

Gillis sat down and immediately began writing his letter, trying to quickly explain his dilemma to the colonel. Several minutes later a quiet knock came from the door as the nurse entered the room. "He's waiting out back," she said. "I caught him as he was leaving. He said he would be happy to deliver your message."

Gillis handed her the letter and then dug into his pocket and gave her one of the silver dollars.

"He will appreciate the money. The kid's family is having a hard time with his dad going to war and all. Do you want him to wait for a reply?"

"Yes please, I am sure there will be one."

The nurse took the letter and closed the door behind her as she left. Gillis could hear her saying something to the guard but the words weren't clear. The willow tea and a cup of whiskey had made his head feel better and now he was very sleepy. He sat on the bed and undressed. He was exhausted from the day's events and fell immediately into a deep sleep.

The knock on the door awakened Gillis. He had slept hard and he struggled to figure out where he was. A voice that he recognized as that of the nurse was announcing dinner as she opened the door. "Ready for a little dinner?" she asked, setting the plate of hot food in front of the pitcher beside his bed. "I hope you are feeling better."

Gillis struggled to wake up and finally sat up on the firm metal bed.

"You seem to be doing better. You may have problems with your memory for a while but I am sure they will give you some rest and time to recoup before your trial."

Gillis couldn't make sense of the whole thing. The only reason he hit the two policemen was that they were stopping him from saving the only true love his life had ever known. "Thank you. A solid meal will taste good. I appreciate all you have done for me," said Gillis as he took the plate and balanced it in his lap and began eating.

"I will be back in a couple of hours. I have a number of things I need to do before I go home but I will look in on you before I go."

"I appreciate that, and hope your other patients will be easier to deal with."

The nurse smiled and closed the door. Gillis was hungry and quickly ate. When he finished he stood and carefully walked about the room for several minutes trying to regain his balance. It was difficult and his head ached but he was slowly getting better and his memory was coming back. On his third pass around the room he stopped at the window and slid back the curtain to look at the guard. It was getting dark but a small gas lantern in the courtyard cast enough light on the guard that Gillis could see him quite well. The guard was quietly sitting in the same chair as before but now something wasn't quite right—the guard's arm seem to dangle unnaturally on one side. Gillis watched the man for several minutes and he didn't move. Could he be asleep? His gut feeling was that there was something wrong, very wrong.

He walked to the door of his room and slowly turned the knob and opened it. The guard he had heard earlier talking to his nurse was not at his post. Now Gillis knew something was wrong, he could feel it in his bones.

He heard a door begin to open down the hall so he closed his door quietly and climbed back into the bed. Moments later he heard footsteps coming closer. They were heavier than the nurse's and he knew it wasn't her. It seemed like forever before he noticed the crystal knob turning. As quick as he could he stretched his arms out to both sides of the bed, closed his eyes and pretended to be asleep. He kept his eyes nearly closed to allow a small slit of clouded view.

The fuzzy figure dressed in black seemed to be carrying a doctor's bag and Gillis could see from the outline that he also wore a derby hat. The stranger turned and faced the bed without speaking a word. Gillis suspected that the man would not turn up the two small gas lanterns on either side of the room like a normal doctor doing their rounds. The dark figure stood over the bed as Gillis struggled to breathe naturally knowing that whoever stood in front of him probably intended to kill him. Slowly, the stranger leaned over and began lowering his left hand toward Gillis's head.

Gillis had turned the handle of the pitcher of water so it almost touched his extended hand. In one quick motion he grabbed the half-full pitcher and with all his might slammed it into the startled man's head. The man stumbled backwards. Water, blood, and chunks of white porcelain showered the floor as the man fell backwards, grabbing his head as Gillis staggered to his feet. The quick movements made his head scream with pain but he knew it was his only chance to escape.

Gillis could see the man on the floor was still moving slightly and he knew he didn't have the strength to fight him. His only hope was to make a run for it. He grabbed his boots and clothes and in his nightgown, stumbled into the hall. Gillis used the wall stabilize himself as he moved down the hall towards the exit door. In the shadows he saw the guard sitting unnaturally against a wall. His eyes were wide open with a look of surprise while a small stream of blood slowly oozed from his forehead.

Opening the door, Gillis staggered into the cool evening air and then stopped to look in both directions. In the shadows a single charcoal-gray horse stood tied. He tried to walk as fast as possible toward the animal hoping he wouldn't stumble and spook the horse. He slipped for a moment and the horse's eyes became huge at the appearance of a stumbling man in a drafty night shirt. Gillis began talking softly as he closed the distance. The closer he got, the more the horse seemed to recognize that he was a man and began to calm. Gillis slowly reached for the tied reins and carefully untied them. A sudden movement by a stranger in the dark might cause the horse to rear back and break away. His bare feet hurt from stepping on unseen objects but he knew better than to stop.

Struggling, with great effort he mounted. With his clothes and boots in one hand and the reins in the other he turned the horse away from the hitching rail. Suddenly he heard the crash of a door being slammed open. Gillis never looked back as he kicked the horse's sides with his bare heels while pulling one rein to the side. Within seconds the horse was at a full gallop as Gillis fought to hold onto his clothes and boots and keep them from falling.

He rode for several blocks before taking a right turn and heading into the darker section of town where few gas street lights burned. From the bottom of his soul he knew the man that had tried to kill him wouldn't give up, no matter the cost. He turned the horse onto a dirt street where the sound of metal horseshoes on the cobbles wouldn't be heard. As he rode he noticed a large barn sitting back off the road in an area that was pitch black. He steered the horse up beside the barn and slid out of the saddle. Carefully, he held the reins in one hand as he put his clothes on with the other. He was dizzy and stopped several times to gather his balance. Putting on the last boot, he took a deep breath of satisfaction that he had cheated death.

As he was burying his nightshirt under a pile of leaves, he heard the sound of trotting horses coming down the street. Gillis reached up and held the horse's muzzle to stop it from whinnying as two riders passed by. All he could see was the men's outlines and there was no way to know if they were part of the group of assassins. Never had he felt so alone. Right now Gillis didn't feel like he had a friend in the world. If he was to survive, he needed one. He walked the horse into the barn and tied him securely to a post. Sitting down in a pile of hay, he covered himself as much to keep warm as to be able to keep an eye open toward the door. He worked his tired body deep into the hay until only his head showed as he lay quietly listening.

Gillis woke with a jerk. He didn't know what woke him but he knew he had fallen asleep and for how long he didn't know. Shivering as he walked to the barn door, Gillis rubbed his arms as he stared out at the starry sky. He couldn't tell what time it was but he knew it was late into the night. For the next two hours he sat quietly waiting until the moon began to set in the west and the brilliance of the stars began to fade. With great difficulty he tried to stand. He was shaky and grabbed one of the stall boards for balance.

When he could walk, he moved to untie the silent gelding that munched on the hay his reins allowed him to reach. After untying the horse, he slowly led him back onto the dirt street. The first rays of the sun were beginning to light the night sky as Gillis shivered. His shirt was still damp and the lightweight jacket he wore did little to warm him. He felt better and despite his head protesting every movement, he decided it was time to move, but to where he didn't know.

He pulled back on the reins to make sure the horse stood quietly as he reached up and grabbed the saddle's horn. Gone was the original adrenaline that had allowed him to mount the horse in one try. Now he struggled to pull himself up into the saddle and at one point his foot came out of the stirrup and he almost fell. It wasn't pretty but eventually he straightened up in the saddle and gave the horse a little nudge with his boot. It was a powerful animal, well trained, with a smooth stride. He would head west out of town toward his father's farm, and try and figure out a plan later.

He had ridden for about twenty minutes and was struggling to stay upright. At times he looked for landmarks but in the dim light of early morning he couldn't remember anything and nothing looked familiar. As he rode flashes of Sandra screaming and begging for his help kept coming into his thoughts.

Up ahead he could see something familiar, the Long Bridge. He knew it spanned the Potomac River separating Alexandria from Washington. That at least verified he was headed in the right direction. He was still riding in the shadows when he noticed the three riders sitting on their horses at the edge of the bridge and he knew they had to be waiting for him. Gillis pulled back on the reins and melted further into the darkest shadows he could find. In front of him, it became more open between the buildings and there was no chance to go much further unnoticed.

He dismounted and used buildings and shrubbery to silently move to one side to get a better look. The men looked tough, not the type to be out on an early morning social ride. Down the street he heard the sound of hooves hitting the cobblestones and turned quickly. Coming up the gentle grade was a troop of soldiers and they were headed toward the bridge.

Immediately, he knew he had to react as the officer leading them rode closer. Gillis hurriedly mounted his horse and kicked him hard with his heels. The horse shot out into the street at a full gallop headed for the officer leading the group.

"Spies, Confederate spies by the bridge," he yelled as he rode toward them. "They are counting troops." The men on the bridge heard the yell and seemed to panic as they turned and began riding away from the bridge at a trot and then quickly into a full run.

The officer's quick reaction sent his men charging forward after the three fleeing men. The soldiers rapidly disappeared in their pursuit leaving Gillis sitting on his horse. With his horse's hooves echoing a thick hollow sound he rode across the bridge and into Alexandria. At a full run he turned his horse and got off the main road as the sun began to rise. He slowed to a trot and rode for ten minutes on the back streets. Unsure of his location, he finally pulled the reins back and stopped.

For a moment his mind seemed to clear and there in front of him was a familiar building with a white picket fence. He thought his mind must be playing tricks on him. There in the yard on the same old bench smoking a pipe and watching the sunrise, was the old man he knew as Sam.

Chapter 21

Gillis nudged the horse toward the hitching rail in front of the fence. With great effort he slid from his horse while holding firmly to the saddle horn. He was very dizzy and his legs were shaky as he walked toward Sam. He wasn't sure what he intended to say, but he knew he couldn't ride much further and needed help. Just before he reached the bench everything went black and he fell hard to the ground.

Gillis awoke in a clean bed and he struggled to see two blurry people in the room with him. As his focus began to come back, Sam spoke. "One of those policemen must have really busted you up, son. It's nice to see you awake—we were worried."

Gillis struggled to sit up as Sam turned to the other man. "You remember Detective Fritz, my son-in-law don't you?"

Gillis nodded. "How long have I been here?"

"You rode your horse in here in the wee hours yesterday and you have been asleep pretty much all day and night. It's almost ten in the morning—you must be hungry. Let's get you fed and then maybe you can tell us what is going on and Logan can tell you what he's learned."

"The horse I rode in on?"

"He's fine. We have him stalled in the barn. Other than me and the boy that helps me, no one really goes back there anymore since they changed this into a boarding house."

Sam lit his pipe and settled into a chair. "We heard the police were looking for you but you're safe here. You need to eat something and then we will change out those bandages. You are still bleeding a bit. You took a hell of a wallop to the head but whoever did the stitching did a fine job."

"I'm not sure if it was the doctor or his nurse. The nurse was good. I hope she is still alive. I think she saved my life."

"What do you mean?"

"I was in the hospital for a couple of days and this nurse was caring

200

for me. There was a guard outside my window and one at the door. When I woke up she was the one that helped me with my bandages. I never saw a doctor until the last night and I knew he wasn't a real doctor. For some reason, I woke up and moved around the room and when I stopped at the window I cracked the curtains and glanced at the guard and he looked dead. I knew they were after me, so I made my escape."

"Do you think it was the same man that has been killing people around here?"

"Well, whoever it was certainly used the same type of weapon on that guard that I saw used before."

Logan listened intently from a chair a few feet away and then stood. "Let's get you something to eat and while you eat we can talk more while I change those bandages."

After some breakfast and two cups of coffee, Logan replaced the bandages. Gillis tried to tell the rest of story but in places his memory failed. He struggled through the part about the medallion, the dead end alley, and the watery tunnel but they seemed to understand. Finally he looked at both men and said, "They have Sandra and I don't know how to save her."

Sam cleared his throat. "We already heard a lot of what you told us. It's all over the streets. Someone is trying to railroad you. The murder of your friend and the abduction of your fiancée made the papers. Your face was on the front page of this morning's paper. Logan and I have known for quite some time there is an abundance of corruption in the police force and unfortunately, you just experienced some of it. There certainly was no reason for the police to beat you almost to death, especially under those circumstances. We both believe it is part of the bigger picture and that the guard who hit you may have intentionally tried to kill you."

Gillis stared at Sam. "You really believe he meant to kill me?"

"We have little doubt. It would have been written up as you assaulting a police officer and the whole thing would in a short time have been swept under the rug."

"Why would they want me dead?"

"You figure things out quicker than any man I have ever met. It probably threatened them. They must have decided you were becoming too much of a risk."

Detective Fritz walked over beside Gillis's bed with a serious look and moved a chair so he could sit down beside him. "One of the reasons I left the sheriff's office was the corruption. I believe there might be a contract out on your life. If I am right, someone wants you dead and I may have a few more pieces of the puzzle on why."

"Do you believe me about the medallion, the dead end alley, and the secret tunnel?"

"If you aren't telling the truth then you have the best imagination of any man I've ever met. Since the murder of Annabelle, we both knew something wasn't right. We also believe your father is somehow messed up in this and hopefully he isn't on the wrong side of things."

"What about Sandra?"

Logan took a second to answer and then smiled. "Of course we will help. I'm still on your payroll, aren't I?"

Gillis reached up and touched his head while he moaned slightly. "First thing I would like to do is to get my mules back here. If I need to make a fast break for my father's ranch, they will be my best mode of transportation."

"Consider it done. I will go over to the livery stable this afternoon and pick them up. Which stable are they at? I will need a note from you releasing them. Hopefully, the guy doesn't read the newspaper regularly."

"Sam, can you somehow get a carriage? I need to ride by the alley where I found the entrance to the tunnel. I believe that is where they took Sandra. Unfortunately, if I am correct, it is probably guarded by the police. I will need some type of disguise to avoid being recognized."

Sam smiled. "I used to play bit parts at the local theatre. I am sure I still have a fake mustache and a wig or two. As for the carriage, I have one out back and a good horse to pull it."

Thirty minutes later Sam gave the reins a shake and a command to go, as the horse and carriage with Gillis as a passenger headed down the road to the alley. Gillis wore a reddish wig and mustache that from a distance looked real.

Gillis turned to Sam. "I always wondered what it felt like to grow a mustache. Actually, it kind of itches."

It took almost forty-five minutes to cross the river and then reach the cross street before riding past the alley. Sam pulled the reins back until the horse was at a slow walk as they passed the alley entrance. There, sitting on a crate was a guard staring back out into the street. Gillis pulled his head back to remain inconspicuous as Sam smiled and waved. The guard waved back as the two of them continued down the street.

"That was a close one," said Gillis.

"Son, I don't think the guard had a clue that you were here with me. With that wig and all, from a distance you might even pass for a woman."

"Thanks a lot, I will remember that," said Gillis.

"With all you said I really don't believe we will be able to get in there. I hope you have another plan up your sleeve."

"If I am correct this is just one of many entrances into this tunnel. For whatever reason, those tunnels were abandoned and for a group like the Fenians, it would make a perfect hiding place. It would give them an easy way to appear and then disappear after a murder. It was pretty ingenious how they hide their symbols in plain sight. Only their group would know what to look for. That finally explains why they guarded the knowledge of the medallion so fiercely. The medallion was the key to how they disappeared and how they kept their society so secret. Whoever is running this show is smart, very smart indeed."

The carriage shook as they went down a poor section of cobblestone road. "If this is an old sewer or water tunnel, there has to be records of it," said Sam.

"My thoughts exactly, do you know where the utilities department might be? My hope is they still have all the maps of the city's tunnels and their access points."

"I have lived here for over twenty years but I've never heard anyone speak of a major tunnel in this area. This city has grown and changed a lot over the years and they have been building water and sewer tunnels under Washington for at least sixty years, maybe more. I seriously doubt anyone around here would remember the really old tunnels. A number of tunnels were abandoned due to unstable soils, too much water and even quicksand, but I don't remember anything about this one. The new ones seem to be better engineered. The ones that had too many problems were abandoned and it wouldn't be out of the question, forgotten. When we get back, I am sure Logan will know where to find the utility department."

An hour later they steered the carriage around Sam's house and headed to the back of the barn. As they turned the corner of the barn, Gillis saw his four mules and a stout horse tied to a hitching rail and Logan standing beside them.

"You got them. Did you have any trouble?"

"No trouble," said Logan. The neighbor boy helped me. With your note and a small tip, the blacksmith was more than willing to get them out of his stable. From the look of the man, I don't think you need to worry too much about him reading the paper. This can be a big city for someone trying to find a person or for that matter, a mule."

Gillis's face suddenly turned to panic. "The medallion?"

"What about the medallion?" said Sam startled by the outburst.

Gillis jumped to his feet. "The medallion I had in the pocket of my jacket—is it still there?"

"I think I know what you are looking for," said Logan as he picked up Gillis's coat from the chair and handed it to him. "You mean this?" Logan handed the medallion to Gillis. "I heard it hit the chair and took it out and set it aside while you were asleep."

"Thank you, thank you so much. I can't believe the police didn't take it. They must have somehow missed it." Gillis's mind seems to wander as he spoke. "I think the reason they missed it was the nurse. She interrupted them when they were going through my clothes. I woke up for only a moment but I remember her throwing two men out of the room. You could tell she was a lady and felt the need to protect me, even if she saw me as a criminal. I can only hope she wasn't a victim of that killer's attack. I never saw her body. Maybe somehow she got out of there before he arrived. I can only hope and pray that she did."

"Do you know where there is another entrance to the tunnel?"

"No, I don't but unless I am mistaken there are numerous entrances and smaller tunnels that may lead to the main one. If I am going to find Sandra, I need to find an unguarded entrance that will allow me to enter unnoticed."

Logan cleared his throat. "Sam told me earlier what you said about the utility department. I happen to know where the building is located, over close to Droit Park."

"Great. Tomorrow we head to Droit Park."

This time Logan drove the carriage as the disguised Gillis rode as the passenger. They crossed Long Bridge and a little over an hour later, Logan pulled the reins back on the horse and pointed to a dilapidated brick building. "That is where the utilities department calls home. Not much of an office if you ask me."

Gillis looked at Logan. "Do you think they will be able to tell this is a disguise?"

"That's a hard question. There is no lack of strange people walking around Washington and perhaps you might just fit in."

Gillis was worried as he stepped down from the carriage and followed the detective to the over-sized oak door that had white painted letters spelling out Water Department. Logan knocked loudly but no one answered the door. Finally they opened the door and started down a poorly lit, narrow hallway. The ceiling reminded Gillis of the tunnel he had found with a rounded brick arch that went for at least ten yards without a window.

"This isn't much better than coming to work in a mine," said Gillis. Finally, the hall ran into another door with a sign over it that read Office. Again Logan knocked a couple of times and waited before shoving the door inward into a large room with hundreds of pipes fitting stacked in shelves. Even the ceiling was tightly designed with more pipes strapped there. The dimly lit room relied on several high windows and a few kerosene lanterns for light. Dusty maps and piles of books were stacked high on every conceivable surface. Large wooden file cabinets crammed with maps and files stood side by side for at least forty feet against one wall.

"Well, it looks like we came to the right place," said Logan. "Hopefully whoever runs this dump can find what we are looking for in this mess." Just then Gillis heard something and turned to look in one corner where he could see the back of a slender, balding man with white hair and mutton chops.

Gillis walked toward the man. "Excuse me, sir, do you work here?"

The man stared at Gillis as he lowered his wire-rimmed glasses to the end of his nose. "You lost? Why, of course, I work here. Why else would I possibly be down here if it weren't for work?" the man said in a thick German accent.

"I didn't mean to be flippant, it's just—" Gillis paused as he struggled to find the right words as he made eye contact with the man.

"Yes, what do you want?" he said in an irritated voice. He walked past an almost clean-desk with a framed painting before continuing on for another couple of feet where he picked up a small irrigation gate valve. Gillis could see the thick wrinkles of the man's face as he looked up at a high shelf. The elderly man had a large nose surrounded by puffy white mutton chops that grew almost down even with his lower lip.

"I know the place looks a mess but everything has a rightful place. You're not from the mayor's office are you?" Gillis shook his head. "Young man, I assure you I know where everything is and that is what counts."

"No, we aren't from the mayor's office but it sounds like you are the man we need to talk to," said Logan inserting himself into the conversation. "We want to get some information on a tunnel that was built in Washington years ago and then probably abandoned."

"What's the name of the tunnel?"

Logan looked at Gillis at the same time Gillis looked at him with a kind of confused look. "We aren't sure but we know the location of one of the entrances."

"Won't help. Let me know when you know the name," he said abruptly. He turned back to his bench and began working.

"Look, are we bothering you?" asked Logan in an exasperated voice.

"Why as a matter of fact, yes, you are. Now if you don't mind I have work to do so would you mind shutting the door on your way out?"

Gillis spoke up. "We know you are busy but we have a terrible problem. We lost our dog down a hole that goes into this abandoned tunnel and we need to find a safe way to get her out."

"People lose dogs all the time. What's it to me?"

Gillis lowered his head slightly. "She means a lot to me. She is a fine dog, very rare, a long-haired dachshund. Most people have never heard of them."

The man stopped and stared at Gillis for several seconds. "Well, I guess I could give you a little of my time for your dog's sake. Now what are the two closest cross streets? That should at least get me in the right neighborhood."

"Gilmore and Birch. There is an alley there and the entrance was on the right side."

"So why don't you just go in there and find her?"

"We would but the tunnel collapsed after she chased something inside," said Gillis.

The little old man went over and grabbed a dusty book off the shelf and started quickly going through page after page with his finger. "Sure you don't know the name?"

"Sorry, I am new to the city and really don't."

"I don't remember any tunnels in that area. I know there hasn't been a tunnel built there for years but let me think about it for a minute." He grabbed a second book and again began rummaging through the pages until he paused and began scrolling down, stopping his dirty finger on a small paragraph. "Might be the Farragut Tunnel or possibly the Lewis Tunnel, let me see here."

Gillis and Logan patiently stood there hoping for the best.

The wiry man shut the book with a pop and quickly crossed the room where he fumbled through a number of maps and books before stopping and closely examined one. Then he returned to the table, opened the dusty book and began scanning it. "Yes right here, according to these records I do think it may be the Farragut Tunnel. The book says construction began in 1801 for a water tunnel and was later abandoned when two men died because of quicksand cave-in. A Mr. William Farragut lost his funding for the project after that. Appears that maybe he was planning to build a state of the art steam-powered plant that would be capable of pumping water to every building within a mile of there. Obviously this Mr. Farragut was way before his time," he said, nodding his head to one side.

"Does the map you looked at show the locations to any of the tunnel's entrances? We have to find our dog."

"Be patient, I'm looking. About four hundred feet south of where you found the first entrance there should be a second entrance at the northeast corner of Gilmore and Post. That's near where they built the Red Deer Diner. There seems to be a pattern—the next entrance seems to be on a northerly course and is about five hundred feet further up the street near where I believe the Tall Pony Hardware now sits. The next one is on Gilmore, halfway between the corner and Maple Street. According to this, that would also be the location of the underground vault where they planned to house the steam plant. I would assume that a vault big enough to house a steam engine would be quite large, so your dog may have ended up there."

Gillis studied the map for a couple of minutes and then looked up at the old man. "How familiar are you with Gilmore Street and could there be other possible locations?"

"Certainly, I often walk that route on my way home. I don't remember ever seeing any tunnel entrances but who knows how many building have been rebuilt over that time period. Sixty years later, a lot has changed. Over the years two major fires have changed a lot of streetscape. It's so hard to recognize things. But yes, I have walked that area many times and may know the location of one of these entrances. It's near the police station. There is a metal door that seems out of place and if I remember right there is a sizable rusty lock securing it. Only makes sense that it could be one of those abandoned entrances. At least it may be a good place for you two to start looking." The wiry old man again pointed to the map. "Here near the police substation, it still looks like an old construction site, lots of trash and old beams, the normal junk a place like that collects over time. The place really hasn't changed much over the last thirty years when they had a fire there."

Gillis pointed again to the map. "Can you show me on here and describe any landmarks that would help us locate these other two sites?"

"That one is south of the Red Deer Diner, probably no more than fifty feet and the other one is right next door to the Tall Pony Hardware. You may have a real hard time finding that one, because they remodeled the front last year and I think they sealed up the access to the alley just south of there."

Gillis put out his hand. "Thank you, sir. We really appreciate your help. Hopefully, we can find our dog."

The man nodded as Gillis and Logan turned and walked out the door, shutting it as they left.

Logan took only a couple of steps down the hall before he reached up and grabbed Gillis by the arm. "What was that all about? You don't have any dog, at least one I know about."

"No I don't, never owned a dog. There was a couple that lived on the farm that had one but I wouldn't have ever considered it mine."

"So why did that old coot open up to you? Hell, he damn near threw us out before you mentioned your lost dog, a dashon?"

"No, it's not a dashon, it's called a long-haired dachshund. They are very rare. Most of them are found only in Germany."

"Okay fine, a dachshund but why the story about your dog?"

"Did you want me to tell him my fiancée was kidnapped? The police are after me. I am being stalked by a band of killers and I need to find their hideout?"

Logan stared at him for a moment. "Good point, but why did he open up and start helping you when you mentioned this dachshund dog?"

"It was only an educated guess on my part if he would react positive or not. When I went past his desk he had a small painting on it. It looked like a portrait of a man and his dog. The man was very slender like this man but a lot younger and the dog was a long haired-dachshund. I guessed that picture was him in his younger years. He must have really cared for the dog to have had a painting done. From what I read, this type of dog is very friendly and has a lot of personality. I guessed he had a close relationship and possibly still has some emotional attachment."

"You figured that out with a quick glance at his desk? Gillis, I think you just might have what it takes to be a detective."

Gillis only smiled and kept walking to where they had tied the horse and parked the carriage. "We don't have much time. Who knows what those devils have done to Sandra. I want to go by the three locations. We still have at least a couple of hours of daylight. Let's check out the Tall Pony Hardware first and then if we don't find anything head over and look around that diner."

It took them forty minutes to travel from Droit Park to where the old man had told them the Tall Pony Hardware store was located and that was with the horse at a fast trot. Logan pulled back on the reins as the carriage slowly stopped across the street from the corner hardware store. It wasn't busy but a slow steady stream of people seemed to be coming and going. An old man with a weathered face and shaggy beard sat in a beat-up rocking chair beside the front door. The man seemed more asleep than awake as the customers came and went but occasionally he would say something to one of them.

"I sure don't see an alley or any kind of doorway that looks like it might lead to a tunnel," said Logan in a discouraged voice.

"When you think about it, it's been here for sixty years. I am sure the entrance won't stand out. I would like you to stay here while I walk across the street and have a chat with that old gentleman. Who knows, he may even know something that could help us." Gillis stepped down from the carriage and casually walked across the street stopping for another carriage as it passed. He felt obvious with the fake wig and beard and was sure everyone knew they weren't real, yet no one said a thing. Gillis walked up to the old man hoping not to startle him and saw an empty glass. The closer he got the more he noticed the stale smell of beer.

Gillis cleared his throat hoping to get the man's attention and it worked. The old man sat more upright in his chair and stared straight at him. "What's your problem, young man?"

"Nothing sir, I was hoping to buy you a refreshment and then in turn trouble you for a bit of information."

"What information are you in need of?"

Gillis didn't like lying but this was an emergency. "My grandfather once worked on a construction job near here building a water tunnel, probably in the range of sixty years ago. I was wondering if it still existed and if it did could you steer me toward any entrances. He said it was called the Farragut Tunnel and it was abandoned after a cave-in killed a couple of the workers."

"You came to the right place, young man. I happened to have worked on that tunnel as a teenager. Now what did you say your grandfather's name was?"

Just then Gillis heard footsteps behind him and glanced around his shoulder to see two police officers approaching. Gillis never turned to make eye contact as one of the officers spoke. "Morning Nicholas, I see you have been keeping a good eye on everything like always. Mind if we put up a poster of a wanted killer on the wall? He's a bad sort, killed two policemen over at the hospital the other night and then escaped. The captain is sure on everybody's butt to find him."

Fear started to overpower him. His legs felt like wet noodles, weak and ready to buckle. He was sure the police would notice the wig and any minute he would be tackled from behind.

Chapter 22

Everything that could go wrong seemed to be happening. Maybe he should throw up his hands and surrender but if he did, there would be no chance that Sandra would ever be saved. Suddenly, he heard a yell for help from across the street as Logan fell from the carriage and landed on the cobblestones with a loud moan. The police ran to help the injured man as Gillis turned to the old man. "My dog's loose and I need to grab him. I'll be back and then we can talk."

Gillis went around the building's corner and out of sight. He continued down the block at a fast walk until he was out of sight before ducking into a small depression in the brick facade. If he ran he would draw attention and that's not what he needed. He had to gain distance in case the old man noticed he looked a lot like the face on the poster. Fortunately, it would be dark in an hour and then maybe he could go unseen by keeping to the darker unlit roads that paralleled the main street.

He continued in a direction that would eventually put him at Sam's house. In the distance he heard a whistle—could it be a police whistle? He wasn't sure. Gillis changed streets and walked further away from the main street as the sun slowly set in the west. Everything was worse than he had imagined and now he was being blamed for the death of two policemen. Even if he surrendered now and told his story his experience told him he probably wouldn't make it back to the police station alive. No, he needed to get back to Sam's house and figure out some sort of plan. Time was quickly becoming his enemy.

For the next hour he tried to blend into the normal traffic of pedestrians, horseback riders and carriages that funneled up and down the streets. Staying close to trees, he remained alert and tried to disappear back into their protection if anything appeared threatening. Finally, daylight turned into darkness and he felt more comfortable moving quickly between the shadows.

Walking in the dark, arousing only the occasional dog, he heard a carriage coming down the street. Silently he backed into the shadows as the sound of the carriage drew closer with a light near the driver. He made out the features of a familiar face, it was Logan Fritz. As the carriage closed the distance Gillis walked out into the street slightly scaring the horse as Logan pulled back on the reins. "Get in quick," said the familiar voice as he slowed to a stop just long enough for Gillis to climb in. "Half the police force is back there searching for you. They have fanned out and are going block by block and we are just ahead of them. Hold on," said Logan popping his whip in the air as the horse began to trot faster.

"What happened back there?" Gillis asked.

"I saw those policemen coming around the corner before you did but I had no way of warning you so I pretended to fall and hurt my leg. Fortunately, you knew what I was doing and got the hell out of there. That old man recognized your picture as soon as you left and the police have been crisscrossing the town trying to find you ever since. It's difficult to avoid raising suspicions in a town where murder has gotten out of control."

"I appreciate the fast thinking and the ride."

"Take a bunch of the bedspreads in the back and throw them on top of yourself and make yourself look like a pile of blankets. It probably won't help if we get stopped but at a distance I think we will be fine."

An hour later the carriage pulled up in back of Sam's carriage house and the two men quickly got out, put away the horse and carriage, and entered the house.

Gillis and Logan walked through the back door where Sam stood waiting in the shared living room. "I was getting worried about you two. I'm sorry I have some more bad news. I was at the grocery store today and they have a fair portrait of you on a wanted poster. They say you killed two policemen in cold blood and they have a five-hundred-dollar reward on your head."

"I don't believe this," said Gillis looking straight at Sam.

"We don't either. If we did we wouldn't be standing here telling you about it. It really sounds to me like someone is doing a pretty fair job of framing you."

"All I can say is thank you for believing in me." Gillis's head went down. He was overwhelmed.

"I still have to find a way to save Sandra, and if need be, I will die trying. I think we have to go to that Red Deer Diner or that old run-down building area of town by the police station. It would be smart to take a look at the diner site first with the other entrance being right next to a police station."

Both Sam and Logan nodded, as Sam put his arm around Gillis's shoulder, "Supper ready. Let's eat and then we can come up with a plan."

A short time later, pushing his chair from the table Gillis said, "I didn't think I was hungry but I guess eating a whole plate of food kind of disputes that a little. Tomorrow we need to take a carriage ride past that diner and see what we've got there. Somehow we will need to get in and take a closer look. Now that we know the police have stepped-up their search for me it will be harder to go unnoticed. I would like to be in front of that diner at daylight before the city comes alive. I think that will be our best chance of going undetected."

*   *   *

The next morning all three men were up early and the horse was harnessed a good hour before sunrise. "We need to leave soon if we want to be there at first light," said Logan, as he checked the harness and tightened one of the buckles.

Logan lit the lantern and soon the carriage was headed down the road at a full trot towards the bridge. Gillis tried his best to bury himself in a pile of blankets. "Do you really think this will work?" asked Gillis in a sarcastic voice.

"No, not really but at least it will keep you quiet," said Logan, laughing quietly.

The two made good time as their horse trotted up the street. It was still barely light and no one was on the street in either direction as Logan pulled to a stop.

"Why don't you take a quick look around and see if you can find anything," said Logan.

Gillis stepped from the carriage and hopped up on the wooden boardwalk that surrounded the brick building that housed the eatery. The brick on the building was quite old and Gillis hoped the building was constructed in a similar time frame as the tunnel.

Quickly, he walked down one direction looking for something that might give him a clue of a possible tunnel entrance. Turning, he started down the opposite side of the building until he stopped in his tracks. The boards on the fence were beginning to rot. He grabbed one board and easily pulled it away. With a snap it broke and Gillis stared into the hole. There in the shadowy background was an alley similar to the one he had found and the men he sought had escaped to.

Quickly he pulled another board away and slid through the small gap into the alley. It was filled with trash and the foul smell of human excrement but there in front of him was a rusted lantern and above it a single charcoal colored brick. Gillis quickly moved to the lantern, careful not to step in the many piles of feces as he moved. Unlike the other dead-end alley, this one had a wooden door that allowed access to the building beside it. He crept up to the rusted lantern which was almost an exact match to the one in the other alley.

Pulling the medallion out of his jacket he almost dropped it. He fumbled with it for a moment before trying to insert it in the key hole but something was blocking the hole. He tried several times but he knew he had run into another dead end. These people were smart enough to try and block every possible access to the tunnel.

Just then Gillis heard something above him and looked up. Someone was opening a window and Gillis tried to slide behind some old lumber out of sight as a woman emptied her chamber pot from the window above. The contents spattered everywhere and the smell was enough to make him gag. Gillis quickly made it back through the small opening in the fence and back to the carriage.

Gillis looked at Logan. "Might as well get going, that entrance isn't going to work. It's plugged like the first one and if a person was to use a sledge hammer to try and open it, the people on the second floor would be hollering for the police by the second swing. We are going to have to find another way."

They rode in silence for a couple of minutes and then Logan looked at Gillis, "Do you smell that? It smells like—"

Gillis interrupted him, "I know what it smells like. Some woman on the second floor emptied her chamber pot down into the alley while I was there and it spattered on me."

Logan smirked. "This can be kind of a crappy job sometimes."

Gillis gave him an irritated look. "I really don't appreciate your humor. Maybe we can stop at that park and I can wash a little of this off."

Gillis kneeled down and tried to wash the smell from his clothes at a small pond in an isolated part of the park. Once he finished cleaning himself the two were on their way again toward the final place where the old German had said there may be an entrance someplace off that street. The thought of the police station in the middle of the block where they needed to look had kept their spirits and conversation at a low level. They turned the carriage down another street and headed to their next possible entrance location.

Logan focused ahead as he talked to Gillis. "I brought a paper along and thought you could sit on that far bench and monitor what is happening. We know there are going to be policemen walking back and forth and at least this way, you can see what I am doing and still keep an eye out. What do you think?"

"Whatever it takes to find that door is what I need to do. Sandra has been a captive for most of a week now and who knows what she is going through. I feel self-conscious with this wig and fake beard. I brought along a pair of specs that may help. Sitting where the police won't be expecting me and analyzing the streetscape makes sense. There has to be an entrance somewhere but God help us if some store keep remodeled and built over it. If that happened then for all practical purposes it may be lost for good."

"Let's not take a defeatist attitude until it's warranted. We have had nothing but bad luck and maybe this one will be different," said Logan.

Gillis nodded and stared ahead as the horse continued to trot along. Logan pulled back the reins and turned to Gillis. "See that bench? I have walked this street before and this bench gives you a perfect view. Take this paper and pretend you're reading but keep your head down. I am going to go down the street and turn around and then tie off over there, a couple shops down from the police station." Just then two officers walked out the door of the building with "Police Station Number Four" written above the entrance.

"Hopefully we can see a pattern develop," said Logan.

Gillis quickly scanned the street. It was wall-to-wall low-level stores and nothing looked well kept. He couldn't see any sign of an alley or spaces between the different buildings and with the exception of one building that had been partially burned, nothing stood out. Gillis stepped down from the carriage with the paper in one hand and turned to Logan. "Good luck. I will be waiting and watching."

Logan shook the reins and steered the horse and carriage back into the middle of the cobblestone street. He went down several hundred yards and turned around before directing the horse over to an isolated hitching post. He stepped up on the wooden boardwalk which appeared to be the only thing that was well maintained and began walking east toward the police station. Taking his time, he closely looked at each building as he went. He walked past the station and noticed the door closed. Continuing down the street he passed a rundown Chinese laundry and the remains of the partially burnt building.

Gillis could see Logan peering into the building from his location but he couldn't see anyone on the street and when he looked back, Logan was gone. Gillis jumped to his feet trying to locate Logan but as far as he could tell he had vanished. He stuck the paper under his arm as he put his head down and crossed the street to the last place he had seen Logan.

As he got closer he could see the building was far more damaged that it appeared from his bench. This had to be the place the old German had described. By bending a board slightly back, a hole just big enough for a man to squeeze through had been created in the small foyer of the dilapidated building. Because it was perpendicular to the street, only a person paying close attention would have ever noticed.

He heard a crunching sound, and the sound of someone walking through burnt debris. Gillis stuck his head into the building and he could see blackened floors, walls and ceiling but a lot of the abandoned store's main structure had been saved and was still intact.

Toward the back of the building he saw the shadow of Logan walking. He appeared to be carefully examining the interior, and then he disappeared again. Gillis wondered if he should follow but he had agreed to stay by the bench and watch and now he stood one building down from the police station.

The next couple of minutes seemed like an eternity as Gillis stood quietly waiting, constantly looking over his shoulder for unwanted company. He was nervous. Gillis decided to follow Logan as he bent back the board that led inside. Almost immediately he saw the shape of Logan moving toward him.

Working himself through the opening as Gillis helped by bending the board backwards, Logan spoke. "I think I found something. Let's get to the carriage where we can talk." Somehow Logan had gotten charcoal on one side of his face and as they turned to walk down the wooden planked boardwalk two older ladies passed. Gillis buried his head and face and looked at the ground as Logan smiled and wished the women a good day.

Gillis looked at Logan. "That was close. By the way you have a big smear of charcoal on your face."

Logan pulled out his handkerchief, spit on it, and then wiped the soot from his cheek. "Let's get going. I may have found an entrance but I'm not sure. If it is an entrance, it may be impossible to open without everyone for two blocks hearing."

Chapter 23

The two men walked past the police station as two officers came out, turned and walked in opposite directions. Gillis couldn't wait. "What did you find? I need to know."

"I think we finally got some dumb luck. That building is so filthy inside that people haven't been using it at all and I believe that is why they didn't find it."

"Find what?"

"The tunnel entrance, there is a tunnel entrance in the back of the building or at least it looks like an entrance. Sometime in the past, this entrance was walled off and probably forgotten but the fire burned enough of a small hole in the back stud wall that I could peer into a small void. I struck a match and looked inside. For a moment I could see a brick wall with a recessed opening the size of a hallway. It appeared round on top and I could only see a little further, so I threw the match into the hole and I got a better view. There's what looks like a heavy metal door inside. The door looks like it is solid and reinforced with wide steel bars and rivets. That's the good part—the bad part is there is a huge lock on the door and it looks rusty and from my quick observation, beat to hell."

Gillis looked at Logan. "Good work. Now at least we know the location of an entrance, even if it's in a dangerous place."

"Yeah, but with a police station only thirty feet away you certainly aren't going to be able to take a sledge hammer and pound on that lock without someone hearing. And even if you are lucky enough to find a key for that old lock it is way too rusty to function. Take my word for it, you will never be able to insert a key into that lock or turn it if you did."

For the next few feet Gillis didn't say anything and then he turned to Logan. "We still have some light left. Help me find a chemist. I need to purchase a few items."

"Like what?"

"You will see. Hopefully he will have what I need."

Climbing into the carriage they were off down the street away from the police station. They turned left and left again to head back in the direction they had come but over one block. Logan looked at Gillis. "At least we won't have to go by that station again today." Gillis only smiled.

Logan pulled back the reins and the horse slowed to a walk. "I can't remember exactly where but there is a small chemist shop around here. I used him on a case, years ago. He's a smart guy and good chemist but a bit on the eccentric side. Try not to let his mannerisms bother you. I think he has smelled too much of his own fumes over the years." Logan tied the horse and the two men walked over to a white door with a small sign that read "Chemist."

"Hopefully he is here," said Gillis.

"Oh, he's probably here. He has way too many issues to deal with to be gone."

"What do you mean by that?"

"You will see," said Logan as he knocked on the door.

Seconds later they could hear movement behind the door and a voice hollering, "Yes. Yes, I'm coming." The door squeaked as the man opened it far enough to poke only his head out. He stared for a couple of seconds at Logan before speaking.

"Detective Fritz, if I remember right. Come in but please be careful not to let any of my friends out. They seem to want to make a break for it every time I open that door."

Gillis had a puzzled look on his face. "Let who out?"

Logan turned back to Gillis and smiled. "The guy loves cats. He must have at least fifty of them. They will be everywhere and if you want to buy something you better not let one of his cats out." Gillis looked down and there was a white and gray spotted cat and it looked like it was ready to scoot between his legs as he began to open the door. Gillis took his boot and blocked the way as he carefully shut the door behind him. He turned to see a smiling older man standing there.

"Love cats, always have, always will, now what can I do for you and your friend here?"

"Oh, this is Clarence." Gillis sent a questioning glance toward Logan.

"Nice to meet you, Clarence. Nice to see you again, detective. Thought you retired."

"Yes, I will someday. Things haven't worked out the way I thought they would. Anyways, my friend here needs to buy some things from you and unfortunately we are in a hurry."

"So what might that be?"

Gillis stepped forward and for the first time realized just how many cats this man actually had. They were sitting on chairs, the floor, and some even nestled on top of counters and they all seemed to be staring at him. "I need a small vial, test tube size, of hydrofluoric acid. Please remember to wax the vial extremely well, and the glass stopper—wouldn't want it to eat through my coat."

"I have that. I don't get much call for it being so dangerous and all. I always keep it locked up in this closet here. You obviously know how dangerous and corrosive it can be. Had a helper once twenty years ago, spilled a little on his crotch. He died from the burns a week later, amazingly powerful stuff."

"Yes sir, I am well aware of its properties and I will make sure the vial and the plug are well coated in a thick layer of wax. When you use it be sure not to breathe it, it would be fatal."

"Wait here, while I prepare the test tubes. The stuff is a little on the expensive side. It will cost you five dollars. Is that going to be all right with you?"

Gillis nodded in agreement and ten minutes later they were getting back into the carriage. As they sat down Logan spoke. "I assume you plan to pour that acid on the lock I found. That vial he gave you looked pretty small. Are you sure it will do the job?"

"Oh, it will do the job all right. Now I need to go by a mercantile and buy a small concealable saw, a lantern, and a couple of candles so we can open that hole large enough to get into the passageway. Do you know of a store close by?"

Logan nodded, turning the horse at the next intersection. It wasn't long before Logan was back to the carriage with the supplies. "Now if my calculations are correct, that acid may take all night to burn through that lock. I want you to slowly drive the carriage past the building and drop me off. I'll take care of the lock tonight. Pick me up in an hour or so, after dark. If there is any activity on the street then drive past and come back every half hour until it's clear. Sooner or later we should catch a break."

"Are you sure you don't want to wait until early morning?"

"We don't have the luxury of time. Who knows what Sandra's situation is. No, I have to chance someone possibly seeing me or a light in the building but I will do everything I can not to let that happen."

It was dark when Logan turned and headed down the street. A man was busy lighting the few sporadic gas lights that adorned the street.

"Wait to let me off until the carriage is blocking his view. If I am figuring this right, I will be able to blend into the darkness and wait until I see him turn away." Gillis put his hand on his chest and was surprised that he could barely feel the small vial through his padded coat.

The carriage slowed to a crawl and Gillis, with tools in hand, hopped down to the street and quickly jogged to a dark spot in the building's façade. There he flattened himself against the building and let the shadows hide his presence. For several minutes he watched the man move from lantern to lantern and he knew the next time the man stopped and looked up to the street light he would make a short dash to the burnt building. The man was getting closer and as he stopped and looked up, Gillis shot from the shadows. He hugged the building walls as he moved to the burnt building and into the darkness of the small dark foyer. Quickly he looked back to see the man lowering his lighting stick and starting to move to the next light. Gillis waited to make his move until the man began to walk toward another lantern post.

Quickly he bent back the board and climbed inside the building. It was pitch black inside and even the sliver of moon outside didn't help. He cautiously stepped an inch at a time not knowing exactly where he was going. After a few minutes and painfully few feet of progress, he hit something with his foot and reached down to touch what felt like a beam. Carefully he stepped over the object and continued on for another ten feet when his hand touched a solid wall. He slid his hand along the wall until he found an opening. Touching the wall he worked himself around it.

Pulling a match from his pocket, he lit the six-inch candle he carried, exposing a blackened room with a hallway leading further back. He studied the area around him and mentally took notes before moving further into the building and away from the street. The crunching of the charcoal beneath his feet sounded loud and he found himself sweating.

Finally, he reached a wall with a twelve-inch-wide hole, the size Logan had described. At that point he lit the lantern and carefully lowered it into the hole, lighting the passage and the metal door. A sense of victory came over him. At last he might have a real chance to save Sandra.

The lock was large, rusty, and terribly beat up just like Logan had described. Taking his small pruning saw he began cutting the wall until the opening was big enough to slip through. Carefully he lowered one leg then the other inside the small chamber and approached the door. Logan was right. It was metal and heavily reinforced with metal brackets. Cautiously he removed the vial from his jacket and stepped closer to the lock. He quickly loosened the plug and then with a handkerchief over his nose and mouth, began pouring the liquid onto the lock until the vial was empty.

Smoke from the chemical reaction started to build and Gillis pushed the handkerchief tighter to his face and hurried to get back through the hole in the wall. Grabbing the lantern, he almost fell as he struggled to get out. He continued to press the handkerchief tightly over his nose and mouth as to not breathe the poisonous vapor. He took one last look toward the street and his getaway and opened the glass door of the lantern and blew it out.

It took several minutes until his eyes had adjusted as he quietly stood in the dark with one hand holding the wall. Suddenly he heard a noise and froze to the point he almost stopped breathing. At least two people were talking and the voices were coming closer. Terror began going through his mind. Had they possibly seen the light? Were they the police? The voices were close, real close and Gillis could make out a word here and there and then the voices seemed to pass.

A large drop of sweat rolled down his nose. He wiped it off with his shirt sleeve before slowly heading towards the street. The smell of the acid was strong and Gillis covered his mouth and nose. He hoped no passerby would notice and inform the police. He made it back to the board that covered the door and bent it back. Looking out on the street, it seemed deserted. Silently he slid out into the shadows of the foyer before moving onto the street, before looking both ways. The street was still dark, silent, and empty.

Gillis stood watching for a few minutes when he could heard the faint sound of horseshoes on the cobblestones. He studied the carriage's shape until he recognized it and then quickly exited and met Logan right as the carriage got to where he was hiding. Filled with adrenaline, Gillis jumped into the carriage. The action caught Logan off guard as he drew his hands back in a defensive posture.

Logan exhaled loudly. "Are you all right? That entrance you made from the shadows sure startled me."

Gillis smiled. "You aren't the only one to have this night take your breath away. That's one spooky old building but I do believe you found an entrance. Hopefully it ties into the main shaft. I poured the acid on the lock and we need to wait until tomorrow and hope that it eats its way through that lock. I can only pray it is as powerful as I remember."

The next twenty minutes were quiet as both men seemed to be in deep thought. "You know, Gillis, even if that tunnel leads to the main shaft there is no telling if we will find her. If we're successful there may be a hell of a lot of people who murder for a living guarding her."

"Yeah, I have been thinking about that a lot too. After looking at those old plans, I believe the main chamber is the only space large enough to operate out of and it is north of where we are. The map showed lots of tunnels but if I am correct we should be able to see their foot traffic and that should lead us there."

"You do know they won't let you take her without a fight and we both know those men know how to fight."

Gillis looked over at Logan. "I know. I will deal with that when I come to it. I'm well aware I am over my head."

"I will be at your side through this." Logan paused. "Hell, I have come this far and I can't turn back now."

"Logan, do you think it's possible my father might be a prisoner there too?"

"There is always a chance. Until you know otherwise, I would try and be positive you'll find him."

Gillis looked straight ahead as the carriage continued down the dark street.

Later they drove behind the boarding house and into the back stable area. After taking the harness off, Gillis led the horse into a stall. He hoped that no one would take notice as Logan pushed the carriage inside.

As the two walked to the door they could see a light on. "At least Sam is still up. I was wondering if he would wait."

Gillis lightly knocked on the door and Sam appeared quickly and opened the door. "Come in, come in quickly and stay away from the windows."

"What's going on?" asked Logan in a worried voice.

"I'm not sure but a man I have never seen before was hanging around down the street most of the afternoon. He leaned against a tree for quite a while like he had nothing better to do. Finally, I went in to get a little tea and when I came back he was gone. He could be no one for that matter but I am always a mite suspicious especially the more we learn about that Fenian brotherhood. It is better to be safe than sorry so don't silhouette yourself against those windows."

"Thanks for the warning," said Gillis as he sat down. "I believe Logan may have found a tunnel that will lead us inside. We hope to try and find our way into the main chamber early tomorrow and find where they are holding Sandra. They probably have a headquarters down there. It's safe and far from prying eyes."

Sam rubbed his chin. "So your plan is to get very lucky and find your way through a bunch of unmarked passageways to a room you have never seen before. Elude who knows how many guards along the way and somehow find Sandra, get her out of wherever she is being held and then escape without anyone being killed."

Gillis looked at Sam. "I don't enjoy how you've painted that picture but yes, that's about it. I don't have too many choices with the police hunting me for murder and the Army thinking I am crazy."

Sam walked over to a small end table and opened a drawer and reached inside. "At least take this Navy Colt with you. By the sound of your plan you will need it. It's loaded and all you need to do is pull back the hammer and fire. I put fresh caps on it today after I saw that man."

"I have only shot a gun a few times since I ran away at fourteen. I guess

I need to remember fast. That is the same type of gun Luke and I traveled here with but the police took it and my derringer when they arrested me."

That night Gillis didn't sleep much with his mind going in and out of what his imagination thought may be in store for him. For several hours in the middle of the night he stared at the dark ceiling and hoped that the next day would somehow go well.

Gillis felt a hand on his shoulder and he struggled to see who held the candle beside his bed. "It's time," came a low voice which he recognized as Logan's. "Let's get a little to eat and then get the carriage out and get going. It should be dark for another couple of hours, and once in the tunnel, the light outside won't matter much."

"We will need a sturdy chunk of two by four about a foot long, an old towel, a heavy hammer, a small pry bar, and the lantern," said Gillis as Logan nodded.

Both men hurried to eat and quickly they were in the carriage and headed back up the street.

"I hope that acid of yours worked," said Logan as they crossed Long Bridge.

"Me too," said a quiet Gillis as the horse maintained a steady trot.

They tied the horse and carriage a street over where someone else had left their horse for the night. With the supplies under their coats, they made their way to the fire-scarred building. The streets were lifeless and it didn't take long for the two of them to make it to the building and quickly slip inside. They lit a small candle and made their way toward the thick metal door embedded in the charcoal-scarred brick wall. The two men could see that the acid had done something in the dim light of the candle but neither was sure of the results and both remained silent. Gillis pulled the sturdy chunk of wood from his coat and wrapped it in the towel.

"Hand me the hammer," said Gillis. Logan handed him the heavy hammer. Gillis put the two by four's flat edge on the lock and with one hardy swing wacked it hard. The sound of the lock breaking as it hit the floor seemed loud and Gillis and Logan stared at each other listening.

After several minutes Gillis finally spoke. "I don't think anyone heard us. Remember, the police station is only one building over and within an hour it will be buzzing with activity."

Logan nodded and placed the towel under the latch and then took the small pry bar from his coat and wedged it under the latch. Logan gently pushed on the pry bar and the latch immediately fell to the floor, the sound muffled by the towel. He smiled. "That acid of yours really works."

Logan took the pry bar and wedged it into the door jam and inserted pressure, but nothing happened. "I think it's stuck—let me pry all around the door and see if I can loosen it." Five minutes later, and what felt like an eternity, the door slightly gave with a squeak. With great effort they were able to slowly and quietly get it to move. It took both men straining to finally pull the door open wide enough for them to fit through.

"So far so good," whispered Gillis. "Hand me the lantern and I'll go first."

Gillis stepped inside the dark tunnel not knowing what to expect. The brick-lined walls and arched ceiling showed a lack of use. Gillis could feel a slight breeze coming up from the narrow passageway. It was almost warm compared to the temperatures of the cold morning. Gillis extended his arm and the lantern to cast light out as far as possible in front them. A thin layer of mud coated the floor and their tracks stood out. Gillis looked at his tracks and then to the level dirt floor. "No one has come this way for a long time. At least it will be easy to find our way back."

"Keep alert, these tunnels can be dangerous."

The two continued slowly along, trying not to make a sound as they walked. Suddenly, Logan grabbed the coat tail of Gillis, "Don't move."

Chapter 24

Gillis froze in his tracks and turned back and looked at Logan. "See those boards in front of you?"

"Yeah?"

"Before you step on them, carefully move a couple and see what is beneath it. Sometimes if the floor of an old tunnel or mine gave out, the miners just put boards across the hole. Who knows how long these boards have been here. There is a good chance they are rotten. We need to make sure everything is solid." Gillis knelt down and moved one of the boards aside as he lowered his light to see better. As he moved the board a small amount of dirt could be heard falling into the darkness under the board.

"You're right, there is a hole in the floor and who knows where the bottom is."

"Let's see if we can go around it. I am pretty sure all these boards are rotten. One more step and you might have been at the bottom of that shaft."

Gillis began testing his footing on the far side of the tunnel and found it solid. He turned back to Logan. "I think there is at least twelve inches of solid floor left on this side of the tunnel and we should be able to get around the hole. Thank God you saw it."

"Let's just keep going. We can't forget where this is when we make our way back."

Carefully, the two men worked their way around the dusty lumber trying not to slip on the thin muddy coating on the floor. Keeping their bodies tight against the wall they made their way past the hole and continued on. Almost falling down a shaft put Gillis on high alert as his eyes searched the dimly lit passage with a new seriousness. He turned to Logan. "There is a set of stairs leading down in front of me, be careful."

At the bottom of the stairs they could hear water and the further they went, the louder the sound of water got. "We can't be too far from the canal.

I am going to slow down so we don't accidentally walk into someone or something."

The floor of the shaft was littered with scattered bricks that had come lose from the ceiling and in places the structural integrity was almost gone. Gillis put his hand on his waist and could feel the heavy, clumsy shape of Sam's Navy Colt covered by his coat. Since he had entered the tunnel he had checked the revolver at least three times to make sure it was still there. He thought of his father and their arguments. He had never wanted to be a fighter or the hero his father pushed him to be. Gillis hated the thought of going to a special school in Ireland for the gifted and what they might have turned him into. His mind wandered to Sandra and how her father had been murdered. Sweat rolled down his forehead and onto his eyebrow and he wiped it away with his handkerchief. He was scared and now he was being forced to be brave.

The sound of Logan stumbling over a half-buried brick startled Gillis. "Are you okay?" whispered Gillis.

"Yeah, yeah, it was just a damn brick. I need to be more careful."

Gillis looked ahead at the edge of the light cast by the lantern and then back to Logan. "I think we are close. There seems to be some type of blockage ahead."

Logan moved up beside Gillis and looked at the debris that went from floor to ceiling. It was mostly big timbers and two by six planking and a fair amount of it was burned.

"Is there a way through?" asked Logan in a discouraged voice.

Gillis took his time shining the light back and forth and then finally turned to Logan. "There must have been some type of fire or explosion. There is brick and burnt lumber crammed everywhere. I don't know if we can get through or not. I will need to probe some more."

Logan, whose waist was at least twice the size of Gillis's, stood back and stared at him. Finally he dropped to his hands and knees and tried to enter one of the tunnels created by the fallen timber. A minute later he crawled back out and stood up.

"I think I am small enough that I can make it through but the passageway is probably too narrow for you."

Logan nodded. "You know I want to go but time isn't on our side. Gillis, you need to go on without me and hope to God you can find her before it is too late."

Gillis made eye contact with Logan. "You *are* going to be here when I get back, right?"

"Where else would I go," said Logan. "Find Sandra and get her the hell out of there. I will do what I can to back you up but it will need to be from here."

Gillis dropped to his knees and looked into the dark opening between the burnt timbers and debris. He could still feel the pain in his head as he started crawling into the thick pile. His small flickering candle fought with the cool breeze coming from beyond his view. As he entered the small hole he could hear sounds like small animals moving about and the faint smell of dung swirled around his nose. On his hands and knees he crawled several yards when he felt something on first one leg and then the other. He dug deep and fought the reaction to scream and throw himself backward.

Turning his head as much as he could, he moved his candle to where he could see his feet. The dull cast of candlelight illuminated two beady eyes of a large rat staring back at him. With an excited flick of his hand the rat disappeared back into the darkness. His hands felt the damp dung that covered the tunnel floor as he continued to crawl.

Minutes later, he stopped and carefully moved objects from his path until he noticed a faint light in the distance. He could not pinpoint the light's source but he knew it wasn't coming from his candle or the small lantern than Logan held back at the entrance. The light made him anxious as he began to crawl more carefully and slowly. He prayed that the light came from one of the main tunnels that might lead him to the larger vault. If his guess and the map were right, there was a good chance that they were holding Sandra there.

Gillis felt something cut his hand and lowered his candle to see. The edge of a rusted band brought blood to his knuckle and a stream of crimson flowed down his wrist. Never in his life had he considered himself a physical person. Deep down he didn't want to be the hero type but his love for Sandra pushed him on. Thinking about his lack of skill with a gun, he prayed that if he found Sandra he would be able to out-smart these men. Mental achievements were what he had always taken pride in. He needed to become mentally and physically tougher than he ever thought possible. Tying the handkerchief tightly around his hand, he continued creeping forward.

He crawled under a large chunk of burnt timber and felt something hard and smooth. He looked up and realized that he was through and was looking at a large dimly lit passageway lined in brick. Exposing enough of his head and hands to pull himself into the corridor, he slowly looked around. In front of him was a catwalk, five feet wide in both directions. To the left, the tunnel melted into the darkness but to the right he could see dim lights that came from where the wall took a bend.

Directly across from him was a narrow wooden bridge that disappeared into another dark tunnel entrance. From the small amount of light that shone in the passage he could see a thin film of mud on the bridge and in the center were what looked like tracks. Gillis took a deep breath. He knew he needed to crawl out onto the brick pavers and start making his way toward the light.

Silently he was giving himself a pep talk when he heard footsteps headed in his direction. Gillis blew out the candle and yanked his body back into the darkness. Looking up, he saw the back of a boot in front of the tunnel entrance. Suddenly it pivoted toward where he hid. Fear overtook him as he fought the urge to panic. He covered his mouth tightly and tried not to breathe. Why on earth would this man stop two feet from where he lay hidden unless he had seen or heard something? Gillis flattened his face into the thin layer of mud on the floor. Then he felt it, the warm sensation of water dripping onto his hand. Immediately he knew the man had stopped to relieve himself.

A minute later, Gillis heard a sound like dirt being ground into the brick and then saw movement as the sound of footsteps seemed to drift away. The thought of being urinated on repulsed Gillis as he crawled back onto the catwalk. Crouching down behind the remains of an old barrel, he carefully surveyed the site. Rusted equipment, rotting wooden boxes and garbage were tightly piled against the wall for as far as he could see. He prayed he could use them for cover.

He listened for a minute and could hear the faint sound of men talking. The light was adequate enough to allow him to see his footing and avoid stepping on the occasional piece of debris that littered the cobblestone floor. His hand felt something on top of the box he used to brace himself. He lifted it up. It was a small chunk of rotting canvas.

Gillis could barely hear the water which was moving slower in this part of the canal. He made it to where the tunnel catwalk began to gently bend. The further he went, the brighter the light became. He looked back to remember the landmarks to his tunnel's entrance. At most, he was only fifteen yards from where it began and shouldn't have any trouble finding it again even in the dark. The light's reflection caught the end of one of the bigger beams. It was several feet in front of his small passage and he would look for that as one of his markers.

Another couple of steps and he could see part of a larger room with a kerosene lantern hanging on the far wall. He knelt down beside a large, wooden box and analyzed the scene. Two men were talking but he couldn't locate where they were. Although he couldn't see what was against the wall closest to him, the far wall had numerous small barred cells that were more the size of cages than a normal jail cell.

A potbellied stove crackled on the far wall where the catwalk melted into the larger room. Moments later a man walked over to it and sat down. Gillis studied the first cell where an older gray-haired man sat on a makeshift wooden bed. He looked tired and emaciated. The next cell looked empty but there was a blanket stretched across one corner toward the back half of the cell. He could see a man leaning against the bars in the third cell. He looked back at the area where the small potbellied stove sat. A pile of split firewood leaned against the wall and beside that an ax was stuck firmly into a round of log used for splitting wood. The man continued to sit in the chair in front of the stove but Gillis could hear him occasionally say something to an unseen person. Gillis studied the old man in the first cell. A heavy lock and chain secured the door of his cage. The next cell with the blanket also had a lock but it was much smaller and obviously not as strong.

Gillis saw another man walk over to the stove. He leaned his musket against the wood pile before pouring himself a cup of coffee. The men were both well-built, tall, and they gave the impression of knowing how to handle trouble. Gillis knew he had no chance of overpowering either of them. The men sat looking toward the stove, but even with their backs to him it would be impossible for him to sneak up on them. With all the dirt and the debris scattered across the floor, it would be suicide.

The old man began saying something to the guards as he tried to pull himself up on the cell bars and to his feet. One of the guards walked over and with his empty coffee cup smashed the old man's fingers and sent him tumbling to the floor, screaming in pain. Gillis had never seen anything to match this kind of brutality. The anger welled up inside him. He wanted to kill these men but without some kind of a plan it was impossible. His mind went back to Sandra. If these men would do this to an old man, what would they do to a beautiful young woman?

As Gillis stared from the shadows he saw the blanket in the second cell move slightly and then there she was, Sandra. Almost like magic he could see her shoulders and head above the makeshift screen. There was a slight sigh of relief and then panic set in. She looked beat up. Her dress was dirty and torn. She stood, her face pale and tired, but she moved to the center of the small cell and sat down without too much trouble. The guards had at least shown her a little respect by hanging a couple of blankets to give her some privacy.

Gillis pulled his Navy Colt from his belt. He had no plan but now he considered charging the two guards. Maybe he would get lucky and kill them before they could pull their pistols or get to their muskets. Sweat oozed down Gillis's forehead as several times he gave himself a count of three to charge, only to stop his count and take another series of deep breaths. He would have to cover twenty yards to the men and charging at a full run would not help him with his accuracy.

He leaned back against the barrel, angry that he couldn't come up with a better plan. A plan that would at least give him a fighting chance, not run into the fight with guns blazing and little chance of survival.

One of the men turned and yelled back to an unseen person. "Shane, wake up, you're on guard duty in a minute or two."

A groggy voice answered, "Yeah, yeah, I hear you."

A third man walked toward the stove while pulling his suspenders up over his shoulders. This man was a good two inches taller and much broader at the shoulders than the other two. He grabbed a cup from the top of a barrel and poured himself some coffee. He looked rugged and powerful and Gillis knew that only the luckiest of shots would stop such a man.

Gillis heard a quiet squeak from behind him. He turned his head slightly to see a large rat cleaning his facial fur only inches from his foot. The rat appeared to have no fear of him and Gillis found that strangely interesting. Slowly, he removed his jacket and held it in both hands. He didn't really have a plan but it had to be better than running at three armed men and maybe more, with five or six shots in his gun. He glanced at the cylinder of the pistol and carefully counted the bullets.

Gillis moved his hand and it startled the rat but to his surprise the rat only moved slightly. If his plan worked at least he might have a fighting chance. He rummaged through his pockets, finding a few coins but nothing he was looking for. Then he reached into his back pocket and it almost surprised him to find his medallion. He set it down beside himself and then began searching for other things.

Finally, his eyes landed on his boots. His stylish boots were adorned at the top with a fine lace of leather, there as much for looks as actually tightening the boot. He carefully removed the lace just as the rat turned and moved back into the pile of debris. Gillis needed the rat to come out again to have any chance of his plan working. In the meantime, he needed a few more items.

Cautiously, he moved to a crouch and looked around. His eyes had become accustomed to the dark and he could make out more detail. He crept down the passageway far enough to retrieve a small, empty paint bucket. He now had most of what he needed. The other tunnel entrance was directly across the bridge from him as he quietly slid an old barrel far enough away from the wall that he could easily fit between them. Then Gillis got the canvas he had found earlier and laid it beside his other items. He was almost ready and now all he needed was for that large rat to come out again.

Moments later Gillis saw movement inside the pile of debris and then the rat appeared. The rodent crawled over close to Gillis's foot, and stood up on its hind feet as if to analyze this strange thing in his pile of junk. Gillis took a deep breath. He knew he wouldn't be faster than the rat's reactions so he had to anticipate the rat's escape route. He lunged forward and threw the coat in the direction he hoped the rat would run. The large rodent jumped and headed for the hole in the garbage just as Gillis had thought and the jacket slowed him down enough that Gillis was able to pounce on the jacket and grab the rat.

With a slight squeal the rat lay trapped inside Gillis's jacket with only its long hairless tail sticking out. He had done it, he had captured the rat, and now he hoped and prayed his idea would work. If it didn't, Gillis was sure the men would kill him and possibly Sandra.

While keeping the coat tightly around the rat, Gillis took the leather string that was almost sixteen inches long and tied the medallion to it. The animal was squirming but the thickness of the jacket allowed Gillis to keep it in place as he tied the other end of the leather string to the rat's tail. After stuffing the jacket, rat, old bolts, and the medallion in the bucket, Gillis stood. He looked to see if the three men were still sitting around the stove with their backs to him and then crept to the water's edge and with all his strength threw it across the water. The bucket landed on the far side of the bridge in front of the other tunnel entrance with a loud, echoing thud. The rat rolled out of the jacket and for a moment stood there looking dazed before running toward the safety of the dark tunnel entrance with the medallion clanging behind him. Gillis dove back to his shadowy hiding place beside the barrel and cupped his hands around his mouth to throw his voice and yelled at the top of his lungs, "Run!"

The sound of the bucket and bolts hitting the floor were louder than Gillis expected. He pulled the old barrel toward himself and threw the dusty chunk of canvas over his body. The sound of the metal clanking along the floor could be heard across the bridge as the rat furiously tried to escape the unknown menace that had grabbed its tail. He only hoped the guards would hear the noise and take the bait.

Chapter 25

Gillis heard one of the men yelling to the others, "He's in the tunnel— quick light the lantern!"

Men were running down the cat walk and across the planks of the bridge yelling as they ran. He peeked from under the canvas only to see the biggest of the three men standing not five feet from him looking around as if he was unsure of what to do. It didn't appear as if he was going to follow the others. These guards were well trained and not stupid, thought Gillis, and he feared that the last guard had become suspicious. Again Gillis fought the feeling of panic. Sooner or later the other two men would catch up with the rat and know they had been tricked and his simple hiding spot would be discovered.

With one quick move, Gillis jumped at the man's back with his pistol raised. The man suddenly turned just as Gillis struck the side of his head with his pistol. The man just looked at him for a second and then his eyes rolled back and he tumbled backwards into the canal with a splash. Instantly, Gillis ran for the cell that housed Sandra, stopping to grab the ax from the block of wood as he ran past. Sandra was staring straight at him in a trance-like look of disbelief. With one quick whack of the hatchet the lock exploded into two pieces and Gillis yanked the cell door open.

"Sandra, it's Gillis! Sandra, we need to run!"

It was like something snapped into place for her as she looked at Gillis and started hurrying out the cell door as Gillis grabbed her hand and began running back out the way he came.

"Save me," yelled the old man in the cell closest to Sandra's. "I am Senator Lenox Baker, please take me, I beg of you." The frail old man stood there, his eyes begging for help. Gillis stopped for a second and then pivoted and ran back. With all his strength Gillis smashed the ax down onto the lock of the old man's cell but it bounced off with a loud clang. The old man stared with a hopeless look of desperation as Gillis turned and the two ran towards the escape tunnel.

"I'm sorry," Gillis yelled back at the man as he grabbed Sandra's hand and began to run, pulling her as he did. She seemed disoriented but Gillis knew he had little in the way of choices: they needed to escape. Soon the other two men would figure out this had been a distraction and would be back to join the fight. The two ran to the small opening at the base of the abandoned tunnel. Gillis stopped Sandra and knelt down to help her enter the small passage.

A shot rang out and a splinter of wood hit Gillis's cheek. Gillis turned and fired back in the direction of the tunnel across the bridge. Then turned to Sandra, "Quick, crawl and when you reach the other side, there should be a friend of mine waiting. Go, hurry!"

Several more shots rang out and Gillis anxiously looked into the darkness of the hole. He could no longer see Sandra's dress but he could hear her struggling as she worked to make it through the maze of debris. If Logan's lantern was still lit, she would soon see it. It is now or never, he thought as he fired two more shots across the bridge and then dove for the small hole. He began crawling as fast as he could through the darkness. Seconds later he could see a small glimmer of light and he knew it was Logan's lantern. He heard another shot and this one was close. Gillis felt a sharp pain in his leg and knew he had been shot, but how bad, he had no idea. He kept moving and as he got closer to the opening he yelled for Logan, "Run, get her out of here, they are right behind me!"

A quick series of shots sent black smoke into the maze of burnt timbers. Going as fast as he could Gillis finally broke from the timber passage into the tunnel. He stood holding his small lantern and as he did he felt a hand grab his ankle, knocking him to the floor. Kicking the hand with his free foot, he ripped his foot from the grip. Madly crawling, trying to get upright he glanced back to see the darkened shape of a man with a thick beard climbing through the opening. Gillis finally launched himself to his feet and ran. Logan and Sandra were nowhere in sight and Gillis hoped they had already made it to the safety of the stairs, and with luck the street.

The bearded man somehow had made it through the tunnel even with his wide shoulders and was now trying to get to his feet. The man chasing him was agile and fast and Gillis knew it would only be a matter of a few more feet before he caught him. In a panic he ran up the brick staircase into the main tunnel. In the faint light in front of him he could make out the scattered boards that hid the hole in the floor. Then he felt a hand grabbing at his shirt and he ducked and threw himself to the wall beside the boards. The man behind him dove at him but the momentum threw him forward into the middle of the rotten boards. The sound of wood shattering and a man screaming filled the tunnel. Moments later he heard a loud thud and then a small cloud of dust arose from the hole.

Gillis needed to find his way to the street and fast. Another shot rang out as he continued to run but felt nothing. Near the entrance he turned and fired blindly back into the tunnel and then dove through the door. He regained his feet and saw Logan and Sandra standing there.

"Run!" Gillis screamed in a panicked voice. Logan turned and fired his pistol several times at the tunnel entrance and then began to run. Gillis, Sandra, and Logan broke into the street as they heard more shots coming from behind them. Down the street, they could see uniformed officers piling out of the station and sound of high-pitched whistles. They could hear the sound of men coming from behind them.

"This way!" Logan yelled pointing in the opposite direction of the police station. "The carriage is down the block and around the corner."

Several of the policemen held muskets and one had a pistol and before the three of them were halfway up the street they could tell the two parties were in full battle.

Logan looked down at Gillis's leg. "Is it bad?"

"No, a flesh wound, keep running. We need to get to the carriage." Gillis could hear more gunfire and took a second to glance over his shoulder. Behind him several bodies lay in the street as more police came streaming out of the station.

The horse and carriage were tied to a hitching post and Gillis helped Sandra while Logan untied the horse and launched himself into the carriage seat. Sandra slid closer to Logan as Gillis hopped up onto the crowded carriage yelling, "Go, go!" Logan snapped the whip, sending the horse into a fast trot.

"Are you sure that wound is all right?" asked Logan, keeping his eyes focused on the reins and horse.

Sandra continued to stare ahead as if she were numb to what was happening until finally she laid her head on Gillis's shoulder. Gillis answered, "I'm fine. I'm much more worried about Sandra and what they did to her."

She sat there staring as the horse trotted along and then suddenly she jerked her head up like she was just waking up. Gillis leaned over and grabbed both of Sandra's shoulders gently. "Are you okay?"

She whipped her head around and looked straight at Gillis. "They tried to starve us to death—they didn't feed us. It was damp and cold. All the men were beat and mistreated. They…" Sandra hesitated, "they beat several men to death."

"Why would they do that?"

"The guard told me it wasn't what they did, it was what their families did."

Sandra began to stare straight ahead as before. Logan looked over at the stoic Sandra. "I hope we can get her back. She must have gone through hell down there." Gillis nodded in agreement. For the next twenty minutes she stared until they went over Long Bridge and the bumpy ride created by the planks seemed to suddenly wake her again.

She looked at Gillis and then began talking. "They told me. I talked to the guards and they felt bad they had to lock me up but said Gillis was figuring things out and was a threat. They were killing for revenge for the Potato Famine in 1845." Then as quickly as she began she stopped.

"I know what she's talking about," said Logan. "Thousands of Irish families died during the famine."

The rest of the trip was quiet and no one spoke until the carriage turned into the yard and over to the carriage area. Gillis helped Sandra down from the carriage and with his arm around her waist walked her to the back door of the house. Out of nowhere Sam appeared and opened the door while he held a lantern high enough that it lit the gravel in front of the doorway.

"You did it, you found Sandra! Is she all right?"

"She's a little beat up, hungry and really worn out but I think she will be okay. Can you pour her a warm bath, and we will need to find her some clothes."

"I think some of Annabelle's clothes might fit. They may be a bit baggy but at least they are clean. No one has done anything to her room since she was murdered."

"Good, let's get her some food and a hot bath."

Sandra looked at Gillis. "Who is this man?"

"He has been helping me," said Gillis. "And a lot has happened since you were kidnapped. As soon as you get some rest I will explain everything." Gillis never saw Sandra eat so fast, as her dainty lady-like mannerisms seemed to vanish.

An hour later Sandra was reclining in what had been Annabelle's large porcelain tub. Gillis put a folding screen in front of the tub and sat in front of it in case Sandra needed help. Finally, Gillis could hear her getting out of the tub and asked, "Are you okay?"

"Yes, that was wonderful. Let me dry off and get these clothes on and I will be down. I'm a little tired but I want to see you for a while before I rest."

Gillis headed back down the stairs and into the kitchen where Logan and Sam sat talking. Sam moved to look at Gillis. "Logan told me most of what he knows but it sounds like you had your hands full. Are you all right?"

"The wound isn't deep. I was lucky the bullet only caught a little skin. I need to wash it out thoroughly so if you could boil some water it would be greatly appreciated."

Sam nodded while Logan asked Gillis, "What happened in there? Sure stirred up a pile of hornets!"

"They had a literal prison down there. We found the senator that vanished, Lenox Baker. He looked really rough and you could see they had been torturing him. I still don't understand this whole thing, why second-generation Irishmen would be so obsessed with getting even twenty years later. Most people have to let go at some time but these people are totally focused on revenge."

Logan looked at Gillis. "A lot of close families were torn apart and some died during that famine. I told you I left the sheriff's office. It was shortly after I left that I met a man named Pinkerton."

"You mean Allen Pinkerton of the Pinkerton Detective Agency? I only know him from what I have read."

"One and the same. He is a man who demands justice and quite frankly he was exactly what I had in mind. He told me that he was approached by a high-ranking aide to President Buchanan. With all the murders and people vanishing Mr. Pinkerton needed to have a select group of individuals to help protect the President as well as other high-ranking officials. This group would work undercover and would deal with any possible threats, internal or external. Apparently, they had done an extensive background check on me and they asked me to join. According to Mr. Pinkerton my knowledge of the Washington and Alexandria area would be a vital component of the group."

Gillis interrupted. "So you are a Pinkerton agent? But what does that have to do with my father and this Fenian Mu group?"

"Do you remember the long trips away from the farm your father took when you were young?"

"Yes, he had a lot of business out of town—but get to the point."

"About eight months ago your father contacted me. I don't know how he knew I worked for the Pinkertons but he did. One day I found a letter in my mailbox from him. He wanted to arrange a meeting. Before that I had never heard of Scully McCabe but what he had to say would blow the lid off everything I knew about assassins and protecting this country."

"Most Irishmen are good hard-working people just like you and me. Unfortunately your father had been forced down a different path. He has been helping me for over a year now and I think you need to know who your father really is—he was raised and trained in Ireland to work for the Fenian Brotherhood. He was one of their top assassins. A couple of years ago he became disgusted by all the senseless killings and decided to switch sides. Now he's working with the U.S. government."

"So let me get this straight," said Gillis. "I assume by what you told me this is not all a coincidence and that Sam living here is not by chance. Nor are you his son-in-law, am I right?"

"Sam is ex-military, a retired major and you're right, we moved him into the boarding house so we could contact your father when he visited his lady friend. We thought we had it figured out. No one would suspect Sam and he could get messages to me as needed, but no one figured her life was in danger. Your father's information was beyond valuable."

Just then Sandra walked down the stairs. "Thank God you came when you did, Gillis. I feel like I lived through the worst nightmare imaginable. Who would have ever believed a group could be so violent and exist here right under our government's nose."

"That is what Logan and I have been talking about. Do you have enough energy to listen to what he has to say about it?"

"Yes, I want to hear," said Sandra, as Sam got a chair and helped her into it.

"Your father was sworn to secrecy and if he ever told you or anyone else it would have been a death sentence," Logan said. "They would have killed him, and you. I am sure he told you about being an orphan and how a rich old man took him in and paid for his schooling. That wasn't just a school and your father wasn't just an ordinary orphan. The old man's name was John O'Mahony and he didn't just happen upon your father or help him out of the goodness of his heart. He was rich and hated anything English." "When your father was young he watched both his parents die of starvation. He was taught that England chose to let Irishmen die because they had no money and they could make better profits elsewhere. This Mr. O'Mahony fought for a free Ireland and lost both of his sons fighting the occupying English troops."

"He started a school in an abandoned castle in a remote part of Ireland and filled it with orphans. These weren't just ordinary orphans. Each child was tested for how smart they were and their athletic ability before they were admitted. If they couldn't meet those standards they'd find themselves back on the streets fending for themselves or worse. Those that made the grade were given a great education, taught how to speak correctly, use proper manners, and other subjects that would allow them to flourish in almost any environment. But all of this had another side, a dark side. They were also being trained in the art of killing, the art of being an assassin." Gillis glanced over at Sandra with a look of disbelief.

Gillis was angry. How could this possibly be true? "This doesn't make any sense—my father couldn't have been an assassin. My father was a loving, caring person who went out of his way to help others. Never once in all the years I lived on the farm, did I see one thing that would make me believe he would do anything even close to that."

"Marrying your mother changed him. For the first time since his family died he experienced love and found something worth living for. I am sure he was a gentleman at home, but you never saw his hidden side. He never wanted to drag you into the dark side of his life. Your father really loves you and I only hope he is all right. He never wanted to send you back to Ireland but they demanded it. He had no choice."

"When you ran away and disappeared, you actually made him happy. By not knowing where you escaped to, you didn't have to suffer the same brutal education your father was forced to endure. You aren't the physical fighter your father was, but it is obvious to everyone that you are as smart. The Fenians wanted you for your intelligence. Brilliant people are much harder to find than brawlers. They intended to groom you for leadership."

Gillis leaped to his feet and walked to the door and then spun around and walked back. He seemed stuck on what Logan had said and wasn't going to let it go. "What do you mean if he is all right?"

"I was supposed to meet with your father several months ago about some important information but he never showed up. He changed the location of our meeting twice that week before he finally settled on an isolated café, but he never showed and I haven't heard from him since."

"So what you are saying is my father is dead?"

"No, that is not what I am saying. I just don't know if he is alive or not. If he is alive and he could, I am sure he would contact us. He said it was extremely important that he give me this information but I don't know what he knows and I never saw him again."

"I find this all hard to believe," said Gillis.

"Your father anticipated you might not believe me. He wanted me to remind you of when you were young. He mentioned Monty and said if you can find him, he will have the answers to most of your questions."

Gillis looked at Logan and then lowered his head before speaking. "That was a special time between my father and me. I never spoke of those times or of Monty to anyone."

"Your father said that somehow you would figure this whole thing out. He has great confidence in you. You might even know where he is."

"I don't know where he is but I may know where the information you are looking for is. We will need to make a trip back to my father's farm to be sure but I am not leaving without Sandra. I almost lost her once and I won't lose her again."

Logan stood. "Tomorrow we can talk further but I need to go back and check in. We sure stirred up a hornet's nest tonight. Hopefully, the police were able to rescue some of those prisoners." He paused for a moment and then looked at the weary Sandra. "I will be back first thing tomorrow and we can talk more. Sam, can you keep an eye on things so these two can get some sleep? They have been through a lot."

"Not a problem," Sam said. "But I need to mention that I saw that man hanging around on the corner again today. I went and got my spyglass to check him out but he seemed to have disappeared. Can't say he was spying on the house but I haven't seen that man before and right now that makes me nervous."

Logan nodded in agreement. "I don't think anyone knows you are here but just in case I will try and bring back some men. I should be back early tomorrow morning. Until then, stay in the house and be careful. We need to discuss a few more things."

Gillis's glance caught Sandra dropping her head and he reached over and caught her from falling. "I need to get her to bed. With a bath and the food, she should feel better tomorrow, but for now she needs sleep."

Logan walked to the door. "Remember, avoid lighted windows and stay safe. I will be back in the morning." Silently he opened the door and disappeared into the darkness.

Gillis helped Sandra up and walked her to Sam's bed. He had changed the linen while she was eating and by the look on Sandra's face she was too tired to notice. "Honey, I love you and you will be fine," Gillis said. "It's time for you to get some rest. Everything will be all right now that I have you back."

Sandra looked at him smiled. "I love you too Gillis, but who is Monty?"

Gillis felt warm inside, and having Sandra back and remembering a fond memory made him smile. "Monty was the name of my favorite creature, a giant wooly mammoth. When I was real young I was fascinated by him. My father would read stories to me about how he would lumber across the countryside with his massive tusks. Monty was our secret, just between him and me and when Logan mentioned Monty, I knew they had really talked. My dad wouldn't have shared our secret lightly."

Sandra's face had barely touched the pillow when she seemed to fall into a deep sleep. Gillis bent down and kissed her cheek as he pulled the blankets up around her neck. After blowing out the candle he headed back to the main room where Sam sat waiting.

As Gillis entered, Sam turned his head. "You still have my Navy Colt, I see. Just double check and make sure it's loaded."

"Do you think they will find this place?"

"No, I don't, but seeing men around here I haven't seen before makes me more than a little nervous. Knowing Logan, he will be back early tomorrow and we can get things figured out. Use the chair or the couch and get yourself a little sleep—who knows what tomorrow is going to bring but keep that pistol close. I have a little whiskey—it might help you relax. My guess is the next couple of days may be interesting, real interesting."

"I appreciate you asking, but not right now. I have a lot of thinking to do. If I am to find my father I have to get back to his farm and there's a lot of territory between here and there. A lot can happen on a long journey like that. I will be interested to hear what Logan has to say tomorrow."

Sam got up and walked toward the kitchen. "Sleep now and I will wake you if I need you. I plan to watch all night—that's why I brewed the whole pot."

Gillis sat in the big pillowed chair and was surprised at the comfort. He laid his pistol on the table next to the chair and looked over at Sam quietly sitting at the table. "Have you ever been scared, I mean really scared? So scared you didn't know if your body would do what your mind ordered it to do? Where we found Sandra was a terrible bad place and I thought I would lose control."

Sam looked at him and made a few movements with his mouth like he was trying to speak but didn't have the words. Finally he said, "I guess that's the real difference between men and boys. Men do what they need to do, no matter what—boys don't. There's a lot of talk thrown around about how tough guys are but no one really knows for sure until the moment they have to face fear head on. If you wouldn't have been afraid down there, there is probably something wrong with you. You reached deep and did what you needed to do. No matter if you are second-guessing yourself or not, there is no doubt what you did took bravery and guts. Now get some sleep."

Closing his eyes, Gillis thought how wonderful it was to have Sandra back. Minutes later his head fell to one side and he began to snore softly.

* * *

It was close to daylight when Sam shook Gillis's arm. "Wake up—we have company and I don't think it is Logan."

Gillis jumped up, grabbing his gun as he rose. Sam had the curtain slightly pulled back and was peering into the darkness. "There is something out there. The neighbor's dog was barking and then abruptly stopped and that ain't like him. I thought I saw movement a couple of minutes ago, but I can't be sure. Go in there and check on Sandra and make sure she is all right but don't light any candles." Sam pulled a shotgun from the closet and continued to stare into the darkness. "I think I will go outside and check on things. It's probably nothing but don't shoot me when I come back in."

Gillis shook his head as he crossed his arms. "Don't worry, I won't shoot you. Do you think it's a good idea for you to go outside? Shouldn't we wait until Logan gets back?"

"We got the stock out there too and I would feel better if I checked. Anyways, I have my trusty shotgun and it is one hell of an equalizer. Don't worry, I will be fine. You don't need much of an aim with this gun. Now go and check on that sweet future wife of yours. I will lock the door behind me. I have a key to let myself back in but I will knock first. Stay back in the shadows and don't go near those windows."

Gillis headed to the bedroom and silently opened the door, letting his eyes adjust to the darkness. He could hear Sandra softly breathing and finally the shape of her body came into focus. Relieved, he turned and closed the door quietly, leaving only a slight crack as he left.

When he got back to the living room Sam had already gone and Gillis checked to make sure the door was locked. He was getting nervous and wondered if there really was someone lurking outside. Walking over to the stove, he picked up a towel and reached for the coffee pot. He poured a steamy black cup before returning to the leather padded chair. The chair gave him an excellent view of the door and the room where Sandra slept. With one hand holding the coffee cup, and the other holding his Colt, he sat down to wait.

Almost five minutes later he heard a soft knock and then the sound of a key in the lock. He heard a voice. "It's all right, Gillis. It's me, Sam."

The door opened and Sam began to enter through the doorway when all of a sudden and without a sound, a well-dressed man appeared behind him. The man bent his wrist back in a ninety degree angle from his forearm and shoved it toward the back of Sam's head.

Gillis launched himself from his chair, throwing his hot coffee in the direction of Sam's face. Sam's immediate reaction was to duck his head to the side and that movement saved his life. An eight-inch rod shot from the man's sleeve, cutting hair and scalp fragments from the side of Sam's head. The impact knocked Sam to the floor. Gillis raised his pistol and without aiming shot several times, tearing two large chunks of wood from the door frame. The well-dressed man yanked his arm back and disappeared from the doorway as Gillis ran towards him.

Leaping over Sam, Gillis made it outside. He swung the gun in all directions but the mysterious man had disappeared back into the darkness. He stood there for a long minute before going back inside and locking the door behind him. Gillis reached down and helped Sam stumble to a chair. Then he grabbed a towel from the kitchen and pressed it against the bloody wound.

"What's going on?" asked a tired Sandra as she appeared in the doorway. "I heard shots." She hesitated. "What happened to Sam?"

Gillis motioned for her to get down. "They found us, stay low. Logan should be back soon and he is bringing help."

Chapter 26

Sandra dropped to the floor and crawled into a dark corner of the room. Gillis could see she was scared and he hated these men for what they had done to her. Sam moaned in pain and reached up and touched the towel. "Where in the hell did that guy come from? I thought I checked everything real well before I decided to come back in."

Gillis whispered to Sandra, "I need Sam to lie on the floor and for you to hold this towel tightly against his wound. I am going to see if I can figure out what they are doing out there."

Sandra slid across the floor and helped Sam down while holding the blood-stained towel in place. "Will he be all right?"

"Head wounds always look worse than they are. He lost a lot of skin but with time, that will heal. The biggest thing is to keep pressure on the wound and keep him warm."

"I will be okay. Takes a lot more than a head wound to stop this old geezer," said Sam with a painful look on his face.

Gillis crawled to the window and looked out. Numerous lights from lanterns were now on in the neighborhood and he knew that the shots had been heard. Gillis heard a movement that sounded like horses and he hurried to the front window while keeping low. He could make out at least six mounted men and he knew he was in trouble.

"Turn the table over—you and Sam need to get behind it. That oak should stop any musket ball. There is a group of riders outside and this could get ugly." Gillis grabbed Sam's Colt revolver and checked the cylinders one by one. All six were loaded. He could feel his stomach tightening as he glanced out the window quickly and then looked over in Sandra's direction. She had done a good job in making sure they were both out of the line of fire. Now it was up to him to fend off whoever was outside.

Someone banged on the door. He turned both pistols in the direction of the door and took a deep breath.

"Gillis, it's Logan, open up. Gillis, can you hear me?"

Gillis jumped to his feet and opened the door to the familiar voice. Logan pointed to the chunk of wood missing from the door frame. "Looks like you had some trouble."

Several soldiers stood outside as Logan and an officer entered the house. It was Major Cates. He saw Sam lying on the floor with Sandra holding the blood-soaked towel on his head. The major hurried outside and barked an order to get a doctor, then walked back in.

"Don't worry, the major brought a dozen men with him and they are searching the grounds. Whoever was out there is gone now," said Logan.

The major saluted Gillis. "Sir, I hope you accept my apologies. You were right and I didn't believe you. I believe you now. Officer Logan informed me of the situation and your part in it. And to make matters worse they tried to assassinate you. Did you get a good look at him?"

"I am sure it was the same man I saw earlier, the man at the restaurant. It had to have been him. I didn't get a good look at him but it was him. He almost killed Sam. I saw the weapon. It looked like some sort of rod. It's got to be some type of spring-loaded device and from what I could tell the weapon is completely concealable inside the cuff of his shirt." Gillis paused for a second and then sat down. "It was almost like the whole thing happened in slow motion. Sam was coming in and then there was this arm silently extending itself toward the back of his head."

Logan put his hand on Gillis's shoulder. "Everyone is okay now. You did a good job."

Gillis looked up and gently nodded. He felt shaky as he stood and walked over to Sandra. "Are you all right?"

Sandra struggled to her feet. "When is this nightmare going to end?"

Twenty minutes later the doctor arrived and the soldiers escorted him inside. Immediately he began working on Sam as Gillis, Sandra and Logan sat around the table drinking coffee and trying to get themselves back together. Abruptly, Logan changed the subject. "The assassin that came for you is known as The Surgeon. They call him that for a reason. His murder scenes are always clean and well thought through. He has been working on and off in the Washington area for the past two years and the amount of information we have on him wouldn't fit in this coffee cup. From what I have been told, he is a normal-looking gentleman of average height and weight. He dresses well and most of his victims never knew what hit them. The majority of his murder scenes are the same. We aren't sure of the murder weapon he uses but we always knew it was him by the small hole in the back of the victim's head. It would kill almost instantly, quietly and with little mess. If it was a spring-loaded rod you saw, it would fit the description of what we know about him."

"I am still a little irritated about you using me for bait." Gillis looked Logan in the eye. "But if my father brought you in on this and told you about Monty then he wanted me involved. I will try and help you as much as I can, but my first priority is to protect Sandra."

"I understand. You said you might know where to look for a clue."

"My father's farm is called Kilmaar Glenn after a beautiful farm he knew in Ireland. He left me a clue that I think I figured out before Luke was killed. I told Sandra about it in the vaguest of terms but I believe the answer is there."

"I am sure by now you have figured out we aren't dealing with regular street thugs," said Logan. "These are the worst of the worst. These men live in cities across the East Coast and beyond. If my source is correct they may even try to kill the President. To our knowledge your father is the only person to ever penetrate their inner circle and if he has the information we think he does, it could bring down their whole organization. At first we believe they wanted to see if you could smoke out your father but now they mean to kill you any way they can."

"I know what we are dealing with and I thought this group was far larger than you were telling me. This is a young country in the middle of a civil war and if the President were to be killed, then who knows what the fallout would be."

"We need to leave for your father's farm as soon as we can and find what you believe is hidden there."

"They know we are here and I don't believe a dozen or more soldiers are going to be enough to protect us if they come hard. It seems to me, we need to leave here as soon as possible and try to disappear into the hills on our way to Kilmaar Glenn. Once we are there, we will be on our turf and the odds will substantially change."

"Sandra, are you able to travel?" asked Logan.

"Yes, I am."

Gillis gave Sandra a concerned look. "I'm not honestly sure she is but I will talk with her tomorrow. In the meantime, have the major and his men settle in until morning. If we leave, I want to leave as soon as it gets dark tomorrow night. If I'm correct, there is supposed to be little to no moon."

Logan nodded in agreement. "I will go tell the major."

Gillis walked Sandra back to her bedroom and quietly said good-night. He was relieved she was getting some sleep. He thought of Sam, whom the doctor had moved across the hall to another bedroom. As he entered the bedroom the doctor met him in the doorway.

"Is he all right, doc?"

"Nasty wound to the head but it will heal. For the next couple of weeks he might have a lingering headache but I believe eventually he will be fine. Thank God it was only a glancing blow. Whatever hit him was one vicious weapon to slice through bone like that."

"Thanks, doc. Will you check back in tomorrow morning and make sure he is doing okay? He is too good of an old guy to lose."

"No problem. I will see you then." The doctor picked up his brown bag and headed for the door.

Gillis took a seat on the wide couch. Tomorrow they would try to make the journey back to Kilmaar Glenn and the safety of his childhood home. If he was right, Brown Haven—the old, isolated cabin down in the meadow could give the answers needed to solve this mess and help him find his father. He wondered if Sandra would be able to travel after the horrible ordeal she had gone through. Tomorrow would be a new day and he would know soon enough.

* * *

A rooster crowed about a hundred yards away and Gillis sprung to his feet before he realized where he was. A sigh of relief came over him as he sat back down and reached for his pistol. He looked at the place where the two mini-balls had torn chunks of wood from the door frame and wished his aim had been truer. He sat there trying to figure out the best way to proceed when Logan walked in.

"Morning Gillis, hell of a night last night. Hope you two slept all right. We got another ten men outside to watch the place and more if we need them. You still thinking you want to leave tonight?"

Gillis sat up from the couch. "Morning already? I didn't sleep at first but I guess I was exhausted because I sure slept the last part of the night. Yes, I want to leave right after dark. I plan to ride my old partner's mule and have Sandra ride my mule, Brandywine. I would also like someone to go to the hotel and get both Sandra's and my belongings and settle any bill we have."

"I will ask the major to take care of it."

"I want Sandra to sleep as much as possible. Have you looked in on Sam to see how he is doing?"

"I checked in on him earlier and he's doing fine. Again, thank you for saving him."

"No thanks needed. Anyone would have done the same thing."

The rest of the day seemed to creep along with numerous discussions as to what would be the safest route for their journey when Gillis heard a knock on the door.

"It's Major Cates. My men are ready to leave whenever you and Miss Richards are."

Gillis opened the door and looked at the major, "I am a little surprised that Colonel Dougell put you in charge of getting me to Kilmaar Glenn. Throughout this whole ordeal, you certainly never thought I was telling the truth and now you believe that I may hold the secret to exposing one of the most lethal murder rings to ever to come to America."

"I understand your concern and reservations, and if you remember I have apologized for not originally believing you. I have been trained to examine all the facts before I come to a conclusion. Honestly sir, your story did not make sense to me and I didn't believe you. The colonel needs this mission to remain top secret and not get out amongst the public. He has seen to everything including our route."

Gillis just stared at him. "Well, do you finally believe me now?"

"Yes sir, all the facts point to you telling the truth from the beginning. I apologize again sir, but I was just doing my job and being careful."

Gillis was mad, and he didn't like this man, even a little bit. "I guess it's time I wake Sandra. It will be dark in another forty five minutes and if we could leave then, major, it would be appreciated."

"Yes sir, my men will be ready. We have your things from the hotel and we will have all but one of your mules packed. Do you want to us to supply you with some horses just in case the mules don't work out for the lady?"

Gillis thought for a moment. "No, we will ride the mules."

"Major, did you find out what happened with those Fenian men in the tunnel? Were the police able to capture them?"

"Logan told me of your part. I must say you are braver than I would have given you credit for, but yes. The police were able to kill five of them and capture another two. They also saved three prisoners, including Senator Baker. They were holding them for ransom and only the government knew."

"That answers a few more questions," said Gillis as he walked over to Sam's bedroom door. Logan was sitting beside the bed as Gillis walked up and noticed Sam's eyes open and alert. "Sam, I wanted to thank you for everything. Without you, I am not sure we would have made it. When this whole thing is over with, I hope to see you again."

Sam's gaze had a look of understanding as he reached for Gillis's hand. "You take good care of that future wife of yours—she's a keeper."

They talked for a few more minutes before Gillis said his good bye and left to wake Sandra. Gillis knocked on the door and to his surprise a chipper voice answered, "Just a minute, I am almost dressed."

Gillis went back and sat at the table trying to figure out exactly what to say. Would she be all right to travel? How had this whole ordeal affected her?

Minutes later Sandra entered the room. "How is Sam doing?"

"He's well, but a better question is, how are you doing?" Gillis stood from his chair to greet her.

Sandra walked up to Gillis and hugged him. "I'm fine now that I am here with you."

An hour later under the cloak of darkness a troop of sixteen soldiers, the major, Logan, Gillis and Sandra were headed down the road and out of town. Several soldiers watched as they left, ordered to stay and watch over Sam. Gillis rode Scotch Daddy and Sandra rode Brandywine. He felt comfortable with Sandra riding such a sure-footed animal. Two scouts rode in front with the major and Logan and two more soldiers rode at the rear of the column. Gillis and Sandra were in the middle leading their mules while two soldiers led another four pack mules behind them. Gillis could tell these men were handpicked and understood how important their mission was but he couldn't shake the feeling of being watched.

As they passed over the last small bridge that led out of town, the sound of horse hooves hitting the bridge planks seemed to echo throughout the darkness and Gillis was sure anyone for a half a mile could surely hear them. He looked over his shoulder and in the distance he could see street lights breaking the almost-complete darkness of the town. He felt different. Gillis had come into this town a naive young man. This trip had changed and hardened him. Never again would he look at things the same way now that he had been touched by such violence and death.

Soon they were on a narrow country road with their final destination being Scully's ranch. For five hard days they rode, making reasonable time. Sometimes they rode by day and other times they rode late into the night. The major's idea was to confuse anyone who might be following them.

It was close to dusk and the troop had ridden down a dark road for close to four hours when the major rode his horse back down the column of soldiers and stopped beside Gillis and Sandra. "My scout says there is a small meadow ahead where we can rest for the night, depending on how Miss Richards is doing."

Gillis looked at Sandra, concerned over her response. "I'm fine to ride on if you chose to. Your mule Brandywine is very nice and smooth to ride but sooner or later I will need a break," she said.

The major could read the concern on Gillis's face and sat for a couple of seconds before making his decision. "If it is all right with you, ma'am, and Mr. McCabe, we will camp in the meadow for a few hours and then leave before light tomorrow. This will give my scouts some time to see if we are being followed as well as scout our route up the road a piece."

Gillis nodded. "We are fine with that, major." When they reached the meadow, Gillis helped unpack the two mules while one of the troopers watered the other two mules. Quickly, Gillis unpacked a few extra blankets and a large piece of canvas for a makeshift tent and set up a place for Sandra. He had just finished squaring everything away when the trooper who had helped water the mules walked up.

"Sir, would you mind if I asked you a question?"

Gillis looked at him with a puzzled expression. "As long as it doesn't jeopardize anything related to this mission."

"No sir, it doesn't jeopardize anything. I would never ask anything that would put you or this mission in jeopardy. My question is . . ." He hesitated trying to find the right words. "There is a rumor that somehow you figured out how the assassins were disappearing by finding a single drop of blood. I would like to know if that is true or not."

"It's partially true. When I first looked into the murders, I was told the assassins seemed to just vanish. One day, I was fairly close to a man who was assassinated and I chased after the murderer. He just seemed to disappear. I know people don't vanish and knew he was wounded and that is what gave him away. I was able to follow his blood trail from the street and into an alley. There in front of a brick wall, I found a perfectly round spot of blood. If the assailant had been moving, the spot would have been oval. So I asked myself, why did he stop? The answer had to be that there was an escape route through that wall and somehow he had to have accessed it."

Suddenly, Major Cates hollered, "Trooper, get over here on the double and quit bothering those people. You have the first shift on guard duty with Trooper Morris. Make sure you plant yourselves back down that road at least a hundred yards and keep a good lookout. I don't want anyone coming in here without us knowing."

Major Cates walked over to Gillis. "I hope my trooper wasn't bothering you."

"He was fine. We were just talking, nothing important."

"Mr. McCabe, I hope you feel like we can work together to make this mission successful," the major said in a stoic, professional tone.

"I am sure I can work with you like I worked with some of the others."

"Others?"

"Other assholes like you." Gillis turned and walked back over to where Sandra was sitting.

"I guess I deserve that," said the major under his breath.

The night was dark and unseasonably cold but Gillis was happy to see Sandra sleeping well as he thought of all that had happened.

The next morning Gillis saw the major, Logan, and several of the scouts talking and he hurried over to join them. "What's going on?" asked Gillis.

"The scout heard a horse about two miles up the road. It was tied in thick timber and there is no reason for it to be there. It's possible it's someone traveling or it could be a Confederate patrol. I know this area has been in Union hands for a least a month but there is no telling if a few patrols made their way through our lines. It is also a possibility that some of those Fenian men knew we were coming this way and somehow managed to get in front of us."

Logan looked at the major with a disconcerted face. "Major, we have no idea how good these people's information is. There is certainly the possibility that we could have a few moles in our system and they might be getting information as they need it."

"Ridiculous. Only you, Colonel Dougell, and I know the route we are taking. There is no possible way they could know our route."

Logan shot back in an angry voice, "For three years this group has run rampant in Washington, and if it wasn't for Gillis, we probably still wouldn't have our first true lead. We have to assume they have someone on the inside." Logan crossed his arms with a look of firm seriousness.

The major took a deep breath. "Then what do you think we should do?"

"I'm not sure. What little information we have points to something big coming down and fairly soon. We need to get Gillis to Kilmaar Glenn as quickly as possible and visit the cabin he calls Brown Haven. I am concerned that we are quickly running out of time," said Logan.

Major Cates broke from the group. "Sergeant Morgan, take five men up the road and inspect the place the scout heard the horse. If there is an ambush, I want it flushed out immediately. If we hear any shooting, we will back you up. Now pick your troopers and get going! Corporal Sanson, take two men and go back down the road a hundred yards and join our rear guards until I send someone to relieve you." The major turned back to Gillis. "I can't afford for you to be part of an ambush. Once they inspect the road and it is clear, we will be on our way."

Gillis nodded and glanced at Logan as he walked back toward Sandra. "Are you doing all right?"

Sandra, with little emotion in her voice, answered, "I'm fine. Let's hope we can get this mess cleared up and be on our way. I am ready to go back to your father's ranch and hopefully get our lives back to some kind of normalcy."

"Who would believe what has happened to both of us. I wonder if my father has somehow gotten back to the farm. I understand now why we had that big fight when I was a teen. He started it because he felt trapped—he had no good choices and now I don't know if I will ever see him again."

"I don't know if he is alive or dead but from what Logan said, he's a survivor. I believe there has to be a good reason that no one has seen him and in my heart I hope and pray he is still alive."

Gillis looked into Sandra's warm blue eyes. "You are an amazing woman Miss Sandra Richards—how did I get so lucky to ever find you?" As he spoke he noticed a couple of the mounts being moved in the back of the meadow and for the first time he saw the outline of a wagon in the moonlight. Gillis was sure it was the same old logging wagon he had seen with Luke when they came down the shortcut from the mountain.

Sandra saw Gillis's attention had switched from her to something else. "What is it, Gillis?"

"There behind those horses, that old logging wagon. It was there when Luke and I came down from the mountain. If it is the same wagon, there is a trail behind it that leads up into the mountain. I remember riding right past an old logging wagon with the axle and several of its wheels broken. Luke led the way but I am sure this is how we rode towards town."

"The way things are going do you believe we need to use it? If there really is somebody out there and they mean to harm us, we need to know how to escape."

"I know but for now we will keep it to ourselves. I don't know these men. I believe they can be trusted but I am not going to gamble our lives on it."

Sandra gently nodded and sat back down as a trooper offered her some coffee which she took. Moments later Gillis and the group heard shooting from up the road and shortly afterward a trooper came running for the major. "Sir, there's at least ten men dug into the forest up the road and it don't look like they are wearing uniforms."

Gillis suspected that somehow the Fenians had found them and he rushed over to Logan. "We need to get out of here and quick. The information my father wanted me to find is too important to be lost here."

More shots rang out from down the road. Logan looked at Gillis. "How can we do that? We're trapped."

"I think I know a way out. There is a trail behind that old logging wagon in the back of the meadow. I remember it from when Luke and I rode down from the mountains and through this meadow. That has to be the same wagon. There is a trail behind that large bush over there," said Gillis, pointing.

Logan looked seriously at Gillis. "I will talk to the major. Start saddling up and get your two pack mules. We still have a fair ways to go and we will need them." Logan hurried toward the major as Gillis walked over to catch his mules who were staring at all the commotion as they grazed. A scout hurried to help him as he led two of the mules from the meadow.

Moments later, the trooper led the other two mules over to some close trees and tied them for saddling and loading. Gillis quickly rubbed the mule's backs with dry grass and put their blankets on. It only took a few minutes to have both riding mules saddled and bridled, and not much longer to tie the packs on. As Gillis tightened the last cinch, Logan walked his horse over to them.

"I'm ready anytime you two are. I talked to the major and at first he didn't like the idea of you leaving the safety of the troops but he doesn't believe things are going well. He has reluctantly agreed. He wants us to meet up at your father's ranch."

The trooper who had been helping Gillis turned to him. "Good luck, sir. We will do the best we can to hold these men off. I hope you make it." Then he saluted.

Chapter 27

Gillis led one of the mules followed by Sandra and last was Logan leading the other mule as they headed toward the old wagon in the moonlight. The sound of shots could be clearly heard from both directions and Gillis strained to figure out where the trail started. Abruptly Brandywine turned and started walking into the brush. The big mule took the lead as they went to his left and then began walking straight for a dark shadow in the mixture of maples and brush. It was as if Brandywine remembered exactly where the trail began and got the rest of the train of animals following in the right direction. The brush and trees seemed to open up and there in the moonlight Gillis could see the darkness of a trail at their feet. He sat back in his saddle and thought how amazing it was that the mule could somehow find her way in the dark and remember a trail it had traveled only once and that was over a month before.

For the next several hours they rode up the steep ridge working around numerous deadfalls and other obstacles. Gillis let Sandra lead because Brandywine seemed to know exactly where they were going. Each time she came to an obstacle she would stop and then, without help, figure the best way around it. Gillis was appreciative of what was happening and the additional confidence the mule gave him carrying Sandra, was much needed.

Hours later as they crested the top of the ridge the sun began to rise over the far horizon. Brandywine worked her way around another fallen tree. Only then did Gillis realize how well the animal had done in almost total darkness. Gillis leaned back in the saddle. "Are you doing okay?"

"I'm fine. What's your plan now?" Sandra asked.

"I honestly don't remember everything between here and the ranch, but I hope to ride until dusk and then camp in a place we can defend. Once we get off this trail, I need to try and remember all the turns and forks in the road and I don't feel comfortable I can do that in the dark. Tomorrow at first light, we will move out. This trail shortens the trip. If somehow the Army can find a way out of their mess, it will probably take them at least few days or so more to get to the ranch."

The group continued on, making good time even though the trail was rough and rocky. Gillis thought how well the mules had done when he heard a yell from behind him. He stopped and looked in the direction of the yell. There lying on the ground moaning in pain was Logan. He was holding his arm close to his body while his horse stood quietly with its reins dangling on the ground with a bloody knee.

"Logan, you all right?" yelled Gillis as he slid from Scotch Dandy and hit the ground running toward Logan. With the animals standing in the middle of the trail it was hard going around them and it took a minute for Gillis to make it back to where Logan sat.

"What happened?"

"I don't know for sure. One minute I was riding along and the next moment I was on the ground. My horse stumbled on something but I don't know what."

"Your arm doesn't look good. I have some clothes we can rip up for bandages and make a sling. Luke said this trail was more of a mule trail than anything else and I should have listened."

"Gillis, you had no choice. I can only hope those soldiers came out on the right side of things and survived. If it wasn't for this trail, I am not sure what would have happened."

It took a few minutes to unpack the clothing needed to make the bandages and it was becoming obvious that Logan wasn't doing better. Sandra and Gillis gently applied the bandage to his bloody arm and placed it in a sling. Then Gillis carefully wrapped the sling so it was tight to Logan's body, as Logan painfully moaned.

"Can you stand?"

Logan nodded and stood with Gillis's careful help. "I think I can ride. It won't be pleasant but we need to reach the ranch and find that information and something tells me we don't have much time."

"We will need to camp and rest tonight but we should be back to Kilmaar Glenn in three or four days, if everything goes well. Then I will send a man to fetch you a doctor."

"I like your optimism and I hope you are right. Come help me get back on my horse. Looking at this knee I think the horse is going to hurt as much as I will for the rest of trip."

Gillis looked at the horse's knee and tried to examine it. "It's a fairly deep cut but I am sure he can make it. If there is one thing I know about horses and mules, they are tough. Besides, neither of these pack-mules are broke to ride and getting bucked off again wouldn't help the situation." Gillis helped Logan get his foot in the stirrup and with a grunt Logan was back in the saddle.

The rest of the day went as well as could be expected with numerous stops to drink and rest Logan's ribs and arm. His face had lost some of its color but he seemed determined not to slow the group and finally as the sun started to set, Gillis pulled his mule up and stopped by a small, open meadow. "We camp here tonight. There is a stream over there and we should be able to hide ourselves back in that timber," said Gillis, pointing to a thick stand of trees at the back of the meadow. Gillis unloaded the two mules and took off their saddles.

Next he set up a small lean-to, to give Sandra some protection and privacy. Sandra cleared a small area back in the trees, got some wood, and then started a tiny fire. Fetching water from the stream, she got some coffee going and gave Logan a steaming cup as he leaned against the base of a large oak tree looking uncomfortable. Up until now, Gillis had felt more at ease that at least two men carried pistols, but with Logan's shooting arm being injured and with sore ribs, Gillis was sure he was in no shape for gun play.

Taking jerky from a bag, Sandra handed out what would serve as their dinner as darkness began to set in. Gillis stood. "I'm going to take a look at our back trail while it is still light enough to see. Hopefully, there will be no sign of anyone following us." He headed back up the trail toward the top of the ridge they had crossed earlier.

Ten minutes later and with it almost dark, Gillis sat on a rock and scanned the country they had just traveled through. For some reason he felt uneasy as if they were being followed, but there were no visible lights on their back trail and Gillis knew how hard it would be to follow their tracks at night. Satisfied, he stood and walked back to camp, joining the others.

In the light of the small fire, Gillis could see that Logan had fallen asleep as he leaned against a tree. Sandra got up and placed a blanket around him as he slept.

"See anything?" asked Sandra.

"Nope, everything was quiet and calm. I am going to get the mules and put Logan's horse on the picket line, and then we can talk."

A few minutes later Gillis walked back to the dimly lit space of their campsite and grabbed a blanket and sat on a log close to the fire, but with his back to the flames.

"You think we are going to have trouble?" asked Sandra.

"I'm not anticipating any but I want to be prepared for it. Staring at that fire will blind a man. Luke taught me that. If it wasn't for Luke I wouldn't be here now."

"He was a good hired hand."

"He was far more than my hired hand, he was my friend. Almost immediately, Luke knew we were being followed and now that I have seen what those men are capable of. I know that without him . . ." Gillis paused. "Anyway, he saved my life."

"I am sorry about Luke. I know you thought highly of him and he would want you to bring these men to justice. You said your dad left you some clues that might tell you where to find answers to this whole thing. You mentioned Brown Haven. Is that another ranch he owns?"

"No, Brown Haven is nothing more than a cabin that sits in a secluded meadow inside Kilmaar Glenn. The cabin was there when my father bought the property and he even lived there for a few years as they built the main residence. Dad decided to rebuild it and call it Brown Haven after his wife's family. From an early age I was banned from going down there. From what we have gone through, my guess is the Fenians came there every now and then on business and they were not the type you wanted your family near."

"Didn't you think that was kind of odd, not being allowed to go down there?"

"My father was a fair and just man but when he said something, he meant it. I always tried to respect that. Looking back, I believe in later years, I wasn't allowed down there because he didn't want me being lured in by those people."

* * *

The next morning Gillis was up before sunrise saddling all the animals with Sandra helping by holding a small kerosene lantern. When he was in the meadow and they were being attacked, the adrenaline was flowing but now the saddles and their loads seemed heavier as he worked through getting each animal ready. Logan seemed stiff and his movement painfully slow as Gillis helped him struggle to his feet.

"Will you be able to ride?"

Logan half-heartily smiled. "Hell yes, help me up into my saddle."

"First we need a little breakfast and some hot coffee, and then we are out of here."

Fifteen minutes later, Gillis led the two mules out of the small meadow followed by Logan and then Sandra pulling up the rear. About midday the trail broke from the ridge and the trio found themselves on a dirt road headed southwest. They passed the small clearing where Gillis had found the shallow grave but didn't stop, nor did he want to discuss it. Periodically, Gillis looked back over his shoulder and he could see pain on Logan's face. They were making reasonable time but there wasn't any way Logan's ribs and arm would stand the pounding of even a smooth lope. Gillis was sure he had a number of ribs either broken or badly bruised.

The next day was slower than anticipated but uneventful and Logan seemed to be getting slightly better. Gillis recognized some of the hills close to his father's ranch.

"We need to come into Brown Haven by the back trail we used, if I can find it. If those men are ahead of us they will probably be setting up close to the ranch. Hopefully Roper and his men have noticed them. I want to get off this road and on to that trail as soon as we can. It will be dark by the time we get to Brown Haven. It's pretty isolated and no one but us has used it for years. There's a good chance they don't know it's there."

They kept riding and Gillis looked down at the road. "Looks to me like we have company. Those tracks look fresh."

Sandra looked puzzled. "How can you tell, Gillis? You're no tracker."

"I'm not, but Wooly taught me a few things to look for and those are fairly fresh. Keep your eyes open and listen for anything that seems out of place. We should lose them when we cut off on that trail I know. If that works, we will wait until dark and then ride to the cabin."

For the next couple of miles the group rode silently and then Gillis saw what he was looking for, the grouping of several large rocks on the right side of the road. "If I remember correctly it's another fifty yards further on the left. My guess is it's going to be a little hard to find."

Suddenly Gillis pointed. "There it is, behind that bush, I am sure that's the trail!"

Logan rode up and looked in the direction he was pointing. "Boy, I don't see it. Are you sure there is a trail there?"

"Follow me, I am positive this is it," said Gillis, as he gave the mule a nudge with his foot and began leading the train of animals into the woods. Once inside the tree canopy the trail was far more visible. It was grown over in parts but the fact that the trail was a good three inches lower than the surrounding ground made it easy to follow. It was tough going with all the blow-downs and low overhanging brush. Roughly four hours later the trail broke from the forest and into a small meadow.

"There it is, Brown Haven," said Gillis with a smile as he pointed toward a small cluster of trees. "Somehow, we made it. The cabin is back in those trees. Let's tie off the animals here in the woods while we still have some light and unpack what we need for the night. I will get a lantern out and we can go inside the cabin."

"What's the matter?" asked Logan as Gillis remained in the saddle.

"I don't have the key; it's up at the ranch."

Logan sat there looking at Gillis and slowly shook his head. "Then break the damn window."

Gillis looked embarrassed for a second but then carefully helped Logan down and began unloading the stock. For the first time Sandra began unsaddling her mule and Gillis smiled to himself in approval. The animals were hungry but Gillis knew that putting them out on the meadow while there was still light could be dangerous so he decided to wait for a couple of hours until the dark of night really set in.

Gillis carried a number of items and a large bag, Sandra carried some cooking supplies and food while Logan carried the lantern in his good arm across the meadow.

"Find a window that makes sense to break," said Logan struggling with weariness and the constant pain. Gillis was tired too and he fought the urge to comment on the obvious. He laughed to himself about never considering the act of breaking a window.

Gillis set his load down in front of the door and began to walk around the cabin, looking for a window. Once he found one big enough to slide through, he broke the pane of glass and worked his way inside. Moments later he opened the door, startling Sandra. Gillis lit the lantern and helped her and Logan inside. Sandra quickly found a bed in one of the rooms and helped Logan over to it. He was exhausted and the moment he laid down, he was asleep.

As Sandra walked from the room she saw Gillis staring at the massive fireplace. "What are you doing?"

"I know you have been through a lot, but do you remember me talking about a book I found in Annabelle Smith's room? That book was mine, planted by my father and it was from my childhood collection. At night my father used to read to me and explain the marvels of the past. Throughout this whole thing he knew I would come looking for him and eventually find the building where his girlfriend was murdered. When I saw that book, I knew my father meant for me to find it. He left a word game, a puzzle, a code to solve in the same manner he used to give me as a child. Somewhere among these hundreds of fossils is a trilobite fossil that could lead me to the answers. Being secretive about things has always been my father's way. See all those fossils embedded in this fireplace? Now our challenge is to figure out which trilobite it is."

"Do you have any idea where to look?"

"No, it could be anyone of them. I will have to use the process of elimination."

Gillis stared at the massive fireplace and almost everywhere he looked there seemed to be a trilobite fossil of one size or the other. Gillis began by thoroughly examining the lower ones. Each fossil he pushed and pulled and tried to slide different angles before turning to the next one. An hour later he sat down and Sandra handed him a cup of hot coffee.

"No luck?"

"That's an understatement. I have checked every trilobite fossil at least twice and each one is solid and firmly anchored into the masonry. I don't see how they could possibly be removed and not at least leave some trace of the activity. A minuscule crack in the mortar, some small fracture in the fossil itself, something, but there isn't anything," said Gillis as he took a long drink from the cup. "Not a clue anywhere, not a thing. My father was clever and I must figure this out." As he sipped Gillis examined the fireplace from top to bottom again determined not to miss even the smallest detail and then he began to focus on the mantel.

Gillis got up holding his cup and walked over to the fireplace for a closer look with the kerosene lantern in his other hand. The extensive mantel was a good eight feet long and stretched much of the width of the entire fireplace. The ends of the mantel were flared back at a sixty degree angle and buried themselves into the mortar. The heavy mantel was made from one beautifully cut and sanded piece of maple held in place by two large end beams. The face of the mantel was an amazing work of craftsmanship and art. It was beautifully carved and detailed by someone with quite a talent. To add even more beauty to the ornate board, it also had been painted by an expert in shading and color variations. The unknown artist had captured the beauty of everything from flowers to branches and their ornate leaves.

"When you found the book on dinosaurs, didn't you tell me your father always liked to hide things in plain sight? So what are you missing?"

Gillis saw the almost unnoticeable wood carvings tucked into a shadow of the returned side of the mantel.

Gillis smiled broadly. "You're right, my father would always hide things in plain sight and if my guess is right, it's been staring me straight in the face and I didn't notice."

The return side of the mantel was facing the part of the cabin that received little light from the windows and Gillis thought without the light of a lantern, no one would ever closely examine this section. His inspection only took seconds before he noticed a tiny trilobite the size of a little finger. It was carved into the wood between two beautiful ornate maple leaves. Carefully, he placed his pinky finger on the shell of the tiny trilobite and pushed. Immediately, the shell moved backwards into the wood and then several wooden leaves and their branches sprung forward almost three inches, revealing a hidden compartment.

Inside the niche was a round tube of thin brass with a removable end. How amazing it was that someone had cut an irregular opening with such skill that to the naked eye it didn't exist. And to locate it in an area of painted shadows showed all the more cunning. Gillis shined his light inside the compartment and then inserted two fingers and removed the narrow, six inch tube and unscrewed the end. The tube was no more than two and a half inches in diameter but Gillis could see a tightly rolled paper tucked neatly inside and after smiling with a sense of achievement, he turned to Sandra.

Suddenly the door of the cabin slammed open and Gillis heard the sound of a gun's hammer being pulled back. "Don't move a muscle or you're dead. If you're smart you will set that lantern down on the floor, slowly."

Chapter 28

"Wooly, is that you?" Gillis recognized the deep, raspy voice.

"Mr. McCabe?"

Gillis picked up the lantern and set it on the table to light the room as Wooly released the pressure from the hammer and slipped the gun back into its holster.

"It's been a while since anyone has heard anything from you. Are you okay? Where's Luke?"

Gillis looked down at the floor for a moment until meeting eyes with Wooly. "It's a long story, Wooly, but Luke was killed. Unfortunately, we don't have a lot of time at the moment. We believe we are being followed by a group of men that are dedicated to killing me and getting ahold of what I think is in this tube."

"Luke was a good man, I am sorry to hear that. I guess you will be glad to know that Roper hired another four men while you were gone. About a week ago, one of the men saw a man with a spyglass watching the ranch and Roper felt you would want him to increase security. What's this brass tube have to do with everything?"

Gillis returned his attention to the tube and with some difficulty managed to retrieve the tightly rolled paper. Laying it on the table he unrolled it and then turned to the others.

"This is a letter from my father to me. Let me read it to you."

Dear Gillis,

First of all I want to express how sorry I am that you have been caught in the middle of all this violence; it was never my plan. By reading this letter I know you have been able to piece together the clues. You are clever, my son, and I am so very proud of you. Hopefully now you understand why I never tried to find you. The last thing in the world I wanted for you was to be a part of this hate-filled group. I knew if something happened to me you would be able to handle what needed to be done. As an orphan child I had few choices and now as an adult I chose to make the right decisions, even if it goes against the very people that raised me. As a group, the Fenian Brotherhood has lost their way in the hatred of anyone English. Their hate has led them to the point of murdering innocent people and exceeds anything a rational person could support. I find their new leader repugnant and evil. This younger group is violent beyond anyone's imagination. It has been difficult but someone had to inform the government what these people intended to do. They are a disgrace to the majority of good law-abiding Irish Brothers.

It is of extreme importance that you get the information on the next three pages to a man in Washington named Logan Fritz. Logan is a good man and I trust him. I have been giving Logan information for a while. With this information you can save a lot of good people. Do your best my son.

All my Love, Your father

Scully

Several minutes later after looking at the papers Gillis looked up with a serious face. "You aren't going to believe all the information this contains. There are lists of all the high ranking Fenian officers in almost every major city on the East Coast. The next sheet is a list of past and future targets and some of the dates they are to be eliminated."

"The last page is a list of secret locations they are using in each city and how to find them. Whoever wrote all this has done a lot of dangerous work and I believe that man is my father."

Gillis kept reading and then his face lost color. "Oh my God, it says here they plan to assassinate the President and they have a date."

"What's going on?" said Logan as he entered the room holding his ribs and sore arm.

"Sorry we woke you but I have something you need to see."

Logan took the bundle of papers and sat by the table and with the light of the lantern began reading them page by page. Several minutes later he looked up. "Do you realize what we have here? Your father has given us all we need to destroy the Fenian Brotherhood. We need to get this in proper hands in Washington immediately."

"Did you notice that Colonel Dougell's secretary, Miss Caden, is circled on the list?"

"Yes I saw that. It's hard to believe. She must have been the leak that enabled them to be one step ahead of us all the time."

Gillis turned to Wooly. "Is it safe to go up to the house?"

"I believe it is. We haven't seen any sign of strangers or anyone watching for at least two days. I think we need to be careful but if we take the path up through the forest we should be able to travel undetected."

Gillis insisted Logan rest for another thirty minutes before they left but finally gave in to his badgering. "Yes, I know how important it is to get this information to Washington but we need to be sure we can get it there. Wooly can make the ride to a safe telegraph office and get this information to Washington. He knows the country around here like the back of his hand and he is good with a horse. While you are resting, Logan, I need you to write a short letter Wooly can use when he telegraphs the message to Allen Pinkerton. Wooly and I are going to go over to the woods and saddle up and put the packs on the mules. We'll be back in fifteen minutes. Please write the letter but don't let your guard down even for a moment. Remember, these people didn't get this far by not being smart. I need a copy of everything."

Logan nodded as Gillis and Wooly headed out the door and across the moonlit meadow and disappeared into the forest. Minutes later Gillis walked back to the cabin and quietly knocked before whispering Logan's name.

"We're ready and here's your letter and the lists," said Logan as Gillis walked into the cabin. Gillis took the letter and shoved it inside his coat pocket.

Wooly led the ride through the forest on a trail that was overgrown and almost impossible to see in the dark. Gillis found himself covering his face to avoid branches that seemed to appear with the sole purpose of hitting him in the face. After about thirty minutes the tired troop broke from the forest and found themselves in front of a small cabin some distance from the main house.

"Follow my lead and don't talk until we are at the barn."

They hadn't made it twenty yards when suddenly there was a voice from out of the darkness. "Who goes there?"

Wooly quickly answered, "It's me, Wooly. Go tell Roper that he needs to come quickly and meet us at the barn."

Sandra rode up beside Gillis and whispered, "Why didn't he tell them you were here and why are we meeting at the barn?"

Gillis leaned back and answered in a quiet voice, "Because the barn is by far the most defensible building on the ranch and he didn't want anyone to know I am here. We need a safe place to talk with Roper and Wooly and if the Fenians are watching the farm they may attack now if they know I am here."

Sandra nodded and then fell back into line behind Gillis as they rode on. They stopped at a long hitching rail in front of the barn and Gillis helped Sandra to the ground and then tied the two pack mules to the rail. As he turned, he heard Roper whisper, "Nice to have you back, Mr. McCabe."

Roper smiled at Sandra. "Nice to see you again, Miss Richards."

"It's good to be back, Roper. Is the farm secure?" asked Gillis.

"Yes sir, Mr. McCabe. I have guards out on the whole perimeter and everything is quiet. I have been having Wooly ride the perimeter woods as much as possible. Good thing he did—I see he found you."

"He did and I appreciate it. Now please help the man on the horse down, that's Logan Fritz. He's pretty beat up so be careful. He's an agent for the Pinkertons and the U.S. government." Roper gently helped Logan down. Logan moaned quietly as his foot touched the ground and then he leaned against his horse.

Roper stood back and looked at Logan. "I don't know who looks worse, you or your horse. What happened?"

"That was one rough shortcut we took and unfortunately my horse stumbled up on the ridge and I regrettably failed to stay on."

"Roper, have a couple of the men unload the mules and then meet me inside the barn. We have some important business to discuss."

"Yes sir, Mr. McCabe."

Sandra turned to Brandywine and in a quick movement gave the mule a kiss on the muzzle and whispered, "Thanks for getting me here in one piece."

Gillis walked inside the barn with Logan, Sandra, and Wooly following. He set out five rounds of wood in a crude circle and then turned to Logan. "Why don't you and Sandra sit down and rest until Roper gets back?"

Logan slowly sat down with the look of pain. Gillis put his hand on Logan's shoulder. "Tomorrow we need to have one of the men ride and get a doctor but tonight you need to sleep in a real bed. I would have asked Roper to take you to the house immediately but you need to hear what I have to say."

Just then Roper walked through the wide barn door and shut it behind him. "Roper, will you lock the door? I need everyone to talk in a whisper. Who knows if the walls have ears and this is too important for the wrong person to hear."

Roper put the large solid board across both doors and tried to move it to make sure it was secure.

Gillis cleared his throat. "What I have to say I must say quickly. What we found in Washington was so far from what I expected that I don't have words to express it. My father is and has been in some way tied to a group call the Fenian Brotherhood. All those business trips he took were tied to this group. Over the years, the men who visited the ranch and stayed at Brown Haven were also part of this group."

"My father Scully chose at some point during that time to switch sides and help the U.S. government stop the Fenians. From what we now know, the Fenian Brotherhood figured out he changed sides and they murdered his girlfriend and possibly him. They also tried to kill me. We found documents with the names of their members, their hiding places, and a list of future targets. On that grievous list was a name that sent panic through me, our newly elected President, Abraham Lincoln. They even have a date and place. Unfortunately it is only three days away."

"I have to believe the Fenian Brotherhood knows I have found the list and they will do almost anything to destroy it. We need someone to slip out of the ranch tonight and make it to a safe telegraph station. The problem is, I am sure they are watching both this place and monitoring all telegraph stations for a hundred miles in every direction. We can't underestimate these people. They were smart enough to remain undetected while committing murders and kidnappings for over five years across most of the East Coast. I need a brave volunteer that knows the land. I am hoping Wooly is my man. He needs to know that everything about this is dangerous and the task may cost his life."

Wooly sat on the log round staring first at Gillis and then the floor before locking eyes again with Gillis. "Guess I know this ground as well as any man here and it makes sense for me to go. I guess I volunteer."

Gillis put his hand out and the two men shook. "You be careful, a lot is riding on you." Gillis could tell by Wooly's stoic face that he understood and was up for the task.

"Roper, I need two of the best horses we have, big strong animals with lots of heart and no bottom. What about that big, six-year-old Morgan? The sorrel you call Kiko, the one with the four white socks."

"That's a great horse and another one would be that five year old Thoroughbred, Gun Runner. Those are our two best animals and they can handle both distance and speed."

"Put Wooly's saddle on Kiko and a pack with food and grain on Gun Runner. I am going to need Wooly to send that telegram from at least two locations to two different people in case there are moles. Wooly, I would like for you to leave within the hour. Darkness is our ally."

"Yes sir, Mr. McCabe. I will be ready."

Gillis turned and looked at a tired and hurting Logan. "Now that we have all this business taken care of, let's get you to the house and into a good bed."

"Sounds good but I will sleep better when Wooly is out of here safe and sound."

"Me too," said Gillis as he turned to Sandra. "Are you ready for a good night's rest in a real bed?"

Sandra smiled and then walked over to Logan and took one arm to help him. Logan had gotten worse and only the severity of the situation had stopped Gillis from finding a doctor. Now Logan was paying the price. Several lanterns were hung throughout the ranch. There was enough light that the three of them easily made it to the house's back door and quietly entered. Lucy looked up from her ironing and quickly came to help.

"Lucy, this is Logan. Let's put him in the room across from my father's and put Sandra in the guest room." Several minutes later and with much care, they moved Logan onto the bed and removed his boots. He was almost immediately asleep.

"Lucy, would you mind drawing a bath for Miss Sandra? I know she would really appreciate it and it will help her sleep. It been a long and hard ride but she did wonderfully!"

Sandra smiled at the compliment. "Thank you, Gillis. I have never felt so tired in my entire life. I am so glad to finally be here and safe."

Sandra looked at Gillis. "Where are you going to sleep?"

"Down the hall but I need to take care of a few things at the barn and make sure Wooly gets out of here safely."

Gillis headed back down to the barn and saw Roper already saddling the horse he called Kiko. "That is one stout horse. Hopefully Wooly doesn't have any trouble but if he does I think that horse could get him out of it."

"Yes sir, Mr. McCabe. I have watched this horse run in the pastures and he is fast and athletic."

Gillis heard something behind him and turned to see Wooly carrying saddlebags that appeared packed. "Wooly, do you have all the supplies you need?"

"I think so. I hope to make it to a telegraph office in Townson. I don't think they will be watching any of them that far out and then I will high tail it to Washington with Logan's letter. One way or another, I will get my message through. Do you want to know my route?"

"No. Who knows what is going to happen here in the next few days and having that information would only put you in more jeopardy," said Gillis as Roper walked in leading another horse. The horse was stout and black and looked to be a thoroughbred. "That horse sure looks like he can run. These two will make a good pair. Be careful for the first few miles, those will be the most dangerous. You should have the advantage after that."

"Will do, boss. It looks like Roper has the packs tightly secured so I guess I will slip out now."

"By God Wooly be careful." Wooly nodded as he stepped up into the saddle. Roper opened the side door of the barn quietly and Wooly and the two horses slipped out vanishing into the darkness. Gillis followed the horses through the doors and then stood silently listening but he heard only the distant crackle of leaves. Finally, he turned and walked back into the barn.

Roper was sitting there waiting. "Now what, Mr. McCabe?"

"I plan to leave here with Sandra in the next couple of days. This place is just too dangerous and I won't put Sandra's safety at risk again. Roper, I want you to go up and watch the main house. I have work here that needs to be done tonight." Gillis walked down to the barn and took his father's papers and put them in an old, out of the way trunk, and then put a few more dusty items on top and around it. For over an hour, he sat and thought about the situation and what his next move should be. He hoped and prayed that Wooly would make it with the papers to a telegraph office and then on to Washington. Eventually he decided he needed rest and began walking back to the house when he saw Roper again. "All the guards in place?"

"Yes sir, Mr. McCabe. Those Fenians will have to be very good to get past our men."

"I hope you are right. I will see you in the morning."

Gillis whispered to the guard stationed at the back door and then silently went inside and down the hall to his father's bedroom and got ready for bed. He was exhausted but his mind whirled as he finally fell asleep.

* * *

The next morning Gillis awoke to sun streaming in his window and knew he had overslept. He hurriedly put on his clothes and made his way to the kitchen. Sandra and Logan sat at the table drinking coffee and Lucy was busy cooking. When Sandra looked up she smiled. "Kind of nice to finally sleep on a good bed isn't it?"

Gillis walked over and put his hand on her shoulder. "Yes, I know this has been tough on you but I want you to know that there isn't another woman in Virginia that would have handled it better." He sat down and looked over at Logan. He looked uncomfortable.

"Did everything go well and you got Wooly and the list out?" asked Logan with an anxious look as he sipped his coffee.

"Wooly is gone—he left in the dark and I listened for a good thirty minutes after that, but I didn't hear a thing. I think that was a good sign. He knows this country better than any man we have and my guess is he is either at a telegraphic office by now or close."

"That's good. I wonder how long it will take before those Fenian boys realize we snuck out and aren't with the troopers anymore. Anyway, I hope you hid the second list well. It is always good to have an alternative plan to fall back on."

"I haven't yet but after breakfast I plan to work on it. I am going to get some things squared away in the barn and then I am going to go over our security with Roper. I figure we rest today and tomorrow we figure out our next move."

Twenty minutes later Gillis excused himself and headed toward the barn. He opened the door and locked the entrance behind him. He kept pushing away the uneasy feeling that the Fenian Brotherhood could attack at any time but if they did, he needed to be ready. For the next two hours he didn't look up as worked in the barn before deciding to take a short break.

It was about noon when he laid his shovel down against one of the barn posts next to an old chest that sat in a poorly lit corner. He stretched his back for a moment before sitting down on one of several log rounds used for chopping wood. Suddenly there was a knock on the door. "Gillis, it's Sandra, open up!"

She sounded scared and Gillis sprung to his feet and quickly removed the dead bolt from the door. As he slipped it off, the door pushed open and Gillis was thrust hard to the ground. In front of him stood a man wearing a derby hat and holding a large knife to Sandra's throat. His neatly groomed mustache hid some of the harshness of his face, but his ice water smile sent terror into Gillis's soul. He knew this man was the person he had heard about, the man they called "The Surgeon". He was the man who had killed Luke and so many others. The Surgeon's eyes seemed to be alive with hatred as he stared at Gillis lying on the ground. The Surgeon grabbed Sandra by her blouse and pushed her into the grasp of one of the other men. The second man grabbed Sandra and put his knife against her throat.

"Get up, Mr. McCabe, and make room for your guests."

Another man came from outside and held a revolver close to Roper's lower jaw. "One stupid move and both of these fine people die. Do you understand me, Mr. McCabe?" The man paused for a moment and then his eyes began examining every detail of the barn.

"Mr. McCabe, I am sure you know why I am here but before we get to our task I have a couple of questions for you. I am dying to know how you were able to figure out how I disappeared and where the entrances to our escape routes were. We spent years preparing those passageways. I must admit it is impressive that one man could figure all that out."

Gillis wiped a little blood from the corner of his mouth where the door had hit when it slammed open. "It was fairly simple. I followed your blood trail," said Gillis, knowing he needed to buy himself some time.

"It was only a flesh wound and I wasn't bleeding but a drop or so, here and there."

"Yes, but when you were moving, the drops of blood were oval and when you stopped I found a drop that was perfectly round and it was in front of what appeared to be a solid brick wall. That meant you stood in that spot for at least a moment. You ran into that alley knowing you could escape and that was enough for me to figure there had to be a door in the wall. Otherwise you couldn't have vanished the way you did."

"But there were other brick walls lining the entire alley."

"There was another clue and a clever one at that. In the whole alley there was only one charcoal-colored brick amongst the burnt red bricks and it was almost at the top of the wall. A brick you wouldn't normally notice unless you were looking up or were looking for it. One brick that on the surface seemed to blend but when you thought about it, it had to be some type of sign that could be quickly recognized."

"Still the masonry was perfect around the door. What made it stand out?"

"The door didn't but there had to be some way of opening the panel and I thoroughly checked the brick. After eliminating it, the only logical answer was the rusted lantern. I tried moving it in several directions before it actually opened. Then I remembered the medallion." As Gillis talked he tried to figure out his next move. Somehow he had to get this maniac to drop his guard but that wasn't going to be easy.

"Yes, we made the man that lost that pay dearly. You don't disappoint me, Mr. McCabe. You are smart like your father. Too bad he was a traitor to his own kind. I am sure you can appreciate what a vile thing he did to the only family he knew, don't you agree, Mr. McCabe?"

Gillis didn't answer. He just stared back at the man. He continued trying to discover a weak point but up until now he could only conclude that this man was vicious, narcissistic, and had all the cards.

"You do know that my men will be coming to look for Roper and me, don't you?"

"I really don't think so. Let's just say your men are preoccupied at the moment and won't be joining us." A smile crept over his face.

Gillis struggled with what to do. These were tough, salty men that had taken the ranch without firing a shot. Now, they were going to get their way or kill Sandra if he resisted. Somehow there had to be a way to defeat them.

The Surgeon continued checking out the barn when suddenly he jerked to a stop at a pile of hay. He was staring at the pile of freshly dug dirt hidden by the hay pile. "So Mr. McCabe what do we have here. Obviously you have been digging a hole, but why?"

Gillis stared ahead as The Surgeon began moving toward the hole and then stopped. "What do we have here? A nice big hole and oh my, there is even a set of stairs going down." The man reached for a rusty horseshoe that hung from a nail on one side of the post and tossed it into the blackness. It hit with a loud splash.

"Stairs to a watery grave." The Surgeon turned and looked at Gillis. "I'm beginning to get bored. Let's talk about the gold you brought from Norfolk and the information your father smuggled to you. Before you answer, I want you to remember if you are lying, I will kill your Negro friend first and then I will start using your fiancée for a whittling stick."

Gillis lowered his head for a moment trying to hide his frustration. "You're clear enough. The gold is in the water at the base of the stairs. The last couple of stairs are broken but the water is only two feet deep and the gold is in boxes off to the right hand side. The water is so brackish you will need to feel around a bit but I have ropes on each box so they can be pulled up."

"You're a thinker, McCabe, and I appreciate that but thinkers can also be dangerous. I wouldn't doubt you have a gun stashed down there somewhere." The Surgeon pulled his gun from its holster and pointed it at Gillis.

"Cian, light that lantern over there and go down and see if those chests are really down there. If they are, bring the ropes back up with you." The

Surgeon stood looking down into the hole for a moment, then moved to a position he could see down into the stairway. Cautiously, Cian started down the stairway one step at a time, shifting his weight to make sure the stair would hold him. Hanging his lantern from a nail in the rafter he finally stepped into the brackish water.

They could hear water splashing and the impatience of The Surgeon came out. "Well, is the gold down there?"

"I don't know. But something else is down here. I can hear it moving in the water."

"It's probably nothing more than a rat. Now bring the ropes back up here so we can bring those boxes up," he said in an impatient voice.

The man called Cian climbed back out of the staircase and stood on the barn floor holding the two ropes in his hands. "Here's the rope."

Gillis noticed how The Surgeon's glance seemed to miss nothing as he continuously surveyed the room. Sandra was scared and Gillis could see the moisture in her eyes. She had gone through a lot and she didn't need any of this.

"Cian, pull them up. We don't have all day."

The man nodded and with great effort began pulling up the first chest. Once on the barn floor he took a hammer off a shelf and whacked the small lock which broke from the blow. Quickly he opened the box. "Wow, you aren't going to believe it. There's got to be at least seventy or eighty pounds of pure gold bars in here," he said excitedly.

"Pull up the other chest. I want to see them both."

Cian leaned over and grabbed the second rope. He began the difficult task of pulling the chest up hand over hand until it too sat on the barn floor.

"Open it!"

Again Cian struck the lock and this time the lock flew off. Then he opened the box's lid. "Same as the other one boss, it's full of gold bars!"

"Go sit over there," said The Surgeon to Sandra, as he walked over to the chests and knelt down and picked up a small bar and examined it. "Yes, it is pure gold and we have Mr. McCabe to thank for it. Now all we need are the papers your father somehow delivered to you."

Gillis continued to stare at The Surgeon but didn't say a thing.

"Look, Mr. McCabe, do you mind if I call you Gillis? Well Gillis, I have told you what I would do to your Negro friend here if you didn't give me the answers I requested. Now are you going to tell us where those papers are or do I begin my handiwork?"

The man holding Roper cocked his revolver and shoved it tightly against Roper's chin, pushing the skin tightly against his face. Gillis raised his voice. "It's in that old trunk over there." He pointed to an aged, dusty trunk sitting among a pile of junk stacked in the corner. "It's there!"

"Let's you and I walk over there and take a look. I know you are too smart to risk the lives of these two but just in case, slowly open the trunk," he said as he cocked the revolver and pointed it at Gillis's head.

Gillis reached down and carefully opened the trunk. "Now freeze," ordered The Surgeon. "Where are they, where's the papers?"

"They're right here. I put a few papers on top to conceal them. Now do you want me to get them or not?"

"Not so fast, Mr. McCabe. I think I can get them for myself. Why don't you move over by your beautiful lady friend so I can keep a good eye on both of you? I want to make sure you didn't hide a weapon under those papers. You can never be too cautious you know." He knelt down in front of the trunk and began to remove the first layer of paper when the papers slightly moved.

"What the hell?" were the last words the man said as the huge cottonmouth water moccasin exploded from beneath the papers, striking The Surgeon squarely in the face. One fang struck deep into his nose and the other one sunk into the skin just below his eyeball. As the man pulled back, Gillis could see the fangs of the massive snake still embedded in the man's face. He screamed in terror. Grabbing the snake with both hands he tried ripping it away. He staggered backward still holding the thrashing body of the snake, his face washed in blood. The whole clash seemed to paralyze the other two guards for a fraction of a second and that was all Roper needed to violently jerk to one side and throw an elbow.

With a powerful punch to the jaw, he sent the man tumbling to the ground. Gillis instantly dove at the other man knocking him off his feet. Gillis rolled over trying to get to his feet only to find the man they called Cian already up and reaching for his revolver. Gillis leapt at him again but he knew he was too late as the man turned and aimed his gun. As he jumped forward Gillis heard the sound of a gunshot. The two men rolled together and then both of them lay still. It took a second but finally Gillis pushed the body to one side and saw Roper holding his revolver slightly lowered with traces of black smoke still escaping from the barrel.

Chapter 29

Gillis glanced down at the feared assassin known as The Surgeon as he lay still on the ground. His leg twitched and Gillis yanked himself backwards before realizing his reaction. He knew the man was dead but his fear hadn't totally faded. Out of the corner of his eye he caught movement. The thick bodied snake was slithering away toward the opening that led to the cellar. Gillis stood there a moment, gave Roper a nod of approval, and then walked over to Sandra, helping her to her feet. He stretched his arms around her and hugged her until she seemed to compose herself.

"Gillis, I'm scared," said Sandra in a trembling voice.

"It will be all right. I'm going to get you out of here and when I do I am going to find a place far away that I can keep you safe for the rest of our lives."

Gillis glanced over and saw Roper peering out the door into the barnyard.

"I'd heard stories since I was a child that there were secret rooms and passageways to hide and escape from the Indians attacks but I never knew where or if they ever existed. I guess I know now. When we get through with this mess I would like to see what is down there but for now there is still a pile of those fellows out there. What do you want to do?"

"Bar the door and let's make sure we have every gun loaded and ready. We will—"

Gillis was interrupted by the sound of shots, lots of shots.

Roper turned to Gillis. "Some of our boys must have gotten loose."

"Maybe, but that sounds like a hell of a lot of shooting and yelling."

Soon a voice was heard. "You in the barn, this is Major Cates, surrender, you are surrounded."

In disbelief Gillis looked at Sandra and then to Roper. "Sounds like the Army to me," he said, as he removed the bar from the door. There in the sunlight stood Major Cates and three soldiers.

"Everyone okay?" asked the major. "Sorry it took us so long."

"We are fine but I don't know about our men or the staff."

"I think the majority of them are safe. The first house we attacked had men guarding it and those men are dead. The house had a number of men and women tied up inside and we are freeing them as we speak. Did you find the message from your father?"

"Yes major, we were able to figure out the clues and find the paperwork my father hid. Wooly rode out with the message last night. Hopefully he has made it to a telegraph office by now and is headed to the Pinkerton's office in Washington."

"Excellent. Did you by chance see the man they call The Surgeon?"

"Come inside major I want to introduce you to The Surgeon."

The major moved inside and immediately saw the three men lying on the ground. "Did you do that?"

"No, Roper killed two and my guard killed the other."

The major looked at Roper. "Good work, son, and tell that guard of yours he did an excellent job also."

Sandra looked at Gillis, questioning as he spoke. "Yes major, the guard did an excellent job. He has always had a bit of a killer instinct in him."

"Where's The Surgeon?"

"That's him over there," said Gillis pointing to the bloody-faced man.

"He's a man that needed to die. He killed so many people with that silent device he has. Did you find it?"

"No, to tell you the truth I think we have all been in a bit of shock, but we can now," said Gillis as he walked over, knelt down and felt the left wrist of the man. "There is definitely something here," said Gillis as he tore back the man's sleeve, exposing a mechanical apparatus. Three tightly set springs of staggered sizes sat on each side of the long shaft. The shaft looked to be about one-quarter inch in diameter and had a patterned X on the end. Gillis pulled The Surgeon's hand and wrist backward as far as he could and then with his finger touched a small bar. The result was immediate, silent and extremely powerful as the shaft shot out a full nine inches.

"So that is how he was able to quietly kill so many and go unnoticed," said the major, staring at the weapon. "I hope there is a hot place in hell for this man—he certainly deserves it!"

Gillis turned to the major. "Last time I saw you and your men, you were outnumbered and pinned down, what happened?"

"You can thank Mr. Fritz for that one. Unbeknownst to me, Mr. Fritz had my superiors send a troop of Pinkertons a half day's ride behind us and I am glad he did. The information your father had was deemed too important to chance. He didn't want a huge troop drawing more attention than was necessary."

Gillis glanced over towards Sandra. "I'm glad he did!"

It took way into the night before everyone finally allowed the adrenaline to settle. After Sandra had gone to bed, Gillis sat at the kitchen table with a cup of hot coffee that Lucy had made. Roper sat across from him looking tired but ready.

"Roper, I need you to send a man into town tomorrow morning and have him wait for a telegram from Wooly. By mid-day tomorrow he should have made contact."

"Yes sir, Mr. McCabe, anything else."

"I want you to check with the major and make sure he is comfortable with everything. I know the men are tired but set a light guard, just a couple of men. I don't think they will be back but we need to be cautious."

"Yes sir, I will do it right now." Roper walked out the back door quietly closing it as he left.

The next day Gillis awoke to the sound of hard rain on the roof and he wondered if it was just a local shower or one that would impede Wooly getting his information through. He walked into the kitchen to see Sandra helping Lucy. "I must have slept longer than I thought."

"You needed some sleep. You haven't got much for a while, but sleeping to noon probably caught you up a bit," said Sandra smiling, as she poured Gillis a cup of coffee. "Wow, I must have really been exhausted."

The knock on the back door surprised Gillis as he turned and saw the major through the small glass window of the door. He quickly rose to open the door and motioned for the major to come in. "Come in, come in, would you like a cup of coffee?" asked Gillis.

"Thank you, I will," the major said as he sat down at the table. "I don't know if you knew but I sent two men into town last night with information for Washington. I wanted them to know we were successful and what happened here. This morning a telegram came in for you and one of my men just rode in with it." The major pulled the telegram from inside his uniform and handed it to Gillis.

Gillis quickly unfolded the telegram. "It's from Wooly, he made it through and he was successful in getting a telegram off to Colonel Dougell. Says he is now on his way to Washington but the rain has slowed him up some."

The major smiled, "Congratulations, sir! You have done a great service to your country, but it will get a lot harder from here on out."

"What do you mean?" asked Gillis.

"You have kicked one hell of a large hornet's nest. These Fenians, no matter how many we kill or capture, will be coming after you. These are the most vicious, depraved group of individuals our young country has ever dealt with." The major paused, took a sip of his coffee and continued. "My orders are to stay here for another week and make sure the farm is secure. Unfortunately I need to head back to Washington. The information you and your father have provided your government is immeasurable. We now have the key to the door that tells us who and where they are. I have to admit at first I totally misjudged you, Mr. McCabe. I have grown to regret my unfounded earlier conclusions. You are a fine, brilliant man, and it's been an honor serving you, sir." The major held out his hand and Gillis extended his, then they shook.

"Thank you, major. I appreciate your comment but what you are really saying is I need to be looking over my shoulder for the rest of my life."

The major lowered his head for a moment then looked Gillis in the eye, "I'm afraid so. No matter how many of the Fenians we get, your name will be at the top of their list. You won't be safe anywhere and I have no idea where to tell you to go. I will keep troops posted around the grounds but eventually we will be pulling out and unfortunately you will be on your own." The major stood, saluted, and headed back out the door.

For the next three days the rains continued and the major's troops took up residence in the barn. Gillis spent most of his time sitting at the desk in his father's office in deep thought. What should he do, where should he go, how could he keep Sandra safe?

On the morning of the fourth day Roper knocked loudly on the door before quickly coming into the kitchen. "Mr. McCabe, Mr. McCabe."

"What is it, Roper? What's all the excitement?"

"A telegram from Wooly, he says he has sent both telegrams and made it through to Washington. He also says the Army has begun rounding up members of the Fenian Brotherhood and killed over fifty of them."

Roper handed the telegram to Gillis as Sandra came running in.

"What is it, what happened?" Sandra asked excitedly.

Gillis finished reading the telegram and handed it to Sandra. "Says they are really taking it to the Fenians, and the President is safe."

"Thank God they got those hideous people," said Sandra. "Now we can go back to living a normal life." Gillis didn't say anything, he just got up and walked back to his father's study and sat down.

* * *

Two days later the sun rose to clear skies and a warm breeze. Gillis asked Lucy to set a single table on the patio off the main house. He wanted his mother's old flowery tablecloth and a vase filled with fresh wildflowers in the middle. Gillis knocked on Sandra's door and when she answered Gillis reached for her hand and silently walked her outside to the table. After they were seated, he seemed to struggle with what he wanted to say and then he began, "You have been through hell and back. I am sorry for what I put you through but amazed at how you handled it. According to the major, my life as I have known it is over. Everything will be more dangerous from now on. On our way back to the ranch I planned to formally ask you again to marry me but now I am not sure that is the best thing. Miss Sandra Richards, I love you with all my heart but with people trying to kill me I can't see you marrying me. If anything ever happened to you I don't know what I would do."

Sandra interrupted in an irritated voice, "Now you listen here, Mr. Gillis McCabe. I am a grown woman and I make my own decisions. There is nothing in my past life that I want to go back to anywhere near how I want to be with you. Now you ask me the question and I will decide the answer, is that clear?"

Gillis looked stunned as he handed Sandra a beautiful ring with a small diamond mounted on top. "This ring belonged to my mother and it is very special to me. Sandra Richards, will you marry me?"

Sandra looked back at him and smiled as a tear rolled from her eye. "Only on one condition."

Gillis was caught off guard. "What do you mean?"

"Throw in your mule, Brandywine, and the answer is yes."

Gillis and Sandra both laughed. "I will," said Gillis reaching over the table and kissing her passionately.

They both stood up and hand and hand started walking down the hill towards the main road. Sandra looked at him, "So Mr. McCabe, where are you going to take me?"

"I've heard there is the most beautiful valley in the whole world near a river called the Greybull in the Wyoming territory. It's big, wild, and free, you interested?"

"You bet I am," she said as she kissed Gillis.

Gillis looked up. A rider just seemed to suddenly appear on a stout, lathered horse. Gillis dropped Sandra's hand and slowly reached inside his coat until he felt the handle of his revolver. No longer would he allow fear to paralyze him as he continued walking toward the man, ready for whatever happened.

"I'm looking for a Gillis McCabe. Would you know where I can find him?"

"What's your business with him?" Gillis asked cautiously.

"Got a letter I need to deliver. The man who sent it paid handsomely for me to deliver it. Are you him?"

"Yes, I'm him. Who's it from?"

"I don't rightly know, but he said if anyone asked to tell them it was from a man that enjoyed Glengyle Scotch, whatever that might mean."

"Where are you from?" Gillis asked the rider.

"About twenty miles outside Alexandria, a decent ride from here, but I made good time."

"Yeah we know, we have ridden it before." He paused. "Any news from those parts?"

"Some, I guess the government is cracking down on a bunch of killers, the ones that have been assassinating people around Washington and Alexandria. They have gotten a whole pack of the lousy skunks."

"That's good news and I appreciate the letter."

"As I said, the man that asked me to deliver it paid well." Reaching into his vest pocket the stranger pull out a small envelope and handed it to Gillis. Then tipped his hat, turned, and nudged his horse back onto the road.

Gillis opened the envelope and pulled out the letter.

"Read it out loud, Gillis," said Sandra.

Dear Gillis,

Hope this letter finds you well. News has traveled fast and what you did for this country was nothing short of incredible. We make a good team. Unfortunately, shortly before you came back to visit I was ambushed. I didn't think the Fenians were suspicious of me and I was gathering more vital information every day. Finally I thought it prudent that I take the information I had and hide it at Brown Haven just in case. I had told the love of my life, Miss Annabelle Smith, to keep the dinosaur book at her home and if anything ever happened to me to tell the Pinkertons and find you. I never thought they knew of her existence and I will carry that burden for the rest of my life. I probably have another three months before my wounds heal enough to ride and until then I plan to stay hidden. I know you're aware of the danger and that was the last thing I wanted to happen but I had no choice. After I heal I will find you. Until I see you again.

Love, Your father

Scully McCabe

Also by Stephen B. Smart

Whispers of the Greybull

Its 1937 and Cole Morgan has lost everything. At his parents' funeral he is offered a job on the massive Greybull Ranch in Wyoming. Years of drought and misfortune have crippled the once proud ranch.

A seventy-year old mystery taunts the owners while even the toughest ranch hands speak uneasily of a sinister presence in the hills.

While hunting for the rogue grizzly bear that killed his friend, Cole stumbles upon a clue to a long forgotten gold mine. Only if he can find the courage and endurance to uncover the mine's location will he be able to solve the ranch's many secrets and maybe stop the dark forces that are trying to take control.

Vanishing Raven

It's 1867 in the Wyoming Territory. Sixteen year-old Raven Dove and her family are on a wagon-train headed for the Oregon Territory. As the wagon train slowly moves through another sagebrush-filled valley near the Yellow Stone Country, tragedy strikes. Raven and the rest of the wagon train vanish from a well-used trail. This is the story of what happened to her and how she fought her way back to freedom and civilization.

Biography of Stephen B. Smart

Life has a strange way of leading us down unexpected paths. My career in writing started very different from most. On a beautiful summer day I took the opportunity to ride one of my larger mules out into the hills above my ranch. Who would have thought that short ride would change my life forever. Suddenly the mule stopped, shook violently and collapsed backwards. The force of the impact knocked me out. The mule and I began tumbling down the hill. Later I would wake to find my boot and broken leg lying on my lap. My chest was battered by the saddle horn and I was unable to move. Through the grace of God, a fisherman heard my pitiful cry and found me.

I have never been known for my patience. As soon as I was off the morphine I picked up a notepad and began working on ideas for a book. My first book, Whispers of the Greybull, would be a Western Writers of America Spur Award Finalist for best new author. My second book, Vanishing Raven, would win a Will Rogers Silver Medallion Award.

Today, I continue to enjoy writing, while as a Landscape Architect, I run a design and construction business called Environment West and a nursery called, Smart Gardens, in Spokane Washington. Cartooning continues to be a lifelong pastime, as well as my passion of hunting and packing the different wildernesses of the west.

authorstephenbsmart@yahoo.com

Made in the USA
San Bernardino, CA
28 June 2017